When You Were Mine

When You Were Mine

Lisa Swift

hera

First published in Great Britain in 2019 by Hera

This edition published in 2020 by

Hera Books
28b Cricketfield Road
London, E5 8NS
United Kingdom

A CIP catalogue record for this book is available from the British Library.

Print ISBN 978 1 78863 853 1
Ebook ISBN 978 1 912973 15 6

This book is a work of fiction. Names, characters, businesses, organizations, places and events are either the product of the author's imagination or are used fictitiously. Any resemblance to actual persons, living or dead, events or locales is entirely coincidental.

Printed and bound in Great Britain by Clays Ltd, Elcograf S.p.A.

For my lovely agent, Laura Longrigg – thanks for everything.

Chapter One

'Don't get me wrong, he's a lovely man. Considerate, sweet – everything I want in my life. It's just that he's, well... not very good.' The woman lowered her voice. 'You know, in bed.'

'Ah.'

Maggie had suspected sex would be at the root of it. Although officially her job was to advise people going through relationship crises, most of the couples who came to see her had what Carol, the oddly prudish manager of Applecroft Couples Counselling Centre, called 'bedroom issues'.

It was rewarding work. A healthy sex life was a key part of any stable, loving relationship and Maggie enjoyed helping people achieve that. Just that day, she'd advised a young woman struggling to put an abusive past behind her, a couple trying to heal after a miscarriage, and a husband and wife in their seventies who wanted to spice things up with a bit of light BDSM.

The irony was that it was well over three years since she'd last been to bed with anyone herself. At the tender age of thirty-four, her sex life had essentially been retired. Maggie was starting to feel a twinge of envy mixed with the sympathy when couples confided their stories to her. Their relationships might not be perfect but at least they had someone to cuddle up with at night.

'There's no need to whisper,' she told the woman, Nicki, flashing her a reassuring smile. 'I know you feel embarrassed, but trust me, you can't tell me anything I've not heard before. Consider me unshockable.'

'That's why I wanted to see you. I mean, a professional. There was no one else I felt comfortable talking to.'

'Couldn't your partner join you?'

'No,' Nicki said, flushing. 'He doesn't know I'm here.'

'How long have you been together?'

'Not that long – three months.'

'And has he noticed you're having problems?'

'No. I didn't want to hurt his feelings. Well, you can't just come right out and tell a man he's not satisfying you in the bedroom, can you?'

Maggie smiled. 'I know; they're fragile creatures when it comes to sexual performance critique. Little loves.'

Nicki laughed. Sensing her client was starting to feel more comfortable, Maggie got up from the sofa they were sharing and went to flick on the kettle.

When she'd started work at the centre five years ago, her room had looked more like a headteacher's office than somewhere people might feel relaxed discussing their most intimate sex and relationship issues. Maggie had dug her heels in right away, insisting Carol invest in a complete refurb. She'd got rid of the intimidating steel desk and high-backed leather chairs and brought in modern, comfortable furniture – a couple of squishy sofas, a glass coffee table. Clients ought to feel they were chatting with a friend over a cosy cuppa, not being bollocked for sub-par exam performance. The only nod to the fact that this was an office rather than someone's sitting room was the brass nameplate bearing Maggie's name and job title – Dr Maggie Nightingale, Relationship Counsellor.

There was even a radio, providing background music from a local station that did a good line in forgettable chart-toppers.

'Hey, is this Route 69's new single?' Nicki asked as a fresh song started.

'Not sure.' Maggie hunted in the cupboard for the coffee jar. 'Their stuff all sounds kind of the same to me.'

'You're not a Jordan Nash fan then?'

'I preferred his earlier work. You?'

'Yeah, love him. Who doesn't these days, right?'

'Just me, I think,' Maggie said, smiling. She grabbed a couple of mugs. 'Tea or coffee?'

'Coffee, thanks.'

When she'd made them a drink, Maggie handed Nicki a mug and sat back down.

'So your boyfriend hasn't realised there's a problem,' she prompted.

'No. I've kind of been faking it.' Nicki looked up to meet Maggie's gaze. 'That's wrong, isn't it?'

'I don't know about wrong. It's definitely a bad idea.'

'I know it's not very modern or feminist,' Nicki said, swirling her coffee. 'But when I look at his little face, all earnest... he'd be miserable if he thought I wasn't enjoying it.'

'Is he enjoying it?'

'Well, he manages to... you know. But he's so uptight, I'm sure he must find it hard work.'

'So what's the problem exactly? Isn't he aware of your needs?' Maggie leaned against the arm of the sofa as she sipped her coffee: her relaxed, open posture signalling she was every inch the non-judgemental, tell-me-anything counsellor lady. Her clients, she knew, felt less embarrassed when they were reminded this was an everyday occurrence for her. Talking about sex, that is. Having it, sadly, was something of a distant memory.

'That's the problem,' Nicki said. 'He's too aware.'

'Too aware of what?'

'Of me. Every two minutes he's stopping to check he's doing it right. "Do you like that, Nic? How about this?" How can I relax when I feel like I'm expected to give a bloody step-by-step tutorial?' She sighed. 'And the poor boy looks so anxious, I end up saying whatever I think will reassure him.' She met Maggie's understanding eyes. 'I really want this to work out, Maggie. That's why I booked a consultation.'

4

'Well it won't work out if you carry on like this. Sex needs to be satisfying for both of you or it's going to cause problems eventually.'

'I know. I just don't know how to talk to him about it.'

Ah, the British: happy enough to have sex but scared stiff of talking about it. Maggie supposed she should be grateful for people's natural bashfulness on the subject. At least it kept her in work.

'Perhaps you could try something new,' she suggested. 'Something to help him learn to read your responses so he doesn't feel the need for constant verbal affirmations, kind of a bonding exercise.'

Nicki frowned. 'Kinky stuff, you mean?'

'Not necessarily. Just something you can experience for the first time together.'

'What kind of thing?'

'Well, how about erotic massage? Treat him to some oils and spend an evening really getting to know each other's bodies.'

Nicki looked thoughtful. 'Yeah, that might work. I could tell him I was feeling tense after a rough day at work.'

'There you go, now you're getting it. Oh, and quick tip: skirt, no knickers. There's not a heterosexual man alive who can resist that one.'

Nicki laughed. 'I hope the man in your life knows what a lucky bloke he is. If you've got one.'

Not one who appreciated the skirt-and-no-knickers gambit, unfortunately. Maggie drained the last of her coffee to avoid giving a reply.

Nicki glanced at the clock. 'Well, looks like my time's up.' She stood and put her coat on. 'Thanks for listening, Maggie, you've been brilliant. It's such a relief to have someone to talk to.'

'That's my job,' Maggie said. 'See you same time next week?'

'Definitely.'

'Bring your boyfriend too, if you think it might be helpful.'

'It'd scare him to death. I'll give the massage and commando combo a go first and report back,' Nicki said with a smile. 'Hey, have you got another client now?'

'No, that's me done for the day.'

'Maggie… look, tell me if this is out of order, but do you fancy going for a proper drink? I've got nowhere I need to be for an hour.'

Maggie felt a twinge of regret. She'd enjoyed chatting to Nicki. It was hard to meet people you could feel that spark of connection with as an adult, and it'd be nice to make a new friend – a female one. As lovely as her best mates Ibby and Other Max were, she longed for a bit of girl-talk sometimes.

'I'm afraid I'm not allowed,' she said. 'We've got this whole code of conduct about socialising with clients.'

'Oh. That's a shame.'

'But when you don't need my advice any more, look me up, eh? Remember, communication's key. If the massage doesn't do the trick, just talk to the boy.' She shook Nicki's hand. 'Good luck.'

Chapter Two

'Okay, what about this one?' Maggie said in the pub after work.

Ibby took one look at the phone and passed it back.

'Nope. Don't fancy him.'

'What do you mean, you don't fancy him? I fancy him if you don't.' She turned the phone round to look at the Tinder profile again. 'He's got abs, Ibs. Actual abs! You know, like the blokes in the shaving ads?' Maggie subjected the surfer in his board shorts to a hard stare. 'Never seen any in real life before. I was starting to think they were a PR stunt by the people who invented Photoshop.'

'Exactly. Meathead gym bunny,' Ibby said. 'I'm not playing second fiddle to the guy's rowing machine. Swipe left.'

'That's seven now, you know.'

'Can't just throw myself away, can I? Come on, who's next?'

'Matthew. Twenty-nine, works in media—'

'Absolutely not.'

'I haven't even shown you his photo yet!'

'You've told me all I need to know. "Works in media" is something people write on dating profiles because they think it sounds better than "ad sales".'

'What's wrong with working in ad sales?'

'Nothing. It's the pathetic attempt to sound cool and edgy that gets on my pecs.'

'Right.' Maggie shoved the phone back. 'I give up. You can find your own bloody boyfriend.'

'Aww, come on.' Ibby put on the face he thought made him look adorable and puppy-like, but which always reminded

8

Maggie of a constipated gerbil.' 'You're better at finding good ones than me.'

'You know I do this stuff for a living, right? You should be paying me.'

'Please, Mags. All I seem to find are weirdos who want me to walk on their backs in their mum's high heels or play *Call of Duty* in the buff.'

'That's your usual Saturday night, isn't it?'

'Yeah, but not with anyone looking. And I'm classy enough to keep my pants on.'

'Fine. But if you don't like the next one, I'm resigning as your official pimp.'

'Better make him good then.'

'Haven't had a text from Other Max while you've been Tindering, have you?' Maggie asked. Other Max and his new girlfriend had been due to meet them at their local, The Blue Lagoon, ten minutes ago. 'If he doesn't get here soon we're going to miss him.'

Ibby grinned. 'He's been here quarter of an hour,' he said, nodding to the window. 'In the beer garden.'

Maggie glanced out. An earnest red-haired man was leaning across one of the tables, saying something to a blonde woman with both her hands clasped in his. She had her back to them but Maggie could easily picture the half-bewildered, half-terrified look that tended to settle on the faces of those confronted with Other Max in freefall anxiety mode.

'Oh God, the poor girl. He hasn't been talking at her like that the whole time?'

'Yep, warning her what awful bastards his best mates are. She must think we're hellspawn by now.'

Maggie knocked on the window, and Other Max looked up. He gaped when he saw who it was.

'Come on,' she mouthed. 'You can run but you can't hide, Other Max.'

'Good timing.' Ibby finished his lager. 'It's his round.'

'Hey, this one looks all right,' Maggie said as they waited for their friend to join them. She passed the phone to Ibby to show him the Tinder profile she'd just found. 'Nat, thirty-one. Researcher for local radio. I think he's a bit adorable, personally.'

Ibby fixed the phone with an appraising gaze.

'Yeah, I could cope with him. Nice eyes.'

As Ibby swiped right on adorable Nat with the nice eyes, Maggie's own eyes widened.

'Shit.'

Ibby looked up. 'What?'

Maggie's gaze had locked with Other Max's girlfriend's. The woman turned red to the roots of her short blonde hair, and Maggie thought for a minute she was going to run for it.

It was Nicki.

Which meant that the boyfriend who couldn't make her happy in bed was ...

Oh God. Poor Other Max.

'Mags, what's up?' Ibby said. 'You look like you've seen a ghost.'

'Nothing. Just... remembered something I need to do at work.'

She slapped on a reassuring smile for Nicki and nodded towards the empty chairs opposite.

'Um, hi fellers,' Other Max said when he reached them. 'This is Nicola. Nicki. My girlfriend.' He guided Nicki forwards, his right eyelid trembling with terror. 'So behave yourselves, okay? Please.'

'Don't we always?' Ibby said.

'No.'

Maggie shook Nicki's hand, holding eye contact as she tried to transmit vibes of guaranteed client confidentiality. 'Nicki. Great to meet you at last.'

'I, Ii,' Nicki said, smiling uncertainly. 'Er, you must be...'

'Maggie.' She nodded to Ibby. 'This is our friend Ibby. Pay no attention to a word he says.'

'Charming.' Ibby shook hands too. 'Nice to meet you, Nicki. Can you tell your boyfriend it's his round please?'

Nicki smiled, relaxing slightly as she absorbed the fact that Maggie wasn't about to drop her in it.

'It's your round, sweetie.'

'It usually is.' Other Max glanced from Ibby to Maggie.

'Okay, I'm going to the bar. Don't show me up me while I'm gone, you two.' He pointed an accusing finger at Ibby. 'You especially.'

Ibby held up his hands. 'Me? Maggie's worse than I am.'

'Maggie doesn't do the Harrison Test. I swear that scared off my last three girlfriends.'

Colour rose in Nicki's cheeks, the full reality of everything she'd confessed about Other Max's sub-par sex technique obviously flooding back, and Maggie jumped in to rescue her.

'Nicki, take a seat.' She looked at Other Max. 'The usual for us, we're not driving. Cheers.'

'So any juicy cases on at the moment, Mags?' Ibby said when Other Max had gone. 'Maggie's a sex therapist,' he told Nicki.

'Relationship counsellor,' Maggie said. 'And you know I'm not allowed to talk about that stuff. Applecroft Couples Counselling takes confidentiality very seriously.' She caught Nicki's eye. 'So do I.'

'I knew you'd say that,' Ibby said. 'Come on, can't you manage a bit of sauce to fill the conversation while we wait for our drinks?'

'No I can't. Professional ethics.'

'Spoilsport.'

'Why don't you tell Nicki about all the blokes you've rejected on Tinder today, if you're so desperate to talk about someone's sex life?'

'Nicki doesn't need to hear what a hot piece of ass I am. She can see for herself.'

'So, um, what's this Harrison Test?' Nicki asked, looking a little dazed.

Maggie groaned. 'You had to ask.'

'The Harrison Test, young Nicola, is a cunning pop quiz I devised to make sure my best mates don't throw themselves away on unsuitable partners,' Libby said.

Nicki frowned. 'So I have to do a quiz?'

'All love interests have to pass it when they do The Meeting of the Friends. Helps sort the wheat from the chaff early on so we don't waste time on wrong 'uns.'

'Sorry,' Maggie said to Nicki. 'He doesn't mean to be rude. Calling people chaff is just his way of showing love.'

'So. The Harrison Test,' Libby said.

'Do you have to, Ibs?'

'We made a pact, didn't we?'

'A drunken pact. In the first year of uni. Fifteen years ago.'

'A pact's a pact. Legally binding for life,' he said, clasping a hand to his heart. 'Right, Nicki. Han Solo, Indiana Jones or Rick Deckard?'

'What?' Nicki said, blinking.

'You have to pick. Solo, Jones, Deckard. And you must show your workings.'

'The best character, you mean?'

'If you like.'

Nicki stared at him for a moment, then gave a what-the-hell shrug.

'Okay, well… Deckard, that's *Blade Runner*, isn't it?' she said.

'Not him.'

Libby frowned. 'Hmm. Okay, go on.'

'Han was cool, obviously, but… I'm going with Indiana. Best costume by a mile.'

Libby turned to Maggie. 'Oh, I like her.'

'Well done,' Maggie said, smiling at Nicki. 'A pass first time. Most people go Solo.'

'So you make all new partners do this? Pick their favourite Harrison Ford character?'

'Not their favourite,' Ibby said. 'The best. Objectively. And the best objectively is Dr Henry Jones Junior, better known as Indiana after the Jones' family dog.'

'Don't even ask,' Maggie said, rolling her eyes. 'He's obsessed with bloody Indiana Jones. We think he might've been bitten by a radioactive fedora as a baby.' She nodded as a fresh glass of wine materialised in front of her. 'Thanks, Other Max.'

'And you'll be pleased to know she passed,' Ibby told Other Max as he claimed his Peroni from the tray.

'Oh God. You did it, didn't you? You Harrisoned her.' Other Max grimaced apologetically at Nicki as he took his seat. 'Sorry, Nic. You get used to him.'

'*Other* Max?' Nicki turned to Ibby. 'Oh. Are you a Max too?'

'No, I'm an Aaron. But it's just Ibby to my friends. As in my last name, Ibbotson.'

'Then why Other Max?'

'Because my friends are dicks,' Other Max said, glaring at them.

Maggie grinned. 'Come on, you know it suits you.'

'We had two Maxes in the gang in the old days, back at Bristol Uni,' Ibby explained. 'Max – Max Prime, if you like – was Maggie's boyfriend. We lost touch when he moved away for work.'

'Fourteen bloody years ago,' Other Max grumbled. 'You'd think I might've earned an upgrade by now.'

'Too late,' Maggie said. 'We'd got used to calling you Other Max.'

'No one even called the guy Max but you. Everyone knew him by his surname.'

Maggie shrugged. 'He'll always be Max to me.'

Nicki smiled uncertainly as she tried to join in. 'So this Max got preferential treatment because he was the one sleeping with Maggie, did he?'

Ibby snorted. 'Oh, you really are new.'

Maggie shot him a warning look. Other Max shook his head, frowning.

'Ah, come on, you two,' Ibby said, grinning. 'She'll find out eventually.'

'Find what out?' Nicki glanced at Other Max, whose face had flushed to match his hair. 'What is it, sweetie?'

'We've all slept with Maggie,' Ibby said, taking a casual gulp of his pint.

Maggie glared at him. 'Yeah, thanks, mate.'

'Well, we have.'

'You don't need to make me sound like Miss Easy Knickers 2003 though, do you?'

Nicki stared at her boyfriend. 'Not you too?'

'Er, yeah. Just the once.' Other Max kept his eyes fixed on his beer. 'We were kids, Nic. Put a load of hormonal students together, drunken shagging becomes kind of the universal hobby.'

Nicki's face was a mask of shock. Maggie avoided her eye. The thought that she'd been giving bedroom advice to someone sleeping with one of her own former partners was easily as excruciating to her as it must be to Nicki.

Nicki turned her attention to Ibby. 'And you?'

'Yep.'

'I thought you were gay.'

'Yep. Right at the good end of the Kinsey Scale.'

Maggie gave her best friend's sandy hair an affectionate ruffle. 'What can I say? I'm that irresistible.'

'I just wanted to check, see if it'd turn me straight,' Ibby said, shrugging. 'I think at that age I had the idea that you wouldn't know until you'd given it a go.'

'It didn't work,' Other Max told Nicki.

Ibby shook his head. 'If anything, it just strengthened my conviction that vagina really wasn't for me.'

'I try not to take it personally.' Maggie pushed back her chair. 'Right, I'm off for a weewee before we go. Er, Nicki, you want to keep me company?'

Other Max glanced at Ibby. 'The girly loo trip. That means they're going to talk about me, right?'

'So I understand.'

'Should I be scared?'

'I would be, given they've just found out they're in a position to compare notes on your sexual performance.'

Maggie tried not to wince.

'Nicki, I am *so* sorry about this,' she said when they reached the Ladies'. 'Don't listen to Ibs, I really do take client confidentiality seriously.'

Nicki was staring straight ahead, her gaze fixed on the hand dryer.

'You slept with my boyfriend.'

'Well yeah, but not recently,' Maggie said, deciding this comment was probably addressed to her rather than the Lagoon's Dyson Airblade. 'I was eighteen.'

'But this is…'

'Unexpected, I know. I could murder Ibby, dropping it into conversation like that.'

'No, this is… great.' Nicki finally detached her eyes from the dryer to beam at Maggie.

She blinked. 'Is it?'

'I don't need to explain the problem now, do I? You've got first-hand experience.'

'I can't remember sleeping with Other Max that well, if I'm honest,' Maggie said. 'It was over fifteen years ago, and we were pretty drunk at the time. I don't remember him being any worse in bed than the average teenage boy.'

But Nicki's beaming smile stayed in place.

'Still. I won't feel embarrassed telling you about Max's sex stuff if you've slept with Max too.'

'Other Max.' Maggie shook her head. 'Nicki, I'm sorry, but I can't be your counsellor for any more sessions. I'd be breaking every ethical code going.'

'Even better. That means we can socialise after all, doesn't it?'

Maggie smiled. 'Yes, I suppose it does. I'd like that.' She patted Nicki's arm. 'I'm glad all the bombshells haven't made the friend-meeting ordeal too weird. Come on, let's go back. Me and Ibby have to get off.'

'Yeah, I should probably get Max – Other Max – back to mine.'

'What's the rush? Are you going out?'

'No, but I've got a bedroom full of massage oils waiting for us.' Nicki lowered her voice. 'Plus thanks to you, I'm not wearing any knickers.'

They went to rejoin the boys. Ibby was just knocking back the last of his pint.

'Right, come on, missus,' he said to Maggie, standing up and linking her arm. 'We'll be in trouble if we're late.'

'Where are you off to?' Nicki asked.

'Applecroft Secondary,' Maggie said. 'It's Coding Club tonight.'

'You two go to a Coding Club?'

'No,' Ibby said, smiling. 'Our daughter does.'

Chapter Three

Amelia Ibbotson-Nightingale stared at the gibberish in front of her, wondering why the heck this had seemed like a good idea.

Okay. Colour. How did you change the colour? You had to find the hashtag, then…

Arghhh!

'This is bullpoo,' she whispered fiercely to Georgia. 'It doesn't *mean* anything.'

'Bull*shit*, Melie. Can you not just say bullshit? You make us sound like total losers when you say bullpoo.'

'Okay, then it's bull… crap. I can't understand any of it!'

'Oh come on, it's not that hard.' Georgia tapped at a hashtag and the background on her website changed instantly from green to pink. 'See? Easy breezy.'

Amelia glared at her best friend. This was their first ever Coding Club, and already Georgia could build websites like she'd been doing it since she was in nappies. Why couldn't she do that?

Georgia flicked her ponytail. 'Weren't you listening to Isaac? He was super clear when he explained it.'

Amelia gazed at Isaac and whispered a sigh. He was leaning over Rory McCallum, showing him how a missing curly bracket could break his whole website. Isaac's long, floppy hair fell over his Wayfarer-framed glasses, and occasionally he'd reach up to push it away.

Amelia wished she could run her fingers through it. Isaac was sixteen, drop-dead gorgeous and the first great love of her life. And the last. There could never be anyone after Isaac Helms.

It was a pity he didn't know she existed.

'Ask him to show you something,' Georgia muttered.

Amelia started. 'What?'

'That's why we came, isn't it? So you could talk to him?'

Amelia flushed. She could think of quite a few things she'd like Isaac to show her, starting with how to French kiss and ending with his sexy six-packed stomach, the one he had when he took his shirt off in her favourite recurring daydream.

Georgia raised her voice. 'Isaac! Can you come show us something please?'

Amelia's blush deepened. 'Georgie, don't!'

'Too late, he's coming,' Georgia said. 'Go on, talk to him. I didn't sacrifice a night with Jordan Nash on YouTube to learn how to design websites, did I?'

Amelia shrank into her chair as Isaac headed over. Her big chance to get him to notice her and she was totally unprepared. What was she going to say?

'What's the problem, girls?' he asked, smiling warmly. The smile burrowed right into Amelia's lovestruck thirteen-year-old heart and nestled there like a contented hamster.

'It's my friend Amelia,' Georgia said. 'Can you show her how to do it, please, Isaac? She really wants you to.'

Oh, she was *shameless*.

Isaac leaned over the back of Amelia's chair to look at her screen, his face level with hers. He was so close, Amelia could smell him.

Arghh, he was wearing aftershave! God, that was mature. She breathed deeply, savouring the scent so she could remember it later. Maybe she could work out what kind he wore and—

'It looks okay to me,' he said, interrupting her wandering thoughts. 'What're you struggling with, Amelia?'

He knew her name! He'd actually said her actual name!

'Um...' She shot a panicked look at Georgia. 'The, er... hashtags. Can you tell me again what the numbers mean?'

'Oh, the hex codes?'

She winced. She knew they were called hex codes, she *knew* that. Why had she called them hashtags?

'Hex codes, yeah. I was listening when you told us, honest.' *I wasn't lost in your perfect sea-green eyes. Nuh-uh…*

He smiled again, and Amelia wondered how she hadn't melted into a puddle of quivering jelly on the carpet.

'It's okay, lots of people make that mistake. The hash symbol's been around since long before Twitter gave us hashtags though.'

He was so smart. She'd bet he was an actual, proper genius. One day he'd probably cure cancer or invent the hoverboard or something.

Isaac leaned over her keyboard to alter one of the numbers, and she watched as the text on her website changed from black to green.

'It's easy really,' he said. 'Every colour has its own unique hex code. So you change the number, hey presto, the colour changes. Nifty, right?'

'Super nifty,' Amelia said, smiling up at him. Georgia rolled her eyes.

'I can give you a list of the most common colours if you want. But I always think it's more fun to play around with the values and see what you get.'

'Me too,' Amelia said, fervently believing she'd formed these deeply held views on hex code experimentation years ago. 'I love coding, it's dead interesting. Thanks for starting this club, Isaac.'

Amelia could tell by the way Georgia was shaking her head that she must be babbling, but this was the first time she'd had him to herself. She had to say something that might make him remember her.

'Well, Mr Wright had the idea,' Isaac said. 'I'm glad he asked me to help, though. It's great watching you lot get enthusiastic about it.'

'I'm enthusiastic. So, so enthusiastic.'

Isaac laughed. 'Glad to hear it. I'll see you both again next week, I hope.'

'Definitely. We wouldn't miss it, would we, Georgie?'

Georgia shrugged.

Isaac was straightening up, and Amelia realised he was going to leave.

'Um, do you like anything else?' she blurted out in a desperate attempt to keep the conversation going.

'What, other than coding?'

'I was just interested in, you know, other stuff I might want to get enthusiastic about.' Amelia tried a casual hair-toss and ended up with a couple of strands in her mouth. Smooth.

'Well, I like music. Me and some friends are in a band actually.'

'*Are* you?' Amelia gazed at him as if this information was the final glacé cherry on the cupcake of her adoration.

'Do you like Route 69?' Georgia's eyes narrowed, and Amelia knew she was testing him.

'Yeah, love them,' Isaac said. 'Jordan's a great songwriter. Wish I could write like that.'

'You write songs too?' Amelia breathed.

'I try to.' He nodded to the door, where Mr Wright, their computer science teacher, was opening up to let parents in. 'Looks like we're finishing. I'll see you both next week.'

'Well, he's a massive geek but he's got good taste in music,' Georgia said when he'd gone. 'Seriously, who says nifty? My nana says nifty.'

'What do you know about music?' Amelia said hotly, resenting this slight on her beloved. 'You only like Route 69 because you crush on Jordan.'

'Well yeah, natch. But some of my crushing on Jordan's because he's super talented, so it's like one of them vicious circle things.'

Amelia groaned. 'Oh God, what a total loser. Why did you let me go on, Georgie?'

'What was I supposed to do, stick my pencil case in your big mouth? At least you talked to him.'

'And I got to smell his aftershave.' Amelia breathed a sigh. 'I can't believe he plays in a band. He's just so totally perfect.'

'Tragic,' Georgia muttered. She nodded to the door. 'Your mum and dad are here for you.'

Amelia stood up and slung her bag over her shoulder.

'See you tomorrow,' she called to Georgia as she headed to where her parents were chatting to Mr Wright.

Isaac glanced up from the PC he was shutting down. 'Thanks for coming, Amelia.'

'You're welcome,' she said, turning beetroot again. Then she decided that made her sound like a six-year-old who'd been told to use their best manners, and added a casual 'no worries'. But Isaac's attention had already wandered elsewhere.

'Hello, sweetie,' her mum said when Amelia joined them. 'How was your first Coding Club?'

Amelia shrugged, because that was the standard response when a parent asked a question like that. Then it occurred to her Mr Wright might be passing on feedback to Isaac.

'Really, really good,' she said, nodding emphatically. 'Dead interesting. I like coding a lot.'

'You're very pink, Melie.' Her dad held a hand to her head. 'Not coming down with something, are you?'

'I'm fine, Dad,' she said, cursing her stupid blush reflex. She pushed his hand away from her, praying Isaac wasn't looking.

'Well, thanks for signing her up,' Maggie said to Mr Wright. 'It sounds like you've stumbled over a hidden talent.'

'I'm pleasantly surprised myself. I must say, Mrs Ibbotson-Nightingale, it's not an enthusiasm Amelia has ever displayed in my classes before.'

'It's just Nightingale, Dr Nightingale. Or Maggie's fine.' She nodded to Ibby. 'This is Mr Ibbotson.'

'Oh.' Mr Wright looked at Ibby. 'Sorry, how rude of me. I shouldn't have assumed.'

Ibby smiled. 'Don't worry about it, happens all the time. Maggie and I aren't a couple.'

'But you are Amelia's father?'

Ibby shot his daughter a fond glance. 'On the days she hasn't disowned me for being just too embarrassing. That's right, isn't it, Melie?'

Amelia rolled her eyes.

'Well, it's very civilised of you to pick her up together like this,' Mr Wright said. 'It's not all divorced parents who are prepared to put their differences aside for the sake of the children.'

'That's okay. We're not divorced either.'

'We live together – I mean, we're a family. We're just not a couple.' Maggie smiled at the man's puzzled expression. 'It's a long story.'

–

'I thought we handled that pretty well,' Ibby said when they were walking home along the beach. 'What do you reckon, Melie?'

Amelia eyed him suspiciously. She leaned towards him and sniffed.

'Oh *God*. Dad, you are so tragically, deeply embarrassing.'

'What?' He looked at Maggie. 'What did I do this time?'

'You're drunk, aren't you?' Amelia demanded. 'You stink of beer.'

'I am not!'

'Right. So you and Mum haven't been to the pub while I was at Coding Club then.'

'No.'

'Dad?' she said, raising her eyebrows.

Ibby sighed. 'I had two pints, that's all.' He frowned at her. 'Anyway, we're the parents. You're not the boss of us.'

'Okay, fine.'

'Good. I'm glad we got that sorted.'

There was silence for a moment.

'Hey, we had a talk at school today about addiction and substance abuse,' Amelia told them conversationally.

'Your mum had more than me!' Ibby said, pointing an accusing finger at Maggie. 'Two large wines. That's nearly a bottle.'

Maggie glared at him. 'Telltale tit.'

Amelia scuffed at the wet sand, making a hole with her toes, and watched as it slithered back to fill the space.

'Do you know that if you drink too much alcohol, it makes your liver swell up and your kidneys turn all yellow?'

'Two pints, Melie. Leave me alone.'

'I'm never going to drink alcohol. When everyone else is going to pubs, I'll be writing the world's most amazing computer programs with—' She bit her lip.

Maggie smiled at Ibby. 'Aha. The mystery's solved, I think, Dad.'

Ibby grinned. 'Come on then, Melie, what's he called?'

'Nothing. Nobody. Mind your beeswax.'

Ibby's phone buzzed just as they passed the hot dog kiosk. He pulled it out and smiled.

'Check it out, Mags. Somebody's irresistible.' He passed it to Maggie. 'FYI, it's me.'

'Nat with the nice eyes,' Maggie said. 'He didn't waste any time getting back to you, did he?'

'Who is it, Dad?' Amelia asked, standing on tiptoes to see the phone.

Maggie held it up for her to see Nat's photo. 'What do you think? Looks like your father's got himself a hot date next week.'

She shrugged. 'S'pose he's cute for an old person.'

'So I've got your approval then?' Ibby asked.

'Dunno. What kind of date?'

He took his phone from Maggie and glanced at the message. 'Pub. He's suggesting a drink at the Sea Pig.'

'You're not going to mess it up again, are you?'

'I never mess them up. They mess them up.'

Amelia rolled her eyes at her mother, who nodded her agreement.

'Just don't mention *Crystal Skull*, okay?' Maggie warned him.

'It's best to get it out of the way, isn't it? No point wasting my time on him if we're clearly going to be incompatible.'

'Ibs, there's more to the perfect partner than his views on *Indiana Jones and the Kingdom of the Crystal Skull*.'

'I dispute that very strongly.'

'Okay, come on.' Amelia took her dad's arm and marched him in the direction of their house. 'We need to start getting you ready.'

Ibby cast a worried glance over his shoulder at Maggie.

'Mags, help. I've got a bad feeling about this.'

Chapter Four

When they got home, Amelia commanded Ibby to sit on the sofa. She looked him up and down, one eye narrowed, like a painter assessing a canvas.

'Melie, you're scaring me.'

Maggie nodded. 'That's the same look she had in her eye when her and Georgia gave the hamster a makeover in primary school.'

'Okay, Dad, look,' Amelia said. 'You've been on like five dates since I started Year Seven, and none of them worked. You're really, really rubbish at dating.'

'I'm a failure. Good to know.'

'You're just old,' Amelia said with an indulgent smile. 'That's why you need me. I'm like... the voice of modern youth.'

'You've been on one date ever. Rory McCallum drank too much Fanta at the bowling alley and was sick on your hire shoes.'

Amelia rolled her eyes. 'That was Year Eight, Dad.' As far as she was concerned, anything that had happened more than six months ago was ancient history.

'I liked Rory.'

'Oh please, I'm so over him. Rory's a loser.'

'There you go then. Something me and him have got in common.'

'Never mind him anyway, we're talking about you,' Amelia said. 'So, first. What will you tell this Nat when he asks what bands you're into?'

'Um, the truth?'

Amelia's eyes widened. 'No! Never, ever tell him the truth. You can't let him find out how uncool you are till he's got to know you.'

'This is doing nothing for my confidence, you know.'

'What you do is, you ask what he's into. Whatever he says, you tell him you're, like, their biggest fan. Then pretend you need to wee and go Google them in the boys' toilets.'

'Under no circumstances be myself. Noted.'

Amelia yanked out her phone and tapped out a message.

'What're you doing?' Ibby asked.

'WhatsApping Georgia.'

'You're not getting me dating advice from Georgia Fielding?'

'Mhhmm.' Amelia's phone buzzed. 'Okay, she's replied.'

Ibby shook his head. 'How do you kids text so quick?'

'So, rule one is from me. Don't get drunk, and if there's karaoke don't do it, and don't try to be funny because you're not.'

'Hang on, that's three rules.' He frowned. 'Wait, no karaoke? What if there's "Don't Stop Believing"?'

'Especially if there's "Don't Stop Believing".' 'Right, rule two is from Georgia. No garlic, no onions, no fizzy stuff. Otherwise you might do a stinky burp in his face. Oh, and no kissing. That's from me again.'

'Why not? I don't see why I shouldn't have a bit of kissing if I'm not allowed onions.' He held up a hand. 'Never mind, I know. Because I'm eight hundred years old and the thought of it makes you gag, right?'

'Well, yeah. But also because if you're rubbish at it he might not want to go out again. But if you wait till, like, the third date, then he might not mind letting you practise a bit.' Amelia looked rather proud of this bit of insight.

Maggie smiled. 'Your daughter is wise beyond her years, Ibs.'

'Right, come on.' Amelia grabbed her dad's hand and guided him to his feet.

'What's happening to me now?' Ibby asked, looking shell-shocked.

'We're going to find you something to wear.' She scanned his jeans and shirt with an unimpressed lip-curl. 'Something that might make you look the tiniest bit non-tragic.'

Ibby cast Maggie a helpless glance as Amelia dragged him from the room, and she laughed at him silently.

'Have fun!' she called after them.

When they'd disappeared to evaluate the contents of Ibby's wardrobe, Maggie threw herself down on the sofa. The wine at the pub had left her feeling drowsy, and she wondered whether she'd have her World's Greatest Mum mug confiscated if she gave in and ordered a Chinese. It was two days until their official family takeaway night.

Oh, what the hell. They could call it a celebration. Amelia had apparently taken to coding in a way neither of her parents had predicted, Ibby's love life had received a much-needed shot in the arm, and Maggie had... well, whatever it was she had. Her friends and family, that'd do. Surely that deserved a celebratory takeaway.

She flicked on the TV for some background noise while she rummaged in the coffee table drawer for the Chinese menu. Amelia and Georgia had left it tuned to some music channel, and Maggie grimaced as the faux-angry yells of Georgia's favourite band, Route 69, blared out.

Jordan Nash. The man seemed to be everywhere these days. She zapped the TV off again.

–

Jordan forced his eyes open. It felt like the lids had started to solidify while he'd slept – if you could call it sleep. There'd been no rest in it. Just that bloody dream again. Her.

The thinly lit room was littered with debris – empty beer cans, fag packets, crumpled paper. He was lying on a sticky, beer-sodden carpet, something plastic digging into his arm.

He picked it up. Apparently someone called Edward Lacura had let his membership of Liverpool Central Library lapse.

Naughty boy, Ed. Use them or lose them, wasn't that the slogan?

Jordan ran one finger along the edge of Ed's library card, picked up a little residue and rubbed it against his gum. Not much, but enough for a bit of morning pep. Still, he could murder a double espresso.

Jordan didn't know Edward Lacura, or what his library book preferences were likely to be. He didn't recognise any of the slumbering forms lying in the wasteland of what must've been a soul-numbing good time the night before. He didn't even recognise the willowy blonde girl snuggled into him, one arm across the crotch of his jeans and a trickle of dried blood staining her upper lip. The last thing he remembered was Riley, the bassist in his band, ranting loudly about their hotel's policy of closing the bar at midnight, and a blurry stranger suggesting they carry the party on at her place.

'Hey,' Jordan said, nudging the girl. His voice shook him. Raspy and hoarse, he sounded like Batman in the latter stages of emphysema.

The girl didn't move.

He tried digging a finger into her ribs.

No response.

Shit! She hadn't OD'd? He'd woken up in some pretty fucked-up situations, but so far he'd managed to avoid any medical emergencies.

But no, she was breathing normally. Just in a deep sleep. He exhaled with relief and nudged her again.

'Hey! Wake up, can you?'

The girl let out a damp-sounding snort and blinked at him.

'Morning, sexy,' she mumbled. 'Some party, wasn't it?'

She was pretty, for all that she looked like death cooled down. A natural tilt to her lips gave her a carefree, mischievous look that reminded him of someone else, and a dimple nestled in the crease of her cheek.

'I'll take your word for it,' he said. 'Look, is this your place?'

'What, you don't remember?'

'Not as such.' He rubbed his temples. 'Christ, I feel like shit.'

'Mmm, you were really putting it away last night. I was worried you might pass out on me at one point.'

He didn't dare ask what they'd been up to when he'd nearly passed out. The girl's suggestive tone and the arm across his groin seemed to be telling their own story.

'Sorry,' he mumbled. 'It's a bit foggy this morning, um... Daisy. It is Daisy, right?'

'God, seriously? You don't even remember me?'

If his head hadn't hurt so much, he'd have aimed for a guilty but hopefully adorable grimace, apologised and extricated himself as graciously as he could. But he was too rough to be charming. It'd been months since he'd had a comedown this bad.

'No. Sorry.'

'Right.' Daisy-or-whatever's lips set into a thin line and she withdrew her arm.

Jordan pushed himself up. A groan escaped as painful white light hit him in the brain with the force of an Acme anvil.

'Riley?' he called out.

Daisy sat up too. She fished out a pocket mirror and started dabbing dispassionately at the bloody trickle emanating from one nostril with a tissue.

'Your friend's gone. We packed him into a limo around four.' She flashed him a tight smile from over the top of her compact. 'You said you wanted to stay. Get to know me better. Shame none of the braincells survived, it was rather fun.'

That accent. She was picking her words carefully, each syllable wrestling with a thickened tongue, but he could still hear the diamond-chiselled tones that screamed 'posh'.

'Where do you come from?' he asked, curiosity forcing its way through other feelings.

'Tipperary. I did already tell you that, but thanks for the renewed interest.'

'You don't sound very Irish.'

She laughed. It tinkled right through Jordan's sore head.

'They whipped any trace of that out of me at Roedean, darling. Anything other than pure RP is a definite no-no in my family.'

'You went to Roedean?'

'I'm afraid so. It's actually The Honourable girl-whose-name-I-don't-remember, if you care to consult your *Burke's*.'

Heiress, right. That made sense. Socialites, models, actresses: they were the only girls he got to meet these days, other than fans.

It was a pity he didn't remember her, he thought with a twinge of guilt. She seemed quite nice.

'So where are we?' he asked.

'My flat in Knightsbridge.'

'Knightsbridge! Jesus, that's miles away.'

Daisy flicked a wrist dismissively as she applied a glistening peach lipstick. 'Oh, take a cab, darling. You can afford it.'

'Are you kidding? I can't call a cab here, I'd have every pap in town on my tail.'

'Well, don't you have a driver? There must be someone you trust.'

Someone I trust…

'I'll call my manager. I guess he'll be worried, if Riley's turned up without me.' He put a palm to his head. 'God, I need some air. Fucking stinks in here.'

He stumbled his way through the unconscious bodies, stupefied with excess, to the door.

'Hey! Jordan!' Daisy called after him. 'Will I see you again?'

'Sure, I'll send you some VIP tickets,' he called back. 'See you, Daisy. Thanks for the memories.'

'It's Lily,' she muttered as he staggered outside.

In the bright sunshine that bathed Lily's quiet, leafy street, Jordan leaned against the wall, gulping in lungfuls of healing fresh air. After a few seconds he lit a cigarette and drew deeply on it, watching the silver smoke as it gradually dissipated.

His eyes followed the smoke upwards to a huge billboard in the distance. From it, the same eyes – his eyes – looked right back at him.

'Big Brother is watching you,' he muttered.

The billboards had been appearing all over London, part of the build-up to the long-awaited new Route 69 album, *Sleepwalking*, which was due out that summer. Everywhere Jordan looked these days he seemed to see his own giant, smirking face – heavily airbrushed, of course, to hide the bags under his eyes and the deepening crinkles at the corners. His skin looked like it was made of melted Action Men.

There was something soulless about the man in the poster – something inhuman. Mecha-Jordan, the Hitbot 4000. Real Jordan shuddered just looking into the dead, empty eyes of his other self.

He'd hoped a cigarette would calm him down, but he could feel himself getting angrier with each drag.

Christ, why did he do this to himself? In what reality could this possibly be mistaken for fun? Passing out in a room full of strangers, so off his head he couldn't even remember who he'd just had sex with. His brain was throbbing, his guts twitched, he was aching all over: he was thirty-three with the body of a seventy-five-year-old.

He wasn't having fun. He wasn't happy. Hell, he was barely existing. He didn't have any friends, not really: just hangers-on and flatterers, fans, people he worked with. He hadn't had a girlfriend, a real one, in years. He was just a lonely, sad-as-fuck loser getting the same cheap kicks night after night, deadening every sense, killing time until the day he finally managed to kill himself.

He didn't feel alive, not by a long way. He felt as empty as the android Jordan staring at him from the billboard. And yet he kept on doing it, night after night, just to feel… well, to feel something. Anything, so long as it punched him good and hard in the gut and left him good and numb in the brain.

What were three platinum albums worth when your life was sliding out of your grip?

Stamping out his cigarette, he found his phone and pulled up his manager's number.

'Craig? Yes, I'm fine. I mean, I'm safe.' Jordan's voice cracked in a sob. 'But I think I need help. Please, Craig. Help.'

Chapter Five

'Help yourself,' Maggie told Nicki, plonking a bottle of wine on the coffee table.

'Thanks.'

When Nicki had poured herself a drink, Maggie filled her own glass. Five p.m. felt a bit early, but she'd sensed Nicki might need something stronger than coffee if she was going to share her progress on the Other Max bedroom issue. There was a difference, of course, between advising Nicki professionally and an informal chat with a friend, but Maggie still wanted to help the pair of them if she could.

'So how'd it go after the pub last week?' Maggie asked.

'Do you get time and a half for counselling me in your leisure hours?'

'Nah, this is just girl-talk,' Maggie said, smiling. 'Plus I want to know how my advice panned out. Professional pride and all that.'

'How did you get into all this anyway? You're the first sex therapist I've known socially, you know.'

'Relationship counsellor.' Maggie shrugged. 'I sort of fell into it really. My undergrad degree was in psychology – as much because I didn't know what to pick as anything. But once I started studying, I was hooked.'

'Why?'

'It sounds a bit cynical, but I loved the puzzle element of the human mind. Unravelling problems, taking things to bits and putting them back together. When I graduated, I decided I wanted to use that to help people.'

'So you trained as a counsellor?'

'Yep, went for my doctorate in counselling and psychotherapy. It was a tough slog, studying part-time with a demanding toddler to care for, but Ibby was amazing as ever. His family have always been there for us too.'

'Why relationship counselling?'

'I'm just a sucker for a happy ending, I guess,' Maggie said, shrugging. 'And more practically, because there were job opportunities locally so it was easier to fit round Amelia. How'd I do with your little problem?'

Nicki sighed. 'Well, it kind of worked. You were right, he was a big fan of the no-pants thing. The massage oils didn't go so well.'

'Really, he didn't like it?'

'Oh no, he was making some very appreciative noises. Never seen him so relaxed.'

'Oh God. Too relaxed, right?'

'Yep,' Nicki said. 'Ten minutes in, he was snoring away. I gave up in the end and watched *The Crown* on Netflix.'

The two women looked at each other. Then they burst out laughing.

'Poor Other Max,' Maggie said, wiping her eyes. 'And poor Nicki. Not having much luck, are you?'

'Well, we can always try again. But I'm going first next time.'

'How's it going otherwise?'

'Really well,' Nicki said, flushing. 'Actually I've been thinking... no, never mind.'

'What? Go on.'

'I think... I know it's not been that long really, but I think I might be, you know, falling for him.'

Maggie smiled. 'I'm glad. He's a great guy.'

'If we could get the sex sorted it'd be perfect. I wish he'd just enjoy it instead of being so anxious.'

'He always was a worrier.'

'Was he like that when you and him went to bed?'

Maggie tried to recall the night she and Other Max had had their single sexual experience. They'd been at the student union – her, Ibby and the two Maxes, plus some giggling pull of Max Prime's and a short-lived boyfriend of Ibby's. Maggie and Other Max had been the gooseberries, forced to keep each other company while their friends were coupled up. A drunken dance, a drunken fumble... oh God, Aftershock shots. Then Other Max's room back at their halls. The sex had been far from mind-blowing, but she didn't remember it being especially bad either.

'No,' she said. 'I mean, it didn't last very long, but he wasn't anxious about it. He seemed to have a pretty good idea what he was doing really, for a first-timer.'

'You were his first?'

Maggie winced. 'Sorry. Forgot we hadn't told you that bit.'

'So if he was okay when he was an eighteen-year-old virgin, why the hell is he so terrified of it as a thirty-four-year-old man?' Nicki stared into her wine. 'Maybe it's me. Maybe I'm the problem.'

'It won't be anything you've done,' Maggie said. 'With me and him – well, it's hard to be nervous when you're that drunk. Plus there was our age, that feeling you've got nothing to prove...'

'So you're saying I'd get better results if I fed him a few shots first? Not really the romantic evening I was hoping for.'

'I'm not saying that,' Maggie said, smiling. 'That wouldn't get at the heart of the problem anyway.'

'But what is the problem?'

She shrugged. 'He likes you, it's as simple as that. More than he's liked anyone in a long time – ever, I should think. I've known Other Max a lot of years, and I know the more he wants something to work, the more anxious he makes himself over it.'

Nicki flashed her a small smile. 'I hope you're right. What can I do about it though?'

'Well... just try again with the massage and let me know how you go.'

'Guess that is the best plan.' She swallowed her wine. 'So how about you, then?'

'Me?'

'Yeah. Any potential boyfriends on the horizon?'

'Oh. No. I've pretty much given up, to be honest.'

'How come?'

'It's sad really, but I've not had many serious boyfriends since Max – I mean, my Max. Only one that lasted a decent amount of time, and that was a car crash in the end.'

'Why, what went wrong?'

Maggie sighed. 'It's hard enough at the best of times, dating when you've got a kid. And our domestic set-up, me and Ibs – let's face it, most well-adjusted blokes would run a mile.'

'Was that what happened with this guy?'

'No. Well, yes, sort of, except I ended it. Dan turned out to be a bit of a snake in the grass.'

'In what way?'

'In a controlling sort of way,' Maggie muttered, picking up her wine. 'He seemed great at first. Affectionate, sweet. Then a couple of months in, he started to show his true colours. Snubbing Ibs, sulking when I wanted to spend time with him, doing jobs around the house that Ibs would normally do whenever he stayed over here. Buying Amelia these expensive presents he knew her dad would never be able to get for her.'

'Shit,' Nicki said. 'Did Ibby realise what he was up to?'

'Yes, but he never said anything. That's Ibby all over, he hates any sort of confrontation.' She snorted. 'Even then, I still believed Dan was a nice guy. I thought it was a bit of blokey jealousy; that Dan would get over it once he'd adjusted to the fact this was how things were.'

'How did it end?'

'He asked me to move in with him – me and Melie. Leave Ibs. I said no, of course. Told him Ibby and Amelia were my family and nothing was going to break the three of us up.'

'What did he do?'

'That was when I finally saw the real him. He just exploded. Launched into this rant about how weird it all was and demanded I choose: Ibby or him.' She shrugged. 'So I told him not to let the door hit him on the way out.'

'Bloody hell. And you've not had a date since him?'

'One or two, but nothing serious. I kind of closed myself off after that, emotionally speaking.'

'And if it had worked out – if Dan hadn't been such a… Dan? What then?'

'How do you mean?'

'Well, do you and Ibs have a plan for that? Falling for someone?'

'Not a plan really. Just a promise,' Maggie said. 'This is the family home until Amelia grows up – that's what we agreed back when we found out I was pregnant – and any boyfriends need to be on board with that. Although it's a pretty moot point as far as my love life's concerned these days.'

'Ibby hasn't given up though. I mean, he's still dating.'

'Yeah, always hoping he'll meet the one, the old romantic,' she said, smiling fondly. 'But he's not had much luck so far. Fingers crossed this date tonight goes well.'

'Nat with the nice eyes?'

'That's the one. Ibby's got high hopes for him.' Maggie cocked her head at the sound of a car pulling up. 'Speaking of, that'll be lover-boy now.'

The front door swung open, and teen footsteps shook the walls as they thundered upstairs.

'Shoes!' Maggie called out. 'And homework!'

'Taking it to Georgia's!' Amelia's voice sailed back. It was followed by the noise of a pair of school shoes tumbling down the stairs.

'Dinner first, Melie.'

'Mum! Can't I eat at Georgie's?'

'No, you can eat at the table with your family. And you can put those shoes away, I'm not doing it for you.' She smiled at Nicki. 'Sorry. Parent mode.'

Nicki waved to Ibby as he trudged into the sitting room. 'All set for your big date?'

'Ugh, don't.' He threw himself into the armchair. 'I wasn't even nervous till Amelia got her claws into me. She's been lecturing me the last week about the dos and don'ts of modern dating. Now I've never been more terrified.'

'You're not going to make the poor boy do the Harrison Test, are you?' Maggie asked.

'Course. Keep the wine chilled, Mags, I may be home early.'

Nicki stood up. 'Right, I'll leave you to your family dinner. Good luck tonight, Ibby. Maggie, I'll, er, keep you posted.'

'On what?' Ibby asked when she'd gone.

'Oh, nothing. She's getting into aromatherapy,' Maggie said. 'Good father–daughter bonding sesh?'

It was a long-standing tradition that on Thursdays, Ibby picked Amelia up from school and took her for a luxury hot chocolate at one of the cafés in town.

'A warm, rewarding nightmare. I just spent an hour listening to Melie going on about how someone called TayTay thinks she's so hot but she so isn't and everyone knows that thing with thingy was such a stunt because he's so far in the closet he's hanging out with Aslan the lion and his woodland pals and it's time she totes got over herself. An *hour*, Mags. Tell you what, some days I miss the Peppa Pig years.'

Maggie smiled. 'Poor Ibs.'

'TayTay, what the hell kind of name is that? Some parents are just cruel.'

'It's a nickname.' Maggie headed into the kitchen and put the wine glasses in the dishwasher. 'Taylor Swift,' she called through the door. 'She's a singer.'

'God, really? You know, I've actually heard of her. I thought it must be some girl at school.' Ibby brightened. 'Hey! I've actually heard of her. You know what this means, Mags?'

'What does it mean?' Maggie asked, coming back in.

'I'm down with the kids. I wasn't even down with the kids when I was one.'

Maggie smiled. 'Your use of the phrase "down with the kids"
might suggest otherwise.'

'Nuh-uh, you are not taking this away from me. I'm on
trend. I'm hip. I'm with it, Daddio.'

'Go on then, what's your favourite TayTay song?'

Ibby's face fell. 'I'm not down with the kids.'

Maggie squeezed his shoulder. 'Well, never mind. I still think
you're with it, Daddio.'

Ibby's phone buzzed as Maggie took her seat again.

'Other Max.' He swiped to answer. 'All right, mate?' He
paused. 'Nic? No, she just left.' Longer pause. 'You what? How
would I know?' He glanced at Maggie. 'Well no, why would
she? She doesn't tell me everything, you know. Hang on, I'll
put her on.' He held out the phone to Maggie. 'Here. After
fifteen years, it's just occurred to him to ask if it was good for
you.'

Maggie took the phone.

'What's up, Other Max?'

'Nothing. Nothing much.' He paused. 'So... Nic was round,
was she?'

'Yeah, I invited her over for a drink.'

'You like her then?'

'I do. You've done well there.'

'I know. I'm hoping she won't realise she's out of my league
till I've wormed my way in with a bit of ginger charm.' He
hesitated again. 'What did you talk about?'

'Girl stuff. Which is code for none of your business. What
were you asking Ibs about?'

'Boy stuff. Which is code for none of your business.'

'Come on. Boy stuff isn't sacrosanct like girl stuff is.'

'All right, I just thought he might know... that you two
might've...' Other Max took a deep breath. 'Mags, am I crap at
sex?'

She laughed. 'After a decade and a half, you suddenly
thought you'd better ring me up and check?'

'Who else can I ask? Go on, am I? You're my friend, you can tell me.'

'Well you weren't great, but neither was I, probably. Everyone's rubbish when they're eighteen. You were better than Ibs.'

'Thanks,' he said, at the exact same time as Ibby's much more sarcastic 'thanks'.

'What about your Max then?' Other Max asked. 'Was he rubbish?'

'No, but me and him were together eight months, we had more time to find out how it worked. You were fine though, I promise.'

'You're not just trying to make me feel better?'

'Okay, if I had one criticism, it'd be... you talked too much.'

That was a lie, but she was banking on his memory of the event being pretty shaky after two Aftershocks and the best part of fifteen years.

She supposed she ought to feel guilty about using informa-tion she'd been given in a professional setting, in confidence, against the poor boy like that. But she really liked Nicki, and she could tell Other Max was smitten with her. If there was a way to help one of her oldest friends find love at last, Maggie was prepared to use all the wiles at her disposal.

'Did I?' Other Max asked.

'Yeah. Checking if you were doing it right. I remember it kind of put me on edge.' Maggie paused to let that sink in. 'Still, it was only your first go.'

'Hmm.'

'Look, what's this all about?' she said, determined to hear it from him. The fact that he seemed to have worked out there was an issue all on his own was a good sign. It meant he wanted to fix things.

He lowered his voice. 'It's Nic.'

'Why, did she say you were crap?'

'No, course she didn't. The way she goes on, you'd think I was the love god of the millennium. That's what I'm suspicious about. Feels like I should have to put in a bit more effort than that for her to... you know.'

'Yeah, I know.' Maggie got a lot of 'you knows' in her line of work, meaning everything from orgasm to anal beads.

'I think she's faking it so she doesn't hurt my feelings,' Other Max said.

Bingo...

'Well, have you talked to her about it?'

'Are you kidding? I'm British, of course I haven't.' He sighed. 'I really like her, Mags. I think that's what's making me so uptight.'

'That and you're Max Castle.'

'Yeah, all right,' he said. 'But honestly, it's keeping me awake. And the more I worry, the worse it gets.'

'She must've noticed something's wrong if it's as bad as all that.'

'I don't know. Maybe. After the pub the other week... well, she seemed to have this big seduction lined up. God, I actually pretended to fall asleep so I wouldn't have to go through with it. I mean, how am I supposed to perform under that kind of pressure?'

'You didn't, did you?' Maggie felt a stab of guilt. 'Okay, look. Come and see me in my lunch break when you're free. I'll give you the full professional service, no charge.'

He exhaled with relief. 'Would you? Thanks, Mags, you're a pal.'

'So what's up with him that he's having to consult you professionally?' Ibby asked when she'd hung up. 'Has his willy stopped working? It was only a matter of time till he worried it into an early grave.'

'New girlfriend so he's gone the full Other Max. He's convinced he's not satisfying her in bed.'

'What will you recommend?'

'I told you, Ibs, I'm not allowed to talk about that stuff. Even if he is getting a freebie.' She glanced at the clock. 'And speaking

40

of love life disasters waiting to happen, haven't you got a date to get ready for?'

Chapter Six

Ibby had never been to the Sea Pig before, but he knew it by reputation. Everyone did. During the summer months it was the noisiest pub on the seafront, popular with tourists and known for getting a bit lairy. But it was still only early April, so it should be quiet enough for him and his date to hold a civilised conversation.

Amelia had a study date at Georgia's so Ibby walked her over first, then made the most of the nice weather by taking the scenic route through town. He made leisurely progress along the quiet streets, their sea-view Georgian townhouses glowing silver under the fading sun, and took deep breaths of the salt ocean air as he tried to get his first-date nerves under control.

Applecroft was a small but tightly clustered little oddity on the Somerset coast, about ten miles outside Bristol. A thriving seaside town at the turn of the century, these days it was a slightly incongruous mix of sedate retirees, holidaymakers and broke students looking for cheaper digs than they could get close to the university campus.

Students like Ibby and Maggie had once been. Most didn't stick around after graduating though, heading off to the big cities and higher-paid jobs. Then again, most didn't have a baby with their best friend in the second year, an event guaranteed to send your life plans ricocheting off in new directions.

When he arrived at the pub, Nat was already there. Ibby recognised him immediately from his Tinder photos, which, he was pleased to discover, had hardly done justice to Nat's nice eyes. He'd been on plenty of dates where the photo had borne little resemblance to the man he'd found sitting opposite him, but the only difference between Tinder Nat and the real thing was the hair, which was a little longer. It suited him.

But it was the eyes that really stood out. They were a deep brown, mellow and lazy with a spark that suggested they could kindle when they wanted. If it all went well, maybe Ibby would get to confirm that theory later. He'd already decided that when it came to Amelia's rule about not kissing on first dates, what his daughter didn't know wouldn't hurt her.

Nat was sitting at a table on a bench, which presented Ibby with his first dating dilemma of the night. Did he go for the civilised position across the table, or slip in next to Nat so that if snogging did appear to be on the cards later, he was in prime position to accidentally-on-purpose bring his face closer?

Right. *Be smooth, Ibs. Play it cool.* The seat opposite; that was the logical choice. Then if things weren't going well, it'd be easy to make a quick escape. Whereas if they clicked, it would be the simplest thing in the world to go to the bar, come back with drinks and slide naturally into place next to Nat.

'Hi,' Nat said when he reached the table. His voice had a gentle, pleasant West Country lilt. 'Aaron, right?'

'Actually it's just Ibby.'

Nat blinked. 'Oh. So do we get to upgrade to first-name terms if it goes well then?'

Ibby laughed. 'It'd still be Ibby. Only my family call me Aaron.'

'All right, Ibby it is.'

Dating dilemma number two. Nat had stood up to greet him, which meant either the matey handshake or the peck on the cheek. Which did he go for?

But Nat was already holding out his hand. Ibby shook it heartily and took his seat.

'For you,' Nat said, sliding a bottle of beer towards him. 'Peroni, right? I remembered from your profile.'

'God, is that really on my Tinder profile?'

'Don't you know?'

'Not by heart, no. My friends wrote it for me. I do remember them making me sound like a second-hand Skoda.'

'That's right. One careful lady owner, barely used,' Nat said, smiling.

'You have no idea how true that is.' Ibby took a sip of his lager. 'Sorry I was a bit late. Had to walk my daughter to her friend's. Apparently they're working on an English essay this evening, which in real life means watching beauty vloggers on YouTube and talking about boys.'

He always tried to work Amelia into the conversation early on, quickly followed by his domestic situation with Maggie, because obviously any potential boyfriend not being okay with that was a major deal breaker. But Ibby was also aware that turning up to first dates with a list of deal breakers, starting with 'not being cool with my daughter' and ending with '*Crystal Skull*', was in itself a pretty basic deal breaker for most right-thinking people. So it followed that he needed to be subtle about it.

'You've got a daughter?' Nat asked, looking interested but not horrified, which was a good start.

'Yeah, Amelia. She's thirteen.'

'Thirteen?' Nat said, blinking. 'Wow. Not to sound like too much of a flirt, but you genuinely don't look old enough.'

'I don't feel old enough.'

'So does she live with you or your ex-partner?'

'With me. And my ex-partner. Only she's not exactly my ex-partner. I mean, she's not my current partner either, don't worry. She's just... Maggie.' Ibby shook his head. 'Sorry, this bit always sounds complicated.'

'We don't have to talk about it.'

'It's fine; it's not secret or anything. Just a bit unusual. People always do a face.' He swallowed a generous mouthful of Peroni, trying not to dwell on Amelia's warnings re stinky burps. 'So

I had a one-night stand with my best friend when we were students. She got pregnant and now we raise the kid together. Just as friends, but we live together as a family.' He narrowed one eye. 'You know, when I put it like that it doesn't sound complicated at all.'

Nat was staring at him.

Ibby smiled. 'See? Told you you'd do a face.'

'Sorry.' Nat shook his head. 'Sorry, didn't mean to be rude. It's just, I've never been out with a dad before.'

'Oh, we're the same as anyone else when you get to know us.'

'Never been out with someone bi either.'

'I'm not bi, I was just… straight-curious. Heavy emphasis on the "was".'

'You don't sleep with women generally then?'

'Heh. I don't sleep with anyone generally.' Ibby laughed, then immediately winced. Why the hell had he blurted that out?

'Sorry,' he said, flushing. 'No, just the once.'

'You slept with a woman one time and you got her pregnant?' Nat said, lifting an eyebrow. 'Bloody hell, talk about bad luck.'

'Are you kidding? Best thing that ever happened to me. Although back when Mags told me, yeah, that is basically exactly what I thought.'

'You love being a dad that much?'

'I love being Amelia's dad. Not that it's all sunshine and sugarplums – I mean, this age especially. Kids are so savvy about stuff now, but they're still just babies when it comes to the things out there that might hurt them. You spend ninety per cent of your time worried sick.' He smiled. 'But yeah. Every day I'm grateful to have Amelia and Maggie in my life.'

'That's sweet,' Nat said. 'And of course it goes without saying that I'm impressed by your virility.'

'Thanks. Me too.'

45

'So what was it like?'

'What, sleeping with Maggie?' Ibby said, eyebrows lifting. 'You really want the gory detail?'

Nat shrugged. 'Sorry. Can't help being curious.'

Ibby pondered a moment.

'It was a bit like dry-slope skiing,' he said at last. 'It's fun, but it's not the Alps.'

'You know, this is shaping up to be one of my more surreal Tinder dates. And I'm including the guy who invited me to his house for a foam party in that.'

Ibby waved a hand. 'Pfft, that's nothing. Amateur stuff. I once had a civil war reenactor.'

'What, so you…'

'Yep. Turned up to what I thought was going to be a picnic in the park, bloke slaps a roundhead helmet on me and shoves a pike in my hand. I had fun getting out of that one.'

'I still win though.'

'Nah. My cavalier beats your foam guy hands down.'

'Not with that one, with another one,' Nat said. 'Four words, mate: Gilbert and Sullivan singalong.'

'Oof,' Ibby said, wincing. 'Okay, you win.'

Nat smiled. 'So really, you barely made the top three weirdest dates I've ever had. Well done.'

'Well, feel free to run now if you want. I'll be honest, it's happened before.'

'And if I prefer to stay?'

'That's happened less frequently.' Ibby looked up from his beer to meet Nat's eyes, which were sparkling with amusement. 'But I'd like it.'

There was a raucous roar from the bar, where a stag do in matching rugby shirts were lining up Jägerbombs.

'Sorry,' Nat said, grimacing. 'I thought it'd be quiet this time of year, that's why I suggested it. If they get too loud we'll move on.'

'Are you from Applecroft originally then?'

'Yeah, man and boy. How about you? You don't sound very Somerset.'

'No, I'm from York,' Ibby told him. 'I moved out for a houseshare when I was at Bristol Uni and ended up stuck here.'

'How come?'

'Well, it was Amelia's fault really. When she came along, I still had another year left on my course. Maggie took a year out before she went back to finish her degree, then when she graduated she signed up to do a doctorate – part-time to fit round childcare, while I got what work I could around Brizzle. By the time we were both done with education, Amelia was in Year Four at Applecroft Primary and we'd kind of bedded in.'

'That must've been tough, juggling study and a kid.'

'Mmm, we had a pretty lean decade cash-wise too. Good thing we had my family to support us or I don't know how we'd have coped.' Ibby paused to take a sip of his beer. 'Anyway, we got through it. Things are pretty good now.'

'So where are you living?'

'The Cedars. You know, the new builds near the town centre? It's actually our old student house, we never moved out. Me and Mags bought the place together.'

'And your parents are up in York?'

'No, they moved here too. Mum, Dad and the youngest of my two sisters. Couldn't resist the call of the sea, they claimed, but they came for me really.' He laughed. 'I was fifteen when I came out to my family. I think the last thing my mum expected was a phone call four years later to say I'd accidentally knocked up one of my housemates.'

Nat blinked. 'What, so your family are all here as well? Plus the daughter and the live-in... whatever? Wow.'

'Well, not Dad any more,' Ibby said, breaking eye contact. 'We lost him last year. But yeah, Mum stayed, and my little sister Beth's still in the area.'

'Oh, right,' Nat said. 'Sorry to hear that. Er, I mean about your dad. Not your mum and sister. Unless I should be, in which case... tell you what, I'll shut up, shall I?'

Ibby smiled. 'That's okay, I knew what you meant.'

It was nice to have confirmation that Nat was as nervous as he was. That was a good sign, wasn't it? That was why Rory McCallum had vommed on Amelia's shoes at the bowling alley. The more you fancied the person, the worse the nerves.

So. Cleared the daughter thing, check. The family stuff, check. What was the next first date bit? It'd been a while since he'd got this far.

Oh yeah. The CV Swap.

'So you work in radio,' Ibby said. 'Researcher, was it?'

'Yeah, Brunel FM. Not nearly as glam as it sounds, I'm afraid.'

'What do you have to research? Playlists and stuff?'

'No, the programme I'm assigned to is one of those phone-in jobs. We usually have some topic of the day, and a celebrity interview on Fridays.'

'What sort of topic?'

'Oh, all sorts.' Nat pulled a face. 'Today it was rising toll fees on the Clifton Suspension Bridge.'

'Enthralling.'

'I know. I have to brief Jim, the host – summarise the various news reports, opinion polls and so on. Then Jim gets to pretend he's an expert without doing any of the leg work.' Nat downed the last of his beer. 'But it's not always boring stuff. On Monday it's accusations of institutional sexism in the student debating society.'

'Do you research the interviews too?'

'Yeah. If it's an author, it'll be muggins here who reads the book, not Jim. Then I summarise it so he can pretend he knows what he's talking about. Or it might be an actor, or a musician – we even got Jordan Nash once.'

'You a fan?'

'Not at superfan level, but yeah, got all the albums. You?'

'I preferred his earlier work.'

'Hey, did you read about him going into rehab? Coke problem apparently.'

'So you want another drink?' Ibby asked, standing up.

Nat smiled. 'Yeah, go on.'

Ibby noticed a couple of the lads in the stag party looking at him as he waited at the bar. He flashed them a friendly smile, which wasn't returned, although they kept their eyes fixed on him. He was glad to get his hands on some beers and hurry back to Nat.

Right. Second drink. It was going well. Time to notch up the flirting a bit.

He put Nat's drink down and slid in next to him, abandoning his seat across the table. Nat smiled, but he didn't comment.

'So what is it you do to pay the bills, Ibby?' he asked.

'I'm a freelance journalist. Well, mostly.'

'Mostly?'

'I've got a bit of a sideline.' Ibby grimaced. 'Look, I'll tell you, but it's kind of weird. Don't do the face at me again, okay?'

'Why, is it weirder than having a kid with your best mate?'

'Not quite that weird,' Ibby said. 'It's… okay, so my dad left me an ice cream van.'

'So you're a freelance journalist and ice cream seller?' Nat shrugged. 'Right, why not? Just last week I went out with a High Court judge who was also a Punch and Judy man.'

'Funny boy. Actually I sell second-hand books.'

'Obviously. What an idiot I was to assume otherwise.'

Ibby smiled. 'I promise it makes sense. There's a dozen ice cream vans on the beach selling ice cream. But I'm the only one selling books.'

'The others must feel like right mugs.'

'They do when their freezers pack up. My books are a good read at any temperature.' Ibby shrugged. 'It's surprisingly popular, actually. People love anything quirky, and there's plenty of holidaymakers in need of an emergency beach read.'

'Is journalism that badly paid?'

'No, but I love being in the van. Plus the people-watching inspires my articles.'

'So was your dad an ice cream man?'

'Just a DIY nut,' Ibby said. 'He always had something he was tinkering with, it drove Mum mad. I think the idea with the van was to turn it into a mini motorhome or something.'

'Does it play a little jingly tune?'

'Yep. "Paperback Writer" by The Beatles.'

'Naturally.' Nat was staring at him. 'Anyone ever tell you you're a bit odd, Ibby?'

'Yeah, my daughter. She usually manages to get a "loser" in there as well though.'

He felt Nat's hand clasp around his under the table. 'Anyone ever tell you you're a bit sexy too?'

Ibby flushed. 'Surprisingly, no. Um, I'm just going to the little boys' room.'

Chapter Seven

Ibby escaped to the Gents', where one of the stag do guys was having a slash. He was dressed in a luminous green mankini, which Ibby guessed meant he was the groom.

'All right?' the man grunted.

'Hiya. Er, congratulations.'

'You having a good night, you and your mate?'

'So far.'

'Glad to hear it.' The man tucked himself back into his mankini and slapped Ibby roughly on the back without bothering to wash his hands. 'You boys look after yourselves tonight, yeah?'

'Um, thanks. We will.'

Ibby stared after him as he left the toilets, then yanked out his phone.

'Mags, it's me,' he hissed when she answered.

'Oh God. You didn't, did you, Ibs?'

'Who is it?' he heard Amelia's voice call.

'Your father!' Maggie called back.

'Oh no. Not *Crystal Skull*?'

'Relax, okay?' Ibby said. 'It isn't *Crystal Skull*.'

'What's up then?' Maggie asked.

'Nat just said I was sexy.'

'Well, no accounting for taste.'

'I think he's going to kiss me, Mags.'

'So what do you want me to do about it?'

'What's going on?' Amelia yelled.

'You're too young to know!' Maggie called back.

'Ew, they're not snogging, are they?'

'Not yet. Maybe in a minute.'

'Did Dad drink anything fizzy?'

'Look, never mind all that,' Ibby said impatiently. 'He's waiting. What do I do?'

'Well do you want to kiss him?' Maggie said.

'Yeah. I think so.'

'There you go then. If he meets even your impossibly high standards, he must be just about the perfect man.'

'But what if I've forgotten how to do it?'

'Don't be daft. It's like whistling. You just put your lips together and blow.' For Amelia's benefit, she lowered her voice. 'Only with more tongue.'

'Right.' He frowned. 'I'm pretty sure that's not how you do it.'

'You know what I mean. Just get lost in his lovely eyes and it'll come back to you naturally.'

'Okay.' He threw back his shoulders. 'Thanks, Mags. You're right, I've got this.'

'That's the spirit.'

'Just one thing first. Harrison Test.' He hung up before she could talk him out of it.

He washed his hands, despite not actually having had a wee, then ventured back to their table.

'You took your time,' Nat said. 'Thought you'd done a runner for a minute. I didn't come on too strong before, did I?'

'Er, no. Just had to make a quick call, check Amelia got home from her friend's.'

'Ah, okay. Dadding.'

'So, Nat. Who would you say is your favourite Harrison Ford character? I mean, if you had to pick?' Ibby asked, in what he hoped was a casual tone.

Nat blinked. 'Sorry?'

'Just making first-date conversation.'

'Oh,' Nat said. 'Kind of off the wall, but I like how you're full of surprises.'

'Come on, you must have a favourite Harrison Ford character. Everyone does.'

'Dunno, never really thought about it.' He paused. 'He was pretty cool when he played the president. What was the one, where he was on Air Force One?'

'*Air Force One.*'

Nat smiled. 'The name of the character, you prat.'

'Oh, right. Marshall.'

'Yeah, that's it. Marshall. I liked him.'

'Right.' Ibby tried not to let his disappointment show.

'Still, I suppose Indy has to be the all-time classic,' Nat said, grinning. 'Just teasing. I know you're a fan, says in your profile.'

Ibby beamed at him. 'I was hoping you'd say that.'

'So what did you think of the newest one?'

Ibby's brow lowered. '*Crystal Skull*, you mean?'

'Yeah. Me and a bunch of friends went to see it the day it was released. Honestly, that bit where they blow up the fridge – I mean, I know everyone thinks it was naff, but it was an amazing effect.'

'You're not serious.'

'What?' Nat said, shrugging. 'Looked pretty cool on the big screen.'

Ibby laughed in disbelief. 'You know the phrase "nuking the fridge" has started replacing "jumping the shark" as shorthand for a franchise being well and truly past its sell-by date, right? Because it's an even more pathetic act of desperation than when *Happy Days* had the Fonz water-ski over a shark to boost ratings? *Crystal Skull* is just the *worst*. I still haven't forgiven Harrison for that.'

Nat blinked. 'Wow.'

'What?'

'It's just, I've never heard someone get that angry about a film franchise before.'

Ibby grimaced. 'Sorry.'

'No, it's great. Everyone should have something they get passionate about.' Nat shook his head. 'Never thought I'd be on a date with someone whose thing was Indiana Jones.'

He looked at Ibby, mouth quirking. Then they both burst out laughing.

'Don't think because I'm laughing it means Indy isn't a serious business,' Ibby said when their shoulders had stopped shaking.

'*Temple of Doom* was just as bad anyway.'

'As bad as *Crystal Skull*? No way!'

'Come on. That bit where they push the dinghy out of the plane and ride it off the edge of the waterfall? They should use "dropping the dinghy" instead of "nuking the fridge".'

Ibby smiled. 'I disagree. But I do appreciate your in-depth Indiana Jones knowledge.'

'Why do you think I swiped right on you in the first place?' Nat's hand reached for Ibby's again, and Ibby wove their fingers together.

Nat was looking at him keenly, his nice eyes not lazy any more but on fire, and not all that nice either – at least, not too nice to be naughty. They were locked into Ibby's, who couldn't pull his gaze away. Didn't want to, not now...

'Good date,' Ibby muttered. He brought his palm up to caress Nat's cheek, and planted a gentle, lingering kiss on his lips.

When he drew away, Nat held his gaze, his lips lightly parted.

'Hey,' he whispered. 'You want to get out of here? Go for a walk on the beach?'

Before Ibby could answer, they were interrupted by the sound of a throat clearing. Ibby looked up to see the man who'd served him earlier – the landlord, he was guessing.

'Oh, right,' he said, glancing at the dregs of their drinks. 'Yeah, we're done with these, thanks, mate.'

'I didn't come for the empties.' The man looked embarrassed. 'Look, lads, it's just – if you can't tone it down, I'm going to have to ask you to leave. There've been complaints.'

'Complaints about what?'

'You know what. I can't have heavy petting in my place.'

Ibby laughed in disbelief. 'You've got to be kidding me.'

The landlord held his hands up. 'Look, don't think anyone's got a problem with the two of you, okay? My nephew's one of your lot, doesn't bother me. It's just that rules are rules, same for everyone.'

Nat snorted. 'Seriously, that's what you call heavy petting? Hand-holding and a peck on the lips? Bloody hell, you must lead a quiet life.'

'All right, no need to get personal,' the landlord said, glaring. 'This is a family place, son. I've got my regulars to think about.'

'Family place? Everyone knows this is the roughest pub on the seafront. I only came because it's always dead out of season.' Nat nodded to the bar. 'That stag party can barely stand, you've served them so many fucking Jägerbombs. The one in the mankini's exposed himself four or five times since we've been here. Yet we're the ones making trouble, are we? By what, being offensively gay in a public place?'

'Nat, don't,' Ibby said in a low voice. 'We were leaving anyway.'

'That's not the point. It's the principle.' He glared at the landlord. 'Who complained then?'

'I'm not at liberty to say.'

'Nat, please! Come on,' Ibby whispered. He looked up at the landlord. 'Look, we don't want any trouble. If you don't want us here, we'll go.'

'Fine. My date wants to go so we'll go.' Nat jabbed a finger at the landlord. 'But don't think you've heard the last of this.'

Flushing with anger and humiliation, Ibby grabbed Nat's arm and dragged him to the door. The eyes of the men at the bar followed them out.

'Can you believe that?' Nat said when they were outside. '2018, Christ!'

'Nat, calm down, okay?'

'I mean, a place like that! It's got the worst reputation in town during the summer season. Couple of blokes go there on a date, suddenly it's playing up the Victorian family values.'

'Come on.' Ibby hooked his arm through Nat's and guided him away. 'Let's not ruin a nice evening, eh? We'll have a walk on the beach like we said.'

He didn't say anything, but he wanted to get them as far as possible from the hostile-looking stag party too. They were probably too pissed now to start a fight, but the intention had definitely been there.

'Sorry,' Nat said, his brow lifting. 'You just... you convince yourself things are changing, don't you? Then this happens. Makes you want to cry.'

'Here. Let's sit down.' Ibby guided Nat to a blue and white-striped ice cream van bearing the name Chilled Reads and sank down against it.

'This is your van?' Nat asked, joining him on the sand.

'Yeah. Bit of a fixer-upper but she's home.' Ibby put an arm round Nat's shoulders. 'Things don't change overnight, Nat. There'll always be people like that, as long as there's human beings with the capacity for being pricks. Sad but true.'

'But he's a business owner. It's illegal to single us out like that, it must be.' Nat shook his head. 'We can't let him get away with it, Ibby.'

'What can we do?'

'Fight back, of course! Hey, you know any lawyers?'

'Not who work for free.'

Nat fell silent, glaring out over the quivering black ocean licking up the legs of Applecroft's Victorian pier in the distance.

'I'll write to the paper,' he said at last. 'He deserves to be exposed as a homophobe, if nothing else.'

'What good will that do? We'll just get accused of snowflaking and told to suck it up. Nothing'll change.'

'It might lose that bastard some business.'

'Okay, if we just want revenge. But it won't change attitudes.'

'Aren't you angry?' Nat demanded. 'I mean, you can get practically apoplectic over bloody *Crystal Skull*, but homophobic discrimination and you're just like, "meh, c'est la vie"?'

'Course I'm angry. But I'm smart enough to know anger won't solve the problem.' He sighed. 'Look, Nat, I had a really nice time tonight. Do we have to end it on a sour note?'

'No. No, you're right. I'm sorry.' Nat looked up to meet his eyes. 'I had a nice time too, till the last bit.'

'So you want to go out again?'

'Yeah,' Nat said. 'Hey, weren't we in the middle of something when we were so rudely interrupted?'

'I think we might've been.'

Nat smiled. 'Good date,' he whispered as he brought his lips to Ibby's for a kiss.

Chapter Eight

'We should get up.'

'You're right, we should.' Jordan nuzzled into his girlfriend's neck, trailing his fingertips over her bare breasts. 'But hey, how about this for a class idea? Let's not.'

She smiled as he nibbled her ear. 'Come on, you randy sod, pack it in. You've got a tutorial in an hour.'

Jordan rolled onto his back, pushed his hair out of his eyes and reached for the packet of Marlboro Lights on his bedside table. 'Oh, bugger tutorials. I'm comfy.'

He lit a cigarette and held it out to her. She took a drag, exhaling a pillar of smoke into the air over their two naked bodies.

'You realise we haven't got dressed for twenty-four solid hours?' she said, passing it back.

'Mmm. Isn't it awesome?'

'The others probably think we've died in here. We should at least make the effort to go into town for coffee or something.'

He stubbed his half-smoked fag out in the ashtray and rolled on top of her.

'You're beautiful, you're naked and you're in my bed. Explain to me, Lanie, why the hell I'd want to go anywhere else.'

She smiled. 'You know you're adorable as fuck, right?'

'I know.'

'And you know I love you to bits, right?'

'I'm a lucky lad.'

'Yep.' She pushed him off her. 'But you're also a slob, and as sexy as you undeniably are, I refuse to let you hide in here shagging your degree away. Time to get up.'

'All right, all right. Spoilsport.' He swung his legs out of bed and flicked on the CD player so they could have some background music while he hunted among the general debris of his bedroom for clean pants.

Lanie shook her head as the familiar strains of Johnny Cash singing 'God's Gonna Cut You Down' filled the room. 'Not Hundred Highways *again*. You must've listened to this album a thousand times.'

'Come on, Johnny's a genius. Wish I could play slide guitar like that.'

Jordan finally located some boxers and pulled them on before throwing himself back down on the bed.

'That's it, is it? You're dressed?'

He shrugged. 'You can't rush these things.'

'You'll be late for your tutorial.'

'Told you, I'm not going. Waste of time at this point, isn't it? Once I've signed on the dotted line I'll be sacking it in and moving down to London with the rest of the boys, so why bother rushing around?' He reached out to brush her fingers. 'We can go for coffee if you want though. Fancy joining me in the shower?'

She pushed herself into a sitting position, frowning. 'What did you just say?'

'No need to look quite so horrified. I thought you liked getting all soapy with me.'

'Not that. Are you seriously planning to quit your course?'

'Well yeah, obviously I am.'

'And when were you going to tell me?'

He stared at her. 'But you knew that's what I'd have to do. This is my dream, Lanie. I'm not going to throw it away just to finish a poxy CompSci degree, am I?'

She grabbed a dressing gown and yanked it over her body. 'Look, I know this recording contract's a massive deal for you, but… well, don't you think dropping out of uni is a pretty huge thing to be considering right now? It's only been a month since the funeral.'

Jordan flinched. 'I know it has, I was there. But thanks for reminding me.'

'You know what I mean. You're grieving. It's no time to be making life-changing decisions.'

'What choice have I got? I won't get an opportunity like this again. If I want it, I have to grab it now.'

'Yeah, and supposing it doesn't work out?' she demanded. 'Supposing the album's a flop?'

He scowled down at the duvet. 'Thanks a lot, Lanie. Your confidence in me is truly inspiring.'

She shuffled close to him and rested her head against his shoulder.

'Don't take it like that,' she said in a gentler voice. 'You know how talented I think you are. But a lot of who makes it and who doesn't is down to luck, isn't it? And it's such a small label. Is it really a good idea, sticking all your eggs in this one basket?'

'Lanie, look. Craig swears he's wangled me the chance of a lifetime here, and that guy knows his shit, all right? This recording deal's everything I ever wanted.' He looked down at her head resting against him. 'And if you really love me, it's what you should want for me too.'

'I do love you,' she said quietly. 'If I loved you a bit less, I might keep my mouth shut. But I don't so I can't.' She looked up to meet his eyes. 'Baby, I'm worried about you. You just lost someone, and this Route 69 stuff's happening so fast. It's scary.'

'Please don't worry about me. I hate you worrying.' Jordan summoned a smile and kissed the top of her hair. 'I'm fine, honestly.'

He leaned away from her to open a drawer in his bedside table, took out a mirror and started shaking powder from a little polythene bag onto the surface.

Lanie cast a worried look at the bag. 'You got more?'

'Yeah, Riley sold it to me last weekend.' He looked up. 'Oh, sorry. Do you want some?'

'I don't want some, no. It's bloody eleven a.m. on a Tuesday, we're not going out clubbing. Anyway, you know how I feel about that stuff.'

'Fine, Captain Sensible, be boring then,' he said with a shrug, taking out a credit card to chop it.

She curled her lip as he rolled up a fiver and two white lines disappeared up his nose.

'I'm not boring, I just don't like it. I don't like watching you do it either.'

'Yeah yeah, just say no, kids,' he said, rolling his eyes. 'We're not in an episode of Grange Hill, Lanie.'

'Don't be childish. You know what drugs can do to people – you better than anybody.'

'It's not like I've started shooting up, is it? You smoke weed.'

'That's not the same.'

'Why isn't it? Loads of people in the industry do a bit of recreational coke. It's no big deal.'

'It is for you.'

He pushed away the mirror and turned to embrace her.

'Let's not fall out over it, eh?' he said gently. 'I will stop when I don't need it any more, I promise – I mean, once things are more settled. It's just, after losing Nana, my brain's sort of... full up, you know? This stuff clears my head, helps me keep focused.'

'It'd help if you weren't filling it up with all sorts of new stuff. Recording contracts and industries and London and... you know, everything.'

'Maybe it would, but what can I do? This is happening now. I can't just ask it to wait till it suits me, it's a now-or-never deal.'

She sighed, wrapping her arms around his neck. 'It just frightens me, thinking of you using that stuff when you're down in London without me.'

'Baby, if I did move to London permanently... you'd be coming with me, wouldn't you?'

She frowned. 'Is that the drugs talking now?'

'No, it's me talking. Would you?'

'You know I couldn't. I've got my life here, my degree to finish. My friends.'

'But you'd visit at weekends? I mean, we'd still be... us?'

She dropped her gaze. 'The way you live when you go down there, with Riley and the others – it's not for someone like me.'

'I'm someone like you.' He lifted her fingers to his lips. 'I can't lose you, Lanie. You're all I've got now.'

'Love… if you had to choose, if it was between me or your dream, what would you decide?'

He frowned. 'You wouldn't ask me to do that, would you?'

'No,' she whispered. 'No, I wouldn't ever ask that. But what would you choose?'

'Well, you.'

She smiled. 'No hesitation. Well done.'

'Not even for a nanosecond.' He drew her to him and planted a soft kiss on her lips. 'Lanie, I love you. I'd always, always choose you.'

'Mr Nash, can you hear me? Mr Nash?'

Jordan shook himself free of his memories and looked up at the nurse waving a hand in front of the flickering TV his blank gaze was fixed on.

'Sorry, Irena, I was miles away. What's up?'

'There's a visitor outside for you.'

She smiled kindly, sending a shiver of guilt through Jordan. They were all kind here, treating him like a proper patient, someone who was genuinely ill, instead of what he was. A failure. Still, that was what he paid Cherry Tree House's extortionate fees for. Smile-deep kindness, on tap.

The room he was in was plush and luxurious, like a hotel suite, but more sterile. Rehab, he'd discovered, was like living in a cross between a hospital and *Brideshead Revisited*.

The sun streamed through the bay windows and bathed him in a golden glow, pink-tinted by the cherry blossom that hung in clusters outside his room. Jordan knew that if he took the trouble to look out, he'd see some of Cherry Tree House's other residents enjoying the well-kept gardens, the heated pool and tennis courts.

He could join them if he wanted – a few of them, hearing Jordan Nash was in residence, had even taken the trouble to look him up and ask if he'd like to. But the patients were worse than the staff, always with that half-pitying, half-contemptuous look on their faces. The doctors tried to tell him he was paranoid, but he knew what he saw.

'Who is it?' he asked Irena.

'Your manager. Do you want to see him? I can tell him you're resting if you like.'

'No.' Jordan reached up to rub the week's worth of beard covering his chin. 'Should've had a shave, eh? Tell him to come on in.'

'Christ almighty,' Craig said when Irena had left them alone. He looked his client up and down, taking in the unkempt beard, the dressing gown, the TV remote gripped in one hand as Jordan slouched in an armchair. 'What the fuck did you do to yourself, Jord? You look like a tramp.'

Jordan didn't answer. He just shrugged, his gaze still fixed on the TV.

'What's this crap you're watching?' Craig asked.

'*Last of the Summer Wine*. They're having a classic comedy marathon on Gold.'

'What, that sitcom where the old codgers ride round Yorkshire in a tin bath?'

'It's not always a tin bath. It was a suit of armour on a tandem in the last one.'

'Here, give me that.' Craig snatched the remote from him and flicked the TV off.

'Oi! Put it back, I'll miss *On the Buses*.'

'God, you really have hit rock bottom.' Craig shook his head. 'I thought you were here to get better. How long is it since you even got dressed?'

'What's to get dressed for?'

'Your fans? Your music? You won't be able to hide in here forever; your life's outside, waiting.' Craig glanced down and grimaced. 'Christ, Jordan. At least put some bloody pants on.'

Jordan followed his gaze and hastily readjusted his dressing gown.

'I can't write songs without gear, Craig. I'm blocked. This is it for me, end of the line.' He snorted. 'No pun intended.'

'Don't talk like that.' Craig rested a hand on his shoulder. 'The lads were all asking after you. Jake and Riley have had some thoughts about a track for the next album.'

'Tell them to go ahead. I won't be making any more albums. Route 69's dead, they'll have to go their own ways.' Jordan was staring at the silent TV, mouth twitching, as if he could still see the exploits of everyone's favourite northern pensioners.

Craig moved in front of the TV, forcing Jordan to look at him.

'Look, pull yourself together,' he snapped. 'Okay, so you're in a slump. You've been in them before, and every time in fourteen years you've yanked yourself out and come back stronger.'

Jordan rubbed his nose.

'I've had a good decade and a half, might as well chuck it in while I'm on top,' he said. 'We both know I'm on borrowed time now. If most of your fanbase are teenage girls, you're basically into dog years once you pass thirty.'

'You've worn well though.' Craig glanced at the shaggy beard. 'Most of the time. Your fans are all ages anyway, not just kids. There's a whole generation who've grown up with you.'

Jordan shuddered. 'Wish you wouldn't say stuff like that. It's... big. I'm not strong enough for big yet.'

'You know what I mean. The fans who've stuck with you stayed for the music. Panic! at the Disco have been going just as long as us, haven't they? And they're charting higher than they ever have. Killers, Muse, Fall Out Boy – they've all got longer vintages than 69 and all still going strong. Hell, Green Day have been around since Queen Victoria was on the tit, but they're still putting out new stuff. Reinvent and evolve, boy, that's the trick.'

'I just don't know if I can be creative without drugs.'

'You were creative when I first spotted you, and back then you never touched that bloody stuff. All you had were your principles and your rage.'

'Well, I was young then.' Jordan smiled, twisting the cord of his robe. 'Tell you what, my nan'd go spare if she knew I'd ended up like this. The only time I ever heard her swear was about "those evil bastards". Dealers, I mean.'

'Your dad?' Craig asked in a softer voice, taking a seat.

'Yeah. After what happened to him, you'd think I'd know better than to go near the Class As. And I did, till Nana… well, you know the story. World's smallest violin, right?'

'I'm sorry, Jord, I did my best to get you off it. A hundred times I've tried to make you realise you needed help. You had to want to quit first.'

'I know.'

'You're the last person who should be shovelling that stuff up your nose. Riley and the others don't respond to it like you do. You get too inside your own head with it.'

'Yeah, well. I'm a fucking poet, mate.'

Craig smiled. 'Ah, there's my old friend the ego.'

'How'd the press conference go?'

'As well as it could, I guess,' Craig said, leaning back in his chair. 'I told them you were withdrawing from public life to spend more time with your collection of vintage French pornography.'

'Come on, what did you really give them?'

He shrugged. 'Had to tell them the truth, didn't I? They'd have found out anyway.'

'So they know I'm in rehab?'

'Well, I called it a health and wellness retreat. "Exhaustion and personal issues", the standard line. But yeah, they know.'

Jordan groaned. 'Jesus. I'll get asked about nothing else in interviews for the next ten years.'

Craig looked at him appraisingly. 'Unless we chuck them something else to distract them.'

'Oh, no. No women. I'm not having any more fake relationships for the media's benefit, Arabella was the last.'

'It doesn't have to be fake. I've got some cracking girls just dying for an introduction. You'd like Katarina, she's a Victoria's Secret model with her own castle.'

'I don't care if she's got twelve castles and three sets of tits, Craig, I'm not doing it. I can't anyway. No dating for a year after getting clean, that's what the doctors advise.'

'But surely just a couple of photos—'

'Look, I said no, okay? I'm not doing that shit any more.'

Craig shrugged. 'Fine. Then if you want your public redemption, you'll just have to come back bigger and better.'

'I told you. I don't know if I can.' Jordan stood up and went to the fridge. 'I should offer you a drink really, shouldn't I? If this is a social call.'

His manager looked worried. 'You're not allowed booze in these places, are you?'

'I was thinking tea,' Jordan said, taking out some milk. 'But you could spare us a fag if you've got one.'

'I haven't, sorry.'

'Bullshit.' Jordan managed to flash something like his old irresistible grin. 'Come on, boss. I can't be expected to quit all my bad habits in one go, can I?'

'Fine, just one then.' Craig produced a packet and handed over a cigarette. Jordan hid it under an upturned mug for later.

'It's not a social call anyway,' Craig said, flinching. 'Not that I didn't want to see how you were getting on. But I did bring news.'

Jordan took in Craig's worried expression. 'Nothing good, I'm guessing.'

'Sylvia. I'm sorry, Jord, she's turned up again. Someone must've said her name three times in front of a mirror.'

'Oh, that's just perfect, when I'm stuck in here. What is it this time?'

'What do you think? Husband number four's booted her out so she's looking to make some cash.'

'How much does she want?'

'She doesn't. She already got paid.' Craig took a folded newspaper from his jacket.

Jordan laid it on the bed. A glamorous blonde woman in the tiniest of little black dresses pouted from the page. Inset was a picture he recognised, a five-year-old version of himself, grinning happily in his trunks in the days when coke meant something fizzy and delicious that his nana let him drink on his birthday. He remembered it: one of Nana's snaps, taken on holiday in Great Yarmouth. God knew how Sylvia had got her hands on it. She'd long disappeared from his life by then.

The headline was *Drugs tragedy of my darling boy, by Sylvia Nash* Not her real name, of course. She'd adopted 'Nash' by deed poll pretty soon after he'd hit the big time.

The first time Jordan's mother had sold a story on him had been early on in his career, when he was just twenty and Route 69's debut album *Mix Tape* had been rocketing up the charts. That one had been little more than a fluff piece, all about the young Jordan's wonderful childhood and prodigy-like musical talent; a pretty impressive amount of knowledge for someone he hadn't seen since he was three. In the years after that she'd resurfaced every once in a while, whenever she'd found herself between wealthy lovers or husbands, wanting money from him to fund surgical treatments and the jetsetting lifestyle she'd become addicted to. And if money wasn't forthcoming, she generally found some way to punish him for it.

Like this, for example.

It would've been enough to make his nana swear, if she'd been around to see it. He'd lost her just after Craig had taken him on as a client and started putting the original line-up of Route 69 together.

Jordan remembered going to the hospital to tell her about it, when she was hooked up to all those horrible machines and barely conscious. He'd told her he'd been discovered, that he was getting his big chance, and he'd felt her squeeze his hand. A week later, she was gone. Two weeks later, not long after the funeral, he did his first line. And fourteen years after that, he did his last.

He glanced at the story again. It was a new low, even for Sylvia, who'd been redefining the term 'new low' for most of Jordan's life.

'She's going into the *Big Brother* house on the back of it,' Craig said.

'Jesus. Is there nothing in my life the woman won't exploit?'

'I'm sorry.' Craig placed a hand on his back. 'If she'd come to me I'd have paid her off, but she went straight to the press.'

'Not your fault.' Jordan turned around. 'I'm sorry if I've let you down, Craig. I do appreciate it, you taking a chance on me all those years ago. You've been a good mate too. The only one in the industry I'd call a proper mate.'

'You were worth taking a chance on,' Craig said, smiling. 'Now come on, star, let's not get sentimental. Stop feeling sorry for yourself and get back to work. I know the old fire's still in there behind that fucking awful beard.'

Jordan sat back down and stared at the TV. 'I did have one new idea.'

'Go on.'

'There's this… it's a dream I keep having. I think there might be a song in it, if I can find an angle.'

'What sort of dream? We're not getting into marshmallow people and rocking-horse pie territory here, are we?'

'No. It's just… a name, really. A refrain. I'm wondering if it's a sign from my subconscious, like this is the song I'm supposed to write.'

'Okay, that sounds positive.' Craig nodded to a notepad sitting on the table. 'Go on, you've got all the time in the world to write while you're stuck in this place. Fill that up and next week I'll stop by with some more for you. If you're a good boy

I might even let you bum another fag.' He shook Jordan's hand. 'Nice to have you back, Jord.'

When he'd gone, Jordan took the pad and balanced it on his knee, staring at the empty white space; wondering if he'd ever be able to fill white space again with the magic words that had come so easily after a line or two of coke.

He stood up, took the cigarette Craig had given him and stuck it behind his ear. That seemed to help, for some reason.

He sat down. Then he stood up again, twitched his mum's shaft-and-tell travesty from the bed and crumpled it in the bin. He took a shower, shaved, pulled on some pants, jeans and a loose-fitting shirt. Then, his own particular brand of feng shui completed, Jordan Nash fixed a picture of the face he needed in his mind and started to write.

Chapter Nine

Maggie stifled a yawn. She cast a surreptitious glance at the clock on her office wall.

'I mean, I love Joanna. We've been married over a year,' her client, Mr Roberts, was telling her. 'But you know how it is, when people have different needs. I bet you get couples with mismatched libidos in here all the time, right?'

'Occasionally.'

'Anyway, it's clear we're going to have to do something,' he said, barely registering her answer. 'She's totally lost interest in sex since she got this new job. Never wants to do it more than once a week.'

'And you'd like to do it a lot more often, I'm guessing?'

'Well, I'm a man, right? A very red-blooded one, if you know what I mean. Do you know what I mean?'

'Yes, Mr Roberts. I believe I know what you mean.'

'But Jo says she doesn't have the energy after work. Miss Nightingale, I'm at the end of my rope.'

'Doctor.'

'Yes, sorry. Dr Nightingale.' His gaze flickered to her chest. 'End of my rope,' he muttered.

It was nearly the end of the Mr Roberts' consultation, and Maggie had hardly said a word the whole hour. He'd spent nearly all the allotted time alternately bragging about his feats of sexual athleticism and complaining about his wife's steadfast refusal to be impressed. Maggie was starting to feel quite attached to Mrs Joanna Roberts. The poor cow was probably glad of her new job, since it gave her an excuse to escape the attentions of her obnoxious, patronising, permanently boner-wielding tit of a husband.

Maggie had had clients like Mr Roberts before, and she could guess exactly what was coming next.

'So anyway, I really think it would be best for both of us if I were to... take some positive action,' he said. 'You know?'

'Do I?'

'Yes, you know.' He lowered his voice. 'If I were to take a lover. It's the only fair way.'

And there it was.

'I don't think you can just order one online, you know.' Maggie paused. 'Okay, you might be able to, but I'd strongly advise against it.'

'I've had interest. There are at least two girls... well, I shouldn't boast. But I can't imagine I'd have much trouble.' His receding hairline glowed with self-assurance.

'Go home, Mr Roberts. Go have a conversation with your wife. And this time, try listening to what she has to say – her wants and needs.'

'But poor Joanna gets so tired. I really think it would be better—'

'Mr Roberts. You want me to give my blessing for you to have a guilt-free affair. I'm not going to do that. And if you really believe that by doing so you'd be doing your wife a favour, you're likely to find your problems in that department will soon be at an end, because you won't have a wife to worry about any more.' She stood up. 'And now your time's up. Goodbye, Mr Roberts. Go home and talk to Joanna.'

–

'God, I had a right arsehole client at work today,' she told Ibby later as she helped him shelve stock in the Chilled Reads van.

'What was it? Kinky stuff?'

71

'I'm not allowed to tell you, sadly. Let's just say there's some poor woman out there who deserves a bloody medal.' She shook her head. 'Client confidentiality's a bugger when you want to offload after a rough day.'

'Too professional for your own good, darling.'

'Tell you what though, it's one of those sessions that makes you glad to be single. Rather that than be lumbered with a selfish little prick like this guy.'

'You'll meet someone one day.'

'Honestly, I'm happy as I am. Men just mean headaches, and I get enough of those worrying about Melie.'

'Mmm. A bit too much lady-protesting going on round here, if you ask me.' Ibby held up a book. 'Ugh, another *Da Vinci Code*. I've got nearly enough to build myself an extension.' He tossed it onto a pile with a load of others.

'Sell many today?'

'Not bad for out of season. And I finished that commission about the effect of Brexit on cream sherry exports.'

Maggie shook her head. 'The life you lead, mate.'

'Is Melie going straight to my sister's?'

'Yep, she's picking her up from school.' Maggie nudged him. 'So come on, spill. How was date number two last night? Good film?'

Ibby smiled as he turned his attention back to the books. 'Yeah. Very good actually.'

'What did you see?'

'Oh, some superhero thing.'

'Okay. Can you be any more specific?'

'Er... I think it was underwater. Or in space, possibly.'

She laughed. 'Snogged your way through all of it, didn't you?'

'Damnable lies. I came up for air at least twice.'

'Is Nat still upset about that knobhead landlord at the Sea Pig?'

'Yeah. He got a letter into the *Post* about it though, which seems to have helped him get it off his chest a bit. We can draw a line under it now, I hope.'

'So we all know what happens on the next date, don't we?' Maggie nudged him again. 'The old third date rule, eh?'

He rubbed his side. 'Mags, can you go easy on the ribs? It's not the seventies, you know. Innuendo doesn't have to bruise like it did in the old days.'

There was the sound of a throat clearing, and Ibby turned to serve the customer who'd just rolled up.

'Can I help?' he asked. 'Oh, hang on.' He snatched up his ice cream man hat and plonked it on his head. It was flat and white with a black peak, embroidered with the slogan *STOP ME AND READ ONE*. 'Right. Now can I help?'

'Have you got *Misery*? Stephen King?'

'Might have. You want raspberry sauce on it?'

Nat smiled. 'Just a Flake.'

'You know, I've had that joke so many times I actually started selling them. Here you go.' He handed Nat a 99 Flake and a book.

'*Bridget Jones's Diary*?'

'Yeah, sorry, fresh out of Stephen King. But you'll definitely like that one.'

'Have you read it?'

'No, but I've got four in stock and I need to offload a couple,' Ibby said. 'By the way, this is Maggie.'

'Hey.' Nat shook hands with her through the hatch. 'Best friend and mother of his child, right?'

Maggie grinned. 'And Nat with the naughty-but-nice eyes. How was the film then?'

'Er, yeah. Good... space bits. I think.'

She laughed. 'So I heard.'

'So, what brings you my way?' Ibby asked Nat as Maggie crouched down and discreetly got on with her shelf-stacking.

'You.'

'Keen. I like that in a man.'

'I just came to ask if you were free later. I'm meeting some mates for a drink over in Bristol if you fancied joining the gang.'

Ibby blinked. 'You're inviting me to meet your mates?'

'Yeah. If you want to. And then maybe we can grab dinner, just the two of us?'

'Um, yeah. Tonight's good actually, my daughter's staying at her Aunty Beth's.'

Ibby flinched. Had that sounded like a proposition? *Oh, my daughter's out, feel free to pop in for a nightcap and some nookie...*

'So, er, that means I don't have to be up early to get her ready for school,' he added. 'If you were planning on getting me drunk.'

Ugh, that was even worse. The natural end to that sentence was obviously 'and having your way with me'. He should never try to flirt, it always went tits up.

'No curfew. Gotcha,' Nat said, winking. 'Nice to know we can stay up late.'

'Where are we having drinks?'

'Our regular haunt, The Admiral. I'll text you the address.'

'Right. See you later then.'

Ibby watched him walk away.

'You know what, Ibs?' Maggie said as she stood up.

'What?'

'I reckon you're on a promise there.'

–

Ibby parked up at the pub just after seven.

On the plus side, he noted The Admiral had a rainbow flag flapping from one window, which suggested that a bit of boy on boy hand-holding in this pub was unlikely to produce too many raised eyebrows. On the minus side, it was right out in town, down by Bristol docks, which meant he'd had to drive. Still, at least there'd be no risk of lagery burping this time round.

And if there was any chance he'd be inviting Nat for a grown-up sleepover later, staying sober wasn't a bad idea. He hadn't had sex in so long, it'd be nice to be fully in the moment if it happened tonight.

'You been before, mate?' the bouncer on the door asked.

'No. I mean, yes.'

The bouncer looked puzzled. 'Right.'

Ibby smiled. 'Sorry, I'm a bit out of practice. I mean, no, I haven't been before but yes, I know it's a gay pub. I'm meeting someone.' He held a hand up about an inch above his head. 'About yay high, dark brown hair, adorable eyes, answers to the name of Nat?'

The man laughed. 'Yeah, I know Nat. You can usually find him in the snug. Have a good night, okay?'

Ibby grinned. 'Cheers.'

When he'd got himself a Coke, he sought out Nat and his friends.

'Ibby.' Nat stood to peck his cheek. 'Glad you made it.'

'Hi.' Ibby glanced around the heaving table. There must've been eight or nine people there, all grinning at him. 'Wow. That's a lot of mates. You want to introduce me?'

Nat nodded to the others. 'This is Talia and her girlfriend Andie. Then there's Colin, Jim from my radio show, Rob, Bazzer, Ashleigh and Pickled Egg Johnny.'

'Pickled Egg Johnny?'

'Yeah.'

The burly, bearded man called Pickled Egg Johnny, double-deniming it in cut-offs and cowboy shirt and sporting an impressively retro mullet, lunged across the table to shake Ibby's hand. 'Hiya. Great to meet you.'

'Everyone, this is Aaron Ibbotson,' Nat told his friends. 'Call him Ibby.'

Ibby sank into a seat next to Nat.

'So, er, how do you all know each other?' he asked, feeling a bit dazed after the flurry of introductions. When Nat had invited him to meet his friends, he'd been expecting maybe two or three max.

'Actually we don't,' Nat said. 'Well, not all of us, although Andie, Talia and Johnny are old friends of mine. Tonight's our inaugural meeting.'

'Inaugural meeting?'

Talia nodded. 'That's right. We're Over It.'

'Good for you. Er, Over what?'

'She means, that's the name of the new group. Over It,' Nat said.

'Group. Oh! Is this a group?'

'Yeah. Jim and Rob aren't members, but they wanted to come along when they heard about what happened. They think it could be quite the story.'

'Sorry, when what happened?' Ibby asked, feeling more confused by the minute.

'You know, that landlord at the Pig chucking us out. I told Jim all about it, and Rob was keen to meet up too after he saw my letter in the *Post*. It's more common than you think.' Nat nodded to Talia. 'Tal, tell him what happened to you and Andie.'

'Me and the missus tried to rent a room in a B&B out in Hesham last month,' she told Ibby. 'Funnily enough, all of a sudden they were fully booked. Despite the big Vacancies sign in the window.'

'Makes me sick,' Pickled Egg Johnny spat. 'They know it's illegal, but they know we can't prove anything either. Fascism, that's what it is.'

'That's why we formed the group,' Nat said, his eyes flashing fire. 'We all know how it feels to be treated that way. Maybe together we can actually make a difference. What do you say, Ibby, are you with us?'

He blinked. 'Who, me?'

Nat nodded to the man with the moustache he'd introduced as Jim, the radio host. 'Jim thinks he can get us a spot on the show. Me and you, to talk about what happened. The publicity would really help the campaign.'

The man called Rob seemed to be taking notes.

'So are you and Nat an item now?' he asked, glancing up at Ibby.

'Er, that's rather personal.'

'I mean, will there be more dates? Come on, we're all on the same side here.'

Ibby had thought this was a date. He hadn't realised it was the start of the people's bloodless revolution.

'Um, I guess there... sorry, are you writing this down?'

'Yeah, it'll help if I work it in,' Rob said. 'People love a blossoming romance. Hearts and minds, boy, hearts and minds.'

'Shorthand...' Ibby suddenly realised why Rob looked familiar. 'Hey, I know you, don't I? You're one of the staffers at the *Post*. We met at a conference last year.'

'Did we now? Well, small world,' Rob said, still scribbling away. 'So how about it, then? Is love on the cards for you two?'

'Nat, I'm really not comfortable with this,' Ibby muttered.

'Sorry. I know it's full-on, but Rob and Jim thought it'd help if they could get the two of us. You know, to be the face of the thing. I knew you'd want to help.'

'Well no, you didn't know that, did you? Because you never bloody asked.' Ibby pushed his drink away. 'Look, everyone, I mean, best of luck and everything. But I really need to get going.' He stood to leave.

'Ibby. Stay, please.' Nat looked up at him with those appealing brown eyes. 'Listen, sorry if we scared you. This is important, that's all. If we don't stand up and be counted sometimes, then what ever changes?'

'I'm sorry, Nat. I am on your side – I mean in principle – but... I just don't have room in my life for this.' Ibby nodded to the other occupants of the table, who were staring at him like he'd just finished a spot of puppy-kicking and was off to shove some little old ladies in front of passing cars. 'Talia. Rob. Er,

Pickled Egg Johnny. And the rest of you. It was lovely to meet you, but I have to go.'

Chapter Ten

When Ibby got in, Maggie was in the kitchen wiggling her arse to Aqua in her dinosaur onesie. He threw himself down on the sofa.

'Ibs? What's up?' she asked, poking her head through the open kitchen door. 'Something happen to your date?'

'Don't call me Ibs any more. Call me Che, face of the revolution.'

'What?'

'Oh, nothing.'

She came in and sat down next to him. 'Come on, you, what's wrong?'

He rested his head on her shoulder. 'The date. Wasn't a proper date. Apparently Nat's a key figure in the Applecroft Gay Resistance and he wants me to be the face of their new Homophobia Sucks campaign.'

When he'd filled her in, Maggie shook her head.

'Only you, Ibs.'

'Oddball magnet, right?'

She squeezed his shoulder. 'You okay?'

'Guess so.' He sighed. 'I liked him as well. Tinder should make them declare any weird obsessions in some kind of screening process.'

'Is campaigning against homophobia weird?'

'Maybe not. But it's a bit of a pisser when what you were expecting was an introduction to his closest friends and what you get is a gang of hardcore campaigners dead set on recruiting you. There were crocheted tams, Mags.'

'Shit, really?'

'And don't get me started on Pickled Egg Johnny. Big mulleted Scouser in short shorts who kept giving me the eye.'

Maggie frowned. 'Pickled Egg Johnny? Why do they call him that?'

'Dunno. Suppose he must eat a lot of pickled eggs.'

'Did you see him eat one?'

'Well, no. But he must do. How else do you get a name like that?'

'Where do they even sell pickled eggs? I swear I've never seen a pickled egg outside an episode of *EastEnders*.'

'Maybe that's his job. Chief pickled egg supplier to the Queen Vic, by royal appointment.'

'So is that it then? Are we scrubbing Adorable Nat off the eligible bachelor list?'

'S'pose so. Shame, since he was the only one on it.'

Ibby was silent a moment.

'Shame,' he said again.

He looked pretty down. Maggie knew he'd had high hopes for Nat.

Well, she'd dealt with an upset Ibby many times in the fifteen years they'd been friends and there was one guaranteed cure for the blues.

'Bangers and mash?'

Ibby smiled. 'What would I do without you?'

'Make your own bloody bangers and mash, I expect,' she said, smiling back.

'Will you do it with all the sausages sticking out like in *The Beano*?'

'Always do, don't I?'

'You're the perfect woman, Mags, you know that?' he said, pecking her cheek.

She headed to the kitchen.

'Well if you've got any fit straight friends, would you mind passing it on to them?' she called through the door. 'We can't all afford to chuck men away at the rate you do.'

'Nah, then I'd have to share you. Anyway, I thought you'd given up on men.'

'I could come out of retirement for one of the Chrisses. Hemsworth, Pratt or Evans, I'm not fussy.'

'I think there's a queue, unfortunately.'

She put the oven on to preheat and poured them a drink each.

'To be honest, after all this time I'd be happy with a nice straightforward shag, no strings attached,' she said with a sigh, handing him a glass of wine and chucking herself back down on the sofa. 'Three years, Ibs. Three sexless, miserable years.'

'Hey. How miserable could they have been when you had my hot and chiselled features to gaze upon?'

Maggie snorted. 'Yeah, triffic.' Her eyes widened. 'Oh God, what if this is it for me? What if I'm destined to spend my life listening to everyone's sex issues while never getting to have sex again myself? I wasn't even paying attention properly last time! If it was my last shag ever, I should've been notified in advance; that's only fair.'

'Okay, if you haven't got laid by fifty I'll rent you a gigolo for your birthday. Happy?'

She patted his cheek. 'You're sweet.'

'You should count yourself lucky anyway. It's been four for me. And I put my pulling pants on tonight and everything.'

'Well, that's your own fault. You either need to lower your standards or close your eyes and think of Harrison.'

'Wouldn't have needed to with Nat,' he muttered.

'Does it have to be the end? He really seemed like he might be the one to tick all the boxes.'

'I think it does. I can't be part of that world, that fight, and it's obviously a big part of who he is.' He patted her knee. 'No reason you shouldn't get back out there though.'

'Dunno. You meet enough Dans and arsehole clients like the one I had today, you start to wonder if there's any decent blokes still available.' She glanced at him. 'Anyway, I can't risk losing the one good man I have found, can I?'

'Mags, stop with that. I've told you a thousand times, the Dan thing wasn't your fault.'

'Never said it was.'

'I can smell the guilt a mile off. It's fine, okay? I know you'd never let anything jeopardise what we've got.'

She sighed. 'But I almost did, didn't I? Blinded by my stupid hormones, or whatever it was that stopped me working out what he was up to for so long.'

'Trust me, Maggie, blokes like that know what they're about. They prey on the good guys because they think believing the best in people is a weakness to be exploited. So bin the guilty conscience and move on, eh? For me.'

'Well, I have to admit I do miss the intimacy of being with someone,' she confessed. 'Even with the non-Dans it's a lot to ask though, isn't it? The whole Ibbotson-Nightingale shebang.'

'I know, same for me. Still, I wouldn't swap our little family for anyone. No matter how many boxes he ticked.'

'Me neither.'

Ibby dragged his fingers along the green spines that ran down the back of her onesie. 'Hey, Mags. You're a professional sex person. You ever wondered how stegosauruses do it?'

'Amazingly, no. We don't get many stegosauruses in for couples counselling.'

'I mean, they couldn't just have done it the usual way four-legged things do, could they? The spines'd do them an injury. They must have had some special position just for them. You know, like… steggie-style.'

'Maybe they did it the same way as porcupines.'

'Why, how do porcupines do it?'

'What am I, David Attenborough?' she said, shrugging. 'So what are the musings on rampant dinosaur sex in aid of then?'

'Just trying to take my mind off stuff.'

'Is it working?'

'Not really. It's just driving home the fact that even stegosauruses have better love lives than me. And they're extinct.' He sighed. 'I really wanted this one to work, Mags.'

'I know you did. I'm sorry.'

'Well, enough feeling sorry for ourselves,' he said, summoning a smile. 'Melie's out and we've got the house to ourselves. Sausages, wine and film night, the next best things to sex.'

She kissed his cheek. 'Perfect. I'll go get the dinner on.'

In the kitchen, Maggie flicked on the radio and grimaced as Route 69 blared out. She turned it off again, deciding she preferred her own accompaniment.

She launched into a bit of S-Club Seven as she bustled about, occasionally adding a little twirl. With Amelia out, she was free to be as tragically embarrassing as she liked.

In the sitting room, Ibby felt the buzz of his phone. He went into the hall, out of earshot, to take the call.

'What do you want, Nat?' he said when he answered. 'Not sure I'm in the mood for talking to you.'

'I wanted to apologise.'

'Bloody right. What the hell was that all about tonight, manning the fucking barricades?'

'I'm sorry. We got a bit overexcited, that's all. I didn't mean to scare you.'

'When you said meet your mates, that really wasn't what I had in mind.'

'It wasn't a trick, Ibby. I just thought you might like to join us.'

'No, you didn't think, Nat, you assumed.'

'Suppose I did.' He sounded ashamed. 'Sorry about that. I should've made it clear.'

'I had thought...' Ibby bit his lip. 'I mean, when I invite someone to meet my friends, that's usually a pretty big deal, you know?'

'I'm sorry. It was a big deal. I... thought you'd want to be a part of this.'

'You know what I thought? And yeah, I don't care if it sounds pathetic at this stage. I thought we'd have a quick drink with your mates, romantic dinner, then maybe, just maybe, a kiss and a cuddle back at mine. Not some bloke called Pickled Egg Johnny and the rest of the Applecroft People's Front.'

'People's Front of Applecroft.'

'Not laughing, Nat.'

'Ibby, please, don't be that way. The guys asked if you'd be involved, and you're right, it's not for me to speak for you, but…' He sighed. 'I thought you'd want to.'

'But you didn't ask, did you?'

'No. You're right, that was out of order. Sorry.'

'Look, it's not that I don't care. Obviously it's important. But there are other important things – things important to me personally, and they come first.'

'Your little girl, right?'

'And Maggie. I'm sorry, but they're my family.'

'So you want to go out again?' Nat asked after a pause. 'Just us next time, promise.'

'No. No, I don't think so.'

'Come on, just because of tonight?'

'No, Nat, because of you. I can't date a personality cult. I want a quiet life and I'm sensing you're not the quiet life kind, are you?'

'Well if it comes to it, I'm not sure I can date someone who's apathetic to the point of self-delusion,' Nat snapped. 'Ibby, I really wanted you to be in this with me.'

'I'm not apathetic.' Ibby kept his voice low so Maggie wouldn't hear. 'I just won't be a figurehead. Sorry, but it affects people other than me, people I love. Anyway, I'd only be shit at it and let down The Glorious Cause.'

'Do you have to be so sarcastic about it? It does actually matter, whether or not you want to get involved.'

Ibby sighed. 'Yeah, I know. Sorry. I just can't, that's all.'

'Aren't you even angry? Because I can tell you, mate, I'm mad as hell. No one's got the right to treat us like that.'

'What's the point? I can't change anything.'

'Why can't you?'

'Because it's not just that guy at the Sea Pig, is it? Those feelings run deep. It's too big for one person.'

'But one person plus one person makes two people. Me and you. And you do that sum a few times over, you've got quite a lot of people.'

'Yeah? And how many does it take to change the world?'

'I always felt it just took one, given the right circumstances,' Nat said quietly. 'But two's better. We owe it to ourselves to try.'

'You might. I don't owe myself a thing.'

'Ibby—'

'Leave it, Nat, can you?' he snapped. 'Listen, I'm not your bloody Mockingjay. I'm not the hero Somerset deserves. I'm not Nelson fucking Mandela. I'm just a slob, all right? Just a regular waste of space like everyone else. I want to come home and drink beer in my pants and raise my daughter and leave the world to sort out its own screwed-up problems. I didn't start them.'

'Look, I know you must've been there too,' Nat said. 'Taken the slurs from so-called mates that they dismissed as "banter", forced yourself to laugh at off-colour jokes made at your expense. I have – hell, we all have. Until one day I decided it was more important to be right than to be liked.'

'It's different for you. I've got a kid, and if I'm going to be part of some public campaign then that affects her too.'

'Exactly. You have got a kid. So tell me this, Ibby: would you give the same answer if it was her?'

'What?'

'If it happened to Amelia. If someone treated her that way, humiliated her, just because she was with someone they didn't think she ought to be with. That's the world she has to grow up in.'

Ibby was silent a moment.

'Sorry, Nat,' he said at last. 'I like you a lot. I think you're right. But I can't help you.'

He hung up.

Chapter Eleven

Jordan sat in his hotel room, cradling his guitar. The expectant eyes of Riley, Jake and Lucas, the other members of Route 69, were fixed on him. Craig was facing away, having a fag out of the window, but to Jordan even the back of his manager's head seemed to be telling him this had better be good.

'Okay, so this is a bit different from the stuff I was writing before I... before,' he told them. His hands were trembling. Coming off coke had done nothing for his anxiety. The doctors had promised this was a withdrawal symptom that would disappear in time, but in the week he'd been out of rehab, it had been getting steadily worse.

'How different?' Riley demanded.

'Well it's still me – us, I mean. It's just got more of a *Mix Tape* flavour than the stuff we've done recently.' He smiled. 'Must've been feeling nostalgic.'

'*Mix Tape?*' Lucas shook his head at the mention of Route 69's debut album. Of the four of them, only Jordan and Riley had been in the line-up back then. 'We don't want to be going that far back. 69's moved on from the angry young man shit.'

'This one's not a protest song. It's kind of a love song.'

'Play it already,' Craig said without looking round. 'We've got lives to live, Jord.'

'I'm sure it'll be great,' Jake, their drummer, said with a reassuring smile.

Jordan frowned. 'Why are you sure?'

'Because they're always great, aren't they?'

'Not when I first write them. It's your job to help me make them better.' He glared at Jake. 'Did Craig tell you lot to go easy on me?'

'Course not.' But Jordan could tell by the guilty wince that he was lying.

He put his guitar down. 'Right. I'm not playing it.'

'Fucking diva musicians,' Craig muttered, flicking his fag away. 'Just think, if I'd worked harder at school I could've been managing a McDonald's in Swindon by now.' He turned around. 'Play the song, Jordan. No one's going easy on you.'

'You promise? No softly, softly for the poor recovering addict?'

'If it's crap then I swear I personally will rip into every lyric and note of it until you're in the foetal position, weeping. Then I'll kick you in the balls for an encore. Happy?'

Jordan grinned. 'That'll do.' He picked up his guitar again. 'Okay, so it's about this girl.'

'What girl?' Riley asked.

'An imaginary one,' he said, shrugging. 'She's kind of... a metaphor for lost futures, I think. The lives we might've lived if we'd chosen another path.'

Jordan struck up the first chord and launched into his song. It was low and wistful, with something – a kind of impotent, self-facing anger, tempered with sadness – simmering below the surface.

'So? What do you think?' Jordan asked when the last note had faded.

Craig was silent a long moment before he gave his verdict.

'I think, Jordan, that we've got a hit.'

Jordan broke into a smile of relief. 'Seriously, you think the fans'll go for it?'

'I do.'

Riley shook his head slowly. 'Tell you what, mate, rehab's done you good. Best thing you've written in years. I might have to go for a break at that place myself.'

'The day you quit gear is the day my elderly nana finally achieves her lifelong dream and gets on *Strictly*,' Craig said. Riley grinned and shrugged.

'We'll get that down in the next few weeks,' Craig told Jordan.

'That fast? We haven't rehearsed it yet.'

'Yep, that fast. I want it on *Sleepwalking* and I want it out as a single in the run-up to the album release.'

'On *Sleepwalking*? But that's done. I wrote this for the next one.'

'It's too good not to be your comeback song, Jord. This is exactly what you need after rehab, a new album with a guaranteed hit to sell it. If we have to postpone release date to get it on there, so be it.'

Jordan blinked. 'Wow. You really do like it.'

Lucas slapped him on the back as the band filed out. 'Coming, Jord? Party in Riley's room tonight. I've invited some girls.'

'Not tonight, I want to practise the song a bit more. You guys have fun.'

When they'd gone, Craig chucked himself into a chair. 'Come on then, star, what're you really doing tonight?'

Jordan shrugged. 'Telly.'

'Jesus. You know, this retro sitcom habit's probably worse for you than the coke.'

'I can't go with them, can I? Too much temptation.' He glanced up. 'But you could sub us another smoke.'

'I thought you were quitting,' Craig said, handing one over.

'I've quit buying. It's a start, right?'

Craig regarded his client with a worried gaze. 'You look knackered, Jord.'

'Yeah, not sleeping so well. It'll get easier, they promised me in rehab.'

'How're you finding it?'

'Tough going, but I'm determined. Seven weeks clean. If I can just keep away from the stuff...' He rubbed his nose with the back of one trembling hand, fighting the craving that reared up whenever he thought about coke. 'I miss the feeling it gave me more than anything. Being invincible. God knows how I'll cope on stage.'

'You'll be okay.'

'I'm not so sure.' He shuddered. 'And the interviews when the new album comes out, and then the tour... Shit, Craig, how'll I manage on tour? It'll be everywhere in the bus, and Riley's... you know what he's like. Maybe I came out of treatment too soon.'

'Don't worry about the tour. I'll look after you.'

Jordan flashed him a grateful smile. 'Thanks, mate.'

Craig was silent a moment.

'You want some company tonight, Jord?' he said in a low voice.

'No. No, not tonight.'

'Come on. It's not good for you, sitting on your own brooding.'

'You can stay if you want.'

Craig snorted. 'What, to tuck you in and sing you a lullaby? I'm your manager, not your mum.'

'Well no, she's in fucking *Celeb Big Brother*, isn't she?' Jordan lit his cigarette and went to lean on the windowsill. 'You can watch TV with me. It's *Keeping Up Appearances* tonight.'

'Christ, you must be kidding. I'm going to Riley's, make sure they don't overdo it. Don't forget we've got photoshoots in the morning.' He approached the window and squeezed Jordan's shoulder. 'Go on, let me find you someone. Nice, clean girl, eh? Bit of healthy company'll do you good.'

'I'm... not supposed to.'

'You're not supposed to date. That wasn't exactly what I had in mind.'

Jordan sighed. 'Check IDs then. No one under twenty-five or they're straight out again.'

Amelia pouted in front of the mirror, her lips coated in her mum's Cherry Berry lippy. It definitely made her look older. Definitely.

She wondered what Isaac would think if he didn't already know she was a Year Nine. If she bumped into him in the street, and he wondered who the pretty, sophisticated girl wearing the Midnight Fantasy perfume was. She'd bought it especially because Georgia said it was guaranteed boy bait, even though it had cost her a month's pocket money.

Three years wasn't such a big gap, was it? If she could just get him to notice her...

Her gaze fell on the music magazine lying on her bed, which had a Route 69 special edition cover. Georgia had lent her copy to Amelia on the strict condition that she handled it with the tender love you might usually show a newborn kitten.

The front bore a photo of Jordan leaning casually, smiling with one side of his mouth in the way that made Georgia go weak at the knees. His arms, heavily tattooed, were folded across his broad chest and his rumpled black hair was in the bedhead style that so many of the boys at school tried to copy.

Amelia's lip curled. He might be Georgie's dream man, but he'd never appealed to her. Apart from being tragically ancient, he seemed kind of full of himself, and she couldn't bear arrogant boys. Plus he was on drugs, everyone knew it. She couldn't understand what her friend found so irresistible about him. Okay, he had that whole Brendon Urie bad-boy thing going on, but please. Geek chic was so much hotter.

Plenty of people did find him irresistible though. Most of the girls in her year crushed on him, and boys wanted to be like him. Even Isaac wished he could be like Jordan.

She glanced again at the confident pose, the cheeky smile. It didn't seem fair that some people could just be that way. Be liked and noticed with no effort at all, while she could run naked down the street and still be invisible.

Her phone buzzed and she snatched it off the bed.

I no sum1 whos into u

Georgia's WhatsApp message said.

Who?

Plz say Isaac Helms

In answer, Georgia sent a photo of the Coding Club session they'd been to after school. She'd managed to capture a pic of Rory McCallum, staring intently at Amelia's back as she worked on her Python project.

Ugh. Rory. She had liked him, for a short while last year. They'd even gone out that one time. But now she was nearly fourteen, and she was so over little boys like him.

Hes lookin @ ur bra thru ur shirt

I no. Children r so tragic

Amelia messaged Georgia back and chucked the phone down on the bed.

Her gaze fell again on the photo of Jordan Nash, and the briar rose inked onto his right forearm. She pulled up her own sleeve and examined the white skin.

What, she wondered, would Isaac think about her if she had a tattoo?

Chapter Twelve

Clara Anderson couldn't believe her luck.

Jordan Nash, the idol of her teen years, the man she'd known, deep in her soul, that one day she'd marry, was in this hotel. And she was actually going to meet him!

'Did Jordan really invite me personally?' she breathed to the thin, hawkish man who'd introduced himself as Route 69's manager, Craig, as she trotted after him along the hotel corridor.

'Sure. Spotted you from his balcony, asked me to see if you'd care to join him for the evening. You'll like him, he's a good lad.'

Like him? She'd been heart and soul in love with him since her brother had bought her *Mix Tape* for her twelfth birthday.

'Just a bit of paperwork to sort out first,' Craig said, ushering her into his own room. 'Sorry, but I can't be too careful. Not with my star.'

—

Jordan was slumped against his headboard, watching TV.

Craig had been gone a while. Perhaps there weren't any girls around tonight.

Jordan wasn't too bothered, although he was a bit lonely. Hanging out with fans never seemed to help though. They didn't know him, and they weren't interested in him as anything other than the lead singer of Route 69. Being with them was just a way of being lonely with other people.

Still. He was longing to be close to someone, even if it wasn't real. To fall asleep next to them and wake up in their arms. Yes, he'd like that a lot...

There was usually a gaggle of local fans hanging round outside the hotels the band stayed at. Routers, they called themselves, which Jordan couldn't help thinking was the shittest fan group name ever. Still, he supposed it was better than 69ers, which sounded like a cross between a sex position and a champion conker. Whenever he or one of the other lads got lonely, there were always girls happy to sign one of the non-disclosure agreements Craig kept handy and favour them with some company.

There was a knock at the door. He flicked off the TV and went to answer it.

'All right?' Craig said. 'Yep, found her. Outside like you said.'

Jordan nodded, playing along. Craig always gave the girls the same line, about Jordan having picked them out of the crowd to be his companion for the night. It made them feel special.

Craig ushered the girl forward. She was rather sweet-looking, with long chestnut hair and a curvy figure.

'Clara,' he said by way of an introduction. 'Clara, this is Jordan Nash. But I'm sure you know that. I'll, er, leave you kids to get acquainted.'

'Hiya,' Jordan said. 'Clara. Nice name. Come on in.'

Clara followed him, temporarily robbed of speech. Her eyes were round as she took in the lavish hotel suite, the huge bed and the guitar propped against one wall. Jordan's actual guitar! She wondered if she'd dare ask him to play it for her.

'You want a drink?' Jordan asked. 'There's a minibar.'

'Um, a gin and tonic would be nice. Or anything really. Whatever you're having.'

'I'm not. But don't let that stop you.'

Jordan mixed her a G&T and chucked himself back on the bed.

Clara stared at the glass in her hand, wondering if she'd just made some massive faux pas. Jordan Nash was a recovering addict, she knew that. And here she was drinking in front of him. That was probably the worst thing to do when someone was just out of rehab.

'Oh God, I'm so sorry,' she whispered. 'You don't drink, do you? I didn't think, I... please don't be offended.'

'No, I do drink. Alcohol dependency was never the problem. I just don't fancy drinking tonight.' Jordan smiled. 'But thanks for the concern, Clara.'

Her heart lurched into her throat. Jordan Nash was sitting on a huge bed, saying her name. She'd fantasised about this so many, many times.

He jerked his head towards the bed. 'Want to join me?'

Actually, no. This was what she'd fantasised about.

Clara floated over and sat down beside him, every thud of her heartbeat audible to her.

'Jordan, I love your work,' she breathed. 'I always have, ever since I heard your first album.'

'Thank you,' Jordan said, although this sort of talk bored him daft. 'I hope you'll like the new one.'

'I know I will.' Her gaze fell on the guitar. 'Is that... is that really yours?'

'No, it's Riley's. He left it here so it wouldn't get damaged while they were partying. Lucas chucked his old one out the window after a row so now he's extra cautious.'

'Oh.'

'Mine's over there.'

Jordan nodded to a desk against the wall. Sure enough, there was a guitar case underneath.

'Can I... would it be okay for me to see it?'

He shrugged. 'Help yourself.'

Clara went to unclasp the guitar. She ran her hands reverently over the curves and strings.

It was an odd sensation. How often had she seen Jordan Nash up on stage, making passionate, life-changing music with this very instrument? And now it was here, in her hands. Hopefully before long, its owner would be too.

'Is this the one you used on *Mix Tape*?'

'Yeah. An old friend.'

'That was the first album I ever owned.' Her colour rose as she joined him on the bed again. '"Missing You" is my favourite song. I even had this done. I traced it out from the sleeve liner notes, so I could have a little piece of it – of you, I mean – always with me.'

She pulled her loose-fitting boho top down so he could see her shoulder blade. There was a tattoo, written out in a close approximation of his own handwriting. *Shut up and live*, it read. One of the lyrics from 'Missing You', the song that had given him his very first hit.

Jordan winced. He knew what a massive compliment it was when fans had his lyrics permanently inked onto their bodies, but bloody hell, it was terrifying. And in his own handwriting, Christ. He rubbed his nose with the back of his hand.

'Wow,' he said. 'I'm glad it meant so much to you.'

Clara nodded emphatically. 'It did. It spoke to me. All your songs do, I mean, they're part of me, they're—'

Jordan interrupted before she got stuck in gush mode. 'Hey, you want to watch TV?'

She blinked. 'TV?'

'Yeah. I usually watch Gold, but you can pick.'

'Um, I thought… I mean, aren't we going to talk, or…' She hesitated. 'You know, get to know each other?'

'We can do both, can't we?'

'I guess.'

Jordan handed her the remote and she flicked on the huge TV. It was tuned to his favourite channel, Gold, and the sitcoms he'd found himself hooked on during his time in rehab. Hyacinth Bucket-pronounced-Bouquet had just fallen into her sister's hedge again.

'You ever watch this?' Jordan said. 'It's dreadful. I must've ⌐sode and it's the same jokes over and over.'

'Then why watch it?'

He shrugged. 'I think it reminds me of being a kid. My nana used to love all those sitcoms. Every Saturday night when I was a little boy I'd get into my pyjamas and we'd have cocoa and watch them snuggled on the sofa.'

'She sounds like a nice lady.'

'Yeah. She was.' He nodded to the TV. 'Change the channel if you like. You're the guest.'

Clara flicked through a few programmes, reflecting on the turn the evening had taken.

She'd gone along to the hotel with a group of friends just in the hope of catching a glimpse of the band. When she'd been picked from a load of other Routers to spend the night with Jordan Nash, one of the most lusted-after men in the country and the one true love of her life, she'd been in ecstasies. Images had flashed through her mind of parties, celebrities, glamour. Being taken into Jordan's big, muscular arms, pressed against his chest and kissed silly before he threw her onto the bed and ravished her. She hadn't, truth be told, expected to be watching *Keeping Up Appearances* on Gold.

She stopped channel-hopping on *Celebrity Big Brother*, where a couple of Z-listers were giggling together in a hot tub.

'That's your mother, isn't it?'

'Yeah,' Jordan said, scowling.

'Who's in the hot tub with her?'

'God knows. Bobby Davro's second cousin or someone, probably.'

She squinted at the screen. 'No it's not, it's Tyler, that guy off *TOWIE*. Who's Bobby Davro?'

He turned to look at her. 'How old are you, Clara?'

'Twenty-one.'

'Bloody Craig, I'll throttle him,' he muttered.

'What?'

'Nothing. Turn it over, please. I can't stand that woman.'

Clara stared at him. 'Your mum? But she's always saying how close the two of you are.'

'She's a liar.' Jordan glared at the figure on the screen. 'Story for you, Clara. When I was a toddler, Sylvia there dropped me off at my nan's while she and my dad went out for the night. Only it must've been a pretty heavy one, because you'll never guess. They forgot to come back for me.'

'Fuck!' Clara's hand flew to her mouth. 'I'm sorry. I didn't mean to swear.'

'No, that's the right response for anyone who's a human being.'

'Did they ever come back?'

'Oh yeah, Sylvia remembered me eventually. Funnily enough, it was right after my first number one. Coincidence, right?'

'And where's your dad?'

'Six foot under, now. He died of a heroin overdose a couple of years after they dumped me.'

'Oh God. You poor little boy.' Clara took his hand and gave it a squeeze.

He shrugged. 'I could go all woe-is-me about it, but my parents ditching me was the best thing that could've happened really. Nana did a better job of bringing me up than Sylvia ever could. I think the hardest thing about having a surrogate parent a generation up was always knowing I might lose her young.'

'When did she die?'

'When I was nineteen. I wrote "Missing You" for her.' He sighed. 'Come on, kid, let's find something fun to watch. I'm sick of that story.'

Clara started channel-hopping again, until Jordan put a hand on her arm.

'Ha! Class.' He grinned at the screen. 'One of the best films ever made, this. *Indiana Jones and the Last Crusade*. Most people prefer *Raiders*, but this one's my favourite.'

'I've never seen it.'

'Good God, really? I had a mate at university who'd have had you burned as a heretic for admitting that.'

Clara didn't know what a heretic was, but she decided not to ask. Maybe it was a reference to some other thing from way before her time.

She'd always known Jordan was older than her, but he seemed so... well, not at all like she'd imagined when she'd watched him jumping about on stage, intense as hell and on fire with his music. This Jordan reminded her of her dad.

'So we're just going to watch this film and then...'

'I'll get you a cab. You shouldn't be walking the streets at this time.'

Okay. She had to try, even if it was just to have a story to take back to her friends.

'I could stay over.' She untangled her hand from Jordan's and slid it seductively along his thigh. 'You seem like you want some company.'

'No, kid. You'd better go home.' Jordan removed the hand from his leg. 'Tonight I'm the sort of company who's only good for a hug and Indiana Jones.'

Clara sighed as she wrapped her arms around him. It was true. You should never meet your heroes.

Chapter Thirteen

It was nearly two months after their conversation about his sex life when Other Max finally shuffled into Maggie's office. A counselling centre was well outside his comfort zone, and he looked a combination of terrified and guilty.

Maggie knew the problem was still there from her chats with Nicki, which had become a regular thing now, but she hadn't liked to press Other Max to talk to her. They'd been friends long enough for her to know he needed to do things in his own time or he'd just get even more stressed.

She swallowed the last of her sandwich. 'All right?'

'Hi Mags.' He was sidling, that was the only word for it. His cheeks had flushed bright red.

'Sit down, can you? You look like a crab.'

He sat on one of her sofas, perching right on the edge as if prepared to bolt if necessary.

'So, er... what do you usually do then? To start things off?' he asked. 'I mean, with your proper clients.'

'Well, I usually ask them to remove their clothes first, then we can proceed with the physical examination.'

He stared at her.

She smiled. 'Joke, mate. I usually start by offering a cuppa.' She went to the kettle. 'Tea?'

'Oh. Yeah. Cheers.'

When she'd made them a drink, she took a seat next to him.

'So I take it the situation hasn't changed?' she prompted.

'It has a bit.' He stared into his tea. 'Nic told me she loved me last night.'

'You don't look very happy about it.'

'I am happy. I'm also terrified. I mean, I feel the same, but...' He gave his head an angsty shake. 'That's why I made myself come here today. Mags, I don't know what to do. You'll help me, won't you?'

There was a note of pleading in his voice that appealed to Maggie's tenderest instincts.

'Course I will. You've got my full professional attention.'

'I just don't understand what I'm doing wrong. I try to focus on her pleasure, plenty of foreplay.' His blush deepened. 'Even Googled it. Trying to find out if there's some technique everyone knows about but me.'

'There isn't,' Maggie said. 'Loads of people think that; that everyone's secretly having better sex than them. It's a surefire way to put you more on edge.'

'So what am I doing wrong?'

'Well... okay, you mentioned foreplay. How much, what kind?'

He nearly choked on his drink. 'You don't want all the details, do you?'

'Come on, Other Max. We've been mates fifteen years. I spend all day listening to people talk about sex. You don't need to be shy with me.' She swallowed a mouthful of tea. 'Plus in case you've forgotten, I have actually shagged you.'

That raised a smile. Other Max relaxed slightly, leaning back against the sofa.

'I just didn't know that was how it worked.'

'You're a paramedic, aren't you? Be a bit clinical, if it helps.'

'Okay, well, there's kissing, obviously. Then, er... I mean, she usually... well, then I... er, breasts.'

Maggie couldn't help smiling. 'Breasts? That's all you're giving me?'

'Yeah. Like playing with them and that. She told me she likes that, they're very... sensitive. Um. And then the other important bits, you know, stroking and kissing and... things.'

He grabbed a cushion and placed it on his lap, carefully avoiding eye contact.

'And what about you?'

'What about me?'

'Well, you've told me what Nicki likes. What do you like?'

He shrugged. 'Dunno, anything. I just want to make Nic happy.'

'I see.' Maggie put her tea down. 'This is your problem, Other Max. You're too bloody nice.'

'You what?'

'Tell me this. What's the point of sex, other than for making babies?'

'Well, it's… fun, isn't it? And a way of being close, I guess.'

'Exactly. It's fun, or it's supposed to be, and you're treating it like an exam,' Maggie said. 'Lighten up. Enjoy yourself. Think about what you want as well as Nic. And for God's sake stop being so damn grateful. She loves you, she's not going to bed with you as a favour.'

'Think about what I want?'

'Yeah. It's great that you're so unselfish when it comes to her needs, but it's not wrong to think about your own. There're two people in that bed. Stop asking what Nic likes all the time and tell her what you like. Or better still, show her.' She leaned round to look into his face. 'Do you find her attractive? Does she turn you on?'

'God, yes, course she does. She's beautiful.'

'Then enjoy that. Appreciate her body, for your benefit as well as hers.'

Other Max looked thoughtful. 'I guess I have been making it all about her.'

'Exactly, and that's putting pressure on you both. It's not just men who can suffer from performance anxiety. If she feels you're obsessed with helping her reach climax, that's going to make it harder for her to do so. You see?'

'Yeah. That makes sense.'

'That's the difference between what's happening now and when me and you did it,' Maggie said, picking up her tea again. 'Back then we were just looking to have some fun. We had nothing to prove to each other.'

'I just want her to enjoy being with me.'

'And she'll enjoy being with you a whole lot more if you take the pressure off. Sex isn't all about orgasm-chasing. It's about trust, intimacy, bonding. Instead of trying to rush her over the finish line, focus on what feels good in the moment.'

He smiled, finally meeting her eye. 'You're good, aren't you?'

'I'm a phoney,' she said, shrugging. 'Strong on theory, weak on practical.'

'Go on, how long's it been?'

'Three years celibate now. Nice to know I'm helping other people to a better sex life than mine.'

'You should get yourself out there.'

'Ugh, don't you start. I literally had this conversation two weeks ago with Ibby.'

'Well, why not? Sign up to Tinder, me and Ibs'll write you a profile.'

'Like we did for Ibs?'

'Yeah. We won't even mention that bloody awful dinosaur onesie of yours, how about that?'

'What's the point? No one decent's going to take me on, not the way things are at home. I'll end up with another Dan.'

'Dan was a jealous, controlling prick. Not every bloke on Tinder's going to be like him.'

'Hmm. But it'd be just my luck to find the ones that are.'

'Doesn't it get you down?' he asked. 'Helping couples with their problems all day with no one to go home to at night?'

'I have got someone to go home to.'

'You know what I mean. A romantic partner.'

She sighed. 'Sometimes. But then other days I'll listen to all these relationship issues and the pain they cause and think I'm well out of it.'

'You been in love, Maggie? Since Max, I mean?'

She looked up at him in surprise. 'Who's counselling who here?'

He shrugged. 'You helped me out, I thought you might like a listening ear in return. Tell you what, I won't even bill you.'

'Gee, thanks.' She looked away. 'Not really had the chance, have I? I mean, there was Dan, but... no. It was only ever Max really.'

'Do you think you'd still be together? If things had worked out differently?'

'Probably not. I'm not sure he was the settling type. And if they had then I wouldn't have what I've got now.' She shook her head. 'No, I'm better off as I am. I do miss a cuddle, but I wouldn't swap Ibs and Amelia for any amount of Maxes.'

'Well, there's a Max here who can help with a cuddle.' He put down his tea and gave her a hug.

'Thanks,' she whispered.

'Just don't give up, okay? Everyone deserves a bit of love. Even us lot.'

'All right, so you've found your perfect woman. No need to get smug,' she said, smiling as he released her. 'Good luck, Other Max. And congratulations.'

Chapter Fourteen

The day smelled like summer. Like flowers and suncream and Cornettos. It was no time to be stuck in school but Amelia and Georgia were making the best of it, sunning themselves on the wall outside the science block after being let out of their last lesson early.

'Hey, do you think I'd look cool with a tattoo?'

Amelia poked her forearm into Georgia's eyeline. Her friend ignored it and fished some strawberry sorbet lip gloss from her bag. She rubbed on a generous smear then took out her phone for a pouty selfie.

'What d'you reckon? Pink glow flower crown or classic flower crown?' she asked as she scrolled through Snapchat filters. 'Hey, can you smell chocolate?'

'Georgie, you know you've got the attention span of a goldfish?'

Georgia sniffed. 'I'm telling you. Chocolate.'

She rummaged in her rucksack again, emerging a few seconds later clutching a Club biscuit triumphantly.

'Told you, didn't I?' She peeled off the wrapper. 'Want some? No, course you don't,' she said before Amelia had a chance to answer. 'You never do.'

It was one of nature's many heinous crimes against humanity that Georgia could guzzle chocolate without ever gaining a pound, while she, Amelia, turned into Muffintop Thunderthighs – Viking chief of the tribe Fattyboomboom – if she so much as inhaled the scent of a Twix.

'Helloooo, Earth to Georgia,' Amelia said, waving her arm. 'What do you think? Not like a big anchor or anything boring. Like maybe a butterfly.'

'He still wouldn't notice you,' Georgia said through a mouthful of biscuit crumbs.

'People notice Jordan Nash.'

'That's not just coz he's got lush tattoos though. He's gorgeous and talented and in a band. Oh God, have you *heard* that new song? I seriously can't even.'

Amelia hadn't heard it yet, but even if she seriously couldn't even either, she wasn't going to give Georgia the satisfaction of admitting it.

'No,' she said with an uninterested air. 'What's it about?'

'Some girl. It's like a love song.' Georgia sighed deeply. 'I wish he'd write a song about me.'

'Isaac says he prefers Jordan's early stuff.'

Georgia snorted. 'Oh, Isaac Isaac Isaac. Can't you have an opinion of your own then?'

'I have got an opinion.'

'Yeah, which is?'

'I prefer his early stuff too.'

'I thought you would.'

'Route 69 are nowhere near as good as Little Mix anyway.'

Georgia smirked. 'I bet you never told Isaac your favourite band was Little Mix, did you?'

'No. But I would if he asked.' Amelia's cheeks flamed under what she knew was a bare-faced lie. 'Don't you dare tell him though.'

'Jordan is so as good as Little Mix. Plus he's hot too.'

'You do know he's ancient, right? He's literally the same age as my mum and dad. Major boak.' Amelia retched theatrically.

'He's still sexy. Sexier than geeky old Isaac.'

'He is not. Isaac's beautiful,' Amelia said hotly. 'Jordan's an old man, Georgie.'

'Shut up!' Georgia wiped her mouth and turned to face Amelia, looking worried. 'He's not really the same age as your parents though?'

'Yeah, like thirty-four. God, can you believe being that old?'

Georgia nudged her. 'Can you believe being that old and still not having a boyfriend? Because your mum and dad can.'

Ugh. Here it came again: The Conversation. Like Georgia and chocolate, Amelia could smell it a mile off.

She remembered the day she'd started Applecroft Secondary nearly three years ago; her mum's parting words as she'd straightened a quivering Amelia's tie at the gates.

'You know I love you very much, don't you, Melie?'

'Yes, Mum,' she'd said, rolling her eyes.

'And Dad does too. And we're proud of you and...' Her mum trailed off, seeing Amelia's eyes darting anxiously from side to side as the other kids streamed past. 'I'm being embarrassing mum lady, aren't I?'

'Little bit.'

She smiled. 'Sorry. I just wanted you to know – look, sweetie, when you make new friends, it's fine if you tell them me and Dad are a couple. We won't think you're ashamed of us.'

Eleven-year-old Amelia's eyes had widened. 'You want me to tell a *lie*?'

She'd been easily shocked back then.

'Not a lie exactly,' her mum had said, looking pained. 'More a little fib. I mean, we are a couple. We're just a couple of friends rather than a couple of... couple.'

'But Mum, why would I tell fibs about you?' the younger, more innocent Amelia had asked.

'Well...' Her mum's face still had the same pained look. 'It's unusual, that's all, the way things are at home. I know kids can be little buggers when it comes to anything that makes you different. We'd hate for you to get bullied.'

But her mum had been worrying over nothing. Amelia had been honest with the kids who'd asked about her family for the simple reason that she was a rotten fibber, and to her parents' relief, she never had been bullied. Plenty of the others had step-parents, single parents, adopted parents – there was even a boy in Mr Carter's class with two mums – and they took it pretty much in their stride. It might've been different if she'd been the year group's official Weird Kid: that title belonged to poor Ava Fishwick, a shy, awkward girl who frequently came to school with Rice Krispies stuck to her hair. But people warmed easily to little Amelia, and they were happy to overlook what was different about her.

Her family *was* different though, there was no getting away from that. No one else in school had a mum and dad quite like hers. There was no bullying but there was curiosity. Of course there was; it was school. Amelia felt like she'd been subjected to a barrage of questions over the past three years, leaving her heartily sick of the subject of her thoroughly modern family.

Georgia, despite having been her best friend since Reception, was definitely the worst culprit. No matter how many times Amelia told her that her home life was totally boring and ordinary, no matter how often Georgia slept over and saw for herself, she just couldn't seem to get her head round it.

'Isn't it weird though?' Georgia said, spluttering crumbs obliviously.

'No.' Amelia was on the defensive at once. 'Shut up. Why would it be?'

'Come on, it must be a bit.'

'I've got a mum and a dad and they love me and they love each other. That's not weird, it's perfect.' Amelia recited the well-rehearsed answer as if it was a mantra. 'I mean, sometimes I used to feel sad I'd never get a baby brother or sister, but I'm over it. I'd rather have my mum and dad just how they are.'

'But it must feel strange sometimes. Like your dad going out with that Nat guy.'

'Why shouldn't he go out with people?' Amelia was working up a good head of steam now. 'Dad's great. He's funny even when he's totes embarrassing, and he always says the right thing to cheer you up, and he's a complete loser but in the best way. It's not all about him being my dad – he's his own person too. I think he deserves a nice boyfriend.' She jutted her chin. '*That's* being unselfish and mature, Georgie. You should try it.'

'Hmm. Doesn't your mum get jealous?'

'I keep telling you, they aren't together like that. They're besties, same as us. You know Dad doesn't like girls that way.'

'Does it scare you?'

'What?'

'When your mum and dad crush on other people.'

'Why should it? I mean, it's disgusting, obvs, but...'

'Well, what if your dad likes his new boyfriend more than your mum? Then he might move out and you'll never see him again.'

Amelia's insides did a sickening flip. She hadn't thought of that. Her dad was just... her dad. Okay, she always parroted the line about him being his own person whenever Georgia started going on, but secretly she felt he was her dad over and above any other stuff.

'He wouldn't do that,' she said in a quiet voice.

'My dad left my mum for someone else.'

And Amelia knew Georgia had barely heard from him since.

'Not my dad,' Amelia said firmly. 'He wouldn't ever walk out on us.'

'And my mum and dad were actually having sex,' Georgia went on, ignoring her. 'He just went because he could get betterer sex off someone else. Your dad's not getting any sex off your mum. And if he was he wouldn't enjoy it because he doesn't like doing it with ladies.' Georgia looked her up and down. 'How did they even manage to make you?'

'I try not to think about it.'

'You know what Pyper told me?' Georgia cast a devastated look at the empty Club wrapper and stuffed it down her blouse into her padded bra. 'She said if one of your parents is gay, it means you can't ever have a baby. Because of inheriting too much eastergen. Or not enough, I can't remember.'

Amelia shook her head. 'You are so fake news, Georgia Fielding.'

'Swear to God.' Georgia licked the end of one finger and solemnly crossed herself. 'Pyper's dad's a gincolologist and he told her.'

'What's a gincolologist?'

'Vajayjay inspector,' Georgia declared confidently. 'He knows everything about sex and making babies.'

'Don't say vajayjay; it's crude. Say foofoo. That's ladylike.'

'All right, your maj, foofoo inspector then. Anyway, it's true.' Georgia stared at her. 'Did you want kids?'

Amelia ran one hand over her tummy. She'd had terrible cramps all day. It couldn't really be true, could it? They'd have told them in Biology.

But what if it was true, and the cramps meant her uterus was shrivelling up from too much eastergen? She didn't know if she wanted to have a baby one day, but it'd be nice to know she could. Isaac probably already thought she was a total loser, and if he knew she didn't have a full set of working girl bits down there then there was no way he'd ever see her as the glamorous sex kitten she was hoping any day now to morph into.

'Well, you can always adopt,' Georgia said in a kinder voice. 'And think of all the money you'll save on condoms—'

'Oh God, it's him!' Amelia hissed, grabbing Georgia's arm. This was what they'd been lurking outside the science block for. A group of sixth formers were streaming out of their last lesson, Isaac among them, chatting to a generously bosomed girl in a crop top.

'Look at you. You've got hcart-cycs-cmoji face, it's so tragic,' Georgia said. 'Be cool, Melie, okay? Try to look like you don't care. I mean, like you care a bit, but not too much.'

'How do I do that?'

'Well, sort of lean a bit. And pretend we're talking about something else, then, like, accidentally catch his eye or whatevs.'

Amelia leaned a bit. Then she jerked straight again as she nearly fell off the wall.

'Hey, are you okay?' Isaac said as he passed, noticing her wobbling.

'I'm fine.' Amelia tossed her hair. 'I was just talking about something else.' Georgia groaned silently.

The girl with Isaac laughed. 'You're a cute little girl. What's your name?'

'Amelia Ibbotson-Nightingale,' Amelia said, trying not to glare. She wasn't sure which description she found more insulting, the 'cute' or the 'little girl'.

'That's a big name for such a small person,' the annoying girl said.

Amelia drew herself up. 'No it isn't. It's my name.'

Isaac frowned. 'I know you, don't I? You're one of the kids from Coding Club.'

Amelia beamed. He'd remembered her! That meant he must've noticed her a bit.

'That's right,' she said, nodding vigorously. 'You help me sometimes when I get stuck.'

Rory McCallum was wandering past, his nose stuck in a book. He glanced up when he bumped into Isaac.

'Whoops, sorry.' He blinked. 'Oh, hi, Isaac.'

'Hiya Rory,' Isaac said. 'Hey, how're you finding Python? Been practising?'

'Yeah, I made a noughts and crosses game.'

'Did you? You're racing ahead.'

'Python's brill. I like seeing what I can do with it.' He beamed at Amelia. 'Hi Melie.'

'How about you, Amelia?' Isaac asked.

Amelia, who spent half her time at Coding Club gazing at Isaac and the other half cursing the jumble of letters and punctuation known as Python, nodded.

'Yeah. Brill.'

'Hey, if you wanted you could come over and I could show you some stuff,' Rory said, flushing. 'Or you could show me some stuff. I mean— I didn't mean you couldn't do stuff. We could work on a project together.'

Georgia nudged her, smirking.

Before Amelia could get in with a firm 'no thanks', Isaac nodded. 'That's a good idea. Rory's really got a feel for it, he could help you. Come on, Kat.' He took his friend's arm. 'See you at club, you three.'

When he'd gone, Amelia glared at Rory. 'Now look what you did. You scared him away.'

'Me? No I didn't. Why do you care?'

Georgia snorted. 'Because she luuuuurves him,' she crooned, clasping her hands together.

Rory laughed. 'You don't, do you? He's way too old for you.'

'No. Shut up.' Amelia nudged her friend. 'Georgie, let's go.'

'Hey!' Rory called after them. 'So, um, did you want to come to mine sometime? I mean, for practice?'

'Oh please!' Amelia called back. 'Get over yourself, Rory.'

'That was mean,' Georgia said when they'd escaped school and were walking home.

'No it wasn't. He needs to know I don't like him like that any more.'

'Yeah, but you could be nice about it. He's always nice to you.'

Amelia flushed with shame. She knew Georgia was right. She didn't *like* like Rory but he was kind of a friend. She'd known him since nursery, he lived on her street. If even Georgie thought she'd sounded mean, perhaps she owed Rory an apology.

'S'pose,' she muttered. 'Okay, I'll say sorry. If I see him.'

'Right.' Georgia unlocked her front door. 'See you tomorrow then.'

It was only a little walk from Georgia's house to 22 The Cedars, where Amelia lived, and since starting secondary school she'd been allowed to do it alone if it was daylight.

She took the next left down a side street, the shortest route. She wasn't really supposed to – her parents always told her to stay where she could be seen – but it was a steaming day and she was desperate to get out of her school uniform and into a refreshing bath. *Horses sweat, men perspire and ladies glow*, her nana always said, and Amelia was glowing like a pig.

There were two men approaching, and she moved to one side to let them pass. But they didn't. They stopped right in front of her, blocking the way.

'That her?' one muttered.

'Must be.' His friend looked down at her. 'Are you Amelia Nightingale?'

Amelia took a step back. 'I'm not supposed to talk to strangers.'

'We're not strangers.' One of the men leaned down to bring his face level with hers. 'I'm Charlie, a friend of your mother's. Maggie, right? You look like her.'

'How come I've never met you then?' Amelia demanded.

'Well, we haven't seen each other since university.'

'You got my last name wrong. Seems to me if you knew my mum, she'd tell you my proper name.'

Charlie glanced at his friend, who shrugged.

'I'm sorry,' Charlie said. 'She did, only… I forgot. What is it?'

'Why do you want to know?'

'Listen, kid,' he said with barely suppressed impatience. 'There's nothing wrong, okay? I'm trying to track down some old friends I've lost touch with, that's all. I wondered if your mum still saw anything of her ex-boyfriend, Max.'

Amelia frowned. 'Max Castle? He's not her ex-boyfriend.'

The other man nudged Charlie. 'She doesn't know,' he muttered.

'Where do you live, Amelia?' Charlie asked.

'None of your business.'

Charlie put a hand on her shoulder. 'Look—'

Amelia jumped back and yanked out her phone. She brandished it at the men. 'Don't you touch me! My dad told me if you touch me I'm to knee you in the nads and call the police.'

Charlie's friend grinned. 'Well aren't you just the little poppet?'

'Melie. Hey, you okay?'

Amelia flashed a look of pure relief at Rory, who'd appeared round the corner.

'Come on, Ben,' Charlie said. 'We're wasting our time here. It's the mum we need.'

Not sparing Amelia another glance, the men strode off.

'What was that about?' Rory asked. 'Do you know them?'

'No.' Amelia's voice was trembling. 'Rory, please will you walk home with me?'

He looked at her in surprise. 'Sure.'

Rory walked to Amelia's door with her and she smiled at him as she unlocked it.

'You know, you're okay. I'm sorry I snapped before, I didn't mean it.'

He smiled back. 'Yeah. I know.'

'Friends again, okay?'

'Course. Hey, um, so did you want to come round for dinner sometime? Practise Python or whatever?'

'Yeah, that sounds nice. Just as friends though, right?'

'Right. Just friends. See you, Melie.'

Amelia's parents weren't back from work yet. Once inside she was careful to lock both front and back doors. The incident with the creepy guys had really freaked her out.

Once the house was secure, she went upstairs to run herself a bath. And when she undressed, she got her second big shock of the day.

Chapter Fifteen

Maggie smiled as she drank tea on Nicki's sofa.

'Someone looks happy. Practically glowing, in fact.'

'Yeah.' Nicki smiled into her mug. 'I am happy.'

'Come on then, what's the gossip?'

'It's just going really well at the moment. New love and everything.' She met Maggie's eyes. 'You know that stage where you can't get enough of each other? I feel like a teenager.'

'So your sex life...'

'God, it's amazing. I don't know what happened, but it's like he changed overnight.'

'Changed how?'

'He's just so confident. I've always fancied him, but it's a massive turn-on, that feeling he knows exactly what he wants in bed. And the way he seems to appreciate me, you know? Telling me I'm beautiful, that he loves me...' She really did seem to have a glow about her. 'He's not been able to keep his hands off me these past few weeks. I've never felt so sexy.'

'Well, I'm glad it worked out,' Maggie said, patting her knee. 'The two of you deserve it.'

'You know, I can't help feeling you had something to do with this.'

'Nope, I'm taking none of the credit. Other Max always had the potential to make you happy. He just needed to find his mojo.'

The TV was on in the background. Maggie's gaze flickered to the screen, where Jordan Nash was sitting on some chat show sofa looking uncomfortable.

'What's this?' she asked.

'Yet another Jordan Nash interview,' Nicki said, rolling her eyes. 'Feels like he's on everything at the moment, plugging his new album. Even I'm getting sick of him.'

'It's not out yet, is it?'

'Not till next week, but the latest single was released yesterday. All he seems to be getting asked about is his drug problem though. And that mother of his.'

Maggie's lip curled. 'Sylvia. Why, what's she done?'

'Don't you know? She's just out of *Big Brother*. Got caught cavorting in a hot tub with some bloke half her age off *TOWIE* and now she's flavour of the month in all the gossip mags. Sylvia Nash's bikini diet. Sylvia Nash's secret hook-up. Sylvia Nash's love cheat heartbreak… you know, the usual crap.'

'Ugh, that poor lad. Jordan, I mean, not the one off *TOWIE*.'

Nicki pulled her gaze from the TV to look at Maggie. 'Didn't think you liked him.'

'I preferred his—'

'— earlier work. Yeah, you said.'

'Doesn't mean I don't pity the man.' Maggie's eyes drifted back to the screen. 'I'm glad he's clean finally. Just hope it lasts.'

'Me too.'

'No one deserves a mother like Sylvia,' Maggie said, suddenly fierce. 'Christ, what a monster. You know, she'd given him up for dead until the day he became a fucking meal ticket.'

'I haven't heard that before.'

'Mmm, must've read it in *Popbitch*.'

'I've never known you get angry like that, Mags.'

'She's a nasty piece of work, that's all. It gets my mum hackles up.'

'But you sound…' Nicki was frowning. 'It seems almost personal. I mean, okay, it's sad, but he's a celebrity, there's dozens of them with high-profile problems. Why take Jordan's to heart?'

'He just looks so… lost,' Maggie muttered, watching Jordan clamp his hands between his knees to hide their tremor.

'You're not even a fan.'

Maggie sighed. 'Suppose I'd better fill you in, now you and Other Max are serious. He's bound to let it slip eventually.'

'Let what slip?'

'Okay, so you remember we told you about Max, the friend we lost touch with?'

'Yeah, your ex-boyfriend. What of it?'

Maggie examined her for a moment. 'Nic, you can never tell anyone this.'

'What is it, Maggie?'

'Promise first. Not a soul. I can trust you, can't I?'

'Well, yes,' Nicki said, blinking. 'If it makes you feel better, I promise.'

Maggie nodded to the TV. 'That's him.'

Nicki's eyes nearly popped from the sockets. 'No!'

'Yep.'

'You are kidding me! Your big ex is… *Jordan Nash*?'

'Yep. Or Max Jordan, as he was then.'

'I don't believe it,' Nicki muttered.

'It's true. Max Jordan, my first love. And my last, at the rate I'm going.'

'But he's… Jordan Nash.'

'To me he's just Max.'

'You know how many women fantasise about being with that guy? And you… you actually went out with him.' Nicki shook her head. 'I can't believe you never told me.'

'I had to be sure I could trust you. There's a tiny number of people who know about me and Max. Even my daughter doesn't know.'

'Why keep it secret? If I'd been out with Jordan Nash I'd want everyone to know.'

'For him, partly. He's already got a mother who'll sell him out to the press at the drop of a hat, he doesn't need me gossiping. And for Amelia. Secondary school's hard enough without it getting out that your mum was once shagging the country's leading sex symbol.'

Nicki's eyes had a glazed, awestruck look that Maggie hoped would wear off soon. That was how people looked at Max all the time, she guessed.

She glanced at him on the TV screen, looking panicked, and not for the first time wondered how the poor man had managed to keep his sanity all these years. She wouldn't trade places with him for any amount of wealth and fame.

'So what's he like?' Nicki asked.

'I don't know what he *is* like. I know what he *was* like.'

'Okay, what was he like?'

'Sweet, when I knew him,' Maggie said, her eyes clouding with nostalgia. 'Sort of an innocent. But passionate, idealistic. He was in a band at uni too, before he got discovered and his manager put the original line-up of Route 69 together. He dropped out in our second year soon after he got his first recording contract.'

'What was that band like?'

Maggie laughed. 'Dire. But Max was good, that's why he was the one who got spotted. They mainly ran on anger. Max's songs were going to tear down social injustice piece by piece.'

'That'd be the earlier work you preferred?'

'Yeah. The industry tamed him, I think. I don't know what happened to all those beliefs that used to fire his music.'

'Why did you break up?'

Maggie looked away while she blinked back a tear. 'Sorry,' she said, forcing a smile. 'Long time ago. I don't know why I should get emotional about it now.' She nodded to the screen. 'Same reason his hands are shaking, poor bastard.'

'Cocaine?'

'Yeah. He lost his nan – well, she was his mum really, she brought him up. It was the worst time for his career to start taking off. He had his new music friends, all happy to help him destroy himself, and he... he pushed us out. All three of us, not just me.' The tear escaped and slipped down her cheek. 'He wouldn't be helped, so... we had to let him go. No one's heard from him in over fourteen years.'

'Haven't you ever tried to get in touch?'

'Ths did, once. Sent an email to his manager asking for it to be passed on. I don't know if it was but he never heard anything back.' She wiped her eyes. 'I hope he'll be happy in the end.'

'Sounds like you never really got over him,' Nicki said quietly.

'I don't know about that. I never forgot him. The boy he was when I loved him.' She smiled sadly. 'I suppose you never do forget your first love, do you? Hard to forget mine when he's on every radio and TV screen in the country.'

'You think he ever thinks about you?'

'Max? Don't be daft. We've not seen each other since we were nineteen.'

Nicki was staring at her, one eye narrowed, like she was working something out.

'Mags... you're a Margaret, right?'

'Eh?'

'That's your name, isn't it?'

'Oh. No. It's a bit embarrassing. My granny was Polish and I was named after her. It's actually—'

'Magdalena?'

Maggie's eyebrows shot up. 'Did Other Max tell you that? I'll kill him!'

'No.' Nicki shook her head. 'Jesus, Maggie. This is... okay, brace yourself.'

She tapped at her phone and after a second a song blared out. Maggie recognised the familiar folk-punk style of Route 69, although it sounded softer than their usual stuff.

'Is this an old one?' she asked.

'No, a new one. Their latest single.' Nicki looked up to meet her eyes. 'It's called "Magdalena".'

Chapter Sixteen

Ibby trudged into the house, feeling that in summer a beachside ice cream van, as romantic as it sounded, couldn't quite compare with an air-conditioned office.

'Melie?'

There was no answer, but he knew from the school shoes lying at the bottom of the stairs that his daughter was in the house somewhere. In her room probably, YouTubing when she should be doing homework.

He went upstairs to the bathroom and swilled his face with refreshing, icy water. There was an empty shampoo bottle on the floor, carelessly chucked there by a teenage girl who apparently didn't know what bins were for.

Ibby opened the pedal bin, chucked in the bottle, then did a double take.

Bollocks! Now? And it just had to be when Maggie was out...

He tapped out a text.

> **Mags, you still at Nicki's? Because unless your cycle's shifted forward a couple of weeks, I could really use some parenting back-up.**

He waited a few minutes. When there was no reply, he went and knocked on Amelia's bedroom door.

'Melie? You okay, sweetheart?'

'No.' Her voice was broken by hiccuping sobs.

'Can I come in?'

'No. I'm too hideous to look at.'

'Okay. Bye then.'

He waited. After a minute, the door opened a crack and a little eye peeped out.

'So can I come in?' Ibby asked gently.

'Where's Mum?'

'On her way home.' *I hope…*

'You can come in if you want. But don't look at me.'

Ibby followed Amelia into her bedroom. She threw herself on the bed and hugged her knees, her eyes red and puffy. Ibby pretended to examine her ancient hamster Smiffy, slumbering in his cage on top of the chest of drawers, while he wondered how to open the conversation.

Okay. He'd grown up with two sisters. He'd lived with Maggie for nearly fifteen years. He was a modern, enlightened guy, the father of a teenage daughter, and there was no need to be embarrassed.

He went over to Amelia's bed and perched on the edge.

'Er, so,' he said, trying to remember a conversation he'd once overheard his dad having with his youngest sister, Beth. 'I understand you're becoming a young woman.' He winced. 'Ugh, sorry. Can I please have that remark stricken from the record?'

Amelia giggled through her tears. 'Dad, you're rubbish.'

'It is my first time, to be fair.' He shuffled closer, relieved to have broken the ice. 'Sorry, I know this is your mum's territory. But you can talk to me too, you know.'

'Okay.'

'So can I get you anything? I can pop to the shops if you need, er, towels or anything. Or if you want a hot water bottle, I can—'

'Dad, it's fine. Mum made me a kit so I'd be ready for when it happened.' She nodded to a shoebox by her bed.

'Did she?'

'Yeah, we've had this conversation loads. I know all about it.'

Ibby ran a finger under his t-shirt collar.

'Thank God for your mother,' he said fervently. 'I mean, I do my best, but I am a bit out of my depth with the girl stuff.'

She smiled. 'That's okay. Me and Mum like you like that.'

'I can manage drinks anyway. Hot chocolate? I could do it with whipped cream on top like we get at the caff.'

'Yes please.'

He went down to the kitchen to make drinks, returning five minutes later with a squirty-cream-laden hot chocolate for Amelia and a tea for himself.

'So why the tears, sweetheart?' he asked, sitting down again.

She sniffed. 'Dad, can I have a baby?'

His tea almost splurted onto her unicorn wallpaper.

'What?' he gasped.

'I don't mean right now.'

'Well, good. I don't think they do your school uniform in maternity sizes.'

'I mean, can I make one? When I'm older?'

Ibby cast a glance at his phone, feeling more out of his depth by the minute. Nothing from Maggie. He had to parent this one out on his own.

'Er, you don't really need my permission, Melie,' he said. 'Me and your mum would love to be grandparents a long, long, long time in the future, but it's your...' He trailed off. Body, he'd been going to say, but that sort of girl-talk felt like Maggie's area. '...choice,' he finished. 'Why are you asking?'

'It's just, Georgia said... she said I couldn't have one. Because of you.'

He blinked. 'Me?'

'She said if your dad's gay it stops your bits working. I mean, the bits you need to make babies.' She burst into tears again. 'And that means Isaac won't ever like me.'

Ibby sighed. The whole of the internet at their disposal, and kids still got their sex education from playground Chinese Whispers.

'That's not true, sweetheart,' he said gently.

'How do you know?'

'Because... it just isn't. Look, who are you going to believe, me or Georgia Fielding?'

'But Pyper's dad's a gincolologist and he told her.'

'What's a gincolologist?'

'A foo— I mean, someone who knows about making babies and things.'

Ibby smiled. 'Gynaecologist, you divvy.'

'Yeah, well, he still knows stuff.'

'Okay, I'll prove it.' He sifted through his grey cells to get at the name he needed, for once thankful for his English degree. Then he snatched up his phone and did a Wikipedia search.

'There,' he said, shoving it under Amelia's nose.

'Who's that?'

'A man called Merlin Holland. He's a biographer. That means he writes books about famous people's lives.'

'Never heard of him.' She frowned. 'Merlin?'

'Yes, he comes from a long line of people with daft names. You've probably heard of his grandad, Oscar Wilde.'

'Was he, like... a writer?'

'That's right. He was gay, quite famously so. But his son Vyvyan still had a kid.'

'Maybe it's just for girls it doesn't work.'

'Melie, I swear to you, it's complete nonsense. I can find you a million other examples if you want them. Trust your dad, eh?'

Amelia wiped her eyes. 'You promise?'

'I promise.' He smiled. 'Now come on, who's this Isaac?'

'Just a boy.'

'A boy you like, right?'

'Yeah.' Amelia breathed a sigh. 'But he thinks I'm just some little kid.'

Ibby frowned. 'Why, how old is he?'

'Sixteen.'

Ibby privately felt a surge of relief that Isaac did think she was some little kid. Being a parent was terrifying enough without sixteen-year-old boys and their attached sixteen-year-old baby-making apparatus taking a shine to his quickly maturing daughter. But he managed a smile for Amelia, who was too innocent for such ideas.

'I guess he must be pretty special if you like him.'

'He is,' Amelia said fervently. 'He's so perfect and his eyes and his glasses are untrue. And he's in a band.'

'Sounds dreamy.'

Amelia looked up at him. 'Dad, you won't go away, will you?'

'Not if you don't want me to, sweetheart. Tell you what: when Mum gets back, how about a PJ evening? We'll watch a film and I'll make pizzas.'

'I mean, you wouldn't leave us? Me and Mum?'

'Why would I do that then, you daft dongle?'

Amelia gave a wet laugh. 'You're such a loser.'

'Only you can make that sound like a compliment. Here, shift your bum.' He shuffled over so he could put an arm round her and she cuddled into it. 'Come on, what's brought this on?'

'Sometimes dads go away. Georgia's did.'

'Sometimes they do,' Ibby said, nodding. 'But I won't.'

'You might if you get a new boyfriend. Like that Nat.'

'Never mind him. Didn't work out anyway.'

Amelia glanced up. 'Not *Crystal Skull*?'

He smiled. 'No, not this time. Just... irreconcilable differences.' He looked into his daughter's damp eyes, almond-shaped like her mum's but in Ibby grey rather than Maggie brown. 'But even if we'd fallen madly in love, I wouldn't be going anywhere.'

'What if he tried to take you away? Like Dan tried to take me and Mum away?'

'Yeah, and what happened to Dan?'

She summoned a weak smile. 'Mum told him to get lost.'

'Too right she did. Your mum would never let anyone break us up, and neither would I. It'd be another big fat "get lost".'

'So you'd never want to go live with someone else instead of us?'

In answer, he bent to kiss her hair. 'Did I ever tell you about the day you were born, Melie?'

'No. Tell me.' Amelia snuggled deeper into his arm. She loved hearing stories about when she was a baby.

'Well, you were all gooey and horrible when you popped out.'

'Ew.'

'I know, right? Your mum got the first cuddle, then the midwife put you in my arms. You looked pretty unimpressed by me. Like you could just about put up with the mummy-shaped thing that brought the food, but the daddy-shaped thing, meh.'

'What did I look like?'

'Ugly as hell.'

'I did not! You're ugly as hell.'

'Seriously. You were all wrinkly, covered in this downy black fluff. You looked like an elderly miniature chimp.'

'No way,' she said, poking out her lip. 'Bet I was cute.'

'Well, I never said you weren't cute,' Ibby said, smiling. 'You were the most beautiful ugly thing I'd ever seen.' His eyes glazed and he blinked a few times. 'And that was it, I was done for. I knew I could never let my tiny chimpy daughter go. I held you cradled in one arm and your mum's hand with the other, and I swore I'd never let anything bad happen to my little girl.'

'Really?'

'Really. Me and your mum made a promise to each other the day you were born, that we'd always put you first. Always.'

'Did you cross your hearts?'

'Yep, and hoped to die. We knew there might be boyfriends in the future – well, we hoped there would be. We were young. But we promised we'd never let that break up our funny little family.' He gave her shoulders a squeeze. 'So I'm not going anywhere, see?'

'Not ever?'

'There might be changes, one day when you're grown up. I might meet someone, or your mum might – I hope she does, she deserves to. But at the heart of everything, there'll always be Mum and Dad and Amelia. You'll always have two parents who love you very much, Melie, and you'll always have a home with us both. I promise.'

She threw her arms around him. 'Thanks, Dad,' she whispered. 'Love you lots.'

'Love you too, sweetheart.' He jiggled her affectionately. 'Now how about this PJ evening, eh? You get into your 'jamas while I ring Mum and check where she is. Then you can tell us all about swoonsome Isaac and his perfect hair.'

'How did you know he had perfect hair?'

Ibby laughed. 'Fatherly intuition.'

He started to stand up, but Amelia put a hand on his arm.

'Oh, Dad? I nearly forgot. There was something weird after school today.'

He frowned. 'Weird?'

'Yeah, some men. They started talking to me on the way home. Tried to stop me getting past.'

'What?' Ibby was on the alert at once. 'Did you tell someone? Did they try to make you go anywhere with them?'

'Dad, don't freak out. It was scary but they didn't, like, groom me or anything.'

'I hate that you have to know words like that.' He sighed. 'But I'm bloody glad you do. What happened?'

'They just kept asking questions. But I said what you told me and they went away.'

'Questions?'

'Yeah, about Mum and some old boyfriend. Max. Who is that, Dad? Not Uncle Other Max?'

Oh shit…

'No. No, it's… an old university friend we lost touch with.' Ibby summoned a smile. 'Tell you what, I'll walk you to school tomorrow. I'd like a word with the head, if there's people like that hanging around. Mum or Nana can pick you up.'

'Dad, there's no need—'

'Amelia Jane.' He pointed to his set lips. 'Stern Dad face, all right? It wasn't up for debate.'

She sighed. Parents could be so boring sometimes.

'Okay,' she said.

'We're just trying to keep you safe.' He stooped to kiss her forehead. 'Now I need to ring your mum.'

He went downstairs to the utility room, his best bet for not being overheard, and checked his phone. There was a text from Maggie to say she'd be home soon, but he couldn't wait for that.

'How is she? Is she okay?' Maggie said when he rang, shouting to be heard over the car's hands-free. 'My poor baby, she must've been so frightened.'

'She's okay. But Mags, we've got bigger problems than periods.' He lowered his voice. 'Max Jordan. Melie said a couple of blokes had been asking questions about you and him when she was walking home from school. Scared her half to death.'

'Oh God. Oh *God!* So soon?'

'Soon? What do you mean?'

'That… bastard!' He heard her slap the dashboard. 'Why couldn't he just leave us alone? Why did he have to drag me and my family into his bloody fucked-up Celebrityland?'

'Mags, what's happened?'

'I'll be home in ten. In the meantime, you might be interested in giving Route 69's new single a listen. It's called "Magdalena".'

Chapter Seventeen

The presenter on the curved green sofa simpered at Jordan. He'd learnt to distrust that simper over the last twenty minutes of his TV interview. The mumsy bob and warm eyes were just a front, he now realised, for a woman who was a cross between Jeremy Paxman and a particularly aggressive squirrel.

'So, your new single's just come out,' the presenter, Connie, said, and Jordan breathed a sigh of relief.

Thank Christ, they were finally getting to the reason he was putting himself through this horror show. Twenty minutes, and this was the first mention of his actual bloody job. That was far less interesting, apparently, than his personal problems.

Connie held up an advance copy of the new Route 69 album. 'This is the second release from *Sleepwalking*, out next week. I must say, it's rather different from anything else you've produced recently. Any reason for the change in direction?'

'A difference in me, I think, Connie,' Jordan said, smiling warmly with his hands clasped between his knees. 'This was the first song I wrote after I'd made the decision to get my life back on track, and I think the tone's a reflection of that.'

'It's a love song but rather a sad one. What inspired it?'

'Something we all have to go through, first love and first heartbreak. It's sad, but positive too. A reminder that while it might feel like our world's crashing down the first time a love affair ends, we will come back from it.'

'Except the singer hasn't really come back from it, has he?'

Jordan blinked. 'Wouldn't you say so?'

'Perhaps his life has moved on, but in terms of having healed... well, that's not the impression I got. How did you feel, writing it?'

Jordan smiled. 'How did you feel listening to it, Connie? That's the more important question.'

He knew that in the Green Room, Craig was nodding approval. He liked it when Jordan flirted with the presenters, it was good for the image.

Connie laughed. 'Well, I won't pretend I didn't shed a tear. Falling in love for the first time, we all believe it will be forever, don't we? And that first broken heart... how do you describe it in the song? "A betrayal of everything love promised"?'

'The sentimental soul I am.' He glanced at the clock, and with a surge of relief started detaching his lapel microphone. He was doing his best to hide it, but his anxiety was in danger of exploding into a full-blown panic attack any second. 'Well, Connie, it's been great to chat.'

'Jordan. One last question.'

'Shoot,' he said, leaning back as he tried to appear relaxed.

'There's been a lot of speculation about whether there was a real heartbreak for you – a real Magdalena. Was there?'

'Well, I hate to be vague but "yes and no" is really the answer. Magdalena isn't so much a person as a symbol. To me she's... let's say she represents the road not travelled.'

'And yet symbolic or not, it sounds like this woman, this first love, is very much at the forefront of your mind. Is the untravelled road one you still wonder about?'

'Well, yes.' Jordan flashed her his most charming smile. 'But doesn't everyone?'

When he'd escaped the studio's migraine-inducing white lights, he hurried back to Craig in the Green Room.

'Good job, star.' Craig put his hands on Jordan's shoulders. 'Nice work with that untravelled road bollocks.'

'Jesus, Craig.' Jordan's voice was shaking, and he reached up to rub his nose. 'What the hell's wrong with me?'

'It's just nerves. You're okay.'

'They promised me it'd get easier. It's not getting easier. It's not getting any *fucking* easier.' Jordan held up a trembling hand. 'See that? More than three months clean. Why doesn't it stop?'

'Here. Sit down.' Craig guided him to a chair. 'It's not withdrawal, Jord, it's you. Your nerve's shattered. It'll settle down once you're back performing.'

'What a nightmare that woman was. Half an hour I was in there and not a single question about the track until right at the end. Just Sylvia and bloody coke.'

He rubbed his nose again. God, if he just had a little bit for tonight, just half a gram. Medicinal. Cold turkey clearly didn't agree with him. Maybe phased withdrawal was the way forward. Riley had some in his room, Jordan could ask him any time...

Craig sighed. 'This is my fault. I've been working you too hard.'

'I don't think I can do the tour, Craig.' He swallowed a sob of panic. 'It's... too much.'

'Look, don't think about that now. Get back to the hotel, relax, have a drink. Watch your godawful sitcoms if they calm you down. I won't schedule you any more interviews in the run-up to the tour. Let me and the other boys do the work, eh?'

'Yeah.' Jordan breathed a long sigh. 'Yeah, thanks.'

Back at the hotel, he cast a glance at the door of Riley's room. He hovered for a moment. Then he unlocked his own door, flung himself on the bed and switched on the TV.

It wasn't sucking him back in. Not this time.

–

Maggie knew there was something going on the second she pulled into her driveway. There were a couple of men leaning on her fence, chatting.

People didn't just stop to have a conversation right outside someone else's front door. They were waiting...

Sure enough, as soon as she got out of the car, one of the men hailed her.

'Maggie! Hey.'

She turned to face him. 'I'm sorry, do I know you?'

'Charlie. From uni? We were in Cognitive Psych lectures together.'

Maggie narrowed her eyes. A couple of men, Ibby had said. A couple of men, scaring her little girl...

'The hell we were. What newspaper?'

'We were, you know.' The man and his friend approached her. 'But since you ask, the *Somerset Chronicle*. This is Ben, my editor.'

'Right. In that case, no comment.'

'We'll pay you good money for an exclusive. Something classy, "local girl that troubled heart-throb never forgot" kind of thing.'

Maggie studied him. About her age, ferret-like features... yes, she remembered him now. He had been in lectures with her, although they'd spoken no more than three or four times.

'Did you follow my daughter home from school, Charlie?' she asked with a bright smile.

'We just wanted to speak to her.'

'Right. Then you might like to recall my earlier statement of no comment, and I'll throw in this for free.' She flipped him the finger and went to unlock the front door.

'Did you know Jordan Nash was still carrying a torch for you?' the editor, Ben, demanded.

'Still no comment.' Maggie was fumbling with the keys but she managed to get the door open.

'Have you met his mother?' he asked as she was about to dive inside. 'Maybe she'll give us an exclusive if you won't. "Gold-digger who broke my baby's heart", I can see it now.'

'You bastard.'

'You'd do better to talk to us. There's plenty of other people we could speak to who'd have no interest in putting your side of it across. It won't play well for you.' He nodded to the house. 'Or your freakish so-called family.'

Charlie grinned. 'Yeah, that's right. We know all about it.'

Maggie turned to fix him with a look of disgust.

'Okay, Charlie, here's my statement,' she said. 'As you seem to remember, I had a relationship with Max Jordan, now known as Jordan Nash, for eight months when we were students. We haven't seen or spoken to each other since then. It ended amicably and we both got on with our lives. The end. If you're looking for more dirt than that, I'm sorry but there isn't any.'

'What about the drugs?'

'He didn't take drugs when I knew him,' she lied. 'Now please do me the kindness of fucking off. Oh, and if you speak to my daughter again I will call the police.' She went inside and slammed the door in their faces.

'Mum?' Amelia called down the stairs. 'What's going on?'

'Nothing, sweetheart. I'll be up in a minute.'

She knew exactly where Ibby would be. It was the place they always went when, like any adults sharing a home and child, they occasionally felt the need to have a 'frank discussion' without Amelia hearing. The utility room.

She found him by the window, peeping through the blinds.

'There's two blokes out there,' he told her.

'Mmm. I can think of a few other names for them.'

'What happened, Mags?'

'Fucking journalists – no offence. Trying to get some dirt on Max.'

'Did you give them any?'

'Like what?' She shook her head. 'Even if I had any I wouldn't, much as I feel like bashing his bloody stupid head against a wall right now. What was he *thinking?*'

'Who knows what he thinks these days?' He turned to face her. 'Think they'll run a story on it?'

'You kidding? Guys like that'd run a story if it was their own mother.'

'What paper?'

'*Somerset Chronicle*. Which means the nationals can't have got hold of it yet. I think that guy just got lucky with a scoop because he remembers me and Max from uni.'

'The redtops'll be all over it once the *Chronicle* run a story though.'

'I know. And that puts all three of us in the spotlight.' She grimaced. 'Ibs, we have to tell Melic.'

'Yes.' He sighed. 'Poor little love, she's having a rotten day.'

Maggie linked his arm. 'Well, come on. The sooner we do it, the sooner it's over.'

'How do you think she'll take it?' Ibby whispered as they made their way upstairs.

'No idea. It's not a conversation I ever thought we'd need to have with her.' She knocked gently on Amelia's door. 'Can we come in, sweetie?'

'If you want.'

They went in and took a seat at each side of Amelia's bed.

'Oh God, what?' she said, glancing up from the magazine she was reading. 'You guys only sit either side of me like that when there's bad news.'

'It's not bad, exactly. Just… awkward,' Maggie said, flinching.

'What is it, Mum?'

'Okay, so… now you know that before we had you, me and Dad were young too, right?'

'Ick. You're not going to tell me some rancid story about what you got up to in the sixties or whatever, are you?'

Ibby smiled. 'How old does she think we are, Mags?'

'Oh, at least seventy, I think,' Maggie said. 'No, Melie, nothing like that.'

'What then?'

'You once asked me why Uncle Other Max wasn't just called Uncle Max. Do you remember?'

'No.'

'Well, it's because we had another friend named Max back at university. He was my boyfriend for a bit too.'

'Ew.'

'I know, it's disgraceful,' Maggie said, smiling. 'Anyway, he was a nice boy, very good-looking. He was in a band. We'd been friends a while and liked a lot of the same things, so we started seeing each other.'

Amelia nodded, thinking of Isaac, and Georgia's undying love for Jordan Nash. She understood the appeal of boys who played in bands.

'So?' she said.

'So, we fell in love. We were happy for a whole eight months, including one long summer together. But it didn't work out,' her mum told her. 'It wasn't anyone's fault. Max had a new group of friends I didn't think were good for him, and he'd been offered a job far away, so... well, even though we loved each other, we decided to break up.'

'Why, if you loved each other?'

'That's just the way it has to be sometimes, sweetie,' Maggie said, smiling a little sadly. 'When you're older you'll understand. It's romantic to think love conquers all, but it doesn't always work that way in real life.'

Amelia looked unconvinced. 'Couldn't you have gone with him to where the new job was?'

'I had my degree to finish. And my friends, your dad and Uncle Other Max. I loved Max, but I didn't want to give up everything else that was important to me to be with him.'

'Then couldn't he have stayed for you?'

'That would've been too big an ask. The job he was offered was once in a lifetime.'

Maggie could see that her daughter, with her thirteen-year-old view of life and love, didn't really understand. But Amelia nodded to acknowledge what her mum was saying.

'Anyway,' Maggie said, slipping an arm around her shoulders, 'if I had gone with him you wouldn't be here, would you, madam? So it worked out for the best. Your dad and me quite like you, you know.'

'Why are you telling me about it? Because of those men?' Amelia asked. 'Or is this about Isaac?'

Maggie glanced at Ibby. 'Isaac?'

'Oh, you'll hear all about him, I'm sure,' Ibby said, smiling. 'He's Melie's dream boy. Sixteen years old with glasses to die for.'

'No, it's not about Isaac,' she told Amelia. 'It's about me. But it affects you too.'

'How? I don't know this Max, do I?'

'He's not called Max any more,' Maggie said. 'He uses a different name now. He's... well, after we broke up he got to be quite well-known. A celebrity.'

Amelia felt a jolt of foreboding. 'Is that why the men came?'

'Yes.' Maggie winced. 'I'm sorry, sweetie, but it's someone you've heard of. Max is actually very famous, now. He's... the lead singer of Route 69.'

'You mean... you can't mean he's...'

'That's right. And he's written a song about me; that's why the men were talking to you.'

'No. No! This is a joke, right?'

Maggie sighed. 'I wish it was.'

Amelia groaned and buried her face in her hands. If she could've dropped dead that second, she'd have felt it was a blessing.

'Oh my *God*,' she wailed. 'My mum's had sex with *Jordan Nash!*'

Chapter Eighteen

For seven days, nothing happened. Ibby rushed out every morning to buy the *Somerset Chronicle*, one of the trashier county papers, so they could check it before Amelia went to school. And every morning, it just carried the usual guff about the various local footie teams' successes/failures or the Duchess of Cornwall visiting Westbury-sub-Mendip.

Maggie was starting to let herself hope that Charlie and Ben had dropped the whole thing. *Local teens go out with each other shock!* didn't sound like much of a headline to her, and that was all there really was to it.

But on the eighth day, the day Route 69's new album was released... there it was. And it turned out that yes, there actually was a bit of a story. Her unusual family was it.

Bizarre sex secrets of Applecroft woman who broke my boy's heart yelled the front page. It was accompanied by a photo of Max and Maggie as loved-up, grinning students and the obligatory one of Sylvia sodding Nash, who was pouting with her usual combination of feigned sadness and collagen.

'What sex secrets are these?' Maggie asked Ibby as they pored over it in the utility room. 'That I haven't done it in three years? Juicy.'

'"To the small seaside community of Applecroft she's Dr Maggie Nightingale, sex therapist to the stars",' Ibby read. '"But to the wild child of the British music scene, Jordan Nash, she'll always be Magdalena, the girl who broke his heart when they were just nineteen".'

'Stars? I had a bloke in once who was a session banjoist for The Wurzels, but if you ask me that's scraping the bottom of the barrel a bit. Go on, tell me what my sex secrets are.'

'"These days, though, the Route 69 pin-up might struggle to recognise his fresh-faced teen sweetheart, as we exclusively reveal the unsavoury *open relationship* she enjoys with her gay lover and father of her young child." Ooh, that's me! Yay.'

'How can you be my gay lover? You'd have to be a woman, wouldn't you? Even then, the usual term would be "girlfriend".' Maggie shook her head. 'Where did these guys train?'

'They don't care if it makes sense, so long as it sounds salacious.' He skimmed the rest of the article. 'Strings of lovers, blah blah, innocent child, yada yada, faux outrage, yawn, then an interview with Sylvia eulogising over how her darling Jordan deserves better and how you're probably to blame for him ending up in rehab.' He looked up. 'Well, could be worse. Anyone with two brain cells to rub together will see they're trying to wring what they can out of a non-story.'

'Yeah, and how many people who read this rag have got two brain cells to rub together?'

'Okay, there's that,' Ibby admitted. 'People forget this stuff quickly though. A few weeks and it'll be done with. There's nothing here interesting enough to tempt the nationals.'

'Hmm. I'm not so sure. Just the "Magdalena" thing is worth a couple of column inches.'

'It's Melie I'm worried about. You know what kids are like. She's going to have one hell of a day.'

Maggie grimaced. 'So do you want to show her or shall I?'

–

When Amelia came down for breakfast, her parents were standing by the dining table, smiling nervously.

'Good morning,' her dad said.

'Mmm,' she muttered, sinking into a chair. As morning greetings went it was more than they deserved, she felt. She'd managed to keep up her sulk over them lying to her about Jordan Nash for a full week now and she wasn't about to break her streak without some pretty impressive grovelling from the pair of them.

'I made pancakes for breakfast,' her mum said brightly.

Okay, that was a good start, grovelling-wise. Pancakes were her favourite.

'Fine, whatever.' Amelia glanced up, suddenly suspicious. 'What for?'

'Well, because you deserve a little treat sometimes.' Maggie winced. 'And… your dad's got some news.'

Ibby frowned at her. 'Yes, thanks, cowardy custard.'

'Oh my God.' Amelia groaned and dropped her head to the kitchen table. 'It's happened, hasn't it? You promised me it wasn't going to happen!'

'Now, we did no such thing,' her dad said. 'We just said we hoped it wouldn't.'

'Can I read it?'

'You're sure you want to?'

'I have to, don't I? Everyone else will have.'

Her dad took a newspaper from the worktop and put it on the table for her. Her eyes widened in horror as she read through the story.

'No,' she whispered. 'No no *no!* My life is over!' She glared at Maggie. 'Mum, how could you do this to me?'

'I didn't do it on purpose, Melie,' Maggie said. 'Funnily enough, I didn't realise at nineteen that my choice of boyfriend had the potential to ruin my future daughter's life.'

'You haven't just ruined my life, Mum, you've actually *ended* my life!' Amelia yelled. 'Like, killed it literally dead. You know that, right?'

'Come on, don't be so dramatic.' Maggie crouched down to put an arm around her daughter's shoulders. 'It's such a silly story, anyone who reads it will know there's nothing more to it than that your mum had a boyfriend at university. That's not too shocking, right?'

'They'll know you've had sex! It says it right on the front page.'

'Well yeah, I've had sex. All your friends' mums have had sex. That's why you've got friends.'

'But they don't have it put on the front of newspapers, do they? And it says stuff about Dad too. Everyone's going to be talking about what freaks we all are.' She folded her arms. 'I'm not going to school.'

Maggie frowned. 'That's not up to you, I'm afraid, missy.'

'Mum, please! If you love me, write me a note. Say I'm sick or something.'

'I can't do that, Amelia.'

'Dad?' She looked hopefully at Ibby with the puppydog face that always worked when she wanted to wrap him round her little finger.

'Ask your mother.'

'She just did ask me,' Maggie said, shooting him a look. 'And I said no, quite loudly, in your hearing.'

Ibby sighed. 'I'm sorry, Melie. It's awful, I know, but you'll have to face your friends sooner or later.'

'Ugh! I hate you! I hate *both* of you to the stupid moon and back!' She jumped up and stomped off to her room.

Ibby cast a helpless glance at Maggie, who couldn't help but smile.

'So that went well,' she said.

He sighed. 'Poor kid. Couldn't we let her stay home, just for today?'

Maggie shook her head. 'You know it won't help, Ibs. She'll just be here fretting herself into fits about it, then have it all to come tomorrow.'

'Yeah, I know,' he said, pinching the bridge of his nose. 'Okay, let's go sort it out before Georgia calls for her. You want to take Good Cop or Bad Cop?'

'Good Cop please. I'm definitely in the baddest part of the bad books, I could use some decent PR.'

Maggie followed him upstairs, where he knocked on Amelia's door.

'Amelia Jane,' he said in a low, stern voice.

'Go away. I hate, hate, *hate* you.'

'No you don't.'

'I'm not coming out,' she said in a pillow-muffled voice. 'Tell school I'm dead. Tell them whatever you want, you can't make me go.'

'Do not force me to test that theory, young lady. Come on, out, now. Georgia and her mum are on their way to pick you up.'

'Dad, how could you not have told me about this?' she wailed. 'This is like the most important thing ever to happen to our boring old family and you and Mum never even told me!' She gasped out a sob. 'And now everyone'll think you two are complete weird perverts or something and I'll be the biggest joke in school and I won't have any friends, not even Ava Fishwick, and Isaac—' Her voice broke off as she gave in to tears.

'Sweetie, it won't be that bad, I promise,' Maggie said gently, nudging Ibby aside so she could try some Good Copping. 'I'm sorry we didn't tell you. It was so long ago, it… well, it didn't seem to matter any more.'

'Didn't matter? That you dated *Jordan Nash*?'

'He wasn't Jordan Nash then. He was just an ordinary scruffy student like me and your dad.'

'Ordinary? Jordan? I don't believe you.' She sniffed. 'I don't believe anything you say any more.'

'You want some details? Will that make you happy?'

There was a pause, followed by another self-pitying sniff. 'Dunno. Maybe.'

'Well, he… okay, so he liked playing beat-em-ups on the Xbox with your dad. And his favourite food was pepperoni pizza and he knew all the words to "Thank You for the Music" by Abba, but he pretended he didn't. And one Saturday a month he used to take me home to Bath to watch old TV programmes with him and Jean – that was his nana.' She sighed. 'He wasn't a celebrity, Melie, not then. He was just a boy. Just… Max.'

'And you… you really loved him?'

'Yes, I loved him very much, once. But like I told you, that was a long time ago. He was a different person then.'

There was silence. Then the door opened a crack.

'Is that all true, what you just said?' Amelia asked in a whisper. 'About his favourite food and that stuff?'

Maggie nodded. 'Every word.'

There was a knock at the front door.

'There's Georgia for you,' Ibby said. 'Come on, Melie. I know it's scary, but you have to go to school. Not optional, I'm afraid.'

'Fine,' she muttered, scowling down at the carpet. 'But I'll hate you both forever for making me do this.'

Ibby's mouth flickered. 'You know, I wish I had a quid for every time you've told me that over the years. Let's see how you feel about your evil old parents tonight, eh? I bet it won't be nearly as bad as you think.'

Maggie grasped Amelia's shoulders and guided her to the stairs. 'Be brave, sweetheart. Just keep your head down, get through the day, and we promise it'll all get better. Come on, I'll wrap you up a couple of pancakes to eat on the way.'

'Sorry!' her parents yelled in unison as they waved her off from the doorstep five minutes later.

'Oh. My. God!' Georgia whispered in the back seat of her mum's car, clutching at Amelia's arm. 'Tell me everything.'

'There isn't anything to tell,' Amelia muttered, nibbling with little appetite on the corner of a rolled-up pancake. 'My mum had a boyfriend at university and he was Jordan Nash. Only he used to be called Max. And they broke up and that was it.'

'What else did she tell you about him?'

'Well, he…' Amelia paused. 'Okay, so he likes pepperoni pizza. That's his favourite. And games on the computer, and old TV, and Abba… except he used to keep that secret so maybe don't tell anyone. Oh, and his nana was called Jan or Joan or something.'

'Arghh, this is gold!' Georgia gave her arm a squeeze so filled with delighted excitement it actually bruised. 'Did your mum tell you what kind of kisser he was? Did he do the shovelling thing?'

Amelia frowned. 'What shovelling thing?'

'You know.' Georgia dipped her head to make sure her mum couldn't see, then demonstrated the shovelling thing, sticking her tongue out and doing a scooping motion.

'Is that a thing?'

'Course. Alfie says girls love it when he does that.'

Amelia had her own private doubts about whether Georgia's fifteen-year-old brother really enjoyed as much success with the opposite sex as he claimed, but she decided now wasn't the time to voice them.

'Ew,' she whispered. 'That's my mum, Georgie.'

'Come on, didn't she tell you anything about what sort of boyfriend he was? She must've told you whether he was good at sex.'

'Why would she tell me that? I don't want to know.'

'Yeah, but I do! Find out for me, please.'

'Um, no.'

Georgia's eyes took on a faraway look. 'I can't believe he wrote a song about how he never forgot her. If he wrote me a song I'd just *die* so I could be happy forever.'

'It's no big deal. Can we please talk about something else?'

Georgia shook her head in a pitying manner. 'Oh, Melie. No one's going to talk about anything else today.' She squeezed her friend's arm. 'And when they do, just remember I'm your bestie, okay?'

At the school gates, a gang of eager girls were lying in wait…

At work, Maggie soon found herself going through the grown-up version of the interrogation her daughter was being subjected to over at Applecroft Secondary.

She'd been naive enough to think the first pair who turned up actually wanted counselling. They didn't have an appointment, but Wednesdays were her quiet days so she'd been able to fit them in for an initital consultation. Carol had shown them in, a husband and wife, and Maggie had ushered them to a sofa.

'So I see from your questionnaire you're concerned about your sex life,' she'd said. 'What's the issue exactly?'

The wife flushed, looking down at her hands folded in her lap. 'Well, we've been married five years and things were becoming...' She glanced at her husband, who nodded encouragingly. '...a little stale.'

'That's understandable,' Maggie said. 'It's easy to fall into a routine. Have you discussed it together?'

The husband, James, leaned forward. 'We have talked about, you know, our private fantasies. Melanie confessed she often thinks about another man to get her excited during sex.'

'I can see why that might worry you, James, but it's really no reason to feel jealous. Erotic fantasy can be a perfectly healthy part of lovemaking; it's not a reflection on your wife's attraction to you.'

'I'm not jealous,' James said, beaming at his wife. 'Actually I told Melanie I enjoyed a bit of fantasising myself.'

Melanie giggled. 'The thing is, Maggie, we discovered we'd both been fantasising about the same person. Isn't that funny? Like a threesome with the Invisible Man.'

Maggie blinked. 'Okay, that's slightly unusual, but it's fine. I'm struggling to see what the problem is, to be honest. It sounds like your communication's excellent. If Invisible Man threesomes are spicing things up for you, by all means enjoy them.'

'Oh, we didn't come for any help in that department,' James said. 'We were actually hoping you might pass on some inside information. To help us progress the fantasy to the next level.'

Maggie stared at him. 'I'm sorry – me personally?'

'That's right. Our fantasy man, you see. It's Jordan Nash.'

Maggie had a number of other so-called clients, all walk-in consultations with no pre-arranged appointment. A middle-aged woman who wondered if Maggie could provide intimate details of Jordan's anatomy, ideally with diagrams or better still, photographs. A couple who wanted to know if Maggie and Ibby would be interested in bringing their so-called open relationship to a regular Thursday night bridge and swingers' party.

But the last one was the worst. A Jordan Nash superfan-cum-stalker, the woman no sooner got through the door than she started hurling abuse at Maggie, who was apparently a heartbreaking slut, a gold-digger (Maggie wasn't sure how that worked, since when she'd known Max he'd barely had the price of a pint) and a worse human being than Hitler, Stalin and the Emperor Caligula all rolled into one. They'd had to get the police out when she'd started threatening physical violence.

At twelve-thirty p.m., Carol came in.

'There's not another one, is there?' Maggie groaned.

'There were another three asking for consultations with you by name, but I told them you were booked up for the rest of the day.'

'Have sex with Jordan Nash, have sex with all the world,' she muttered.

'Maggie, I'm sorry. I'm going to have to send you home.'

'What?'

'Well, there's no point you being here, is there? You've got no pre-booked appointments this afternoon, and I doubt we're going to get anyone genuinely wanting a consultation.'

Maggie stared at her. 'You're not seriously suspending me because fourteen years ago I went out with someone who later became one of the most famous men in the country? That hardly constitutes professional misconduct, Carol.'

'Now, calm down. No one's getting suspended,' Carol said. 'Look, I know it's not your fault. It's a distraction, that's all.' She patted Maggie's arm. 'Take the rest of the afternoon off, go home, get some rest. This'll soon blow over.'

Maggie sighed and reached for her handbag. 'I guess it's for the best. I'm sorry.'

When she pulled into her drive, there was a gang of journalists waiting.

'Oh, I do love the smell of doorstepping in the afternoon,' she muttered. 'So much for the nationals not giving a shit.'

'Dr Nightingale, is it true Jordan Nash never got over you?' one yelled.

'Was he a good lover?'

'Did you get over him?'

'How does your little girl feel about your teenage exploits?' another shouted. 'Humiliated? Ashamed? Proud? Like mother like daughter, eh?'

'No comment no comment no comment!' she yelled as she fought her way to the door.

–

At about the same time as her mum was getting sent home from work, Amelia was rather enjoying herself.

It'd been excruciating at first. The Routers of her year group had formed into two camps. There were the ones like Georgia, girls who loved Jordan Nash so much they couldn't wait to become her best friend and get all the gossip on what he was like in real life. Then there were the others, the hardcore who suddenly hated her with a passion for having the nerve to be the daughter of the woman who'd beloved's heart.

But Amelia soon found that for someone life feeling invisible, being adored and hat bad. She was suddenly being noticed – more than noticed. She was a star. And the other camp of note was the boys, who were interested without the jealousy. Positive attention from boys wasn't something her little thirteen-year-old ego could resist.

Georgia became her self-appointed minder, officiously filtering all questions when the pack descended at break times.

'Okay, everyone, let her have some air,' she said, waving them back. She nodded magnanimously to one girl. 'Penny, Amelia will answer your question next.'

'Eeeek! Thank you *so much*, Amelia,' the pigtailed girl with the Route 69 rucksack squeaked. 'So I just wondered, um, is it true Jordan's got a tattoo of a bluebird on one of his bums?'

Amelia had no idea, but she nodded knowledgeably. She didn't want to lose credibility this early in her career, and really, who was going to prove her wrong?

'Yep, on the, er, right bum. My mum said.'

There was a shriek from the gaggle of girls, who immediately started waving their arms to be the next one favoured to ask a question.

At Coding Club, her newfound celebrity even earned her some attention from Isaac.

'Sorry, did I do something wrong again?' she asked when he wandered over.

'No, that all looks good,' he said, giving her screen a cursory glance. 'I just wondered if it was true. About your mum and Jordan Nash. Everyone in school's been talking about it.'

Amelia puffed herself up. 'It's true. She's Magdalena. From the song.'

'Oh my God! That's so exciting for you.' Isaac favoured her with one of the tummy-melting smiles she lived for.

'Yeah,' said the girl who just a few hours earlier had declared be over. 'It is pretty exciting. Maybe he'll come to

ask your mum if she kept any of his old demo know the sort of thing he wrote when he han me.'

'I think Melie's probably a bit bored of talking about this, Isaac,' Rory said, glancing up. 'She's actually had people on at her about Jordan Nash all day, actually.'

Amelia glared at him. He hadn't said a word to her that whole day, though she'd been either courted or reviled by everyone else. Rory was the only one who'd seemed totally uninterested in this new development in her life and popularity. And when he did finally open his big mouth, it was just to scare Isaac off again.

'No I'm not,' she said. 'I like talking about it.'

'Well, Rory's right, we're not here to chat. I should probably see if anyone needs help,' Isaac said, somewhat reluctantly. 'If you could ask about those demos though, Amelia?'

She beamed. 'I will. I'd love to.'

'He doesn't like you, you know,' Rory said when Isaac was gone. 'He only wants to talk to you because he thinks you can get him those tapes.'

'Oh, what do you know about anything?' Amelia poked her tongue out at him and turned back to her program.

Chapter Nineteen

Ibby picked Amelia up from Coding Club and they walked home together.

'How was your day then?' he asked.

'It was okay.'

Ibby smiled. He knew that in teenage-girl speak, that constituted a ringing endorsement.

'No one was mean to you about Mum?'

'Some people. But most people were nice.'

'Glad to hear it.' He squeezed her arm. 'Only a couple of weeks till the summer holidays anyway. By the time you go back, it'll all be forgotten.'

'I guess,' Amelia muttered. Actually, a return to obscurity didn't sound particularly appealing after her day as the centre of everyone's world, but she couldn't quite bring herself to admit her parents had been right. It was a slippery slope, that sort of thing. They might start getting ideas.

She linked her dad's arm as they walked past The Blue Lagoon and through the market square. The town's ancient buttercross – a rudely fashioned stone cross where medieval market traders and their customers had once gathered between Plague outbreaks – stood proudly in the centre, mounted on graduated circular steps.

'I take it this means you're talking to me again?' Ibby said, glancing down at the arm threaded through his.

She shrugged, which he knew was teen for yes.

'Did you have a nice day, Dad?' Amelia asked after they'd walked in silence for a little while.

Ibby blinked. 'You're asking about my day?'

'Yeah.'

'Wow. Someone's in a good mood.' He shrugged. 'Nothing to report. I'm the least visible of the three of us, no one knows me to ask questions. Uncle Other Max and Nicki popped by the van this afternoon to ask how we were all doing, but that's all.' He cast a worried glance in the direction of The Cedars. 'Your mum texted though. She's had a bad time.'

'What happened?'

'She got ambushed at work by Jordan Nash fans. One sounded pretty nasty.'

'Nasty?'

Ibby glanced down into his daughter's worried face. 'Not very friendly, that's all I mean,' he said gently. 'And I'm sorry, sweetheart, but I think there are more journalists waiting at home.'

'You mean they could put us in more newspapers?'

'I'm afraid so,' her dad said vaguely. His eyes had fixed on something in the distance.

'Dad?'

'Hmm?'

'Dad!' Amelia nudged him. 'You've gone all stary. What're you looking at?'

'What? Oh, nothing.'

She followed his gaze to a man. He was about her dad's age, sort of cute for someone old, with big brown eyes. She'd seen him before somewhere...

The man stopped when he reached them. 'Ibby. Hi.'

Her dad nodded curtly. 'Nat.'

Amelia's eyes narrowed. So this was Nat. She didn't know what had gone wrong with him and her dad that they'd decided to stop going out, but since she was Team Dad, she knew it must be Nat's fault.

'How've you been?' Nat asked.

'Good,' Ibby said. 'You?'

'Also good.' Nat smiled at Amelia. 'You're Amelia, right? Your dad's told me all about you.'

'Has he?' Amelia said in her frostiest tone.

'Yeah. He thinks you're pretty awesome. Are you?'

'Depends who's asking,' Amelia said, tossing her hair. 'I mean, yes.'

'So, um, how's it going with Over It?' Ibby asked.

'Great, we're really starting to get some exposure,' Nat said. 'You know we got an open letter of apology off that landlord? He wrote to the *Post* after Rob's piece.'

'That's something, I suppose.'

'And more people are coming forward to tell their stories. I'm discussing it on Jim's show in a couple of weeks.' Nat's dark eyes searched Ibby's face. 'Although they wanted us both. I told them you wouldn't be interested though.'

'Thanks.' Ibby nodded. 'Well, nice to catch up.'

Nat put a hand on his arm. 'Ibby, wait. I've been hoping I might bump into you. It's just... funny you should mention Over It.'

'Is it?'

'Yeah. Because the fact is, well... I'm not.'

'I see,' said Ibby, who didn't. 'Not what?'

'Over it.'

'You're not in Over It?'

Amelia rolled her eyes. 'Oh God, this is *tragic*. Dad, he's telling you he likes you, okay?'

'Are you?' Ibby asked Nat.

'Er, yeah. Sorry, when I practised that it sounded witty and charming. Not, you know, naff.' Nat lowered his voice. 'Ibby, look, I've been thinking about you a lot these past few months, and... okay, you don't want to be part of the campaign, that's your choice. But we had something, didn't we?'

'Nat, I'm not doing this here,' Ibby muttered. 'I'm with my daughter.'

'Sorry. Sorry, I know. I just don't want to give up on us.'

'I said not now, okay?' Ibby said, frowning. 'It's not appropriate to be discussing this in front of Amelia.'

'Oh, don't mind me,' Amelia said cheerfully. 'I'm learning lots.'

'Well, will you call me then?' Nat said.

'I don't know, Nat. I get the feeling you and Over It come as a package.' Ibby glanced at Amelia. 'And we've got stuff going on at home at the moment, as you'll know if you saw the *Chronicle* today.'

'I didn't.'

'Well you're about the only one in town,' Ibby said. 'Come on, Melie. Mum's waiting.'

'So will you give me a ring?' Nat said. 'I told you, Ibby, you don't have to get involved in the campaign. I'm sorry I put that pressure on you, it was out of order.'

'I'll… maybe. Let me get this family stuff out of the way, then I'll have time to think about dating again.'

'Dad, what's Over It?' Amelia asked as they carried on home.

'Oh, it's this campaign group he's in, fighting discrimination. Me and him experienced a bit of homophobia that first night we went out.'

'What, somebody was mean to you because you're gay?' Amelia's brow knit with protective ferocity.

'It does happen sometimes, sweetheart. I wish it didn't, but it's the way of the world.'

'And Nat wants you to fight back?'

'He wants me to, but I don't. That's why we stopped going out.'

'But why wouldn't you want to?'

Ibby frowned. 'Pardon?'

'If someone's mean to you for such a stupid reason, you should fight back! Dad, it's bullying. You told me I should stand up to bullies.'

'This isn't the same as what happens at school, Melie. It's more complicated than that.'

'It sounds the same to me.'

'Well, the man who was rude to us has said sorry now anyway.'

'Bet he didn't mean it though.'

'Look, I didn't want to do it because I didn't want you to get dragged in, okay? It's a public campaign and our family doesn't need that kind of attention.'

'Dad. We were on the front page of a newspaper today because Mum's ex-boyfriend is Jordan Nash. I think we can deal.'

'Less of the sarcasm, madam. I've made my decision and that's that.'

'But—'

Ibby put on the most dad-like of his dad faces. 'Amelia Jane, this is not up for discussion. End of conversation.'

'Okay,' Amelia muttered. She knew there was no point arguing once he unleashed her middle name.

'Good girl.' Ibby's eyes widened as they turned into The Cedars. 'Oh sweet Jesus. What is that, every hack in Britain?'

Amelia clutched at his arm.

'Dad, I'm scared,' she whispered.

'No need to be.' Ibby tried to sound more confident than he felt. 'It's our house, they can't stop us getting in. If they speak to you, don't answer, all right? Not a word, even if they provoke you.'

Gripping Amelia's hand, Ibby marched them into the mob of journalists. Neighbours watched from doors and windows as he shouldered his way through the sea of flashbulbs and sweating flesh.

'What's your relationship with Maggie Nightingale?' one hack yelled, waving a dictaphone in his face. Ibby swatted it away.

'Are you sleeping with her?' another asked. Ibby held on tighter to Amelia's hand. Nearly at the door...

'How well do you know Jordan Nash?'

'Have you slept with Jordan Nash?'

'Are you sleeping with him now? What's Miss Nightingale's current relationship with him?'

Bloody hell, they were obsessed. It was amazing he and Maggie ever got anything done, they apparently spent so much of their time bonking Jordan Nash.

They reached the door finally. Ibby groped in his pocket for the key, willing himself to be calm; steady.

'How do you feel about it all, darling?' one of the journalists asked, taking hold of Amelia's shoulder.

Ibby's arm shot out at once. He shoved the man roughly away.

'Touch her again and we get the law involved,' he growled. He glanced down at Amelia, who was round-eyed with terror. 'No need to answer that, sweetheart.'

'Come on, Mr Ibbotson,' the man said with an ingratiating grin. 'You want to get your side across, don't you?'

'My official statement is no comment.' He lowered his voice. 'My unofficial statement is fuck off. Now fuck off.'

He finally got the door open and dragged Amelia inside. He slammed it closed, exhaling through his teeth.

'Dad…' Amelia whispered.

'I know, Melie.' He bent down to give her a hug, and she sagged in his arms.

'I was so frightened.'

'They'll go away soon, I promise. They can't hurt you, my love.'

Maggie came hurrying down the stairs.

'Oh, thank God you're home,' she said, enfolding them both in a hug. 'Melie, sweetheart, are you okay?'

'I… think so,' Amelia said, her voice shaking.

'Ibs, what do we do?' Maggie asked.

'Wait it out, I guess. Give it a couple of days and it should blow over.'

'Will they all run stories on us, all those different papers?'

Ibby grimaced. 'Probably.'

'But Melie's a minor,' Maggie said in a low voice. 'That can't be allowed.'

'Even so. Those guys know the law, and they know how far they can push it.'

Maggie glanced down at Amelia. 'Sweetie, why don't you go have a bath and get your 'jamas on? I thought you and your dad might like to spend some quality time together tonight. That'll be nice, won't it?'

'Why, Mum, where are you going?' Amelia asked. She looked younger suddenly, eyes round with fear.

'I've… got plans with Nicki I can't cancel.' Maggie kissed her hair. 'I'll be back in no time though, I promise.'

'You don't really have to go out, do you?' Ibby asked when Amelia had disappeared.

'Yes. I need Nicki's help with something, then I'm off on a road trip.'

'Road trip? Where to?'

'I'm not sure yet. All I know, Ibs, is that tonight I'm going to track down Max fucking Jordan, and when I find him I'm going to wring his bloody neck.'

—

'Okay, so where are the band right now?' Maggie asked.

Nicki typed Route 69's website address into her browser.

'Exeter. It's the first gig on the album tour for *Sleepwalking*. They're playing Bristol next week though.'

'Can't you wait till then?' Other Max asked. He was sitting next to Maggie on Nicki's sofa, his girlfriend on his lap and the laptop on hers.

Maggie shook her head. 'Has to be tonight. If that means a two-hour drive to Exeter, fine, I'll drive to sodding Exeter.'

'Why the rush?'

'Because tomorrow every newspaper in the country is going to be carrying this bloody "Magdalena" story. I want Max to sit on it before Melie has to go through any more of this doorstepping bollocks.' She stood up and walked to the window. 'Ugh. There's about ten of the buggers out there now. Wonder if they fancy giving me a lift to Devon.'

'Will he be able to sit on it?' Other Max asked as she sat back down.

'He must have some legal muscle, surely. And Amelia's a minor; it has to be against the law for them to harass her, even if I can't stop them going for me. How much are tickets, Nic?'

'They're sold out.'

'Shit! What about other sources?'

Nicki tapped it into Google. 'Some from touts.' She grimaced. '£350 a pop.'

'That much?'

'It's his first gig out of rehab, isn't it? There's a lot of interest in this one.'

Maggie sighed. 'Well, needs must. Go ahead, here's my credit card.'

'So what's the plan once you're there?' Other Max asked.

'Oh, he'll talk to me,' Maggie said, her eyes flashing. 'After what he's put my family through? I guarantee it.'

'How will you get to him though?'

'Hmm. Nic, can you do another search? I want you to Google "I had sex with Jordan Nash".' She paused. 'No, wait, use one of the others. Otherwise you'll just get stuff about me from that *Chronicle* article. Try the bass player, Riley Michaels. He had a reputation, even back when Max first knew him.'

Nicki tapped it in. 'What exactly are we looking for?'

'Fan forums, blogs, tweets. All bands have groupies, and they're the biggest band in the country. I want to know how, where and when those guys get laid.'

'Um, Mags, what're you planning?' Other Max said.

'Oh, don't worry, I'm not going to shag my way in. I just need one of them to think I will so I can get backstage.'

'There must be an easier way. Who was that manager of his – Colin or something?'

'Craig,' Maggie muttered darkly. 'Craig Harvey.'

'Did you know him?' Nicki asked.

'We never met, no. Max used to talk about him a lot.'

'Maybe there's a way we could get in touch with him,' Other Max said.

Maggie snorted. 'Craig's been making his living off keeping Max catatonic and controlled since he was nineteen years old. That guy did more than anyone to crowbar him away from his real friends. I wouldn't trust him further than I could kick him.'

'Won't the band recognise you?' Nicki asked.

'No. Riley's the only one left from the early days, and I never met him either.' She scowled. 'Just cleaned up his mess.'

'His mess?'

'He was Jordan's first dealer, the one who got him started on coke,' Other Max told her. 'Nasty little fucker.'

'Oh. I see.' Nicki scrolled down the results on her screen. 'There might not be anything, you know, Mags. Guys like that are savvy. They've got all sorts of ironclad legal bumf they make girls sign before they'll drop their pants.'

'But the fact you know that suggests this stuff still gets out.'

'Oh! You're right,' Nicki said. 'Here you go. There's a whole thread on this teen fan forum, girls saying they've spent the night with Riley.'

Maggie curled her lip. 'Teens?'

'Yeah. All over the age of consent, but still, ick.' Nicki scrolled down the thread. 'BDSM stuff being talked about here. Some of these girls are sixteen, Mags.'

'Jesus. Not much older than Melie.' Maggie shook her head at Other Max. 'What a world he got himself into, eh?'

Other Max looked sober. 'Jord wouldn't do that stuff.'

'How do we know what he'd do any more?' She nodded to Nicki. 'Okay, what've you found?'

'There does seem to be a common element. This manager bloke, Craig. He picks up girls for them at the stage door after gigs.'

'Well that's… seedy.'

'Yeah. Would he know your face?'

'Not unless he reads the *Somerset Chronicle*. I told you, we never met.'

'And does he read the *Chronicle*?' Other Max asked. 'They'll have someone monitoring Jordan's press, won't they?'

'Hmm. Possibly not the regionals, or not on a daily basis anyway. If Max had seen it, I'd have expected to have heard from him by now.'

'So are you going to take a shot at it?' Nic turned to look at her. 'No offence, but you'll have ten or fifteen years on the rest of them.'

'Yeah, thanks for the reminder. I might not be twenty, but I want it more.' Maggie thought for a moment. 'Nic, you're my size. What've you got in your cupboard that's really trashy?'

'Just what're you implying, Mags?'

'Come on, you must have something for when you and Other Max play paramedics and nurses.'

'Well… I have got the outfit I bought for a Tarts and Vicars party at my mum's.'

'Go on, what?'

'Leather miniskirt, red, and matching crop top.'

'Perfect.'

Other Max nuzzled into the back of Nicki's neck. 'You didn't tell me you had a leather miniskirt.'

'Well, you'll have to wait for me to model it for you. Tonight it'll be busy seducing Jordan Nash.' She looked thoughtful. 'Tell you what, when I get it back I bet it'll sell for a fortune on eBay.'

'It's Craig I need to impress,' Maggie said. 'Come on, Nic, stop giving Other Max inappropriate thoughts and help me get dressed. I want you to make me look like a complete trollop, then I'm off to Devon.'

Chapter Twenty

Fuck me, I'm old.

Maggie wiggled her hips uncomfortably as she waited in the queue. Either gigs had got a lot less fun since she'd become a mum or she'd been deluding herself that they ever had been. The warm, close air was redolent with sweat and beer, and she felt sticky all over.

Why were leather clothes such a turn-on for some people? Okay, she knew leather was big in the BDSM community, and she'd counselled plenty of couples who were into that scene. That was fine, obviously, if it was what floated your boat. But they never mentioned the bloody chafing, did they? Or the sweating like a bitch on heat. She'd kill to swap the fetish gear for a hot shower and her lovely dinosaur onesie. She was missing *Planet Earth* for this too.

See, this was how she knew she was getting old. Only the chronically middle-aged wanted to swap tight leather and rock concerts for fluffy nightwear and David Attenborough.

She hadn't thought much on the drive down about how she'd feel seeing Max again. All she'd thought about was how pissed off she was with him, and the gang of journalists sieging her home. But now, outside the venue with a huge illuminated billboard of the band overhead – Max front and centre, looking down at her – she was starting to feel… strange. She'd almost think the feeling was excitement, if she wasn't so bloody angry.

They finally got inside, although a few people who'd bought forged tickets from iffy touts were turned away. Maggie let herself breathe again once hers had passed scrutiny. £350 but it was genuine.

She queued for a drink then slid into her seat near the back. Her plan was to stay there until the gig seemed to be winding down then sneak off to the stage door and grab herself a nice, visible spot.

As she sipped her iced lime and soda, she wondered how Max was going to cope tonight. Not that she wasn't still planning to tear him a new one over everything he'd put her family through, but... his first gig since rehab. She couldn't forget the surge of compassion she'd felt when she'd seen him on TV: shaking, vulnerable, afraid. The bad-boy tag never had suited him, not when you'd known him.

She found herself sitting rigid in her seat as he appeared on stage, holding her breath. Everyone around her was doing the same, but they were driven by anticipation. Whereas Maggie's dominant emotion was fear.

Would he have a meltdown, right there in front of a sellout crowd? He'd put her through hell, and yeah, she'd hated his guts for most of the past week, but to see him face that sort of public humiliation...

She didn't need to worry though. He seemed a little hesitant when he first appeared, but as soon as he got the guitar in his hands he was all charisma. The crowd broke into wild applause, roaring his name. *Jordan, Jordan...*

'Good evening Exeter!' Jordan yelled into his mike. He grinned. 'Bet you were worried I wasn't going to show up, right?'

There was a ripple of laughter through the audience as Jordan muttered something over his shoulder to the drummer.

'Okay, I know you lot like this one,' Jordan told the audience. 'Jake, over to you.'

The drummer counted them in for the first number – 'Equinox', a fan favourite from their second studio album.

There must have been two, maybe even three thousand people packed into the venue, but Max made it sound like he was talking to each and every one of them personally. As she watched him perform, the easy charm that kept his audience captivated, Maggie realised her mouth had twitched into a smile.

Most exes had the good grace to disappear once they were out of your life, but for Maggie, it was never going to be that simple. Max had gone from her life but he'd never been out of her gaze – on posters, on TV, on the magazines and album covers that confronted her every time she went shopping.

But she'd learnt to live with it. That was Jordan Nash – a contrived, half-artificial personality with some passing resemblance to a boy she'd once loved. It wasn't Max. And as time went on and his image evolved, it became easier and easier to separate the boy Max Jordan from the man Jordan Nash. Over the years he'd changed his hair, the way he dressed – even his eye colour.

But now... now he was really there, in the flesh after fourteen years. And no amount of new tattoos, dyed hair and coloured contact lenses could distract her from those familiar features, that voice... that smile.

Suddenly, without her permission, her brain was presenting her with a picture – a bashful boy with a guitar, playing her a song in the days when she'd believed love was forever.

I wrote it for you, Lanie. I think I write them all for you, really...

When he started playing 'Magdalena' to thunderous applause, Maggie snuck out to find a place near the stage door. She couldn't bear to listen to that song again. Although she flicked it off whenever it came on the radio, she hadn't been able to avoid hearing it: every shopping centre and supermarket seemed to have the bloody thing playing on a loop.

She couldn't understand why he'd written it now, after all these years. It seemed to be about... no, not seemed. It *was* about her and Max. The life they'd missed out on, together. The choices he'd never made.

When she got to the stage door, there was already a throng of young girls waiting by the barrier. Without seeming to push, but with her subtly bossy mum elbows on, Maggie set about finding herself a good spot. The gig would be over soon, and Max's manager would turn up looking for girls.

–

Craig scanned the crowd of excited R outers who'd congregated outside the stage door. None of them gave him more than a fleeting glance. They were on the lookout for Jordan or one of the other boys; anyone else was invisible.

Tonight he was after someone special, someone for Jordan. The poor lad had been shaking like a jelly before the gig, but once he'd got out there he'd done them all proud.

Craig was prepared to do all he could to shield his star from the excesses of the tour bus and Riley, a reckless libertine who wouldn't know a moral if it leapt up his backside and started playing swingball with his tonsils. But Jordan deserved some sort of reward for what he'd put himself through this evening, and sex was a healthy enough pastime for the boy – healthier than binge-watching fucking *Are You Being Served?* anyway. Jord needed interaction with real people.

Craig had been doing this a long time and he knew Jordan's type. Not too young, unlike Riley, who favoured teens. Curvy, cute. A bit of mischief in the eyes, a warm smile.

No, there was no one, he realised with disappointment. Plenty of good-looking girls, but none Jordan was likely to go for. Maybe he'd have better luck at the hotel.

He was about to turn away when his glance fell on someone hovering to one side. Unlike the others, who were peering over him in the hope of seeing the band, this one seemed to be trying to catch his eye.

Craig ran his gaze over the hourglass figure and long, silken legs poking out from the girl's leather mini-skirt. Bit of meat on her but not too much, the way Jordan liked. Clean, healthy, sober, and not too young – after the Clara girl, Jordan was adamant he'd throw out the next one if she couldn't prove she was at least twenty-five. Yes, this one might do the boy some good.

He beckoned to her and after the obligatory show of 'who, me?' surprise, she fought her way through the other girls to clutch the rope.

'Been to the gig, have you, darling?'

The girl nodded shyly.

'What did you think?'

'Oh, it was amazing,' she breathed. 'Jordan was amazing. I think it was his best one yet.'

'Superfan, eh?'

'I love him so much.' Her eyes widened. 'Oh my God, do you work for him?'

'That's right.'

Maggie fluttered her eyelashes, trying to look a combination of demure and vixenish in what she imagined was typical groupie style. She shook her long copper hair so it fell over one shoulder.

'Oh my God!' she said again, clapping a hand to her mouth as she did her best to channel Georgia Fielding. 'You seriously know Jordan Nash? In real *life*?' She could hear her own italics and they disgusted her. But, needs must...

'I'm his manager.'

'But you look so young.'

Craig kept his face fixed. After fourteen years of dealing with Jordan's fans, he liked to think he was impenetrable to flirting.

She was good at it though, this one. If he wasn't such a cynical bastard, it might've made a dent.

'How old are you, kid?' he asked.

Kid, that was a good one. Maggie wondered what she could get away with. Admitting to anything over thirty was a definite no. Geriatric groupies: not a turn-on.

'Twenty-five,' she ventured, trying not to grimace.

The man cocked an eyebrow.

'Er, six. Twenty-six. It's, um, my birthday.'

Craig's mouth flickered. The girl was late twenties if she was a day. Still, Jordan was always telling him to steer clear of the young ones.

'Okay, twenty-six it is,' he said in the patronising tone that came free with his job. 'What do they call you, darling?'

'Magdalena.' She giggled. 'Funny, isn't it? Just like the song.'

Another obvious porky, Craig thought. No one was called Magdalena who wasn't a sodding Mother Superior.

'I couldn't believe it when I first heard it,' Maggie said, in a breathy voice she hoped was more Marilyn Monroe than smoker's cough. 'It was like he'd written it just for me. I can't tell you how it felt.'

Like having a teapot forcibly inserted up one nostril. But this bloke didn't need to know how it felt to have your private life laid bare-arse naked for the nation to gawp at by your ex. She was saving her rage for Max.

And still it wasn't enough. She could tell Craig was only half convinced.

Okay, if he was determined to make her work for it, it was time to crack out the inside knowledge.

'I loved the new album,' she said. 'The, er, *Hundred Highways* influence really stood out.'

Craig raised an eyebrow. 'Johnny Cash fan, are you?'

She nodded. 'I adore the *American Recordings*, that rawness in his voice. I bet Jordan likes him too, doesn't he?'

Craig was surprised – a rare occurrence. Even for a hardcore Router, that was some pretty in-depth knowledge.

'*A Hundred Highways* is his favourite album, actually.'

The girl beamed. 'I knew it!'

Craig fixed her with another appraising stare. Sensing she was nearly at her goal, Maggie arranged her face into a simper, sticking her chest out a bit for good measure.

'I bet I like everything Jordan likes. I'm really his biggest fan.'

For a moment, she thought it was too much. But finally, Craig broke into a grin.

'Look. How would you like to come and meet the band? I'm sure Jordan and the boys would want me to give you the VIP treatment, with it being your birthday.'

Yes! Nutcracker Suite. Maggie forced herself not to grin triumphantly. Instead she kept her eyes wide, batting her eyelashes furiously.

'Oh my goodness, seriously? Oh, thank you, thank you!'

Craig unhooked the rope and Maggie followed him through, ignoring the jealous glares of the real fans. He opened the door to the backstage area and flashed an ID at the security guard.

'Do you have any girlfriends with you?' he asked her. 'I can send someone to fetch them.'

'No,' she said, peering over him to try to get a look at the band. 'There's just me.'

He glanced at her in surprise. 'You came to the gig on your own?'

'Yeah. None of my friends could make it.'

Shame. That meant he'd have to come back to pick out girls for the others. He hoped there wouldn't be an argument over this one. He was determined to save her for Jordan – something told him the lad would approve.

He wasn't wrong. As soon as they came into view of Jordan, who was lounging against the wall blowing morose rings from a cigarette he definitely wasn't supposed to be smoking indoors, Craig saw his eyebrows shoot up.

'Oh my God,' Jordan whispered. His face lifted into a delighted smile. 'Oh my God, it's you!' He frowned. 'It... is you, isn't it? I'm not dreaming?'

'Yes, you enormous bastard. It's me.'

Craig turned to look at the girl, and he almost staggered backwards. It was as if she'd transformed into a different person.

Her brow had knit into a determined frown, and her eyes flashed in Jordan's direction. Not with lust either: with pure, solid rage. Long gone were the ingratiating simper, the thrust-out chest and schoolgirl giggle. She'd pulled herself up to her full height and was looking seriously dangerous, even in the face of Jordan's incomprehensibly ecstatic smile.

'What the hell is going on?' Craig demanded. 'Do you two know each other?'

But the girl ignored him. She strode towards Jordan, who didn't seem able to take his eyes off her, even when it became clear exactly what she was striding towards him to do.

With a resounding crack, she brought her palm crashing into his cheek.

'You absolute prick, Max!' she yelled. 'What the fuck did you think you were playing at? Do you even know what you've done?'

'Lanie, please—'

'Do *not* call me Lanie!'

She was staring intently at his crotch, and her knee had a crooked, purposeful look to it. Sensing she was planning on introducing the two to each other in the near future, Jordan tossed his fag away and cupped himself.

The rest of the band had gathered around now to see what the noise was about. They stared at the scarlet-faced hellcat glaring at their lead singer while he hung desperately onto his privates.

'What is all this?' Riley demanded. 'Who's this mad bitch, Craig?'

Craig shrugged in bewilderment. 'I picked her up from the stage door. She seemed as normal as they ever do. Soon as she spotted Jordan, she went completely mental.'

'You'd better call security,' Jake said. 'She looks ready to hurt someone.'

'No! Wait,' Jordan said. 'Let her alone, I know her.'

Riley shook his head. 'Did you book this, Jord? Is she a dominatrix or something?'

'No. Well, I don't think so. She's... an old friend.' He nodded to Maggie. 'Guys, this is Maggie, Maggie, the guys. Jake, Riley, Lucas, and, um, you seem to have met Craig.'

'Delighted to make their fucking acquaintance.'

Her gaze was still fixed on his balls, and the expression on her face strongly suggested she was planning to reinsert them into his body as soon as he was brave enough to uncup himself. This was not how the reunion had gone in his favourite recurring Maggie dream.

'She told me her name was Magdalena,' Craig said. 'I thought she was bullshitting me to get backstage.'

'Er, no,' Jordan said, his eyes darting from one incredulous face to another. 'No, that's her name. Magdalena Nightingale, we were at uni together.'

Jake shook his head. 'Oh no, mate.'

'You told us you'd made her up!' Lucas snapped. A dangerous look had appeared in his eyes too. Jordan wished he had a few more hands to cover his other sensitive areas.

'I did make her up. Sort of. I mean, I went out with her, yeah, but I just used it in the song because I liked the name.'

'Then maybe you could've shared that information with the bloody press!' Maggie hissed. 'Because right now, a wide selection of Britain's finest muck merchants are camped out on my doorstep, all of them desperate to get some dirt on the so-called love of Jordan Nash's life, this arch bitch who dumped him when he was nineteen and left him with a broken heart that'll never heal.' She shook her head. 'That's a lot of coincidences for a made-up woman, Max.'

'Why does she keep calling you Max?' Jake asked.

'Because that's his name,' Riley said. 'Well, it used to be. Max Jordan.'

'Right. Let's have some calm,' Jordan said as he tried to take control of the situation. 'Look, Lanie – I mean, Mags. Can we go somewhere private? I'm sorry, I never meant to cause trouble for you.'

'Yes, well, don't say sorry to me – although I was sworn at and almost punched by one of your delightful fans today, so actually, yeah, you probably should. But Amelia's the one who should really get an apology.'

'Who?'

'My daughter. My daughter who got followed home from school by a couple of creepy blokes demanding all the details of how Mummy did it with Jordan Nash back in the day.'

Jordan laughed. 'You're not serious. You've got a kid?'

'Yeah I've got a kid. I'm thirty-four, Max. What's so funny about that?'

'Nothing. Sorry, I didn't mean to laugh. It's just... you know.'

He hadn't been able to stop himself. Maggie, who'd drunk her way around every pub in Bristol, never happy to call it a night unless she'd danced on at least one table. Maggie, who he'd piggy-backed to their halls a hundred times when she'd been hammered, giggling and yelling 'Giddyup, horsey!'.

And now she was a mum.

He felt a sickening jolt when he realised what else it must mean.

'So you're married?'

For the first time, he noticed her face soften.

'No. No, I'm not with anyone. It's... kind of complicated.'

Relief flooded his throat.

'Mags, can we go to my dressing room? I can't stand here hanging onto my balls all night.'

She sighed. 'Fine, come on. I need you to do something for me.'

Chapter Twenty-One

'So... how've you been?' Jordan asked when he and Maggie were alone.

'We don't have time for small talk, Max. There's a vulnerable thirteen-year-old relying on me and if you don't throw whatever legal weight you've got at getting this story shut down, I swear I will never forgive you.'

'Thirteen! Your daughter's thirteen?'

'Max, come on. Get on the phone and do what you need to do. It's only been in the local press so far but it looked like every hack in Britain was on my doorstep this afternoon.'

'So you had her while you were still at uni?'

'Yeah, thanks for the maths lesson. Get on with it, can you?'

'Who's the dad? Is it someone I know?'

'Max!'

'Right. Yeah.' He pushed his hands into his hair. 'I can get Craig onto Ebony, the band's lawyer. But I'm not sure how much help it'll be, La— Mags. I've tried it before with the crap Sylvia puts out and the press always find a way round it.'

'But Amelia's a minor. You must be able to stop them publishing anything about her.'

'That's true.' Jordan took out his phone and dialled. 'Craig? Sounds like the nationals have got hold of our story. Yeah, me and Maggie, but they've got her kid involved too. Can you get Ebony to put the thumbscrews on, then we'll see what we can do to protect the little girl? Cheers.' He hung up. 'Okay, he's on it.'

Maggie breathed a sigh of relief. 'Great.'

'So who does the kid belong to apart from you?'

'It's not important.' She stood to leave. 'See you, Max.'

'What, that's it? You storm back into my life, slap me round the face and now you're just sodding off again?'

'I came to get you to fix the mess you made with that bloody song. Now you've done it. What's to stay for?'

'Maggie, sit, please,' Jordan said. 'Look, I get that you're pissed off. You're right, I've been an idiot. But at least wait till I hear from Craig.'

She hesitated, then sat back down. 'Just until I know the story's been shelved.'

Jordan smiled and leaned towards her.

'So do you still see the others?'

'We don't have to talk, do we?'

'Come on, don't be like that.'

'Okay, you want to talk, we'll talk,' she snapped. 'What the hell was that song about, Max?'

'Well, it was about us, wasn't it?'

'I know it was about us. What I want to know is why, after fourteen years, you decided to write a song about us.'

'I was in rehab and it just… popped into my head. It never occurred to me they'd go looking for you.'

'Jordan Nash's lost sweetheart? Of course they bloody would. And I asked why you wrote it, not where.'

Jordan rubbed his hair. 'Not sure I know myself. I can't stop thinking about you lately. I mean, all three of you,' he corrected hastily. 'That life I left behind.'

'Why?'

'Guess I missed the old gang.'

'Missed us? After fourteen years? Jesus, talk about a delayed reaction.'

'I don't know why either. I feel like I'm waking up, Maggie, since I quit coke. I'm just… not sure to what.'

'Missed us,' Maggie muttered. 'And yet you didn't write a song about Ibby, did you? It had to be me.'

The ghost of a grin flickered over Jordan's face. 'No, well, not much rhymes with Ibby.'

Maggie finally allowed herself a small smile.

'You two still close?' Jordan asked, pleased to see her frown lift. This was more like his dream. In his dream she always smiled.

'Closer than ever.'

'And Other Max, you still see him?'

'Yeah. We all stayed in the area.'

'What're they up to?'

'Other Max is a paramedic at Bristol Royal Infirmary. Not married but there's a girlfriend he's serious about. Ibby's a journalist in an ice cream van. Don't ask.'

'Husband? Boyfriend?'

'No,' she said, smiling. 'His standards are too high.'

'Right. The Harrison Test.'

Maggie laughed. 'It's an ongoing problem.'

'And what about you, Mags?' he asked quietly.

'I'm a counsellor. Helping people with their relationship issues.'

'A counsellor, seriously? Wow.'

'Yep. Dr Nightingale, if you don't mind.'

'Bloody hell,' he muttered. 'You're all so grown-up. And... your relationship issues?'

'I told you, I'm not with anyone.'

'What about the kid's dad? Is he involved now you're not together?'

She frowned. 'Why're you so interested in that?'

'I'm not, I'm interested in you. Why are you so cagey about it?' Jordan groaned. 'Oh God, it is someone I know, isn't it? Tell me you and Other Max didn't fall into bed with each other again.'

'It's not Other Max.'

'Then who?'

She looked away. 'Look, if you must know... it's Ibs.'

Jordan couldn't stop himself laughing, through shock more than anything. 'You what?'

'Ibby. He's my daughter's dad. And yes, he's involved, and yes, it all works, and yes, that's part of the reason I want this story shut down. Being thirteen's hard enough without Mum and Dad and Jordan bloody Nash to complicate it.'

'Seriously? Ibby? As in Aaron Ibbotson, your best friend Ibby?'

'Yes, Max, that Ibby.'

'Ibby who's always been one hundred per cent gay? That Ibby?'

'That Ibby.'

'And he's the, you know, biologically he's the father?'

'Isn't that what I just said?'

Jordan shook his head. 'So you and Ibs...'

'We had some sex, we've got a kid, we raise her together; it's really not that weird. Move on, Max.'

'But you were never a couple?'

'Course we weren't. Just drunk, horny and stupid.'

'Right,' Jordan said, feeling dazed.

'No girlfriend for you at the moment, I'm guessing, if Craig's out pimping fuck buddies for you after gigs,' she said, lip curling. 'Or is there? Is that how it works: a woman a night on tour and a spare for when you get back?'

Jordan flushed. 'It's not like that.'

'What is it like?'

'I can hardly just meet someone down the pub any more, can I? It's isolating, the constant cycle of touring and promoting. Okay, yeah, I get lonely sometimes. Doesn't mean I don't respect them, the girls.'

'Right,' Maggie said, still regarding him with the same expression of distaste. 'What about your mate Riley, does he respect them? Rumour goes he likes them young.'

'Well I'm not Riley.'

'What happened to that fiancée you had – the model, Arabella or whatever? I thought there was a big wedding planned.'

'Probably,' he muttered.

She frowned. 'What?'

'I wouldn't believe everything you read. Arabella was part of the image, that's all.' He leaned forward to take her hands, then thought better of it and leaned back again. 'I'm done with that shit now, Mags, I swear.'

'What, so… are you saying the engagement was fake?'

He snorted. 'They've all been fake – every so-called relationship. Manufactured, just like me.'

'Christ, Max,' she murmured. 'How the fuck have you been living?'

Jordan choked back a sob. 'I know. But it's over now, it has to be.' He jerked as his phone rang. 'That'll be Craig.'

He picked up. 'Did she manage it? Yes?' He broke into a relieved smile. 'Best we could've hoped for, I guess. I'll speak to Ebony tomorrow, we'll get it all sorted.' He hung up.

'So?' Maggie said.

'Ebony's got it off the front pages but sorry, she had to chuck them something. There'll probably be a couple of paragraphs in the gossip sections. But they won't mention the kid, just us.'

Maggie exhaled with relief. 'That'll do.'

'I'm talking to her tomorrow to see about getting protection in place for your daughter. I can't guarantee you won't still get a few paps turning up though.'

'That's fine. I don't care about me, just Amelia.'

'Maggie, I'm really so sorry.'

'Me too.' She stood to leave. 'Thanks, Max.'

'Won't you stay a bit longer? We could have a drink together.'

'No, I need to get home to my family. Thanks for helping though, I appreciate it. And I'm sorry I slapped you.'

'Can I… would you visit me again? It's been nice seeing you.'

'I don't think that will work, do you?'

'It could. I'm Jordan Nash, I could make it.'

'No, Max. I can't be part of this, I've got a life.' She squeezed his shoulder. 'Look after yourself, eh? Remember who you really are.'

And as quickly as she'd reappeared in his life, she was gone.

Chapter Twenty-Two

'Max. Max! Are you listening to me?'

Jordan groaned. 'Lanie, I know you hate me right now, but could you please speak a bit softer? My brain's fried here.'

'Where the hell have you been?' she demanded. 'Two days you've been off the map. Two fucking days! Do you know how worried I was?'

'Can you stop? You're my girlfriend, not my babysitter. I'm a big boy, I can look after myself.'

She curled her lip as she ran her gaze over him, lying on the sofa in the same clothes he'd been wearing when he'd headed down to London the Saturday before. He knew what he must look like. His matted hair badly needed a wash and his eyes felt like golf balls in his skull.

'Yeah, it really looks like it, doesn't it?' she said. 'Why weren't you answering your phone?'

'Look, we'll talk about it later, okay? I'm too tired to do this now.'

'Tired, right. Is that the euphemism we're employing for today's post-bender comedown?'

Jordan groaned again, pulling a cushion over his ears to muffle the sound of her voice.

'Where've you been then?' she demanded. 'Have you got a girl down there, is that it?'

'What? No! Come on, baby, you know I'd never do that to you. I love you.'

He stretched out a hand to her, but she batted it away.

'Yeah, you love me enough to let me worry myself sick, leaving you endless voicemails while you're off powdering your nose with those waste-of-space new mates of yours. I didn't know if you were dead or...

or God knows what. If it's like this now, how do you think we'll cope after you move?'

'It won't always be this way,' he muttered.

'It can't always be this way, Max. Because if it is, I can tell you now I won't be any part of it.' She picked up a packet of paracetamol from the coffee table and threw it at him. 'Here. Fix your head, then I recommend having a long, hard think about how you might fix yourself.'

'Where are you going?' he asked as she slung her bag over her shoulder.

'Where do you think? Lectures. Some of us do still have degrees to finish.'

There was the sound of the front door unlocking, and Ibby came in. He frowned when he clocked Maggie's black expression. 'What's up, Mags?'

'Ask Hunter S Thompson over there,' she said, jerking her head towards Jordan. 'Maybe you can get through to him, because I'm so bloody close to writing him off as lost.' She pecked Ibby's cheek as she passed him. 'See you later.'

When she'd gone, Ibby pushed Jordan's feet off the sofa and threw himself down beside him.

'So I take it I just witnessed the end of another blazing row,' he said.

'Yeah,' Jordan mumbled. 'Well, more of a blazing shout. All I had to do was show up.'

'Where've you been since Saturday, Jord?'

'Riley's place.'

'You could've called. She was worried. We all were.'

'I just wanted to switch off from everything for a few days. Maggie won't ease up on me at the moment.'

'Tough love, mate. She hates watching you snort your health away.' Ibby examined him. 'You look like shit, you know.'

Jordan summoned a weak smile. 'Love you too, Ibs.'

He opened the paracetamol packet Maggie had chucked at him and popped out a couple, gagging as he swallowed them down dry.

'Coffee?' Ibby said.

'Yeah, thanks.' Jordan pushed himself to his feet. 'I'll be back in a minute.'

Ibby watched him head for the door.

'Do you have to, Jord?' he said in a low voice.

'Just one line. Hair of the dog. I won't feel human till I do.'

Ibby's concerned gaze followed him from the room. Jordan could feel it, burning into the back of his neck. And his friends wondered why he'd felt the need to go off grid for a few days, away from worried eyes that judged without understanding.

When he came back downstairs, a couple of mugs were steaming on the coffee table.

'I got us a present while you were away,' Ibby told Jordan as he claimed his drink.

'Did you? What?'

Ibby opened a drawer in the coffee table and waggled an Xbox game at him. 'Ta-da! Picked it up the other day.'

Jordan grabbed it off him. 'Arghh, Counter-Strike! Ibbotson, you legend! I've been waiting ages for this.'

'So, what do you think? Lads' night in with a few beers and some truly top-quality violence this Friday? Other Max says he's up for it.'

Jordan grimaced. 'Friday?'

Ibby shook his head. 'Come on. You're not going down there again?'

'There's just… I said I'd go to this party. I don't think I can get out of it now.'

'Right. Saturday then?'

'I'm not coming back for a week. We've got a couple of new songs to rehearse so I've arranged to kip on Riley's floor.'

'You'd think you'd moved there already,' Ibby muttered. 'You're not going to abandon us for your band clique, are you?'

'Course not.' Jordan put the game down on the table. 'Ibs, I'm sorry. It's just manic at the moment, getting ready to move and fitting in rehearsal time on top. We'll do a proper lads' night before I go, promise.'

'Hmm.'

'Anyway, I'm not exactly moving to Argentina, am I? It's only a couple of hours on the train. I'll be back all the time.'

Ibby smiled, a little sadly. 'Just don't forget us, eh? I know we must seem pretty dull compared to your London set, but it wouldn't be the same round here without you.'

Jordan smiled back. 'Don't be daft. Couldn't forget you lot, would I?'

—

He was dragged from his daydreams by Riley's voice, coming from somewhere behind the curtains that enclosed Jordan's bunk on the Route 69 tour bus.

'Will one of you go tell that boring bastard to get up?' he was saying. 'Fuck knows why, but Carla's desperate to meet him.'

A feminine voice mumbled something Jordan couldn't hear and Riley gave a lecherous snort.

'Jordan, you miserable twat!' he called out. 'I know you can hear me. Get yourself out here before I come and drag you out.'

It was always like this when Craig wasn't around to keep Riley on his lead. Jordan felt like he was clinging onto recovery by a thread every time his manager left him alone.

'Don't, Ri,' he heard Jake say in a low voice. 'Here, I'll go ask him.'

A second later, the drummer's face appeared through the curtains.

'You coming to join the party, Jord?' he asked quietly. 'Some pretty girls.'

Jordan shook his head. 'I can't,' he muttered. 'Not if they're all coked up. Can you tell them I'm asleep?'

Jake regarded him for a moment, then turned to call over his shoulder.

'Sorry, ladies, he's dead to the world in here. Tour fatigue. Maybe later, yeah?'

After Exeter the tour bus headed to Southampton, then to Bristol, before winding its way north.

Craig brought Jordan the major tabloids every day so he could check for news of Maggie and her family, and he was relieved to see that Ebony's machinations had done the trick. There were a couple of gossip pieces about Magdalena Nightingale, the real-life woman Jordan Nash had loved and lost, but nothing about Ibby or the kid, Amelia.

If Jordan had hoped his run-in with Maggie would exorcise the dreams that had been torturing him, he was wrong. If anything, they became more frequent: flashbacks to his old life, back when to Maggie and Nana, the two people who'd loved him best, he was still a boy called Max. And then there were the other dreams, dreams of a parallel present, that frequently caused him to jerk awake. They seemed so real. Him and Maggie, together still with a home and family... the road not travelled. Or the road Aaron Ibbotson had travelled in his place.

He thought a lot about his old friends. Maggie was a counsellor, Other Max a paramedic. What did Max Jordan do by comparison that was so bloody amazing? Okay, the fans adored him. He was proud of his work, especially from the early days. But he wasn't helping people like his friends were – just the opposite. The press were forever denouncing him as a dreadful role model for the kids who admired him, and shit, they were right, weren't they? Apart from make music, what had he done for the past fourteen years other than get fucked up?

By the time the band reached Leeds two weeks later, stop nine of a twenty-date tour, the shaking in Jordan's hands was so bad he could barely smoke a cigarette without causing a fire hazard. The only time it stopped was on stage.

Craig had gone on ahead with the luggage. When they pulled up outside the hotel, their manager was waiting.

Jordan frowned. 'You don't normally meet us off the bus. Something wrong?'

'For you there is,' he said, grimacing. 'Jord, *she's* here. She was threatening to cause a scene so I stuck her in your room. Tried to pay her off but she wouldn't go without seeing you.'

'Oh God, not Sylvia,' Jordan groaned, lighting a cigarette with a trembling hand. 'What does she want?'

'She wouldn't tell me. Says it's for your ears only.'

He sighed. 'Right. Let's get it over with.'

'Hey. Star.' Craig rested a hand on Jordan's arm as he started to walk off. 'Happy birthday, eh?'

When Jordan got to his room, Sylvia was seated at his dressing table, practising her photoshoot pucker in the mirror. Either that or she'd had another batch of lip fillers since he'd seen her last.

'Darling!' She stood to air-kiss him on both cheeks, without ever actually touching him, then sat back down. 'It's been such a long time. How've you been?'

'You know how I've been. In rehab for cocaine dependency, like you give a shit.'

She pouted. 'Now, Jordan, that's not fair.'

'Come on, Mother, cut the crap. What is it today? I'm guessing you're not here to drop off a birthday card.'

'Is it your birthday?'

Jordan snorted. 'What, don't you know? You were there.'

She dropped the affected simper and turned back to the mirror. 'That was another life, darling. Another Sylvia.'

'So what is it? Getting married again?'

'No. At least, not just yet.'

'Right. Then how much are you after?'

'Not a penny, I promise you. I'm actually rather flush since I became a celebrity in my own right. Your coke meltdown couldn't have come at a better time.'

'Christ, you're something.' Jordan threw himself down on the bed, laying on his back as he fumbled to light another cigarette.

Sylvia laughed. 'What on earth's wrong with your hands?'

'Withdrawal.' He gave up on his fag and tossed the lighter to one side. 'I'm sure you remember it. What do you want then?'

'A drink, for a start. Have you got any of the good stuff?'

'No.'

She smiled. 'Like hell you haven't.'

Sylvia unzipped the suitcase at the foot of his bed, rummaging in it until she found what she was after. She drew out a bottle of single malt and proceeded to pour herself a generous glass.

'Help yourself, why don't you?' Jordan said drily.

'You having one?'

'Not with you. So come on, why are you here?'

'Why must you interfere with my little hobbies, Jordan?'

He frowned. 'What?'

'I had every editor in London salivating for an exclusive after they'd hunted down your girlfriend and her daughter.' She tossed back her whisky in one. 'We're talking thousands, darling. The next thing I know, you send the legal heavies in and it all gets shut down. A poxy couple of grand I got from that local rag, that's all.'

'Good.'

'I can never understand why you aren't grateful to me. If Route 69 tracked album sales against every time I made a media appearance, I'm sure there'd be a correlation.'

'Look, Sylvia, you can exploit me as much as you want—'

'I gave you life, darling. You can hardly begrudge me a little return on that.'

'You can exploit me as much as you want,' Jordan repeated, 'but keep Maggie and the kid out of it. Otherwise I'm cutting you off for good, I mean it.'

'You wrote the song, didn't you?'

'Yeah,' Jordan said, scowling. 'Don't know what I was thinking.'

'I would have thought your Magdalena would be grateful. It was a beautiful romantic gesture, the sort any girl dreams of.'

'Maggie's not any girl. And I don't think many girls dream of having their private lives invaded by a bunch of greasy hacks.' He turned onto his side to flash her a look of dislike. 'Well, present company excepted. So you're here to recoup your losses, are you?'

'I told you, Jordan, I don't want money,' Sylvia said, examining her long, hot-pink nails. 'I've got something far more lucrative lined up, if you'll just play ball.'

'What is it?'

'A reality show. I've had a producer interested in a Nash family fly-on-the-wall thing. Perhaps we could involve your girlfriend too, if she wanted to make some money for the little girl's college fund. We could be the British Kardashians.'

'Not a chance. There you go, you've had my answer. Now get out.'

'Jordan, I wish you wouldn't be so closed-minded. You are so like your father sometimes.'

'What part of "get out" didn't make sense to you, Sylvia? Go on. I'll see you when your tits start sagging again.'

He got up and held the door open for her.

'Won't you even consider it?' she said as she stood to leave.

'Not while there's breath in my body and blood in my veins.'

She held one perfectly manicured nail against his throat. 'You'll regret this, Jordan. I needed this.'

'Yeah, yeah. Go on, piss off. Go see if *I'm a Celebrity*'s recruiting, gobble a few kangaroo bollocks with Cannon and Ball.'

With a last glare, his mum wiggled her backside out. Jordan slammed the door behind her.

When she'd gone, he lit a cigarette, smoked it to the filter and burst into tears.

He finally got it. He finally understood what the flashbacks meant, what his brain was trying to tell him. Why he'd felt compelled to write the song that had caused so much trouble.

His old friends, the ones he'd tossed aside so he could be Jordan fucking Nash. They all had meaningful jobs, friends, family. Other Max had his girlfriend, and a rewarding job helping others. Maggie and Ibby had each other and they had their little girl.

What did he have? For family he had a mother who'd sell him for organs if she ever caught him sleeping. For friends he had a band, people he had little in common with except hedonism and loneliness. Where other people were falling in love, Jordan Nash was finding empty comfort in the arms of strangers. And all the while, the fans lapped up phoney relationships with high-profile women designed to generate maximum publicity for his 'brand'. That's what he was – not a man but a brand. A product.

Even Craig, his only real friend – the one person who'd remembered that today was his thirty-fourth birthday – was on the payroll. Jordan had never managed to work out how much of his manager's attitude to him came from genuine affection and how much was based on the fact that his client had made him a very, very rich man.

When Jordan had been a boy, he'd wanted to be like his idols. Write songs like Springsteen, Cash and Dylan. Charm the crowds like Freddie, evolve like Bowie. More than that, he'd wanted to change the world, to fight back against unfairness, against elitism, bigotry and privilege, with his music as a conduit for his stinging sense of injustice.

Now, Jordan Nash *was* the elite – the privileged. He was a wealthy man, an admired man and very much a desired one. Yet somehow, he was nothing, had nothing. Nothing compared to the loved and loving lives of the friends he hadn't valued enough when he'd had them, and who he now missed with an ache he couldn't quell.

And Maggie, the one woman he— but what was the point of brooding? It was too late now.

Jordan gave in to tears and regret for a while. When he was all sobbed out, he hit the booze.

'…and make sure you say please and thank you, and if Nana asks you to do something you do it right away, okay?'

Amelia rolled her eyes. 'I know, Dad, I'm not five.'

'Less of the attitude, missy. Nana's been looking forward to having you stay so I want you on your best behaviour.'

'Dad, stop worrying. You and Mum just have a nice time.'

Ibby smiled and gave her a squeeze. 'Well, I guess as daughters go you're not so bad.'

They stopped at one of the three-storey townhouses overlooking the beach and Ibby knocked on the door. It was opened by a stylish young woman in her mid-twenties with elaborately curled black hair.

'Hiya Beth,' he said. 'Mum not here?'

'She's popped to the shops. Despite the fridge groaning with snacks, she suddenly realised she had *absolutely nothing in* to spoil our Melie rotten with.' Beth held out a hand to Amelia. 'What do you think, chick? I had them done this afternoon.'

Amelia examined the shining pink nails.

'They're so pretty,' she whispered reverently.

'Aren't they? Chanel Nuvolo Rosa. Don't want to lose my reputation as the glamorous aunty. Oh, and guess what?'

'What?'

'I bought you a bottle too.'

'Arghh, brilliant!' Amelia lunged forward to hug her round the waist. 'Thanks, Aunty Beth.'

'So what do you say, Melie? Girly makeovers tonight? You need to get yourself beach-ready now you've broken up for summer.'

'Why, are you staying over too?'

'Yep. You know me, can't resist a sleepover.'

Amelia brightened. As much as she loved her nana, a night of manicures and celebrity gossip with Aunty Beth was a big improvement on watching *Coronation Street*.

'Come on then, Melie, let's get this pyjama party started,' Beth said, ushering her in. 'I understand I've to ask you about someone called Isaac and his divine glasses.'

'Thanks for this, sis,' Ibby said when Amelia had gone upstairs with her overnight bag. 'After everything that's gone on recently, a night on the tiles feels like just what me and Maggie need.'

'Hardly a chore spending time with my favourite niece, is it?' She leaned forward to peck his cheek. 'Go on, Aaron, go enjoy yourself. Love to Mags.'

When his sister had disappeared inside, Ibby turned his steps homewards to grab a quick shower before he met up with Maggie, Other Max and Nicki at Fuzzy Duck's cocktail bar in town.

It had been a great suggestion of Maggie's, a night out for their little gang. Ibby's mum Suze, as doting a nana as ever let her granddaughter get away with murder, had been delighted to offer babysitting services so he and Mags could take a bit of quality time for themselves.

Quality time. The phrase made him smile. It did occasionally amuse him – the way the two of them were exactly like an old married couple, only without the actual couple bit.

It wasn't how he'd thought his life would turn out, but he loved it. He loved his family, his friends, his ice cream van. Okay, a boyfriend would be nice, and he had to admit Nat had been popping up quite often in his thoughts since they'd run into each other earlier that month. Overall, though, he was happy. It wasn't the life he'd predicted, but it was a good one.

He felt some mild trepidation as he turned the corner onto The Cedars. He always did now, ever since the day he'd come home to find every hack in Britain on his doorstep. It was just reflex though, there was nothing to see. All was serene, the air laced with delicious floral scents, the only sound the calls of the songthrushes who made their home in the trees that lined the pavements. Not a soul was to be seen that July day except old Mrs Pinkerton next door, sunbathing in a deckchair.

Things had gone satisfyingly quiet again since the Ibbotson-Nightingale household had found itself at the heart of a media circus two weeks ago. Whatever legal stuff Jordan had thrown at the press seemed to have done the trick. None of them had come near Amelia, whose life had settled back into its usual routine as the novelty of her connection with Jordan Nash had worn off. Maggie had been targeted a few times – there was the odd photographer, and a journalist who'd masqueraded as a client. They seemed to be cherishing a forlorn hope she might have something meaty on Jordan she'd been keeping back. Nothing she couldn't handle though, Ibby reflected fondly.

Mrs Pinkerton waved when she saw him, and he approached the hedge to speak to her.

'Any trouble today?' he asked.

'No, all quiet on the western front,' she said. 'It's been four days since I spotted the last one. I think we're yesterday's news at last.'

'Thank goodness for that, eh? So sorry, Mrs P.'

'Oh, now, don't be silly,' she said, waving a hand. 'No one blames you, or Maggie either. Besides, it was really rather exciting.'

Ibby laughed. 'A bit too exciting for my taste.'

'I must admit, I quite enjoyed it. The ladies at my luncheon club are still gossiping about The Day the Newspapers Came. I'm expecting to dine out on the fact I know the two of you for a good few years.'

Ibby was patting his pockets.

'What's wrong, love?' Mrs Pinkerton asked.

'Oh, just remembered I gave my key to Amelia. She's lost hers.'

'Can you get in?'

'Yeah, there's an emergency back door key under the mat. I'll see you later.'

When Ibby reached the back porch, he frowned. There was something in there that certainly hadn't been that morning.

What the hell was it? It looked like a pile of... Jesus, it was moving! Was it a rough sleeper?

Ibby approached what he'd originally thought was a bundle of clothes and prodded it. The old homburg the man was wearing bobbed sleepily.

'Wuh?' the figure grunted.

'Come on, mate, you can't sleep here,' Ibby said gently. 'Let's get you up, eh?'

'Hm?'

'You've had too much to drink. There's a hostel down in town where you can sleep it off, I'll help you get there.'

A hand emerged from the tatty coat and pushed up the hat to reveal a face he hadn't seen in the flesh for fourteen years.

'Hey, Ibs,' it slurred. 'How've you been?'

–

Maggie pulled out her mobile. No messages. Ibby had been due to meet her in Fuzzy Duck's half an hour ago. Held up by his mum while dropping Amelia off, she guessed. Suze Ibbotson could chat for England.

She wished he'd get a shift on. She was bored of sitting on her own, and Other Max and Nicki weren't arriving for an hour.

A red-haired girl slid onto the stool next to Maggie's. She didn't look much more than twenty and had obviously been out for some time, if the state of her drooping eyelids was anything to go by. She pulled out her purse and blinked at the contents, applying her tipsy maths to the handful of coins.

Maggie smiled to herself. The girl was a student, she'd bet anything. That'd been her fifteen years ago, coppering up for just one more.

'Couldn't lend us twenty pee, could you, hun?' the student slurred. 'I'm just short of a small pinot.'

'I think I can spare that.' Maggie rummaged in her jeans pocket and handed over a fistful of change. 'There you go, all yours.'

The girl beamed as she examined the coins, calculating that she now had enough for an upgrade to a large pinot. 'Cheers.' She glanced over Maggie's shoulder, noticing she was alone. 'Oh sorry, were you saving this seat for someone?'

'My friend, but he's running late. Take it, please.' Maggie shot the girl a friendly grin. 'Maggie.'

'Julia. Thanks for the drink, Maggie.'

'No worries.'

Julia stared intently into Maggie's face, or as intently as she could through the wine haze. 'Hey,' she said suddenly. 'I know you from somewhere. Don't I?'

Maggie stiffened. Her friendly grin disappeared.

'Absolutely not. You've never seen me before in your life.'

'I do, you've been on telly or something. Were you on *Britain's Got Talent*?'

'Sadly not. Apparently the ability to gargle Ed Sheeran hits with Heineken doesn't cut it, or so my daughter tells me.'

'Ooh! Are you that double rollover winner?' Julia scanned the coins in her palm. 'Should've held out for a fiver.'

'I wish.' Maggie let out a resigned sigh. 'I suppose you'll work it out eventually. I'm Jordan Nash's ex-girlfriend, Maggie Nightingale. Old news round here now.'

'Bloody hell! You're Magdalena? *The* Magdalena? You jammy mare!'

'Yeah. Jammy old me.'

Julia lowered her voice. 'So what's Jordan like in real life?'

'He is – was – kind of sweet, I guess. When he wasn't being a total arsehole, anyway. The answer to that depends on when you catch me, to be honest.'

'How come you broke up? Did he cheat on you?'

Alarm bells started to ring in the back of Maggie's brain. She looked up to meet Julia's too-innocent green eyes.

'No,' Maggie said cautiously. 'It's what he started doing to himself that was the problem.'

'The drugs, you mean?'

'Yeah.'

'But before that, what was he like? He obviously never got over you.'

Maggie flashed Julia a brilliant smile. If Ibby had been there, he'd have recognised that as the signal to drag his friend away before she got herself into trouble. But Ibby wasn't there.

'Well, he was fantastic in bed. Gold-star athlete. Full marks from all judges.'

'Really?'

'Yep, multiple orgasms every night of the week. The boy wasn't happy unless we were at it three, four times a night.'

'You're kidding!'

'Swear to God,' Maggie said, crossing herself in a perfect imitation of Georgia. 'And talk about packing downstairs! Ten inches or the Lord strike me dead.'

She glanced up, but no bolt of lightning appeared from the ether. Maggie took this as a sign that if there was an Almighty, he, she or it was firmly on her side.

'No!' Julia was practically toppling off her stool, she was leaning so far forward.

'Uh-huh. At uni we used to call him…' Maggie hesitated. What sounded good? Jimmy Three-Legs? Marky Mark's Stunt Penis? Mr Lunchbox? '…um, The Schlong.'

'Really, that was his nickname?'

'It's a shame really, about his other career. He had a real talent for it, but the injury put paid to all that. So he had no choice but to turn to his second love, music.'

'What other career?'

'Oh, don't you know?' Maggie said, lifting her eyebrows. 'He was an actor. Adult films. Amateur of course, bit of beer money, but he was definitely going places in the porn industry. Then…' She shook her head sadly. 'Bam, right in the middle of a gang-bang scene. Todger sprain. Doctors said he'd never work again.'

Julia smiled uncertainly. 'You're winding me up.'

'Whatever gave you that idea?' Maggie nodded to the girl's handbag, sitting between them on the bar. 'Go on, turn it off.'

'You what?'

'The tape recorder. You must've worked out by now you're wasting your time.'

Julia hesitated, then pulled out a dictaphone and pressed Stop. 'How'd you guess?'

'Far too eager, I'm afraid. And you're not the first journalist who's tried the undercover chat-up. They usually send good-looking blokes though.' She examined Julia, who'd dropped the drunk act and was sitting up straight, apparently not at all embarrassed at being caught out. She'd go far in the biz, once she got the hang of bare-faced lying and deceit. 'What paper?'

'*Daily Recorder.*' Julia sighed. 'I'm only a trainee. This could've been my big break.'

'Why the sudden renewal of interest? I've got nothing to add to what's been printed about me and Jordan, all our secrets are out.'

'My editor had a hunch you might know where he is.'

Maggie frowned. 'He's on tour, isn't he?'

'What, didn't you hear? No one's seen him since he didn't turn up to his gig in Leeds last night.'

'Last night? You mean he disappeared on his birthday?'

'Was it his birthday?'

'Yeah, his thirty-fourth.'

'Oh, right. Well, everyone's going crazy trying to find him. His mum was the last person to talk to him and even she doesn't know where he's gone.'

Maggie sat up straighter. Max missing… oh God, he hadn't gone on a coke bender after some sort of showdown with Sylvia?

But she'd have to worry about him later. Right now she had a nosy hack to get rid of. She fixed her face into an expression of careless nonchalance.

'Well if he's hiding then I'm the last person he'd confide in,' she said. 'Until a brief run-in over that bloody song, we hadn't seen each other in fourteen years. And given that during that run-in I slapped him and came very close to kneeing him in the balls, I can't see me being added to his Christmas card list. Not that I'd want to be, after what he put my family through.' Her phone buzzed on the bar. 'Hang on.'

She picked up. 'Okay, where are you?'

'I popped home to change after I dropped Melie off.' Ibby sounded worried, and a little out of breath. 'Mags, can you get a cab back? Sorry, but something's come up.'

'What is it?' She felt a flash of panic. 'Melie's okay, isn't she?'

'She's fine. It's Max.'

'Can't he make it?'

'Not Max Castle.' He lowered his voice to a whisper. 'Your Max. Max Jordan.'

'M—' She stopped herself, aware of Julia watching her. 'What about him?'

'He's here, that's what.'

Chapter Twenty-Four

'Ibby,' Jordan groaned as his old friend made a valiant effort to pull him to his feet. 'W'm Mags?'

'On her way.' Ibby let the arm he was tugging drop. 'Christ, Jord, meet me halfway here, there's bloody six foot odd of you.'

But Jordan had fallen into a doze again.

'Right.' Ibby retrieved the spare key from under the mat and opened the door. Then he grabbed Jordan's arms and, with a mammoth effort, dragged him inside. He'd have a few bruises in the morning, but that was going to be the least of his worries.

When Ibby had got him in, he sagged against the fridge for a moment. Then he locked the door, drew all the blinds and crouched down beside the semi-conscious Jordan.

What the fuck had the man taken? Was this an overdose, should he call an ambulance? If he did it'd be on every front page in the country tomorrow.

With difficulty he stripped Jordan of the tatty coat and hat he was wearing. There was a nearly empty whisky bottle under one arm. Ibby hid it in a cupboard out of sight.

God, he was a state. He'd been sick down his clothes at some point. His half-open eyes were red-rimmed, his skin deathly white.

Ibby held open one eyelid. The pupil was glassy but it looked the right size, not dilated as it would've been if Jordan had been doing coke. Perhaps he was just drunk.

Lucky they had a mate who was a paramedic. He tapped out a text to Other Max. Ibby knew he'd bring Nicki, but that was okay, they could trust her. And she was a nurse, wasn't she? Two medical professionals had to be better than one.

Ibby looked at Jordan, spread-eagled on his back like he'd been doing snow angels, and groaned. Jordan Nash, superstar, passed out on his kitchen floor. Bloody brilliant, just when things had started to go back to normal.

He tried to get Jordan to lie on his side in the recovery position, but he was conscious enough to resist and immediately roll onto his back again. Ibby settled for turning Jordan's head to one side and slapping his cheeks to stop him blacking out completely.

Ten minutes later there was a knock at the back door.

'Thank fuck you're here,' Ibby said to Other Max when he opened up.

'What's up, Ibs? That text sounded serious.' Other Max's gaze took in the carnage on the kitchen floor. 'Christ almighty. Is that... what's he doing here?'

'God knows. I found him in the porch.'

Other Max came into the kitchen, Nicki following. Her eyeballs practically jumped out of her skull when she saw who was there.

'Oh my *God!* That's... I mean it's...'

'Jordan Nash,' Ibby said. 'Well spotted. Can one of you healthcare types check him over? I don't know what he's taken but he's none too perky.'

Jordan started moaning softly.

'But he's... here,' Nicki whispered. 'Jordan Nash, actually... I mean, he's really... holy shit!'

'Not the time to get starstruck, Nic. We could be looking at a serious medical emergency.' Ibby produced Jordan's whisky from the cupboard. 'He's had most of this bottle, I think. Maybe pills too. Maggie said when she saw him two weeks ago, he seemed... well, he could be a suicide risk. Help him, guys, please.'

'Right,' Nicki said, snapping out of her initial shock as the severity of what Ibby was saying sunk in. 'Max, this is your area. Can you tell what he's taken?'

Other Max was already on his knees, looking Jordan over.

'Hair grip.'

Nicki removed one from her hair and handed it to him. He jabbed it into Jordan's arm a couple of times. Jordan gave an irritated humph and flung his arm across his body out of the way.

'Well, he's responding okay to stimulus. Good sign he hasn't taken anything to numb his nervous system.'

He pulled open Jordan's eyelids to examine the pupils.

'I checked them too,' Ibby said. 'They're okay, right? Not dilated?'

'Hard to tell. He's got coloured contacts in.'

'Shit, has he?'

Other Max slid the contacts to one side to examine the pupils. He exhaled with relief. 'No, they're okay.' He leaned towards Jordan. 'Breathing's regular, heart rate's fine. He's just drunk, Ibs.'

'Like, in need of a stomach pump drunk? If he has to go to hospital, the press'll be all over it.'

'In need of a fuckload of water. It's alcohol poisoning but not at its most severe. He's not blacked out completely, and he's not showing signs of hypothermia or seizure.' Other Max looked at Jordan's soiled clothes. 'Seems like he got some of it up, that's good. We just need to keep an eye on him, make sure he doesn't choke on vomit, and get him rehydrated as quickly as we can.'

'Right.' Ibby went to the tap and filled a pint glass, then handed it to Other Max.

Jordan was muttering now as he started to regain consciousness.

'That's it, Jord, wake up,' Other Max said gently. 'We need you to drink this.'

'Hiya, mate,' Jordan whispered, blinking at him.

'All right?'

'You look… older.'

'I am older. Still a looker though, eh?'

Jordan gave a wet-sounding laugh. 'Hey, you got a cig?'

'Not on me, sorry.'

''Kay.' Jordan submitted to being raised slightly and helped to drink the water.

'It's not good for you, smoking,' Other Max told him.

Jordan summoned a wonky grin. 'Made of plants though, right? Must be one of my five a day.' Other Max laughed and pressed more water on him.

Ibby was impressed. It was funny, Other Max was anxious as hell in his everyday life, but when it came to his work he was calm, collected – the ultimate professional. Ibby could see what he was doing: keeping Jordan talking, stopping him falling back into the stupor. Sleep was dangerous right now.

'How've you been, Jord, okay?' Other Max asked in a light, conversational tone. He held up the now empty pint glass to Ibby, who took it to the sink for a refill.

'Not so good,' Jordan mumbled. 'Where's Mags? I want to see Mags.'

There was the sound of the front door unlocking. Ibby sagged with relief.

'She's here, thank God.'

Jordan blinked hard, as if for Maggie's sake he was trying to force himself to sober up.

'What took you so long?' Ibby asked as Maggie came in.

'Journalist. I couldn't just rush off, she already suspected I knew where he was.' She glanced down at Jordan. 'Shit, look at him. What the hell's he taken?'

'Just booze, we think,' Nicki said. 'Ibby found a bottle of whisky on him.'

Jordan flashed her a weak smile. 'Hey, my Lanie.'

Maggie sighed and knelt by him. She took the water from Other Max.

'Here, let me.'

She helped Jordan drink some, slipping her arm around his back.

'Came to see you,' Jordan slurred, dropping his head to her shoulder.

'I know. Thank you. Drink some more of this for me now.'

Jordan sipped the water obediently, his cloudy gaze fixed on her.

'Why did you come to see me, Max?' she asked.

'Missed you. Wanted to… get away.'

'I think your other friends might be worried about you.'

'Not got other friends.'

'Why did you want to get away? You were supposed to play a gig last night, you know.'

'Sylvia,' Jordan muttered.

His droopy smile had transformed into a black scowl.

'Did she upset you?' Maggie asked in a gentler voice.

'Yeah.'

Maggie rubbed his back. 'Poor Max. She's an awful person.'

'She said… stuff. Stuff about you and the kid, putting you on TV. Told her to shove it.' Jordan smiled. 'Like it when you call me Max. No one calls me Max any more.'

'Here, have some more water.' Maggie looked at Other Max. 'How much does he need to drink?'

'As much as we can get in him. And you'll need to watch him tonight, he's a choking hazard.'

'You didn't take anything, did you, Max?' Maggie asked.

Jordan blinked. 'Like what?'

'Like coke or something.'

'Nope. Don't do coke no more.'

'Anything else then? Pills?'

'Pills?'

'I mean, you didn't try to hurt yourself?'

He blinked, head bobbing, and she could tell he was about to pass out again. She pressed more water on him till he'd revived a little.

'Max, did you hurt yourself?' she demanded again.

'You mean…'

'Did you try to kill yourself? We need to know so we can help you.'

'No. Not that. Just wanted to… forget.' He was heavy against her arm. 'Missed you so much,' he whispered. He glanced around the blurry shapes of his old friends. 'All of you.' He blinked at Nicki. 'Not you. You're new.'

'Yep. Um, hiya. Big fan actually. Hey, you think you could sign my—' She caught Other Max's eye. 'Right. Not the time. Maybe later.'

'I think he's coming out of it a bit,' Maggie said.

'Lanie, can I stay?' Jordan whispered.

'You can stay tonight. Tomorrow, when you're sober… we need to talk.'

Other Max nodded. 'That's right, don't leave him alone. Make sure he sleeps on his side too.'

'And in the morning,' Ibby said, 'we can work out what the hell we're going to do with him.'

Chapter Twenty-Five

Jordan woke up and immediately wished he hadn't. His head felt like the A65 on a bank holiday weekend.

The searing white lights of a television studio were in his face. Shit, he hadn't passed out during an interview?

Except… no, the lights were fading. Not TV. Hangover. Serious. Bastard. Hangover.

What'd happened yesterday? He remembered drinking… oh Christ, so much whisky. Bribing the driver who'd turned up to take him to the gig, begging him to take him far away from his life and all the people in it. In his drunken mind he'd wanted to get somewhere he could feel safe. And then…

But it was hard to think with a pair of feet in his face.

Funny, he didn't remember going to bed with anyone. Come to think of it, he didn't remember going to bed at all. Whose place was this?

Jordan ran his hand over one foot and up the leg attached to it. It was kind of rough for a girl. Kind of… hairy.

'Jord, stop. You're tickling me,' a man's voice said from the other end of the bed.

Right. Well this was new.

The figure sat up and groaned. 'You know, I'm told a lot of people dream of waking up in bed with Jordan Nash. Personally I'd prefer a bacon sandwich.'

'*Ibby?*'

'Yeah, I lost the toss when we were deciding who'd have to bunk up with you. By which I mean, Maggie told me no way and I was getting you.'

'This is a dream. Has to be a dream,' Jordan muttered.

'Sadly not. It's really me.'

'I haven't seen you since…'

'Yesterday. Memory's a bit shaky today, I'm guessing?'

Jordan pushed himself up with an effort. 'Where am I?'

'What, don't you recognise it? This used to be your room.'

Jordan blinked at the familiar walls. Different wallpaper, bed, furniture. But it was true. This was his room, his nineteen-year-old self's room.

'This is… our house. Me and you and Maggie and Other Max…' He shook his head. 'Now I know it's a dream.'

'I promise it isn't. 22 The Cedars, our second-year student house. Me and Mags own the place now.'

Jordan glanced down at the too-tight t-shirt and boxers he was wearing. 'These aren't mine, are they?'

'No, they're mine. And a hell of a job we had getting them on you.'

'Where are my clothes?'

'In the wash. They were pretty manky, you were sick on them.'

'Oh God, I wasn't. Did Maggie see?'

''Fraid so. She had to help me strip you off and get you cleaned up. Oh, and that disguise, the rancid coat and hat, went straight in the bin.' Ibby shook his head. 'Where the hell did you get a homburg?'

'Hesham Scarecrow Festival,' Jordan mumbled, rubbing his temples.

'Eh?'

'Got my driver to drop me off there so he wouldn't be able to tell my manager where I was, must've been early yesterday morning. Nicked it off a scarecrow in someone's garden.'

'You seriously walked from Hesham to Applecroft in that state? It's two miles.'

'Must've done. To be honest, it all goes a bit blank after I mugged the scarecrow.' Every word Jordan spoke pounded his brain. 'Where'd you find me, Ibs?'

'You were paralytic in our back porch when I got home yesterday. Thanks for that little heart attack, by the way.'

'Why couldn't I sleep in your old room?' Jordan asked as he adjusted to this bizarre new reality.

'That's Amelia's. Anyway, Other Max thought one of us should keep an eye on you, make sure you didn't do a Hendrix. And I don't mean playing Woodstock.'

'Other Max was here too?'

'Yep. Nice to have the old gang back together, eh?'

'He doesn't still live here as well, does he?'

'No, he's in a flatshare with a couple of other paramedics. Just me, Mags and Amelia.'

'Amelia...' Jordan's exhausted brain started to catch up. 'The kid, right? Maggie's kid.'

'Well, I think I should get some of the credit.'

'She's really yours?'

'Yeah. Why shouldn't she be?'

'But how did you and Mags even do it?'

Ibby laughed. 'You want me to draw you a diagram? Same way you and Mags used to do it, mate.'

He shook his head. 'I just can't picture it.'

'Good. I'd thank you not to try.'

'When did it happen? Right after I moved out?'

'Yeah, Jord. I got so upset when you went, it turned me straight.'

'Are you being sarky now? I'm too hung over to tell.'

'Course I'm being sarky. It was a one-off, that's all,' Ibby said. 'Mags was gutted when you two broke up. She was feeling down one night, Other Max was out, much wine was consumed, and... well, it was sort of a hug that got out of hand.'

'You're telling me.'

'I was trying to cheer her up.'

'By knocking her up?'

'That was a somewhat unforseen side effect, yes.'

'Is she here now? The little girl?'

'No, she's staying at her nana's so she missed all the drama, thank God. So come on, what's your plan?'

Jordan closed his eyes. 'Plan?'

'You just did a runner from a major national tour, Jord. There's a manhunt going on trying to find you. You must have a plan.'

'I hadn't really thought this far ahead.' Jordan swallowed a gasp of panic. 'It was all just... too much. I had to get away, before I cracked up.'

'I'm not sure a booze binge is going to help with that.'

'No.' Jordan pulled his knees up and hugged them. 'But it numbed it for a bit.'

'Just what is it you're trying to numb, Jordan?' Ibby asked quietly.

'God, I don't know. Loneliness. Futility. Self-loathing.' A sob bubbled from Jordan's throat. 'Ibs, you ever wonder why musicians do drugs, or have casual sex?'

'Because they can?'

'No. No, that's not it. It's not just money, or access, or boredom. It's... you know, when you're on stage you can do anything, fucking anything. That's what it feels like. You're unstoppable, and everyone out there's screaming your name, and they love you. They don't know you, but they love you.' Jordan felt feverish, his voice trembling with nervous excitement. 'It's addictive, that adoration. So when you're off stage, you look for something to fill that gap. Sex to feel loved, although those women don't know you any more than the crowds at the gigs. Coke to feel unstoppable, even though you know the whole time you're shovelling it up your nose that you're faking it.' He laughed, rubbing his nose. 'And that's the pathetic thing, Ibby, about all of us. It's insecurity, in the end. Because what we really need, what we're gagging for, is for people to fucking *like* us.'

Ibby blinked. 'Woah.'

'Sorry.' Jordan ran a palm over his forehead. 'It's just... toxic, in the end, that brand of love. I finally worked that out the day

Sylvia turned up to sell me on some family reality show, how messed up the whole lifestyle is. All of a sudden, I wanted out.'

'So you took coke as a substitute for being on stage?'

'To an extent.'

'Right.' Ibby looked thoughtful. 'You're like Sherlock Holmes, Jord.'

Jordan frowned. 'Eh?'

'Sherlock Holmes. He only did coke when he wasn't on a case. As a substitute for the mental stimulation he got solving crimes.'

'Holmes did coke?'

'Yeah, and morphine,' Ibby said. 'Watson hated him doing drugs, he was forever bollocking him about it. Doctors, right?'

'I did not know that.' Jordan managed a smile through his sore head. 'Ibs, I never realised how much I'd missed your random trivia.'

'So you're really quitting?'

'I'm going to quit the band. But quitting Jordan Nash, that's not so easy, is it? Everyone knows me. I get followed by press, by fans – I've had to take out five restraining orders against stalkers just this year. Believe me, becoming a celebrity is a lot easier than stopping being one when you've had enough.'

Ibby shook his head. 'It's another life, yours.'

'Yeah, and I don't want it.' Jordan reached out to grab Ibby's hand. 'Can I stay, Ibs? Just till I get my head together.'

'I don't know, Jord. We've got a kid.'

'Sorry. I don't know who else to turn to.'

Ibby examined him. 'Really? You've not got anyone?'

'My manager, maybe. But he's... part of it. I need to cut free.'

'I'll talk to Maggie. We'll do what we can for you.' Ibby swung his legs out of bed. 'But first things first. You want a coffee?'

'God, I'd sell whatever's left of my soul for one. Black, please, three sugars.'

'How many?'

'Three. Heaped. I need the energy. And a couple of ibuprofen wouldn't go amiss.'

'All right, I can manage that.'

'Couldn't whisk me up a raw egg with a dash of tabasco while you're at it, could you?'

'Okay, now you're pushing it. We don't do riders.'

'Hey.' Jordan put a hand out to touch Ibby's arm as he passed. 'Thanks, mate.'

He nodded in acknowledgement. 'Old time's sake, eh?'

Ibby knocked on Maggie's door on his way downstairs. Three slow knocks, two fast. Then he carried on to the utility room.

She joined him there a few minutes later, still in her clothes from the day before and looking exhausted. It'd been a long night for both of them.

'So, how's the patient?' she asked.

'Hung over.'

'Well, that much I could've guessed.'

Ibby shook his head. 'He's not good, Mags.'

'He'll soon sleep it off.'

'I mean his mental health, poor bugger. I really don't think he should've gone on tour so soon after quitting coke. What could his manager have been thinking?'

'That it'd be good for a bob or two, I should imagine,' Maggie said, scowling. 'Those people don't give a shit about him as a human being. He's just a cash cow to them.'

'What're we going to do with him? Every hack in the country's out there looking for him.'

'Well, what's his plan?'

'Oblivion, by the sounds of it. He didn't seem to have thought much beyond getting drunk and getting out.'

'So he doesn't want to go back?'

'No. Says he's quitting.' Ibby lowered his voice. 'Mags, he wants to stay a while. With us.'

She frowned. 'I hope you told him he couldn't.'

'No, I said I'd talk to you.'

'Ibs, come on. He can't stay here.'

'It wouldn't be for long. He just needs somewhere to hide out for a bit.'

'We've got Melie to think about. She always comes first, that's what we agreed.'

'We can't just chuck him out though, can we? Christ, you saw the state of him. Another binge like that and he could kill himself.'

'He's a drug addict, Ibby! An alcoholic too, maybe. There must be somewhere else he can go.'

'If there was, why would he come to us?' Ibby dipped his head to look into her eyes. 'I can't help feeling we could've done more for him. Back when he started hurting himself.'

'We did all we could.'

'Still. He'd lost his nan, he was in pain. We were the closest thing he had to a family.'

'You can't help someone who doesn't want to be helped.'

'And now he does want to be helped.' Ibby took her hand. 'He came to us, Maggie. We're the only ones he trusts, after fourteen years. What does that tell you about the state of his life?'

'Well… maybe we can find somewhere else for him while we help him get back on his feet.'

'Where? The shower cubicle in Other Max's shared flat?'

'I can't have him near my daughter. He's an addict. He's not safe.'

'She's my daughter too, Mags. I want to protect her just as much as you do.'

Maggie's frown lifted a little. 'I know.' She lowered her voice. 'Ibs, they could find out.'

'How could they?'

'If we let him in again, if he was part of our lives…'

'I know, I know, it's risky. But we can't just throw him out, can we? He's vulnerable and he reached out to us. We owe him, Mags.'

'Melie's vulnerable too, isn't she? She's a child. Our child.'

'He's not dangerous. He's Max Jordan, how could he be?'

'Isn't he though? Addiction changes people. So does fourteen years.'

'Okay, look. Let me get Jord his coffee then we'll—'

'No need, I put the kettle on,' a deep voice said from the shadows.

Ibby looked round. Jordan was leaning by the door to the kitchen.

Maggie frowned. 'You were listening?'

'Sorry, I didn't mean to. Just came to find out where you'd got to.'

'How much did you hear?'

'Enough.' He sighed. 'Mags, you're right. Your kid comes first. Just give me till this afternoon to sort something out then I'll piss off out of your lives again.'

'Max, I didn't mean—'

'Honestly, it's fine. I'm not your problem. I'm mine, and it's time I started taking responsibility for that.'

'But where will you go?' Ibby asked.

He shrugged. 'Got a big house in Devon I've barely lived in. I can try the recluse act, hide out there till the press eventually get bored of me.'

'Alone?' Maggie said.

'Yeah.'

'I don't think that's good for you, Max.' She watched his hands shaking. 'You should be with people.'

'Who? Sylvia? The band? They're the only people in my life now.' He turned away. 'I'll make the coffee. Don't worry about showing me where everything is, I'll find it.' He glanced around him. 'So weird being back in this place.'

Ibby shot Maggie a meaningful look as Jordan left the room.

She sighed. 'All right, I know.'

'Did you see his hands? Poor bastard.'

'But there's still Melie, isn't there?'

'Come on, Mags, you're a counsellor. That means you care about people,' Ibby said. 'Max Jordan meant a lot to you once. Don't tell me you could forgive yourself if you just wrote him off.'

'No. No, don't suppose I could.' Maggie smiled. 'You're some guy, Aaron Ibbotson, you know that?' She squeezed his hand. 'Okay, he can stay. Just for a little while.'

Ibby gave her a hug. 'I knew you'd want to help him.'

'Let's ask if Melie can take a holiday at Nana's for a week. We'll make sure he's gone before she gets home.'

Chapter Twenty-Six

Ibby went upstairs to phone his mum while Maggie joined Jordan in the kitchen. She found him struggling to spoon coffee into three mugs.

'White, one sugar for you, right? And plain white for Ibs. See, I remembered. Bollocks!' Jordan grimaced as coffee granules skittered across the worksurface.

'Here, let me help.' Maggie reached out to take the spoon from him.

'No! I can do it.'

'Sorry. Go on.'

Slowly and with a great effort of concentration, Jordan finished filling the mugs.

'There.' He flashed her a weak grin. 'Better leave the boiling water to you though, I reckon.'

'Good call.' Maggie nodded to his hands. 'Getting worse, isn't it?'

'Yeah. Hangover's not helping either.' He held up a hand and regarded the trembling with a detached curiosity. 'They said in rehab it'd stop in time, but I'm not sure it's withdrawal. I think it's me.'

'Does it ever stop?'

'When I'm on stage. When I'm drunk.'

'That's not the solution, Max.'

'You think I don't know that?' He turned away, his face working feverishly. 'Wish I knew what bloody was.'

She put a hand on his arm. 'I'm sorry you had to overhear, before. Look, when I said you were dangerous to Amelia, I didn't mean… it's not that I think you'd hurt her.'

'I knew what you meant.' He turned back to face her. 'I'm recovering from addiction but I'm not dangerous, Mags. It's a psychological dependency. I mainly need to be away from the stuff.'

'Still, she's thirteen. Impressionable. You, your problems, it'd be… at least disruptive for her.'

'I know.'

'And it'd be a big ask of a kid, sharing her home with a stranger and keeping secret who that was. You know, half her schoolfriends are madly in love with you. Well, with Jordan Nash.'

'I'm sick to my throat of people I don't know being in love with me,' Jordan said fiercely. He shot her a glance. 'I'm sorry, Mags. About yesterday. It was a hell of a thing to do to you, turning up in that state.'

'I could've done without the medical emergency, certainly. Thank God for Other Max or we would've had to get an ambulance out.'

He winced. 'Was I really that bad?'

'Bad? We thought you'd tried to top yourself.'

'No. I've been low lately but I wouldn't do that.'

'Max, if you've come off coke just to get hooked on booze…'

'I'm not hooked. It was just… a moment of weakness. I wanted to wipe it all out – put things back how they were, somehow. Magical thinking, right?' He glanced around the familiar kitchen, cleaner than he remembered, not so heavy on the pizza boxes and beer cans, but otherwise just the same as when he'd left. 'Still, here I am.'

'If Amelia had found you instead of Ibs, do you know what that would've done to her?'

He flinched. 'Sorry. Never occurred to me. I didn't even know this was your house.'

She frowned. 'But last night you said you'd come to see me.'

'All I remembered was that this was our place, the four of us. That it was the last place I'd been happy.'

'You're a bit of a mess, aren't you?' Maggie sighed. 'Poor Max.'

'Oh for God's sake, don't "poor Max" me. I feel pathetic enough as it is.' He smiled. 'Like to hear you use my real name though. Makes me feel like a person again.'

'You were always a person, you big idiot,' she said, smiling back. 'Give us a hug, eh? It's good to see you.'

He let loose a tear as he put his arms around her.

'Thanks, Maggie,' he whispered.

'Suppose I should wish you a happy birthday too. Two days late and the happy's probably not all that appropriate, but...'

'You remembered?'

'Course I remembered,' she said, giving him a squeeze. 'This is actually the Birthday Special hug. You know, I charge my regular clients extra for the cuddling service.'

'You offer that? Didn't know you relationship counsellors were supposed to give practical demonstrations.'

'Well, we have to pay the mortgage.' She let him go. 'Nice to know you can still crack a joke.'

'Nice to know I can still make you smile.'

'Max, me and Ibs have talked, and... look, you don't need to go right away. Stay a week, take a bit of breathing space. You'll be safe with us.'

'Really, can I? What about your daughter?'

'Ibby's on the phone now, arranging for her to stay at his mum's till next weekend. It's the first week of school holidays so she'll enjoy being right by the sea.' Maggie glanced up at him. 'But if you're staying you'll need to follow a few house rules, okay?'

'No staying out after midnight and no bringing home unsuitable girls, right?'

'No feeling sorry for yourself and no more binges,' she said, tapping his chest. 'Today's the first day of the rest of your life, Max Jordan.'

'Yeah. Wish it didn't come with such a bitch of a headache.'

'Well, that serves you right, doesn't it?'

'God, you really are a mum.' He looked down at her. 'Missed you, you know.'

'We missed you, too. You know, Other Max never did get a promotion to just Max. I think unconsciously we were always saving your place.'

'You're not understanding me,' Jordan said softly. 'Not you plural, you singular. You, Lanie. I missed you.'

Maggie looked away, flushing. But before he could say anything else, there was a knock at the door.

'I'll get it!' Ibby called. 'Jord, stay out of sight.'

Maggie shot Jordan a worried look. 'Who's that?'

'Not your daughter, is it?'

'Can't be, Ibs just spoke to his mum. Maybe it's Other Max come to check on you.'

'Or maybe it's the press.'

She nodded to the utility room. 'Go hide in there. Whoever it is, me and Ibs'll get rid of them.'

—

Ibby opened the door to a tall, bony man who could've been anything from forty to sixty, his shrewd, deep-set eyes looking out from a heavily lined face.

'Yes?'

'Max Jordan. I want to speak to him.'

Ibby's expression didn't even flicker.

'I'm sorry, you must have the wrong address. My name's Ibbotson.'

The man flashed him a humourless smile. 'Nice try, son. I know he's here. Maggie Nightingale's place, right?'

'Look, if you're from the press—'

'I'm not. I sent the press to Aberdeen.'

'You did what?'

'I told them Jordan had family connections in Aberdeen and if he was hiding out, that'd be the most likely place to find him.'

Ibby blinked. 'Oh.'

Maggie came into the hallway and scowled at the man.

'You. What're you doing here?'

'Come on, Magdalena, let me in,' Craig said. 'I don't think we want to be chatting in full hearing of your neighbours, do we?'

Maggie glared for a second, then jerked her head for him to join them inside. Ibby locked the door behind him.

'Who is he, Mags?' he asked.

'Max's manager. And pimp.'

Craig smiled. 'Well, where is he?'

'Not here,' Maggie said, folding her arms.

'I wasn't born yesterday, darling. Ten minutes in a locked room with me, his driver spilled everything. I know he was dropped off a couple of miles away and I worked out pretty sharpish where he must've been heading.'

'Maybe you were given faulty information.'

'I doubt that somehow.' He glanced at a pair of Givenchy trainers on the shoe rack.

'They're mine,' Ibby said.

'Are they? Look pricey.'

'Er, personal.'

'Funny, they've got the same fag burn in the left toe as Jordan's.'

'Mmm. I should really cut down.'

'Look, Craig, it seems to me that if Max has disappeared then he doesn't want to talk to you,' Maggie said. 'Just go, okay?'

'I'll go if Jordan tells me to go. I need to know he's safe, at least.'

Maggie snorted. 'Like you care.'

'Why wouldn't I? I've known him a long time.'

'Yeah, and you've bled him dry for all of it,' she snapped. 'He was a boy when you got your claws into him, a boy who was grieving. And look what you turned him into.'

'I made him a star.'

'You made him a zombie,' Maggie said in a low voice. 'He's lucky to be alive, the sort of life you've been encouraging. Casual sex, drugs, booze and God knows what else.'

'Not drugs. I never encouraged that. And what're you, his mother?'

'Someone who actually gives a shit about him is what I am – so no, definitely not his mother. And if you want to get your hands on him, you'll have to come through me.'

Ibby barged past Craig to stand at her side. 'And me.'

'Guys, it's okay.' Jordan emerged from the sitting room and rested a hand on Ibby's shoulder. 'Let him come through.'

'For God's sake, Jord, keep away from the windows,' Ibby hissed.

Jordan nodded to Craig. 'Here, come with me. The utility room's the place for private chats in this house.'

Craig followed him through to the kitchen, Ibby and Maggie trailing behind.

'Max, are you sure you want to talk to him?' Maggie said.

Jordan pushed open the door to the utility room. 'Don't have much choice, do I? He's here now.'

'All right, here.' Maggie picked up a basket of washing and shoved it into his arms. 'Since you'll be in there anyway.'

Jordan blinked at it. 'What's this?'

'Laundry.' She slapped his arm. 'Need to earn your keep, eh? Make sure you separate the whites.'

'What does she mean, earn your keep?' Craig asked when they were alone in the utility room.

'I'm staying here. Just this week while I work out what I want to do next.'

'Jord, what's the deal with these people? Who are they, some ex and her lover?'

Jordan plonked down the basket of laundry and started sorting it into piles. 'Old friends. They live here with their little girl.' He glanced around the room. 'I lived here too, a long time ago. It was our student house.'

'But who *are* they? What do they do? Why would they help you?'

'They're Maggie and Ibby. She's a counsellor, he's a journalist. And they're helping me because they remember that before I pushed them away so I could be a star, we used to be close.'

'Journalist! Shit, Jordan! You go on the run and first thing you do is get into bed with the bloody press?'

'Heh. Pretty much,' Jordan said, remembering how he'd woken up. 'It's fine, Craig, I trust him. These are the only people I do trust right now.'

'Come on, Jord, what's going on? Why are you hiding out up the arsehole of nowhere in your old student house?'

'Can't you work it out?' Jordan held up Amelia's PE top and dropped it into the whites pile.

'Jordan. Fucking leave off that and look at me.' Craig grabbed his arm and forced him to turn around. 'I've had every editor in London on the phone demanding to know where you are, all the remaining venues on the tour insisting on compensation, and on top of that I personally have been worried sick about you, you little bastard. Now come on, you owe me an explanation.'

'I'm sorry, boss.' Jordan choked on a sob. 'I just couldn't do it any more.'

'What happened? Sylvia?'

'No. Me. Had an epiphany. Or a breakdown, whichever you choose to call it.'

'You're really refusing to do the rest of the tour?'

'Not just the tour. I'm refusing to do the rest of my career. I'm done, Craig.'

Craig stared at him. 'You don't mean it.'

'I bloody do.'

'But… what about the band? What about me, Jordan? I took a chance on you, got you your big break.'

'I'm sorry. I never meant to let you down. But…' He held up a trembling hand. 'See that? I feel like I'm going insane. My brain's all chaos, I don't sleep, I… I can't do it, Craig. Can't.'

'Then we'll cancel the tour and get you help, proper medical help. But you can't give up on your music. I won't let you.'

'That's not your call to make,' Jordan said. 'Craig, tell me this. Are we mates?'

'What?'

'Are we mates, or are we manager and client? Answer me.'

'With you, I've always felt we were both. None of the others. Just you.'

'Then it's time to choose. Because you can one hundred per cent believe that from this day forward, I quit.'

'You don't mean that. Music's part of you.'

'Not quitting music, quitting fucking Jordan Nash. I don't want to be that guy any more, he makes me sick.' Jordan's voice was hurtling towards fever pitch. 'What even is he? He's comatose, Craig, he's… something dreaming, something dead. I'm dead when I'm him.'

'You don't mean it,' Craig said again, a note of pleading creeping into his gravelled tones.

'I've never meant anything more in my life. For the sake of my sanity I'm quitting the band – the industry. And just maybe, when everyone's finally stopped giving a shit about me, I can build something like a normal life. One where I meet girls the usual way instead of you serving them up to me like… toys in a nursery. Where coke isn't on every clean surface, offering to wipe my brain. Where I can have real friends who like me for my own sake, like the ones I had before all this.'

'But what about your music? You need to write, it's who you are.'

'Maybe. But I'm at a point in my life where I want to do that for myself, not anyone else.'

'And performing? Don't tell me you don't love it.'

'I do,' Jordan admitted. 'But I can't help thinking performing's like coke. For someone like me, it's... the wrong sort of fun.'

'You're absolutely sure?'

'I am.'

'Right.' Craig collapsed onto a chair and buried his face in his hands. 'Then tell me what you need from me,' he mumbled.

Jordan rested a hand on his manager's — his ex-manager's shoulder. 'Thanks, mate.'

'Just tell me what to do, before I talk myself out of it.'

'Did you speak to the press?'

'Yeah, soon as I worked out where you'd gone. Sent them on a wild goose chase to the other end of the country.'

'Good work,' Jordan said, nodding. 'They'll be back eventually though. I'll write a statement for you, just saying I'm taking time out while I address my personal problems and that I'd appreciate privacy at a difficult time. The usual.'

'They'll want to know where you are. They won't let it drop.'

'Then fudge it. Hint I've gone abroad. The fact 69 never broke through in America works in my favour, doesn't it? I could disappear over there.'

'Where will you really go?'

'That pile I bought in Devon, I suppose.'

'You shouldn't be alone, Jord. You're not strong enough.'

'I'll have to be.' Jordan managed a smile. 'Don't worry, I'll cope somehow.'

'Anything else you need?'

'Yeah, could you get some of my clothes sent on? And some cash, I'd better avoid using cards. Razor, hair gel, contact lens solution... oh, and chuck in a packet of fags. Address them to Maggie Nightingale.' He paused. 'Actually, you'd better not have them sent here. I'll text you her work address.'

'On it.' Craig stood up and shook Jordan's hand. 'Take care of yourself, star.'

'Thanks, boss. Thanks for everything.'

Craig left Jordan to his laundry. He stopped in the kitchen, where Maggie was doing the washing-up.

'So he's quitting,' she said.

'Heard that, did you?'

'No, but he told us he was going to. What will you do now the gravy train's dried up?'

'I'll get a limited edition of *Sleepwalking* out, for a start. Last ever Route 69 album, we can name our own price.'

'Should've known you'd find a silver lining.'

'Keep an eye on him, okay?' Craig said in a low voice, approaching her. 'He needs to be with people to get better. He needs normality. And for some reason, you and the boyfriend are the only ones he trusts right now.'

'What do you care what he needs?'

'I bloody do, you know. I'm not such a tough old bastard.'

The crack in his voice was unmistakeable. Maggie turned to look at him.

'Wow,' she said, blinking. 'You do, don't you?'

'I've been responsible for him since he was a lad, haven't I? Maybe I wasn't the world's cuddliest surrogate dad but I did get attached, yeah,' Craig said, shrugging. 'You'll look after him? You and your boyfriend?'

'He's not my boyfriend. And yes, of course we will.'

'And will you make sure he's not left to himself? He thinks too much, that boy. Thinking's poison to him right now.'

'We'll do whatever we can.'

He patted her arm. 'There's a good girl.'

With a nod, he disappeared.

Maggie sighed as she turned back to her washing-up. It felt like a baton of some sort had just been passed, and Max Jordan, a man who until recently she and Ibby had never expected to see again, now belonged to them once more. With everything Max had going on in his life now – his anxiety, his addiction, his fame – that was one hell of a responsibility.

Chapter Twenty-Seven

'You really shouldn't have got her the UGG boots,' Maggie said as she and Ibby braved the Bristol traffic on their way back from the shops that afternoon. She nodded to the bags on the back seat containing a few essentials for Amelia, who'd shot up since the last summer holidays. 'They're not exactly summer wear, Ibs. And bloody hell, how much?'

'Well. She deserves a treat, doesn't she? Getting evicted from her own home. She's been begging for these for ages.'

'How many features do you have to write to pay for those?'

'Never you mind.'

'You make it sound like we're sending her to military school. She's not getting evicted, she's going to spend a week with her doting nana.' Maggie shook her head. 'No wonder she's such a Daddy's girl. Spoil her rotten, you do.'

'I just want her to know Mum and Dad haven't forgotten her.'

'It's not for long. Anyway, she'll have the time of her life down on the seafront while the weather's like this.'

'I know. Can't help feeling guilty though.'

'Melie'll be fine. Max… well, him I'm not so sure about.'

'What did his manager say? He needed normality?'

'Yep, and I left him a big dose of it,' Maggie said. 'Once he finishes the washing there's a whole to-do list. Dusting, hoovering, scrubbing the limescale off the bath – should keep him busy.'

Ibby turned the car down the shortest route to his mum's place.

'I hope you're not using our house guest as slave labour, Mags.'

She shrugged. 'Bit of domesticity won't do him any harm. I bet he had people to do all that for him before.'

'I think he spent most of his time in hotels,' Ibby said. 'Strange idea, isn't it? No roots, just moving from one identical room to the next.'

'He never had many roots, did he? Only his nana. Guess that's why when he needed help, he found his way back to us.'

'Yeah.' Ibby glanced at her in the rearview mirror. 'You did the right thing, you know. Letting him stay.'

'I know,' she said with a sigh. 'I just hope we can help him.' The car slowed to a stop and she glanced at the long line of stationary traffic ahead. 'Stick some music on, will you? Looks like we'll be here a while.'

Ibby flicked on the car radio and the familiar strains of 'Magdalena' blared out.

Maggie grimaced. 'Not that music. Turn it over, for God's sake.'

He tuned to another station, where a presenter was waffling.

'Why do you think he wrote it?' Ibby asked.

Maggie shrugged. 'Dunno. He keeps talking about untravelled roads. I think he wonders what his life would've been if things had turned out differently.'

'Do you think he has feelings for you, still?'

'I think he misses being nineteen, before fame swallowed him up. Not sure it's really about me.'

'I'm not so sure.'

'How can he have feelings for me? I'm not that girl he loved, Ibs,' she said sadly. 'There's an ocean's worth of water under the bridge.'

Ibby frowned at the radio. 'Hang on, I know that voice. It's Jim.'

'Jim?'

'Nat's boss, the presenter of the show he works on. He was there that night at The Admiral.'

'And how did it make you feel, being treated that way?' Jim of the soup-strainer moustache was asking his guest.

'Humiliated, obviously,' the guest said. 'And ashamed.'

Ibby blinked. 'Bloody hell. Nat.'

'Is this it?' Maggie asked. 'The phone-in he wanted you to go on with him?'

'Must be.' Ibby turned it up.

'Ashamed?' Jim said.

'A reflex reaction, but yeah,' came Nat's voice. He sounded very self-assured. Ibby wasn't sure he'd be able to keep his voice that steady on live radio. 'As any gay person of a certain age will tell you, you spend a lot of your early life being conditioned to feel ashamed. I'd naively thought things were changing, that kids who identified as LGBT now wouldn't have quite such a rough ride. Then something like this happens and you realise it isn't quite the brave new world you'd started to believe in.'

'And the man you were with. How did he feel?'

'The same, I think.'

'Yet he's not here with you.'

'He wasn't comfortable speaking publicly about it, which is understandable. It takes a lot of resilience to stick your head above the parapet. You run the risk of making yourself and those close to you a target.'

'Aren't you afraid of becoming a target?'

'I'm always afraid,' Nat said, his voice exuding dignity. 'But sometimes it feels like afraid or not, you have to stop seeing it as someone else's problem and step up.'

'Right,' Jim said. 'Let's see who's on line one.'

'Hi Jim, thanks for taking my call,' came a Scouse voice Ibby recognised. 'I just want to say, I think it's fantastic someone's finally taking a stand on this. Businesses round here have been taking the pi— the Michael for too long, and it's time we made it clear we won't tolerate illegal discrimination in our communities.'

'Ha!' Ibby said.

Maggie glanced at him. 'What?'

'Pickled Egg Johnny. Nat set that call up.'

'That's him, is it? Yeah, he sounds like the kind of voice that'd have a mullet.'

'Okay, next we have Terry from Applecroft,' Jim said. 'Terry, I understand your pub was the setting for this incident?'

The Sea Pig's landlord cleared his throat. 'Yes. Er, hi Jim.'

'He was the one who asked us to leave,' Nat said.

'Look, I've apologised for this already,' Terry said. 'My nephew's gay, I've got no issue with it.'

'Yeah, you said. "One of your lot" was the phrase used, if I remember.'

'It's just that if you're going to be doing that kind of thing, it should be in private.'

'Right. The old "behind closed doors" chestnut, haven't heard that one in a few years,' Nat snapped. 'Well perhaps you'd like to tell me, Terry, why it behoves me and my date to act with more discretion than the average heterosexual couple?'

'I mean, when it's out in public and everything...' Terry said, sounding awkward.

'You got a wife, Terry?'

'A girlfriend.'

'Do you ever hold her hand in public? Give her a little kiss?'

'Well sometimes, but—'

'Do people stare? Are they shocked?' Nat said. 'I mean, I'm just wondering why, in these days of supposed tolerance and equality, it's upsetting to be reminded that same-sex couples need to feel physically close to each other too.'

'Listen, it's like I said at the time,' Terry said, recovering his equilibrium as he found his way back to his core argument. 'Same rules for anyone, gay or straight. We're a pub, not a nightclub, and it's not right to have that sort of thing going on.'

'Well I grew up near your pub and it's the first I've heard of it. Is this a policy you brought in just for us, by any chance? I mean, the fact you had some big hairy bloke in a mankini popping his bits out every five minutes didn't seem to be too much of a problem for you.'

'Doesn't let anything faze him, does he?' Maggie said.

'No,' Ibby said absently. 'Shush now. I want to hear where this goes.'

'Okay, look,' Terry said. 'If you really want to know, I did it for your sakes.'

'That was generous of you,' Nat said. 'For our sakes how?'

'Those other lads who were in. They're good blokes at heart, regulars of mine, but they'd had a lot to drink—'

'Mmm. Some might say a responsible landlord would've stopped serving them when they started struggling to stay upright.'

'They'd had a lot to drink,' Terry went on, ignoring that comment. 'I was worried things might… you know, kick off. I didn't want to see the pair of you get hurt.'

Nat laughed. 'Seriously? You thought they were planning to start a fight so rather than asking them to leave, you threw us out?'

'Well, they were big lads, weren't they?'

'You see, Jim, this is exactly what I'm talking about,' Nat said. 'This sort of victim-blaming, making those who've suffered discrimination responsible for their own mistreatment because they dared to deviate conspicuously from the norm, is what's poisoning our communities. We're better than this, people.'

'He's very passionate,' Maggie said, sounding impressed. 'Reminds me of Max when he was young.'

Ibby didn't say anything. In his gut, a niggling feeling was making its presence felt. The feeling he'd made a huge mistake.

There were a few more callers. Some fundamentalist type who started selectively quoting scripture – you always got one, but Nat put him down pretty effectively. Then a lovely old lady Ibby wanted to hug, who called in to say her late brother had been one of 'the gays' and she thought it was wonderful that people like him could now live their lives in the open. By the time the traffic into Applecroft started flowing more freely, the show was coming to an end.

Ibby was swamped with feelings of admiration and respect. Nat had been eloquent, passionate and charismatic throughout and Ibby felt anyone who'd listened would have to be on his side.

And he couldn't help remembering their first kiss that night in the pub – a joining that at the time had seemed pure and tender, before it had been sullied by the shame and humiliation that Nat rightly pointed out they'd been conditioned to feel from schooldays.

'We have one final caller before we go,' Jim said. 'On the line I have Amelia Ibbotson-Nightingale, who tells us she has a personal connection to this incident.'

Ibby stared in horror at Maggie.

Maggie shook her head. 'Now come on. Don't overreact.'

'I'll kill her! I'll bloody kill her!'

'Ibs, calm down. She's only trying to help.'

'Here, reach in the back and chuck those UGG boots out the window, will you?'

'Hi Jim,' Amelia's voice said from the radio. 'Thanks for having me.'

'Where the hell's my mum?' Ibby pushed down on the accelerator.

'Not too fast,' Maggie said. 'It's a thirty zone.'

'How old are you, Amelia?' Jim asked.

'Thirteen and eleven twelfths. It's nearly my birthday.'

Jim laughed. 'And do you have a view on this issue?'

'Yes I do,' Amelia said. 'My dad was the one who went on the date with Nat, and I wanted to say that people who are mean to people just because they're gay or girls or they haven't got Beats or whatever are just bullies. They do it because they're insecure and the only way they can feel good about themselves is by making other people feel bad, which is totally tragic really, isn't it, Jim? I think it's people like that who should feel ashamed, not my dad. Because he'd never be mean to anyone, ever.'

'Wow,' Maggie said, blinking. 'Is that really our Melie? She's so confident.'

'She's so grounded,' Ibby muttered, swinging the car down his mum's road.

'Well said, Amelia,' Nat said. 'Hey, you're a natural, you know. Jim, she'll be doing your job in a few years.'

'I haven't finished,' Amelia said.

'Okay, go on,' Jim said, amusement in his voice.

'I also wanted to say that my dad really liked Nat, and if it hadn't been for the pub man making it weird then I bet they'd be boyfriends now.'

'Oh my *God*,' Ibby groaned.

'Don't tell her off, Ibs,' Maggie said. 'She thinks she's doing you a favour.'

'And Nat, I think you should ask my dad to go out again,' said Somerset's newest radio star. 'He wants to. He hasn't had time to go on dates for a bit, that's all, because of stuff with my mum. You know, the stuff in the papers about her and Jordan Nash.'

Maggie's eyes widened. 'Oh no. She's dragging me in now.'

'Yeah, not so funny any more, is it?' Ibby said.

He pulled into his mum's driveway, jumped out of the car and hammered on the front door.

'Oh, hello, Aaron love,' his mum said when she answered.

'Mum, where's Melie?'

'Well, she's… in your dad's old shed, I think. Playing with her toys.'

'She's playing with her phone. She's on the bloody radio, Mum!'

He jogged round the back of the house and yanked open the shed door, where Amelia was just hanging up. She shrank back when she saw the look on his face.

'Do you know how very, very grounded you are, young lady?' he thundered.

Maggie put a hand on his shoulder. 'Ibs. Go easy, eh?'

'What on earth did you think you were playing at?' Ibby demanded. 'That's my private life, Amelia Jane. It's not your business to be shouting about it on the radio.'

'It is too my business,' Amelia said, sticking her chin out. 'You're my dad.'

'That doesn't mean you've got the right to manage my life for me.'

'It means she gets upset when people are mean to you,' Maggie said gently. 'Because she loves you.'

Ibby's brow lifted slightly. 'That wasn't sensible, Amelia.'

Amelia hung her head. 'I just wanted people to know it was bad,' she mumbled. 'Make them understand it hurts people. You wouldn't tell them so I had to.'

Ibby glared for a moment. Then he sighed. He was a soft touch, he knew it, but he could never be angry with her for long.

He went into the shed and sank down by her. 'I know you were only looking out for me,' he said, slipping an arm around her. 'But you didn't have to tell Nat I liked him, did you?'

'But you do like him.'

'Well you like Isaac. I bet you wouldn't be impressed if I turned up at Coding Club and told him.'

Amelia's eyes widened. 'Are you going to?'

Ibby smiled. 'No. But I won't say I wasn't tempted.'

'Anyway, that's different. Nat likes you too. And you weren't doing anything about it so... I just helped a bit.'

'He might've liked me once,' Ibby said, sighing. 'Think I've burned that bridge.'

A smile flickered over Amelia's features. 'Dad, didn't you hear the last bit of the show?'

'What?'

'He does still like you. He asked if you'd have dinner at his house next Saturday.'

Chapter Twenty-Eight

'And then, right, and then...' Maggie could tell Amelia was struggling to put her epic humiliation into words. 'Mum, Georgia came over and she made us *turkey dinosaurs!*'

'But you love turkey dinosaurs.' Maggie tucked her office phone under her ear so she could eat lunch while Amelia offloaded about the trials of staying with a nana who still thought she was five.

'Yeah, but not when my friends are there! They're little kid food.'

Maggie nodded to Carol as she dumped a large parcel on her desk. She eyed it curiously, trying to remember what she'd bought.

'Nana's just trying to make sure you have a nice time, sweetie,' she said, stripping off the sticky tape. 'She knows turkey dinosaurs are your favourite so she got them specially. It's not fair to complain when she was only being kind, is it?'

'No,' Amelia muttered. 'But she treats me like a baby. Like when we went to the beach today.'

'Go on, what did she do?'

'She made me wear Grandad's baggy old Sex Pistols t-shirt over my bikini,' Amelia said in a pained voice. 'Then Rory came past with his dad, and Mum, I was *sooooo* embarrassed.'

Maggie was glad Amelia couldn't see her smile.

'Well, you're only staying a few more days. Just remember, having you there makes her happy. She gets lonely since Grandad died.'

She felt a twinge of guilt, thinking about Max pottering around their house while Amelia remained in not-very-blissful ignorance at Nana's. Her daughter would have a strop the size of Eurasia if she found out her parents had lied to her about their ongoing relations with Jordan Nash, again. But what choice did they have? You couldn't ask a kid to keep something as big as that a secret, it just wasn't fair.

'When shall I come home, Mum?' Amelia asked. 'Friday? I don't want to miss Telly Takeaway Night.'

'Better wait till Saturday. Your dad's sanding the skirting boards, there's a lot of dust. We'll do Telly Takeaway Night then instead.'

Today was Tuesday. They'd told Max he could kip in the spare room until Saturday, when Ibby would drive him to his place in Devon.

Maggie finally got all the tape off her parcel, wondering with amusement how she was going to break the news to Ibby and Max that the three of them were going to have to do a bit of sanding.

Well, she'd promised Max normality. It did make her smile, thinking that while the nation's press scoured the country for Jordan Nash, superstar, the man himself was back at her house working his way through the dirty washing.

'Why's Dad sanding the skirting boards?' Amelia asked.

'Because he's a man, and there comes a time in every man's life when he needs to sand skirting boards.'

Maggie opened the cardboard box, stared, and quickly closed it again.

'Got to go, Melie.'

'But Mum—'

'We'll talk later, sweetie. Be good for Nana.'

When she'd hung up, Maggie peeped inside the box again, just to make sure her eyes hadn't been playing tricks.

Inside was a pack of cigarettes, a pile of clothes, and what looked like about ten grand in bundled notes.

Jordan looked down at the basket of whites he'd just removed from the washing machine. He held up a sprigged summer dress of Amelia's, now a fetching zombie-flesh grey, and grimaced.

It was Ibby's fault. Jordan had located the culprit, hiding innocently in the pocket of a pair of men's tennis shorts. A blue sock. Who the hell kept a spare sock in their tennis shorts?

He cast a proud glance at the concoction steaming on the cooker. At least that was one thing he could do right. His nana had taught him some top-notch culinary skills that hadn't quite atrophied in the years he'd been surviving on hotel food and takeaways. He'd raided the fridge and cupboards and managed to find the ingredients not only for a pretty awesome chicken curry, if he said so himself, but for homemade garlic naans as well.

He'd enjoyed it too. He hadn't realised how much he'd missed pottering about in his own kitchen – well, Ibby and Maggie's kitchen, but it still kind of felt like his. It'd been a struggle, the tremor in his hands making every pinch of spice a challenge, but he'd taken it slow and he'd got there. And he hadn't had a craving the whole time either.

It was something he could get used to, cooking. Cooking for others especially. There was an amazing feeling of triumph bubbling away in his pot with the garam masala.

Maybe he was a dinner party guy. Maybe that was the road not travelled. Destiny had meant him to be a dinner party guy, and now, at last, he could be.

Well, till the end of the week anyway. Then Amelia would be coming home and he'd have to go to his Devon mansion, a place he'd slept in only once or twice before. It was too big, too empty, like a house in an old horror film. Cooking for one in his sterile brushed-aluminium kitchen wouldn't be the same as cooking for Ibs and Maggie here.

There was a large canvas photo of the three of them – Maggie, Ibby and Amelia –mounted above the dining table.

All of them were beaming, Ibby and Maggie each with a proud arm stretched around the shoulders of a little girl who grinned at Jordan with Maggie's lopsided smile. She was a cute little thing, probably about seven or eight when the photo was taken and very like her mum.

They looked gloriously happy, which made Jordan smile. Still, he tried to avoid letting his eyes wander to the picture if he could. He felt unsettled, if he looked at it too long – his friends' happy family a reminder that no matter how kind and welcoming they'd been to him, he didn't belong here.

He heard the front door unlocking.

'Honey, I'm home!' Ibby called.

'In the kitchen,' Jordan yelled back.

A second later Ibby joined him.

'Something smells nice. What've you made, Jord?'

'Chicken tikka masala.'

'Sounds good.' Ibby tasted a spoonful and stuck his tongue out. 'Yeesh!'

'What? Is it shit? It is, isn't it?' Jordan was more nervous waiting for feedback on this curry than when the early reviews of an album were due.

'No. Spicy,' Ibby gasped. He filled a glass at the tap and downed it in one go.

'Oh, right. Sorry. Might've fumbled a bit more cayenne into it than I meant to.'

'Here.' Ibby went to the fridge and took out some cream. 'Stir a bit of that through. Otherwise you might see Maggie's head do that Tom and Jerry thing where the top pops off like a volcano.'

Jordan grimaced. 'Ibs? Got a confession to make.'

Ibby's eyes flickered to the cupboard where he'd stored the remains of Jordan's whisky.

'For God's sake. I'm not an alcoholic, okay?' Jordan said.

'Never said a word!'

'I had one glass of wine while I was cooking. A small one. Is that allowed?'

Ibby shrugged. 'You're a grown-up. So that's your confession, is it?'

'No,' Jordan said, squashing his eyes closed. He pointed to the basket of greyish washing.

'Oh God.' Ibby knelt to examine it. 'Well, it's fixable, probably. A few hot washes should get most of it out.'

'It was your fault. You had a sock in your pocket.'

'Why would I have a sock in my pocket?'

'You tell me, mate.'

'Slander, that is.' Ibby stood and clapped him on the back. 'Mags'll be half an hour yet. Want to leave your curry on simmer and come have some fun?'

'You trying to get me into bed again?'

'Not that much fun, sadly for you. No, but you could be just the wingman I've been looking for.'

—

'Left! Left!' Ibby was yelling when Maggie arrived home, clutching the cardboard box like it was worth a small fortune. Which, technically, it was.

'I am going left!'

'More brakes, Jord, or you'll go off the… there! Told you. Now you're in the water, you tit.'

'This never would've happened if you'd let me be Yoshi.'

'I'm Yoshi. I'm always Yoshi.'

'Um, boys?' Maggie said.

Ibby paused the game and turned around.

'Jordan turned all our pants grey,' he said, pointing an accusing finger.

'I did not!' Jordan protested. 'Ibs did it. He's been smuggling his lucky sock to tennis matches.'

'Never mind that.' She dropped her box to the floor. 'Max, do you mind telling me why the postman delivered enough cash for a Russian mafia bribe to my office today?'

Jordan frowned. 'What?'

'Take a look. I've felt like there was a bomb under my desk all afternoon.'

Jordan peered into the box. 'Oh right, yeah. It's from Craig, I asked him to send some bits.' He drew out the packet of cigarettes reverently. 'Thank God. I've been gagging for a cig.'

'Never mind your nicotine habit. What about all this cash? We can't have it lying loose in the house.'

'Why not?'

Maggie smiled indulgently. 'I know you've been inhabiting a very different world for a while, Max sweetie, but in this one, ten grand is quite a lot of money. Like a third of my annual salary kind of money.'

'Actually, there's twelve.'

'Twelve grand!' Ibby shot up so he could peep into the box. 'Fuck me.'

'You want some?' Jordan said, holding out a bundle of fifties.

Ibby stared at it, then looked at Maggie. 'Can I?'

'No you bloody can't.' Maggie snatched the money off Jordan and stuffed it back in his box. 'Max, you can't keep that here. What if we get burgled?'

'But I need to pay for stuff,' Jordan said. 'I can't use my cards, they could trace me through them. You've got a safe, haven't you?'

'No we've not got a safe. Who the hell has a safe?'

'Fine, then I'll buy you a safe.'

'Gee, thanks.' She shoved the box into his arms. 'Go on, go stash it out of sight. Ibs, tomorrow you can nip into Bristol and buy a good, sturdy safe. Max'll pay you back out of his wads of filthy lucre.'

'Buy a safe from where, our local heist-proofing supplier?' Ibby said as Jordan jogged upstairs to hide the box of money.

'I don't know, Google it.' She sniffed. 'What's that? Smells amazing.'

'I made dinner,' Jordan said as he came back in, trying not to look too proud of himself. 'Chicken tikka masala. I baked naans too.'

Maggie raised her eyebrows. 'Actually baked them? Wow.'

'Yeah, I enjoyed it actually. Nana's recipe, we used to make them together when I was a kid.'

Maggie smiled. 'Oh, well. If it's one of Jean's recipes then I know it'll be good.'

Jordan gave an involuntary shiver. That was the first time he'd heard anyone use his nana's first name in over a decade. There was no one but Maggie who could use it now, no one who'd known her. The two women in his life had always got on well, bonding over the same guilty pleasure, *Midsomer Murders*, and their shared belief that Jordan was an idiot.

'I'll serve up,' he said, heading for the kitchen.

'Seen his hands?' Ibby whispered to Maggie.

'Yeah. Steady as a rock.'

Chapter Twenty-Nine

Amelia was bored.

It was raining and she was confined to quarters. She pushed the Weeble sitting on the chest of drawers in her bedroom at Nana's and watched it bounce back up. It'd been hers since she'd been a toddler, an old toy of her dad's. In fact, the whole room didn't look much different than it had when she was three.

Her little cousins, Aunty Jenny's kids, were up in York, and Aunty Beth didn't have a family yet. In Applecroft Amelia was the baby of the Ibbotson family, and at Nana's she wasn't allowed to forget it.

It wasn't that she didn't like visiting Nana. She actually quite enjoyed a bit of babying sometimes, though she'd deny it to the death if anyone dared say so. But really, a whole week's stay was just too much. With the eight o'clock bedtimes, no TV in her room and worst of all, no Wi-Fi, she felt like was going mad.

She missed her room. She missed YouTube, and keeping up to date with the latest fan theories on where Jordan Nash had suddenly disappeared to. She missed her mum and dad. She missed Smiffy, her incontinent elderly hamster.

And then there was the curfew. It was great, having the beach right on the doorstep. She'd had some fun times with Georgia, Rory and the other kids listening to music, sunbathing, exploring rockpools – although officially, of course, they were far too mature for crab-hunting and doing it purely for nostalgia. But as soon as five o'clock hit she was summoned back to Nana's for dinner and *The Chase*, leaving her friends, whose more liberal parents had furnished them with packed meals, to enjoy the sunshine without her.

She was getting Isaac-withdrawal too, now school was out. Georgia had suggested seeking him out at the milkshake bar in the town centre where the older kids hung out, but Amelia's nana didn't like her going out of sight.

'Morning, love,' Nana said as she bustled into Amelia's room with a washing basket and started picking things up off the floor.

That was another thing. She never knocked. Didn't she know teenagers needed their own space?

'So I'm losing you today, Melie,' she said, ruffling her hair. 'I'll miss having you about now I've got used to tripping over you.'

It was Friday. Amelia wasn't due to go home until tomorrow. Had Nana forgotten?

'That's not—' Amelia began. Then she stopped. 'Er, yeah. I've had a lovely time though, thank you for having me to visit.'

'Well, we can have a nice long lunch in the conservatory first. I got Cheestrings. Then I'll drive you back and you can chill out in your room for a bit before Mum and Dad get home. Best to go before the rush hour traffic hits.'

Ugh, chill out. Who said 'chill out' any more?

'Thanks, Nana.' Amelia gave her a hug, because as tragically embarrassing as her grandmother was, she loved her to bits. 'I'll get packed.'

—

Jordan was bored.

He'd done everything on Maggie's list of chores, prepared a pasta bake for dinner and was now slumped on the sofa watching *'Allo 'Allo* on Gold. But it wasn't giving him much joy. He wished Ibby was there for a *Call of Duty* marathon. Or Maggie for a chat and maybe, if he was lucky, another amazing hug.

Was that allowed, thoughts of hugging Maggie? Jordan's head was finally starting to feel less chaotic but his feelings for his ex confused him.

They certainly weren't platonic. Everything that had caused him to fall in love with Maggie the first time round was still there, improved by age. Under other circumstances, Jordan would have been seizing the second chance fate had chucked him with both hands.

But these weren't other circumstances, they were his circumstances. He was an addict – clean, but still an addict. Dating was dangerous while you were in recovery, that's what his doctors had told him. It was too easy to swap one addiction for another: the euphoria of falling in love. People could get hurt.

They didn't say anything about a love you never fully let go of in the first place though, did they? whispered a voice in Jordan's brain. He shook his head to silence it.

Logically, he knew that any romantic pursuit of his ex-girlfriend wasn't a good idea. He'd broken Maggie's heart once before by failing to be the man he ought to have been. He couldn't risk doing that to her again, even if she still had feelings for him.

Did she still have feelings for him? Okay, she was warm, and funny, and kind, but that's the sort of person Maggie was. A hug for an old friend in trouble didn't have to mean anything, did it? He'd felt a connection when she'd held him – he thought he had – but his head had been all over the place that day. And it had been fourteen years since the last time she'd been in his arms, he reminded himself. He was deluding himself with dreams and nostalgia, he had to be – the wishful thinking of a man who desperately needed something to hope for.

Still. As the time approached for him to leave The Cedars, Jordan was haunted by the knowledge that if he let Maggie Nightingale disappear from his life a second time without at least trying to do something about it, he'd spend whatever decades were left to him regretting it.

He was due to leave tomorrow for his place in Devon. God knew what he'd find waiting for him there – a Glastonbury's worth of journalists, probably, and a lonely, empty house.

Jordan held up his hand and watched it shake violently. It had definitely been getting better, but whenever he thought about leaving this place, off it went again.

He'd been happy here this last week, had felt safe, normal – not at all like Jordan Nash. Back in his old house with his old friends, it was almost like the last fourteen years hadn't happened – like he'd been given the chance to hit reset on his life and start again from the point when he'd chosen the wrong path.

But it was an illusion. The last fourteen years had happened. The deepening crinkles around his eyes were testament to it.

Well, he could get some Wii practice in, at least, keep his thoughts out of the dark. He fired up the console and loaded *Call of Duty*.

–

Late that afternoon, Amelia waved goodbye to her nana and unlocked the front door. Mum and Dad wouldn't be home for at least half an hour so she had a bit of time to catch up on what was new in the online world. Her fingers were twitching to get at the Wi-Fi.

Her parents were bound to ask why she was home early, but it wasn't her fault, was it? Nana had forgotten, and Amelia couldn't stay when she wasn't expected, it'd be bad manners. If the house was dusty from sanding, she could just stay in her room. It was no big deal.

When she unlocked the door, she frowned. She could hear a voice, yelling at some game.

'For God's sake, where are you going, you stupid… arrrgh! I mean, can't you even shoot straight? I thought you bastards were supposed to be highly trained.'

'Dad?' she said as she entered the sitting room. 'You sound weird. Why aren't you at the van?'

Amelia almost fell into the dresser when the man in her dad's chair leaned round.

'*You!*' she whispered.

'Um. Hi.'

She'd suddenly found herself face to face with the man everyone was talking about – the celebrity whose disappearance had triggered myriad conspiracy theories, helplines for worried fans and a national manhunt.

Jordan Nash.

Chapter Thirty

Jordan held up his hands to the mini Maggie who'd just burst in on him.

'Look. Kid. Amelia. Don't freak out, all right?'

'You!' Amelia hissed, flattening herself against the dresser. 'You're… you're Jordan Nash! Aren't you?' she demanded, as if he could attempt to deny it.

'Look, it's okay. I'm meant to be here, I promise.'

'I don't believe you. You broke in.'

'Why would I break in?'

'Dunno, to steal stuff.'

Jordan raised an eyebrow.

'Okay, then to…' Amelia paused. 'Because you crush on my mum. You probably broke in to… make her go out with you.'

'I'm here because your parents are old friends and they said I could stay a few days. I used to live here, you know.'

'No you didn't. This is my house.'

'I mean before there was a you,' Jordan said, standing up.

'Don't come any closer!' Amelia yanked out her phone. 'I'll knee you in the nads and call the police.'

Jordan smiled. 'Your dad tell you to say that?'

'Yeah.'

'Tell you what, why don't you give him a ring instead?'

Amelia eyed him warily. 'You're on drugs.'

'Not any more.'

'Drugs kill you and rot your brain.'

'I know. That's why I don't take them any more.'

She glanced at his arms. 'My best friend says she wants lush tattoos like yours when she's old enough.'

'Does she? That's scary.'

'I think they look stupid.'

'Right.'

'She's totally in love with you.'

'I think I'm a bit old for her, don't you?'

'That's what I said. I told her you were super ancient.'

'Thanks.'

'Like, the same age as my dad.'

'Actually your dad's two months older.' He nodded to the phone she was pointing at him. 'Go on, call him.'

''Kay,' Amelia said. 'But you stay where I can see you. I can still knee you in the nads while I'm on the phone.'

'I'd expect no less of your mother's daughter.'

Amelia rang her dad.

'Dad, I'm at home.' She lowered her voice. 'There's a man here. I mean, not just a man, it's... Dad, I'm not lying, it's Jordan Nash.' She paused. 'What? You did *what?* No it's not okay! I can't *believe* you guys! Ugh!'

'So I'm in the clear for housebreaking, right?' Jordan said when she'd hung up.

'He's coming home,' Amelia told him sternly. 'He says he'll be here in ten minutes and we're not to go out.'

'I think that's unlikely, since I'm in hiding.'

Amelia stared at him for a moment, her eyes lingering on the rumpled black hair and tattooed arms she'd seen so many times in miniature, on TV screens and magazine covers. They didn't quite seem to match the *Star Wars* lounge pants and baggy t-shirt he was wearing – which, now she looked at them, she recognised as belonging to her dad.

'You wait there,' she said eventually. 'I have to check some stuff.'

She bounded upstairs to the office, where she'd left her laptop, then did a Google image search for Jordan Nash.

The top photo showed Jordan in a smart suit at some awards ceremony, his arm around a tall lady with her big boobs spilling out of a slinky sequinned dress. Amelia blinked at it, trying to reconcile the man in her sitting room with the one in the photo. Then she put on a YouTube clip of Route 69 performing live.

It was just too weird, she thought as she watched Jordan jumping around on stage. Jordan Nash! In her house!

Even after she'd found out about him and her mum, she'd never quite believed in him as a person. Celebrities were... they were kind of like stories. If Amelia had walked in to find the Easter Bunny hopping around the house, she'd have accepted it more readily.

She clicked on the News tab of her Google search and skimmed down the headlines.

Jordan reunites with ex Arabella Collins, claims close friend. Lovebirds in hiding as wedding plans revived

Jordan spotted in Antigua with new love

Route 69 split – Nash supergroup in the pipeline?

Jordan back in rehab after drugs relapse

Sylvia Nash exclusive: mother's fears for missing addict son

There were loads of them, all claiming Jordan was in one place or another and no two agreeing. Not one suggested he might be hiding out in the sitting room of a modest semi-detached house in the suburbs of Bristol.

When Amelia had finished, she drifted back downstairs, wondering if she might not have dreamed the whole thing after all. But no, Jordan Nash was still there. He'd reclaimed her dad's chair and started playing *Call of Duty* again. She threw herself down on the sofa and fixed him with a suspicious stare.

'You don't need to watch me, you know,' he said. 'I'll be right here, not stealing stuff.'

Amelia carried right on watching him.

'Hey, have you got a bluebird tattoo on your right bum?' she asked after a minute.

'I consider that rather a personal question.'

''Kay.'

She stared for another long moment.

'Why'd you write a song about my mum?'

'Well, because...' Jordan hesitated. 'To be honest, I'm not sure. Suppose I missed her.'

'She didn't miss you.'

'Brutal.'

'She never even talked about you till you wrote your stupid "Magdalena" song. She doesn't need a boyfriend, she's always saying.'

'I didn't come here to be her boyfriend. We're friends, kid, that's all. You've got friends who are boys, haven't you?'

'Yeah, one,' she said, thinking of Rory.

'You're not going to tell anyone I'm here, are you? I'm hiding.'

'Who from?'

'The newspapers. My mum. My band.'

'Why do you need to hide from them?'

Jordan held up a hand and watched it tremble. 'I just do.'

'Why's your hand doing that?'

'Not sure. It only does it sometimes.'

Amelia watched it, frowning.

'Maybe you're poorly,' she said at last.

'Think I might be a kind of poorly. But I'm getting better. So will you tell anyone?'

Before she could answer, her parents came bursting in.

'I got your mum,' Ibby panted.

Amelia stood up. 'Well?' she said, folding her arms.

Maggie shook her head. 'Oh no. Don't do that face at me. I taught you that face.'

'Mum, you lied to me! You said I had to stay at Nana's because Dad was sanding the skirting boards. Not because the most famous person in *the whole country* was staying here.'

Jordan leaned round his chair and waved. 'Hello.'

'How could we tell you that?' Ibby said. 'It's supposed to be secret, Melie. Jord's in hiding.'

'I can keep secrets! I'm great at keeping secrets. Why didn't you trust me to keep the secret?'

Maggie looked pained. 'Well, you're... you know.'

'A kid?'

'Gobby, I was going to say.'

'You'd probably ring the bloody radio about it,' Ibby muttered.

'Everyone's been looking for him,' Amelia said, pointing at Jordan. 'A load of Routers think he's disappeared to start a supergroup with Liam Gallagher and Dave Grohl.'

Jordan blinked. 'Do they? Bloody hell, wish they were right.'

'Georgia says she cries every night because she's so worried about him. It's cruel not to tell me he's here.'

'Well what Georgia says and reality are two very different things,' Ibby said. 'Come upstairs, Melie, and we'll explain.'

'Fine. Don't want *him* listening anyways.' Amelia stomped off to her room.

Maggie grimaced at Jordan. 'Sorry. It's a shock for her, that's all.'

'She won't tell anyone where I am, will she?'

'It's a big secret for her to keep. At the end of the day, she is only thirteen.'

'But we'll try to make her understand why that would be a really, really bad idea.' Ibby glanced at Maggie. 'This might require a serious bribe, Mags.'

She sighed. 'Okay, come on.'

They found Amelia staring at the formerly white cotton dress hanging on her wardrobe door. A few hot washes had got it to a passable pearl grey, but it was far from snowy.

'My dress.' She turned to her parents. 'That's my favourite dress! Why's it gone that ick baby vom colour?'

Ibby winced. 'There was a bit of a laundry accident.'

Amelia went to her drawers and opened the top one. 'All my white knickers and socks! They're all baby vom colour.'

'Yes, well, Jordan didn't mean to. We can get you new things.'

She stared at him. 'You let *Jordan Nash* wash my pants?'

Ibby shrugged. 'He wanted to help with the chores.'

'Oh my *God!*' Amelia threw herself face down on the bed. 'This is so *humiliating!*'

Maggie sat down beside her. 'Come on, drama queen. It's not that bad.'

'It really is,' came a muffled voice.

'Now, sweetie. We're going to ask you to be really mature for us, okay? You need to promise you won't breathe a word about Max being here to anyone.'

'Don't see why I should. You lied, Mum.'

'Melie, this isn't the time for a sulk. Max Jordan came to us for help and we promised to keep him safe. You know, it can be very difficult for someone who needs help to ask for it. Can we trust you?'

Amelia sat up. 'You didn't trust me to tell me he was here, did you?'

'We just didn't want you getting dragged into things while we worked out what to do for him,' her dad said. 'If it leaks out to the press, we could find the house under siege again. No one wants that, do they?'

'I wouldn't leak it,' Amelia said.

'No,' Maggie said carefully. 'But someone else might. If you told them.' She held up a hand as Amelia opened her mouth to protest. 'I mean, if you let it slip out by accident.'

'I wouldn't tell. I promise I wouldn't.' Amelia paused. 'Oh, but couldn't I just tell Georgia though? I won't tell anyone else, I swear.'

Ibby shook his head. 'Georgia Fielding? You might as well get a megaphone and shout it off the Houses of Parliament.'

'Melie, you can't tell anybody,' Maggie said.

Amelia scowled at the bed, feeling hard done by. To have your home invaded by a stranger, a mega-famous stranger everyone was talking about, and then told you can't even score a few popularity points out of it with your friends – how totally unfair was that?

'Of course, there is an important birthday coming up for somebody soon,' Ibby said, examining his nails. 'And did I hear a rumour the new iPhone's out?'

Amelia looked up at once. 'Oh God, Dad, really?'

'I think if you can prove you're mature enough then your mum and me might be able to club together. But just one big present, that's all.'

'You promise?'

'If you promise not to tell anyone about Max,' Maggie said.

'I promise.' Amelia would've promised to shave her head and wear a sack to school if it meant getting an iPhone.

'There's our girl.' Ibby gave her a hug, followed by Maggie.

'And while Max is here, remind me, what's the first rule of this house?' Maggie said, raising an eyebrow.

'Be kind to each other,' Amelia mumbled.

'That's right. I know it's a hassle, having a stranger sharing your home, but it's only for one more night.'

'Why do his hands shake like that, Mum?'

'Because he's... not very well.'

'Not very well how?'

'His mental health. He's got very bad anxiety, and I'd say he was at risk of depression too.'

'Because of stopping taking drugs?'

'Because of a lot of things,' Maggie said. 'That's why we told him he could stay. There's not many people in the world who care about Max Jordan except us.'

'Are you kidding?' Amelia said. 'Everyone *loves* him. Most of the girls at my school crush on him.'

'I mean people who really care about him, not strangers who have a crush on him because he's famous. Family and friends.'

'What about his mum? She's always on TV saying how he's her little boy and stuff.'

'His mum's... not a nice person,' Maggie said, frowning. 'She likes his money but she doesn't care about Max. She abandoned him when he was small.'

'You mean abandoned like, she just left him? That's horrible!'

Maggie felt a surge of pride that even the concept of a mother like Sylvia was enough to appal her daughter. Maggie might've been making it up as she went along for the last fourteen years and she certainly wasn't the Instagram-perfect mum, but Amelia had never known a home that wasn't full of love.

'I know, sweetie,' Maggie said, giving her a squeeze. 'His nana was more like his mum, but she died a long time ago.'

'So he hasn't got anyone? Not even a dad or a grandad?'

'Not anyone except us.'

Amelia experienced a twinge of pity.

'Okay. I'll try to be nice.'

'Thank you.' Maggie bent to kiss her daughter's hair. 'Now what about Telly Takeaway Night? I fancy pizza, don't you?'

Amelia's eyes widened. 'We're not having *him* at Telly Takeaway Night?'

'Well yeah,' Ibby said. 'We can't just send him to his room while the three of us scoff down a Domino's, can we?'

'Can I stay in my room then?'

'No, you can come be sociable,' Maggie said. 'Friday night's family time.'

'Jordan's not family,' Amelia muttered.

'No, but he is our guest. Be polite, Melie. He's going tomorrow.'

Chapter Thirty-One

'So. Telly Takeaway Night,' Jordan said when they were settled in the sitting room. 'What's it all about, Amelia?'

'Um, telly and a takeaway?' she said, rolling her eyes. Her mum shot her a warning look.

'Yeah, it pretty much does what it says on the tin,' Ibby said. 'We usually chuck PJs into the mix, but Melie was too embarrassed to let you see her in her frilly nightie.'

'Dad!' Amelia said, staring at him in horror. 'It's not a nightie!'

'I think Jord's probably more interested in your mum's sexy dinosaur onesie anyway,' Ibby said, grinning.

Jordan smiled. 'Ann Summers number, Mags?'

'Yep,' she said, rummaging in the coffee table drawer for the pizza menu. 'Their Stegosaurus range.'

'Oh my *God!*' Amelia buried her face in her hands. '*Please* can I just have takeaway in my room?'

'Nope,' Ibby said. 'You can stay here, be embarrassed by your parents and get a delicious pizza-y reward or you can have sprouts with extra broccoli upstairs.'

'Ugh! This is totally unfair.'

Her dad cleared his throat with a sound that came out a lot like 'iPhone'. Amelia dug her fists into her chin and prepared to sulk quietly.

They ordered a Domino's, with Amelia, Ibby and Maggie settled on the sofa and Jordan in the armchair.

'Here you go, Melie.' Ibby offered her the TV remote. 'Since you're generous enough to grace us with your company.'

'No thanks.'

'You're not going to sulk all night, are you, teenage-face?' Maggie said, jiggling her.

'I'm not sulking,' Amelia said sulkily. 'Just don't want to, that's all.'

'Fine. Your mum can then.' Ibby handed the remote to Maggie, who started channel-hopping.

'Do you mind if we leave earlyish tomorrow, Jord?' he asked. 'I've got a date in the evening, don't want to be back too late.'

'Have you?' Jordan said. 'Who's the lucky man?'

'Nat. Social justice crusader with lovely eyes.'

'Sounds like my kind of guy.'

'Well, tough luck. I saw him first.'

'Is it serious?'

'Third date. We had a couple of false starts but... yeah, got a good feeling about him.'

'You could stay another night if you want, Max, save Ibs hurrying about,' Maggie said. 'Now Melie's seen you, there's no real rush.'

'I would like to hear how Ibby's date goes,' Jordan said, smiling.

'Stay then. Melie won't mind, will you, sweetie?'

'No,' Amelia mumbled, which anyone who was paying attention should've been able to tell meant yes. But her parents weren't paying her much attention. They were too busy laughing and chatting with stupid Jordan Nash.

It'd always been the three of them and now suddenly there was someone else, an outsider. Only he wasn't acting like an outsider. He was making *her* feel like one.

Jordan being there reminded Amelia that her parents had had a life before she was born – that they'd lived here with other people, their friends. For her it'd always been Mum and Dad and Amelia, but for them there'd been a time before that, a time when the future baby Amelia had been completely unthought of.

She didn't like it.

Jordan shifted in his armchair, hiding his awkwardness behind a smile. He was very conscious of the little girl's eyes fixed on him.

He'd been happy here. Felt like he'd slotted easily back into Maggie and Ibby's lives. Like the three of them were students again – playing console games, drinking wine, having a laugh. He'd enjoyed helping around the house, feeling that the place was still, to some extent, his own home. It was the last real home he'd had, after all.

And while he knew Maggie and Ibs were worried about him, there wasn't that patronising pity he'd imagined from the strangers responsible for him in rehab. They'd trusted him; hadn't hidden the alcohol or sharp objects, or worried about leaving him alone. They'd just been there when he needed them, like people who cared about him. Like mates.

And now the kid was here and suddenly they weren't just three mates any more. His old house hadn't been preserved in a timewarp, waiting for him to pick Max Jordan's life back up. This was a family home now and he, Jordan, was the intruder.

It was a relief to put it off for another day, but on Sunday he'd have to go: leave the three of them to their warm, happy home while he shut himself up in his empty mansion. Despite his friends' presence on the sofa opposite, he'd never felt so alone. Or so afraid.

There was a knock at the door, and Jordan instinctively flinched.

'Pizza! Triffic. First there gets the extra garlic dip.' Maggie bounced up to answer it.

'Oh God. What's she doing now?' Jordan said, frowning at the TV. A new programme had just started up.

Ibby followed Jordan's gaze to a tearful Sylvia Nash on the screen. 'You want me to turn it over?'

'No, leave it. I want to know what she's up to.'

'And if anyone, anyone, has information on where my Jordan is now, I'm begging you to come forward,' Sylvia sobbed. She held up a laminated photo of him, like the ones of missing persons in police appeals — as if he wasn't one of the most recognised faces in the country. 'I'm offering a reward for any news.'

Jordan snorted. 'You'd almost think those were real tears.'

'They probably are,' Maggie said, coming back in laden with pizza boxes. She dumped them on the coffee table next to a pile of plates. 'If you're getting out of the public eye, she's going to find herself in the dole queue pretty soon.'

'Ha! You're right,' Jordan said. 'Well, that thought's cheered me up a bit. You guys want a glass of wine?'

'Sounds good to me,' Ibby said. Maggie nodded too.

'Amelia? You want, um, a Fruit Shoot or something?'

Amelia rolled her eyes. Fruit Shoot, as if.

'No thanks.'

Jordan headed to the kitchen. Maggie watched him go, smiling slightly.

She'd been concerned about him drinking when he'd first come to stay, worried that after ditching coke, his next poison was going to be alcohol. Addictive personality, they called it, didn't they? Jordan had been an addict, so had both his parents. The idea that addiction was in his blood had occurred to her plenty of times before.

But in the week he'd been there, he'd been the picture of moderation: just a glass or two of wine with them in the evening, while the whisky he'd had with him when he arrived remained untouched in the cupboard. She was starting to think the only thing Max Jordan had ever really been addicted to was oblivion. Now he didn't need that, he apparently found it easy enough to abstain.

'Shit!' Jordan said when he came back in with the wine.

Maggie raised her eyebrows and jerked her head in Amelia's direction.

'Ugh, sorry,' he said. 'Sorry, Amelia. I'm not used to being around children.'

Amelia shrugged. 'I don't care. Kids at school swear all the time.'

'Well your mum and me do care.' Ibby nodded to Jordan as he handed him the wine. 'Cheers, mate.'

'Just got taken by surprise, that's all.' Jordan pointed to the TV, where the cameras were panning around a stately home that seemed to be on an only slightly smaller scale than Buckingham Palace. It was surrounded by journalists. 'That's my house.'

Ibby's eyes went wide. 'Sh— I mean, woah! Jord, that's where you live?'

'No, it's where I don't live. But I own it, yeah.' He shook his head. 'What is this, a Jordan Nash *Through the Keyhole*? Pretty sure I never agreed to have Keith Lemon picking bits of body hair out of my plughole.'

Maggie grimaced. 'Nice, Max.'

'Sexy as ever, eh?' he said, winking as he helped himself to a slice of pepperoni pizza.

'It's a news programme,' Ibby said.

A voiceover kicked in.

'It's now over a week since anyone heard from Jordan Nash, one of the biggest names in British music and sex symbol for thousands of fans,' a female voice said.

'This sort of thing ever go to your head?' Maggie asked.

'Yep. I'm talented and gorgeous,' Jordan said, tossing his hair. 'I'll allow you to gaze upon me, Mags, my darling, but there may be a charge.'

Against her will, Amelia found herself smiling. Jordan could be pretty funny. She just wished he'd stop making her gag by flirting with her mum right in front of her. The least her mum could do was tell him to get over himself instead of acting like she enjoyed it.

'His disappearance led to national shock,' the voiceover said. 'There have been impassioned appeals from those closest to Jordan for him to reveal his whereabouts, including his mother and bandmates. Meanwhile, some fans are in a state almost approaching bereavement.'

'She likes a bit of drama, this reporter, doesn't she?' Jordan said.

'Sky News,' Maggie said.

'Ah, right.'

The camera cut to a tearful Router who didn't look much older than Amelia.

'I j-just don't know what I'll do if anything's happened to him,' she sobbed. 'Jordan's my w-world. I'll die if he's hurt.'

'This sort of thing's not so fun,' Jordan muttered. 'What's Craig playing at? He was going to give a press conference.'

'Now we go to his manager, live from his offices in London, for a statement,' the voiceover announced.

'There you go,' Ibby said.

The picture cut to Craig, looking weary and sallow. Jordan felt a twinge of guilt. He knew his disappearance must've caused Craig a lot of headaches. Cancelling a major tour part way through was no one's idea of a good time.

'There has been much speculation in the press about the whereabouts of my client Jordan Nash,' Craig said. 'I have spoken with Jordan since his disappearance—'

There was a collective gasp from the gathered journalists.

'—since his disappearance,' Craig said, raising his voice over their shouted questions, 'and he's safe and well, albeit in a state of exhaustion from the rigours of a national tour so soon after his recent addiction battle. He has asked me to make a brief statement on his behalf, to the effect that he will be taking a break from his career while he focuses on his personal problems. Meanwhile, Route 69 will disband and Riley, Jake and Lucas will pursue solo projects. I'm sure we all wish Jordan a speedy recovery.'

'Where is Jordan, Mr Harvey?' a journalist called.

'Is it true he's in hiding?' another asked.

'I knew they wouldn't let it lie,' Jordan muttered.

'Jordan asks that you respect his privacy at this difficult time,' Craig said. 'While I'm not at liberty to divulge his location, I can say that he's in the best place for him. Somewhere he'll be well looked after and hopefully able to top up his tan. Thank you.'

Jordan laughed. 'Good misdirection from the man with the mike.'

'Yeah, I bet they're not all immediately bombing it in the direction of Weston-super-Mare,' Ibby said.

Jordan looked sober. 'They're likely to get what they want on Sunday though. I can't imagine that bit of subterfuge is going to stop them staking out the house.'

'Could you actually go abroad?' Maggie asked.

'Leaving the country doesn't appeal right now.' Jordan shivered. 'I kind of want to stay near you guys. Sorry if that sounds pathetic, but... I haven't got anyone else. Helps me feel grounded.'

'Well, we're not so far away,' Ibby said gently. 'And we're just at the end of a phone on the tough days.'

'Was that really your house?' Amelia asked Jordan in a quiet voice.

'Yeah. That's where I'm going on Sunday.'

'What about all those journalists? Some came here once and they were horrid. One grabbed at me.'

Jordan grimaced. 'Sorry about that, kid. My fault.'

'But how will you get past them?'

'There's a back entrance. If I'm lucky I might be able to sneak in without them seeing. And if not... it'll be brute force, I guess,' he said, shrugging. 'I've done it plenty of times before.'

'And then you'll be on your own in your giant house?'

'Yeah.'

Amelia was silent a moment.

'Here you go, Jordan,' she said, handing him a tub from the coffee table. 'You can have the extra garlic dip.'

Chapter Thirty-Two

It was after midnight and Amelia was still awake, listening to Smiffy running in his squeaky wheel.

It'd been a difficult night – for her anyway. The grown-ups had enjoyed themselves, getting a little bit tipsy while they watched a film. Amelia had sat in silence, feeling left out.

It wasn't that she didn't like Jordan. Actually he seemed a lot nicer than she'd imagined. She just hated the way he was *there*, being the centre of attention with his fame and his stupid problems, making her mum giggle in that totally bleurgh way, eating the last Chicken Stripper out of their Domino's order.

The way he flirted with her mum was the worst thing. Okay, in principle she was fine with her parents dating. It was pretty rancid to think about them kissing and having sex and stuff, but she knew all adults did that. She often told Georgia she'd like her mum and dad to get nice boyfriends, and she'd even intervened with her dad and Nat when she could tell the way they'd ended things was making him unhappy.

But her mum getting back together with Jordan Nash... for some reason, she couldn't stomach it.

Amelia's mum often said she wasn't bothered about having a boyfriend and it was years since she'd last been out on a date. Still, Amelia didn't think she'd mind her having one, just as long as it wasn't Jordan. She couldn't bear the idea of him becoming part of their lives permanently, coming between her and her parents, taking them away from her.

Plus, dating someone as famous as Jordan wouldn't be like her mum having a regular boyfriend. They'd probably be in newspapers all the time, and everyone would want to know every little thing about their lives.

Okay, Amelia's friends would be impressed – for a bit, anyway – and she might be more popular at school. They'd have more money too, and maybe get to go to the sort of glamorous parties she'd seen Jordan at in magazines. Amelia couldn't deny there was a part of her that wondered what it would be like, living that sort of life. But if it meant Jordan being in the house all the time and photos of him snogging her mum on the front of newspapers and creepy guys following all of them around… she shuddered, remembering the day the journalists had come and how afraid she'd been. No, totally not worth it.

So she knew it would be the easiest thing in the world to let Jordan go away on Sunday and have everything at 22 The Cedars fall back into its right place. For the last hour she'd been trying to get to sleep safe in the knowledge that she'd soon have her parents and her home all to herself again.

But she couldn't. Something in her soul was gnawing at her.

Every time she closed her eyes, pictures ran through her brain. Pictures of a huge, creepy house with Jordan all on his own in it, scared to go outside where nasty journalists were waiting to grab him. Of that horrid woman, his mum, who'd left him when he was tiny and pretended to cry about him when she really just wanted his money. Of his hands, shaking because he couldn't stop feeling afraid. In spite of herself, when she thought about Jordan and how lonely and frightened he must be, it moved her tender little heart.

And her mum had said Jordan might get depression. Amelia knew about depression. Georgia's mum Sally had suffered from it after her friend's dad walked out on his family.

It wasn't just like feeling sad. Sally had needed to see a special kind of doctor and take pills, and Georgia and her brother and sister had been sent to stay with their grandparents for a little while. Amelia's mum had told her that depression was like being the saddest you could possibly be, like Amelia had been after

Grandad died, but being trapped in it so you could never feel happy. Sometimes it was so bad, it made people actually wish they were dead.

Finally she got out of bed and crept to her mum's room.

'Mum?' she whispered, knocking softly.

There was no answer, so Amelia went in. She could hear her mum snoring, like she always did when she drank wine before bed – a habit Maggie fiercely denied in the face of all the evidence.

Amelia flicked the bedside lamp on and shook her.

'Hm?' her mum said, blinking sleepily. 'What's up, sweetie? Bad dream?'

'No. Mum, did you mean it when you said about Jordan maybe getting depression?'

Maggie pushed herself up. 'Why are you asking, Melie? It's very late.'

'Depression's horrid, isn't it? When Georgia's mum had it, she couldn't go to work or anything. She just stayed in bed.'

'It's a nasty, nasty thing,' Maggie said. 'But Max is getting better, I think, now he's decided to quit his band.'

'But if he's all on his own, he might get worse again.'

'Well, we'll keep in touch. Me and your dad and Uncle Other Max have promised to ring him every day.'

'Mum…' Amelia winced. She was about to do a far, far better thing than she had ever done, and it was tying her in knots. 'Mum, I… I think you should ask Jordan to stay.'

Maggie blinked. 'Stay here?'

'Yeah. Just until he's better. And I don't think he should ever go live in that house.' Something about Jordan's mansion had really upset her. 'He should get a little house like ours. And a puppy so he won't be lonely.'

'I thought you didn't like having him here.'

'I don't. I mean, it feels weird, having someone living here apart from us. But I don't want him to be sad, like as sad as after someone dies, for ever and ever.'

Maggie looked at her for a moment.

'You know, Amelia Jane, I never stop being amazed that you came from me,' she said softly. 'That's a lovely, kind, grown-up thing to do, my love. To put what you want to one side for someone else.'

Amelia scuffed at the floor. 'I just don't think people should have to be sad and alone.'

'Come here.' Maggie pulled her daughter to her for a tight hug. 'I'm so proud of you right now.'

'Mum, you're embarrassing me,' Amelia muttered.

'I know. It's what I do best.'

'So will you ask him to stay?'

'I'd like to. I know your dad would too, if you're happy with it. You come first, you know that.'

'Mum?'

'Hmm?'

'Will you and Jordan… is he going to be your boyfriend again?'

Maggie smiled. 'Now why would you think that?'

'Well, you said you used to love him, and now you keep smiling at him and laughing. And I know he likes you because he wrote that song and he's always doing heart eyes at you.'

'Heart eyes?'

'Yeah, like the emoji.'

'Don't worry about that,' Maggie said. 'Even if I wanted a boyfriend, it wouldn't be Max. Love affairs are the last thing he needs to be thinking about right now.'

'What about when he's better?'

Maggie hesitated.

'Melie, when me and Max were a couple… it was a very long time ago. He wasn't this person he is now, this famous person. That makes things a lot more complicated.'

'So you won't?'

'I am fond of him. But I think it's unlikely, now, that we'll be more than good friends.'

'You promise?'

'No, I don't promise. I only say it's unlikely. I'm talking to you like an adult now, Amelia, because you've been very mature tonight. Understand?'

Amelia understood. She wasn't getting the answer she wanted, but she was getting respect and honesty.

'I love you very much.' Maggie kissed her daughter's hair. 'Now go to sleep, sweetie. I'll talk to Max tomorrow.'

—

'Hiya,' Maggie said when she got back from the supermarket the following evening. 'Here's your death sticks.'

Jordan caught the packet of fags she chucked him. 'Cheers, Mags. How much do I owe you?'

'Eighty quid.'

He grinned. 'Nice try. I'm not that out of things.'

'Well, worth a shot,' she said, grinning back. 'Tenner, thereabouts. You won't smoke them when Melie's around, will you?'

'Course not.'

'Where is she, in her room?'

'No, she's sleeping over with the friend who's in love with me,' Jordan said, pulling a face. 'Ibs walked her round before his date. You sure she'll be okay?'

'She won't say anything, if that's what you mean. The bribe we offered guarantees silence.'

'You're sure? It's a lot for a thirteen-year-old to keep quiet about.'

'She promised us; that means we can trust her. You've not really seen the best side of her yet. Honestly, she's a great kid.' Maggie smiled. 'That reminds me, there's something I need to talk to you about.'

'What?'

Maggie dumped her shopping bags in the kitchen and came to sit beside him.

'Max, if we invited you for an extended sleepover, would you stay?'

He blinked. 'Sleepover?'

'Yeah. How do you fancy a holiday on the south-west coast till the media circus dies down? Because me and Ibs would love to have you for a month or two. I don't think isolation's the best medicine for you right now, is it?'

'Stay here? Oh my God, Mags, you really mean it?'

'Course.'

'Seriously, that'd be... I'd love to.' His eyes shone at the prospect. 'What about Amelia though? I'm sensing she's not keen on me intruding into the family group.'

'No, kids that age are pretty territorial. But she's the one who invited you.'

'Amelia invited me?'

'Yep. Came into my room in the middle of the night and told me I was to invite you to stay till you were better.'

'Why would she do that?'

Maggie shrugged. 'She's a sweet little thing. Between teenage sulks, her better nature usually prevails.'

'I thought you were worried I was dangerous.'

She nudged him. 'Come on, you know I didn't mean it like that. I was concerned, that's all, with the coke addiction and then the booze binge. Don't worry though, you've proven yourself responsible this past week.'

He looked thoughtful. 'That was nice of Amelia, when she'd probably rather have things back how they were. I'll thank her tomorrow.'

'Oh God, don't. She'll be so embarrassed.'

'Well, can I get her a thank-you present?'

'Now presents, she likes,' Maggie said, smiling. 'It's her birthday at the end of the month actually. Thirty-first of August.'

'Her fourteenth?'

'Yeah, she's the baby of her year. She's currently cursing the fact she was two months premature, otherwise she'd have another year's grace before starting her GCSE subjects. My fault apparently, should've kept my legs crossed till my due date.'

'Two months! God, poor Mags. You must've been scared to death when the contractions started.'

'Well, I think labour alone would've been enough to trigger the mother of all panics. But Ibs was there to hold my hand.' She smiled fondly. 'He was always there.'

'What do you think I should get her?'

'That's up to you. Just nothing too decadent, please. And nothing alive. It's enough work getting her to clean out the hamster.'

'I'll have a think.' He glanced at Maggie. 'So… just the two of us tonight.'

Maggie laughed. 'Don't get any ideas.'

'Had one idea.'

'What?'

'If we play *Mario Kart*, will you let me be Yoshi?'

Chapter Thirty-Three

Ibby brushed down the shirt Jordan had loaned him and knocked on the door.

'Um, hi,' he said when Nat answered. He held the bottle of wine he'd brought out in front of him. 'Alcohol. I've heard it's going to be the next big thing.'

Nat smiled. 'Come on in. I made us a chicken thing.'

'A chicken thing?' Ibby said as he followed him into an open-plan sitting room.

'It has got a proper name. Something French and sexy. Only I forgot, sorry.'

'Googled it, right?'

'Yeah,' Nat said, grinning. 'Tastes all right though, I checked. Otherwise it would've been a sexy takeaway chicken thing.' He planted a kiss on Ibby's cheek as he took the wine. 'Thanks for coming.'

'Thanks for asking me out again. More than I deserved.'

'Well. You've got your daughter to think about, I know that.'

'I was going to ring you, you know. There's been family stuff going on.'

'I heard,' Nat said, ushering him to a small dining table. 'So is it true? Maggie and Jordan Nash?'

'Yeah, he was at uni with us. Not sure why he suddenly decided to write a song about her.'

'You never mentioned you knew him.'

Ibby took his seat. 'Well, name-dropping your celeb pals on first dates – not really a turn-on, is it? Anyway, we've not seen him for years.'

'Where do you think he's disappeared to?'

'Who knows? Somewhere hot and debauched with plenty of busty girls in bikinis, knowing him.'

Nat scanned his outfit. 'You're not channelling him tonight, are you?'

Ibby ran a finger under Jordan's designer shirt collar. 'Well, you know. Thought I'd make an effort.'

Nat opened Ibby's wine and poured them a glass each.

'Look, Ibby,' he said, taking a seat opposite. 'Let's do the elephant in the room before we get too cosy.'

'Over It, you mean?'

'Yeah.'

'They're not here, are they?' Ibby asked, peering under the table.

'Very funny,' Nat said, smiling. 'Look, I'm sorry I pressured you to get involved. And I didn't mean it when I called you apathetic. I was angry about what happened, that's all.'

'No, it was fair. It's important, I know that. And of course I want Melie to grow up in a better world than we did. But... Nat, I'm not like you. What you said, on the radio, I couldn't have done that.'

'It's fine. It's not for everyone.'

'I mean, if I tried that, I'd... I don't know. I just wouldn't have the nerve to shout about my opinions that way.' Ibby looked up to meet Nat's eyes. 'You were amazing, you know.'

Nat laughed. 'I was scared stiff.'

'You were amazing,' Ibby said firmly. 'Passionate, dignified. I bet there wasn't a person listening who wasn't in our corner.'

Nat cocked an eyebrow. 'Our corner now?'

'Our corner.'

'We did get a load of emails expressing support after the show. I mean, there were also a few telling me I personally was an unnatural abomination who'd burn in hell, but the nice ones far outweighed them.'

'Doesn't it bother you, stuff like that?'

'Nah, I'm an atheist.'

'Seriously. Does it not upset you? I'd be dreadful with anything like that.'

'Well, I've developed a thick skin over the years. So is that why you didn't want to be on the show?'

'One reason. I'd be devastated if Amelia became a target for that kind of thing. She doesn't know there's that much nastiness in the world.' Ibby sighed. 'I hate knowing that one day she'll have to find out.'

'You know, she's had a few fan letters of her own since the show,' Nat said with a smile. 'That's some kid you've got there.'

'I know. And I claim most, if not all, credit.' He shrugged. 'Maggie helped.'

'You need a child's perspective to remind you it is pretty simple, really. Don't be mean. Just be a decent human being, basically.'

'She doesn't hold back when she thinks she's in the right,' Ibby said, relaxing as he sipped his wine. 'Takes after her mum.'

Nat stood up. 'Right. Nat's Chicken Thing. I'm patenting that.'

'Yum. My favourite.'

'What're Maggie and Amelia up to while you're playing out with me then?' Nat asked as he served up the food.

'Melie's at her friend's having a sleepover. Maggie's...' He hesitated. 'I'm not sure. But I hope she's having fun.'

—

Maggie folded her arms. 'Fix.'

'Mags, you just drove off a bridge into a load of steaming lava.'

'Exactly. Fix. There never used to be steaming lava there.'

'Right. So you're accusing me of hacking into the game, changing the code to include additional steaming lava then subtly nudging you into it.'

'Aha!' Maggie jabbed a finger at him. 'So you admit it.'

Jordan laughed. 'You know, you haven't changed a bit. You're still a terrible loser.'

'And you're still a terrible cheat.'

Their eyes met for a moment.

Jordan frowned. He'd had a bit of wine, enough to make him tipsy if not actually drunk, but Maggie seemed... different. Softer. Little touches, lingering glances...

Did she want him to kiss her?

'I'll get us another drink,' Maggie said, turning away. 'I'm sure Ibs won't mind if we steal his shiraz.'

'How do you think his date's going?' Jordan called as she headed into the kitchen.

'Well, he's cocked it up innumerable times in his Ibby way and Nat still seems keen. If he hasn't gone off him by now, this could actually be it.'

She came back and handed him a glass of wine.

'And what happens then?' Jordan asked.

'What happens when?'

'Well, how does it work if one of you meets The One? That's got to complicate things.'

'Melie comes first, that was always the deal. Her needs before ours.'

'Yeah, but you do have needs. You as well as Ibs.' His gaze flickered to hers. 'You can't have given up on love.'

Maggie shrugged. 'Pretty much. I had a bad experience in my last relationship and after that... blokes just felt like more trouble than they were worth, to be honest.'

'Well, Ibby hasn't given up. If it works out with this Nat, what happens? He moves in? Ibs moves out?'

'Nothing changes. Boyfriends are fine, but 22 The Cedars remains the family home until Melie's grown up.' Maggie smiled. 'Apart from the times we're providing a safe haven for rock stars in hiding, obviously.'

Jordan laughed. 'Well, if another one turns up I'll be happy to top and tail.' He stretched his arm over the back of the sofa, wondering if Maggie would object to him putting it around her. 'You haven't really given up on love though?'

'I've given up looking for it. I'm at a point now where it has to come to me.'

'When was the last time you were in a relationship?'

'A few years ago. Dan.'

'You said you had a bad experience. What happened?'

'He didn't get on with Ibs.'

'Seriously? Is it actually possible to not get on with Ibs?'

'You wouldn't think so, would you? But somehow this guy managed it. Anyway, obviously that was a deal breaker.' She laughed. 'I spend my life worrying my clients'll suss I'm a fraud. The relationship counsellor who's only had a couple of relationships.'

'Don't you miss being with someone?'

'Not enough to try navigating the dating minefield again. I miss sex sometimes, but I've learnt to live without it.' Jordan's arm slipped to her shoulders, and she smiled. 'So how about you? Any real girlfriends among the fakes?'

'A few, but nothing really serious. We were on tour so much, relationships were tough to keep going. Sex was always available, you know that, but... well, it all felt so empty after rehab.'

'What will you do now all that's behind you?'

'Just be me, I suppose. Live my Average Joe life.'

'You'll never be average,' Maggie said, squeezing his knee. 'Anyway, I meant with your music. This could be your chance to take it in the direction you want.'

'Yeah. I guess.'

'Can you get your guitar sent over, work on something new?'

'Not sure I'm in the mood for writing at the moment, Mags.'

'Best thing for you, mate.'

'It goes with that whole life though,' Jordan muttered, half to himself. 'Music means coke and girls and... pain. Everything I wanted out of.'

'To Max Jordan, music meant music.' She rested her head on his shoulder. 'You were going to set the world on fire.'

'I was young.'

'You believed. That was one reason I fell for you.'

He planted a soft kiss on her hair. 'Still the happiest I've ever been,' he whispered. 'That's what "Magdalena" meant. You, me… innocence. Love.'

She smiled. 'Sentimental after half a bottle of wine, aren't you?'

'I'm sentimental all the time. I just keep it well hidden so it won't damage my street cred.'

She ran one finger over the black briar rose tattooed on his arm. 'You need to write, Max. It's part of you.'

'You know, don't take this the wrong way, but sometimes you really remind me of Craig.' He looked down at her. 'Were you a fan then?'

She snorted. 'What, of you?'

'Okay, no need to be quite so brutal. We creative types are fragile, you know.'

'Sorry.' She forced her mouth straight. 'Sorry, I didn't mean it like that. It was just strange, listening to you after you became a star. I'll be honest, I went out of my way to avoid it. Well, until you were everywhere and I couldn't.'

'So you didn't like any of the albums?'

'I liked the first one,' she said, shrugging. 'That song you wrote for Jean was beautiful.'

'"Missing You". You knew I wrote it for Nana?'

'Who else could you have written it for? I could hear you in pain while you sang it. Broke me up a bit.'

'Aww, Mags…' He kissed her hair again. 'But you didn't like the later stuff?'

'Honest answer? It all got a bit samey, when you took your soul out of it. I missed the heat. Missed the passion. Why'd you stop writing protest songs?'

'Didn't chart as well as the other stuff,' Jordan muttered.

'So you sold out.'

'No. I just geared my sound to what the fans wanted. Nothing wrong with that, is there?'

'You see, this is it, there is something wrong with it,' Maggie said, tongue loosened by her third wine of the night. 'Because you didn't just sign a record deal when we were nineteen, Max, did you? You let them buy you, lock, stock and soul. Lost your mind to drugs, your personality to a persona – this Jordan Nash character – everything that was unique about your sound to that platitudinous easy-pop you started churning out. We were lucky there was any of the real you left by the time we got you back.'

'Don't go easy on me just for old times' sake, eh?'

'I'm sorry, but you need to hear this,' she said, gazing unflinching up at him. 'And you want to know a secret? After fourteen years, Max Jordan was still the empty seat whenever we went to the pub. I don't think we ever quite gave up on you.'

'Wait a minute.' Jordan pushed himself up straight. 'Mags, what did you just say?'

'I said we missed you, if you want me to paraphrase.'

'Not that. About my platyoctopus easy-pop.'

'Platitudinous,' she said, smiling. 'A word I may well just have made up. You know, I'm baring my soul here. Is that seriously what you're going to take away?'

But Jordan didn't hear her.

'I've got three platinum albums.'

'Elevator dross.'

'People are saying I'm peaking. That *Sleepwalking*'s my best work.'

'Yes-men. Flatterers.' She shrugged off his arm and stood up. 'I need to find something up in the loft.'

Jordan stared as she left the room. 'Mags? Where are you going? Mags!'

After twenty minutes, Jordan was starting to wonder if she was ever coming back.

'Maggie?' he called to the house at large.

'Coming!' came a muffled voice.

Five minutes later Maggie reappeared, covered in dust with her hair sticking up at odd angles. She had a cassette player hoisted on one shoulder and a battered cardboard box under her arm.

'Woah,' Jordan said, blinking. 'Is that a ghetto blaster?'

'Retro, right? Hope it still works.' She put it down on the floor and plugged it in.

'What's going on, Mags?'

'Something I want you to listen to.'

Maggie rummaged in the box and produced an old Memorex tape labelled 'MAX'. She put it in the cassette player.

Jordan smiled as his nineteen-year-old voice yelled at him, backed by the wailings of his university band.

'Can't believe you kept these.'

'Course I did. I bet they're worth a fortune.'

'They probably would sell for a bit, you know. I don't think there're many recordings of me with these guys.'

'Do me a favour and don't tell Melie I've got them, will you? I denied their existence when she tried to get them off me to impress some boy.'

They fell silent, listening to the teenage Jordan. It was one of his rage-against-the-world songs, about fighting inequality, standing up, being counted.

'Hear that?' Maggie demanded. 'That's the angry young idealist who made me fall in love with him. *That* is Max Jordan.' She smiled. 'Lead singer of – what did you guys call yourselves, The Pheasant Pluckers?'

'Yeah,' Jordan said, smiling too. 'Bloody hell, I was angry, wasn't I?'

'You cared. You cared about everything, then.'

'Thanks, Mags,' he said softly. 'I needed that. I'll ring Craig and get him to send my guitar.'

'That's the spirit. Here, let's listen to another. Might help you feel inspired.'

Chapter Thirty-Four

Amelia lay on Georgia's bed, kicking her legs in the air while she painted her fingernails Glitter Bomb Blue.

'...so Pyper thinks he's probably bought his own island,' Georgia was saying as she experimented with different-coloured lip glosses in front of the mirror. 'But I definitely think he's run off with Dua Lipa. When's the last time anyone saw her, right? Can't be a coincidence.'

'Georgie, can we pleeeease talk about something else?'

Amelia had begged Georgia to invite her for a sleepover so she could escape an evening watching Jordan Nash making googly eyes at her mum, and now Georgia seemed determined to talk about nothing else but that man. Amelia was actually glad, now, that her parents had made her promise not to tell that Jordan was at theirs. If Georgia knew, there was no chance she'd ever want to talk about anything else.

'Come on, aren't you interested in where he's gone?' Georgia asked, snapping a quick selfie. 'You were last week.'

'Yeah, but we know where he's gone now. That man on TV said he was on holiday or something.'

'They have to say that though. I still think Dua got him.' Georgia threw back her head and gave a despairing groan. 'God, how lucky is she? Hope it doesn't last.'

Amelia wondered if her friend would be quite so in love with Jordan if, like her, Georgia had been faced with the unglamorous sight of the country's sexiest star cooking scrambled egg that morning in an old pink dressing gown of her mum's.

'As if he'd go for Dua,' Amelia said.

'Oh, right,' Georgia said, rolling her eyes. 'Because your mum's the only woman he'll ever truly love blah blah boring. Yeah, we know. You never stop going on about it.'

OMG, how unfair? Georgia was the one who wouldn't shut up about him, not her!

'No,' Amelia said, scowling. 'He's too old for Dua.'

'No he isn't. That'd mean he was too old for me.'

'He's *seriously* too old for you, Georgie.'

'Isn't, isn't, isn't!' Georgia poked her tongue out, which Amelia felt rather proved her point.

'Fine, he isn't then. And he's sunbathing in the Bahamas while Dua rubs suncream on him. Now can we talk about something else?'

There was a knock at the bedroom door and Georgia's mum came in with a plate of snacks.

'Thanks, Sally.' Amelia helped herself to a crustless sandwich, being careful not to get crumbs on her sticky nails.

'You're very welcome, sweetheart.' Georgia's mum smiled fondly at Amelia. The two girls had been best friends for nine years now, ever since Reception class. 'So what are your parents up to tonight?'

'Dad's out on a date.'

'Oh yes, the man from the radio. You were very brave to call in like that.'

Georgia rolled her eyes. 'Mum, don't. Rory keeps telling her she was amazing too, she's getting all vain about it.'

'Well, Melie, I'm sure your mum will appreciate a night to herself,' Sally said. 'A bit of pamper time.'

Amelia just hoped her mum hadn't started snogging the face off Jordan Nash the minute she was out the door. Yeah, she said she didn't want him as her boyfriend, but Amelia had seen the way the two of them looked at each other. Exactly the way she wished Isaac would look at her.

Had she made a mistake, leaving them alone? However boak it was, maybe the sensible thing would've been to keep an eye on them. When it came to Jordan, she had a strong feeling her mum wasn't to be trusted.

—

Jordan and Maggie lay on their backs on the carpet, listening to the last of his old demo tapes.

'You know, I really wasn't bad,' he said.

'All right, Mr Ego.'

'Seriously. I always remember us being total wank, but we sound okay on these.' He rolled over to look at her. 'Hey. Maybe I should get them released as an album. *Jordan Nash: The Early Years.*'

'That's the wine talking.' Maggie rolled onto her side too. 'They were good songs though.'

'You used to come to every gig.'

'Yeah,' she said, smiling. 'Your first groupie. God, you were sexy when you were performing. I thought I was the luckiest girl in Bristol when I was the one who got to take you home.'

'Just Bristol?'

'The whole of the North Somerset area.'

Jordan reached out to twirl a strand of her hair around one finger.

'We were happy, weren't we?' he said softly. 'Before Nana died and I— before it all went wrong.'

'We were kids. Life was simple.' She sighed. 'Getting drunk, making love, sleeping in. No responsibilities. You miss it?'

'God, yes.'

'Mmm. Me too.'

'We're a bit drunk now, aren't we?'

'Yep.'

'So what was the next thing on your list?'

She smiled. 'Never you mind.'

'We haven't changed so much, have we, Mags? Okay, we're older, and you've got a kid, and I've got – had – a major international music career—'

'Nicely shoehorned.'

'Thanks. But we're still us underneath it all.'

'Suppose we are. Our lives change and our bodies change but inside we're the same.'

Jordan scanned her figure. 'You look the same outside to me.'

'Says the man with an army of lithe young groupies eternally ready to show him a good time.' She patted his leg. 'Well, I'm glad old times' sake makes you blind to any post-baby wobbly bits I haven't managed to shift in the last fourteen years.'

'Come on, you know that's bollocks.'

'What, you haven't got an army of groupies?'

'No, I have.' He blinked. 'I mean, I could have. Fans, not groupies. Disrespectful.'

'Sorry,' Maggie said, penitent but amused.

'I mean bollocks to your wobbly bits.'

'Oh, right. Bollocks to your bits too, mate.'

He punched her arm. 'I *mean*, you've not got any wobbly bits. Except good wobbly bits. I'm a big fan of all and any wobbly bits belonging to you.'

'You've always been a charmer, Max Jordan.'

'I know.'

'And you can stop giving me those come-hither rock god eyes. I can't do with being smouldered at.'

'Those're just my regular looking-at-stuff eyes. Very much stay-thither, I swear.'

'Yeah, and I can see what stuff you're looking at with them.' She reached out to tilt his chin up so his eyes were level with her face rather than eyeball-to-nipple with her chest.

He laughed. 'God, I missed all this.'

Her finger was still under his chin. Then somehow, without either of them quite realising how it happened, his lips had connected with hers.

'Sorry,' he said, pulling back immediately. 'Sorry. Accident.'

Maggie flushed. 'Max...'

'Lanie, don't be mad. It was all the nostalgia, I... forgot we didn't do that any more.'

'Look, it's not that I don't want to. It'll complicate things, that's all. You've got enough going on.'

'Does it have to complicate things?' Jordan said, looking at her intently. 'It was simple when we were young. Kissing is simple, isn't it? So is making love.'

'When we were young you weren't Jordan Nash.'

'I quit Jordan Nash, Mags. Now I'm just me.'

'Mmm. Just mega-rich, mega-famous, universally adored little you.'

'None of that stuff matters. It's just smoke and mirrors, the whole thing, just... nothing. Air.'

'But there's still Amelia.'

His fingers were brushing her hand, and she could feel herself wanting to give in. She longed to lose herself in his lips, in his arms, just once. Just tonight. God, it'd been so long... and they'd done it so many, many times before.

'Amelia's not here.' Jordan slid one palm to her cheek. 'What do you say, Lanie? Doesn't count if it's nostalgia.'

Maggie paused a long moment.

'No,' she said at last. She took his hand from her cheek. 'We shouldn't have finished the shiraz, should we? It's affecting our judgement.'

'My judgement's just fine.'

'Max, please. I need to do some good, sober thinking before we go down that road.'

He sighed. 'Okay. Sorry.'

'Don't be sorry. I hate you being sorry.' She shuffled over. 'Look, how about a nice, chaste nostalgia cuddle instead?'

He smiled as he wrapped his arms around her. 'I could go for a nostalgia cuddle.'

Over at Nat's, Ibby hadn't quite reached the cuddling stage. In fact, for the past half hour he'd been wondering if there was some smooth way to segue from the pudding stage to the cuddling stage without being too obvious.

It'd gone well. The conversation had flowed easily. Nat's Chicken Thing (TM), which had turned out to be chicken breasts in a tomatoey sauce, was just like Mother would've used to have made if Ibby's mum had been any good at cooking. And Nat had got Ibby's favourite, pistachio Viennetta, for pud too, which was either a lucky guess or something else Mags and Other Max had felt it necessary to include in his Tinder profile.

'That was delicious. Thanks, Nat,' he said when he'd polished off a second helping.

'Glad it did the trick,' Nat said. 'More wine?'

'Sounds good to me.'

There were candles on the dining table. The flames danced in Nat's gorgeous eyes as he filled their glasses. Ibby wanted to get those eyes good and close so he could have a nice, long, sexy gaze into them. Unfortunately there was currently what seemed like an ocean of Formica between him and Nat, although he was sure it'd only been a small table when he'd arrived.

'So… what do you say to drinking these on the sofa?' Ibby said, deciding it was time one of them bit the bullet.

Nat smiled. 'Was thinking of suggesting that myself. For about the last hour, in fact.'

'I'd still have respected you.'

'Never seen a man eat a bowl of Viennetta so slowly.'

Ibby patted him on the cheek as he passed to go sit on the sofa. 'The best things come to those who wait, young Nathaniel.'

'It's Nathan actually.'

'I like Nathaniel better. It sounds like two parents had an argument about whether to call their kid Nathan or Daniel and decided to split the difference.'

'I'll write to the deed poll people tomorrow.'

Ibby slapped the cushion next to him. 'Come on then.'

'So what do you want to do now?' Nat asked when they were sitting side by side.

Ibby shrugged. 'I thought we could talk some more.'

'Ah, but what would you say if I told you I had every Harrison Ford film ever made on Blu-ray and a sixty-inch HDTV?'

'I'd say how do you want me, big boy?'

'Here.' Nat pressed a button on a remote control and a framed print of Helvellyn over the fireplace slid up to reveal a TV screen. Or home cinema was probably the more accurate description. It was *huge*.

'Blood-*y* hell,' Ibby said, blinking. 'Hey, think I saw this trick once before in an episode of *Thunderbirds*.'

'Impressed?'

'Very.'

'As a seduction technique, you really can't beat Wall's Viennetta and an enormous telly.'

'Well, there are those who say size doesn't matter.' Ibby shuffled round to face him. 'I'm not one of them. So are we going to sit here all night having what can only be described as banter, or are you going to kiss me?'

'I was waiting for you to make the first move.'

'You're the host. It's up to you to initiate the after-dinner snogging.'

Nat stretched both arms around Ibby's neck and planted a soft kiss on his lips.

'There. Happy?'

'Well, it'll do for now.'

'Hey,' Nat said, suddenly serious. 'I'm glad we got things sorted out, Ibby. You know, I think we could have something good here.'

'Me too,' Ibby said. 'Nat, are we... I mean, are you telling me...'

'That I'm taking down my Tinder profile? Yeah.'

'Think I'll get Melie a fancy case to go with that iPhone,' Ibby muttered.

'What?'

'Just thinking what a massive balls-up I nearly made of everything. Thank God for kids who can't mind their own business.'

He drew Nat to him for a deep kiss, his arms twining around Nat's back as they pressed their bodies close. Nat's fingers toyed with the buttons of Jordan's borrowed shirt.

'Nat,' Ibby panted when they broke apart, his shirt hanging open. 'You got something you push in this place that makes a bed pop out of the wall?'

'I've got a bedroom, if that's any use to you.'

'Nice, is it?'

'Mmm. Very Playboy Mansion.'

'Zebra-print wallpaper?'

'Goes with the leopard-skin bedspread.' Nat planted soft kisses across Ibby's bare chest. 'You, er, want to go see it?'

'I'll give it a look over if you want. Pass on some decorating tips.'

'I was hoping you might.'

Maggie was dreaming.

It was a good dream, the kind you didn't want to wake up from. The kind that these days was the consolation prize for her lack of a sex life.

She'd had it before: half dream, half memory. Her and Max, in bed. Only not in their dingy student rooms with their unmade single beds, trying to find a position that wouldn't end up with one of them falling on the floor. They were in a king-sized bed with satin sheets, enjoying endless rounds of silken, satisfying lovemaking with never a thought of having to break off for lectures.

Maggie wriggled pleasurably as Dream Max slid his hand up her back, caressing her shoulder blades with his fingertips.

'Lanie,' he whispered, the name he always called her when they were alone. He kissed her collarbone delicately. 'Never let me go again.'

'I won't. Don't stop, Max.'

'Careful, darling,' he murmured. 'We're not alone.'

'What?'

She was woken by the sound of a throat clearing.

'Comfortable?' Ibby said.

Maggie blinked. She was lying on the sitting room floor with her head against Max's chest and one of his hands up the back of her top.

'Ugh. We fell asleep.' She extracted Max's hand from her clothing. 'Max, why are you feeling me up?'

'Hmm?' he said, blinking awake. 'Oh. Sorry, Mags, did I sleep-grope you?'

'Yeah, you'd better have been asleep.'

'Had a good evening, have we?' Ibby asked, quirking an eyebrow.

'All innocent, I promise.' Maggie stood up and brushed down her clothes. 'We got a bit sleepy after stealing your shiraz.'

'And randy?'

'No randiness has been enacted.'

Jordan shrugged. 'Gave it my best shot though, mate.'

'First rule of good guesting: no violating the lady of the house,' Ibby said, wagging a finger at him.

'So, how about you?' Jordan asked, standing up too. 'Did my favourite shirt have a good night out?'

Ibby smirked. 'Might've.'

'He's smirking,' Maggie said to Jordan.

'He's smirking like a man who has no moral high ground from which to judge us for a bit of sleep-fondling,' Jordan said. 'Come on, Ibby. Share.'

'I may have had some Viennetta and an ogle at Nat's massive telly.'

'Viennetta, is that code for some sort of sex thing?'

'Nope, I had an actual double helping of Viennetta.' Ibby flicked some dust from his collar. 'But I did also enjoy some pretty top-notch hanky panky, yes.'

'He looks very proud of himself,' Jordan said to Maggie.

'I was rather awesome,' Ibby said. 'Nat didn't do badly either.'

'So are you and Adorable Nat officially a thing then?' Maggie asked. 'Now you've consummated your relationship with Viennetta and shagging?'

Ibby's smirk spread into a grin. 'Yup. We ceremonially deleted our Tinder profiles.'

Maggie gave him a hug. 'Good for you, Ibs.' She glanced at the clock. 'Jesus, one a.m.! Come on, you boys, bed. And when Amelia gets back, none of us did anything more risqué tonight than Ludo and cocoa, okay?'

Chapter Thirty-Five

As soon as Amelia got home, she was suspicious. Her parents seemed to be in ridiculously good moods for no reason at all.

Her dad was on the sofa, reading a book. Reading a book and... humming.

'Dad?'

'Hmm?' he said, looking up. 'Oh, hi, Melie. Didn't hear you come in.'

'Why're you making funny noises?'

'I'm humming a jolly little tune.' He leaned over to kiss her cheek. 'Did you have fun at Georgia's, my love?'

She shrugged. 'It was okay. What about your date?'

'Very nice, thank you. The ice cream provision was first rate.'

'You didn't mess it up again, did you?'

'Nope. Actually we thought we'd make a regular thing of it.'

She blinked. 'You mean, like... you're going to be boyfriends now?'

'I do. Thanks for arranging it for me.' He stood up. 'I'll go read in my room until dinner's ready, I think. Somewhere I can enjoy my humming with no one to criticise it. Be good, sweetheart.'

He wandered off, looking a bit like he was floating.

Amelia headed into the kitchen. Her mum was at the sink, wiggling her backside to some cheesy music while Jordan peeled veg next to her.

'Whoops,' he said as he reached over Maggie to get something off the draining board. He put one hand on her bum to guide her shimmying hips out of his way. 'Careful with the twerking, Mags. Hot-blooded men in the vicinity.'

Amelia actually heard her mum giggle. Jordan nudged her when he spotted Amelia in the doorway.

'Hello, sweetie,' Maggie said with the hint of a blush. 'Back already?'

'Yes, back already,' Amelia said, folding her arms. 'Why, am I interrupting?'

'We're just making the Sunday roast,' Maggie said without making eye contact. 'Um, do you want to go hang out in your room? It'll be a while yet.'

'No, I think I'll wait right here. Where I can keep an eye on things.'

'It doesn't need three of us, Melie. Too many cooks and all that.'

'All what?'

'You know, that saying about there being too many cooks.'

'Why, what do they do?'

Maggie glanced at Jordan. 'What do too many cooks do, Max?'

'Spoil broth, apparently.'

'What's broth?' Amelia demanded.

'It's a kind of soup,' Jordan said.

'Why're we having soup? We never have soup on Sundays.'

'We're not actually having soup,' Maggie said, shooting a patronising grown-up smile to Jordan. 'That's just the saying. When you get too many cooks, they can't work together so they spoil the soup.'

'That's a stupid saying.'

Jordan went over to Amelia and clapped her on the back. 'Well, personally I'd say we could use another cook. You can help me with the veg if you want, kid.'

'No thanks.'

Maggie recovered her composure enough to put her mum voice on. 'Well you're not just standing about, Melie. You can come help or you can go upstairs till it's time to eat.'

'Fine. I'll be upstairs then.' Amelia pointed at Jordan. 'You. No touching.'

Jordan watched her stomp out.

'Whoops,' Maggie muttered to him.

Amelia marched upstairs and straight into Ibby's bedroom, where he was reading in the red Chesterfield armchair he'd bought with a bit of cash his dad had left him. He'd always wanted one, although he still hadn't got around to buying the smoking jacket and pipe he felt were really needed to set it off.

Amelia threw herself face down on his bed and groaned.

'Funny,' Ibby said. 'I could've sworn this was my room.'

'Dad, I'm worried about Mum,' Amelia said, her voice muffled by his pillow.

'Why, sweetheart?'

'She's being weird.'

'She seems happy enough to me.'

'That's what I'm worried about.' Amelia rolled over and stared at the ceiling. 'What did Mum and Jordan do while you were out last night?'

'Listened to music, I think.' He paused, trying to remember Maggie's cover story. 'Er, possibly they also played Ludo.'

'Do you think she might like him? I mean, *like* him, like him?'

'What's brought this on, Melie?'

'Because he used to be her boyfriend and he wrote her that song and now he's in our house. And everyone totally hearts him, like Georgia and all the girls at school. *And*, I just saw him touch Mum's bum.' She sat up. 'And Dad, I'll tell you something. It looked to me as though she liked it.'

'I'm sure he was just being friendly.'

'Friends don't touch your bum. That's flirting.'

Ibby put his book down. 'Would it be so bad if your mum did like him? It's been a long time since she had a boyfriend. And she seems happy having him around.'

Amelia scowled at the bedspread. 'I don't know why it has to be him, that's all.'

'Don't you like him?'

'He's okay,' she said, with no real conviction. 'But… Dad, I don't like the way he acts like she's his friend.'

'But she is his friend.'

'I mean, he acts like she's *just* his friend. Not yours. Not mine, like she's not my mum.' Her eyes filmed with tears. 'Like I never happened and they never stopped being girlfriend and boyfriend and they want to make me go away so they can go back to how it was before.'

'Ah. That's it, is it?' Ibby went to sit by her on the bed. 'Melie, your mum loves you very much,' he said gently. 'She'd never, ever want to make you go away.'

'She didn't want to have me though, did she?'

'No, she didn't plan to have you, which is a very different thing. She wanted to have you very much – we both did. Mum would never wish you hadn't happened, any more than I would.'

'Then why does she act like that with Jordan? Giggling and being silly like a kid?'

'Well, when adults like someone that way, it can make them feel as if they're kids again,' he said, smiling as he thought about Nat.

'Oh *God*.' Amelia flopped back down and turned to bury her face in the pillow. 'So she does like him.'

'I think she might do. But if she's happy then we should be happy for her, shouldn't we?'

'What about Jordan?' Amelia mumbled. 'I bet *he* wishes I'd never been born.'

'Come on, he doesn't at all. He's really very nice, you know.'

'He wants to go back to how things were. He wants this to be his house again and Mum to be his girlfriend again and me never to have happened.'

'Melie, that isn't true.'

'Wish I'd never asked him to stay,' she muttered.

282

'It was a very kind thing to do,' he said, stroking her hair. 'You'll like him when you get to know him, I promise.'

'Don't you mind he's here?'

Ibby frowned. 'Me?'

'Yeah. Aren't you frightened he'll try to take Mum away, like Dan did? I bet he thinks we're weird.'

'Max Jordan isn't like Dan. He's a good man – an old friend. Anyway, you know your mum wouldn't let that happen.'

'She might. If she likes him too much.'

He patted her shoulder. 'Let me have a word with her, eh? She never meant to make you feel you weren't wanted. She loves you to pieces, same as always.'

Amelia, trapped in determined self-pity, just sniffed.

Ibby headed to the kitchen. He caught Maggie's eye and jerked his head towards the utility room.

'Oh God, what?' she said.

'Parent stuff.'

'Don't mind me,' Jordan said, peeling potatoes. 'Go right ahead.'

Maggie followed Ibby into the utility room and closed the door.

'Is Melie upset because she saw Max tap my bum before?' she asked.

'It goes a bit deeper than that, I think. It's not that she minds you having a boyfriend so much as the idea of it being him. She thinks he's monopolising you.'

'He's only been here nine days. And she was at your mum's for most of that.'

'Still. She's worried he wants to replace her or something. Go back to how things were before she was born.'

Maggie frowned. 'Did she say that?'

'Yeah.'

'It's true Max has got the past on his mind at the moment, Melie might have picked up on that. But it's really not about her.'

'I know that and you know that, but Melie doesn't know that. She's thirteen, she thinks everything's about her.'

'Course she does.' Maggie sighed. 'We've been thoughtless, haven't we? It's natural she might feel pushed out. I'll talk to her.'

'Mags, what is going on with you and Jordan?'

'I'm… not sure. We nearly kissed last night, but I shut it down.' She looked up. 'But I wanted to, Ibs. It wasn't just the nostalgia or the wine, I really wanted to.'

'You never did get over him properly, did you?'

'I thought I had, but now he's here… there's a lot that needs sorting through.' She sighed. 'Wish it was simple. Your first love turning up back in your life after fourteen years is going to be awkward at the best of times. If he also happens to be one of the most famous men in the country, hiding out while he deals with a substance abuse problem, that's just bloody soap opera.'

'Do you think you'll get back together?'

'No idea. But if we do, I need to know Melie's going to be okay with it. And that you are.'

'Don't mind me, I just want to see you happy. But do mind Melie.' Ibby looked at her. 'She asked if I was scared he'd be another Dan. I haven't got anything to worry about, have I, Mags?'

She shook her head. 'Max isn't a Dan, you know that. Anyway, I'd never let that happen again.'

'Good. Because I've got a lot more to lose this time.' He dipped his head to look into her eyes. 'Maggie – whatever happens with Jordan, you won't forget, will you?'

She placed her hand on his cheek. 'I swear to you on my life, Aaron Ibbotson, it's the one thing I'll never forget.'

He gave her a hug, squeezing her tight. 'You know I love you, right? Always and forever.'

'Still the best thing in my life,' she whispered, closing her eyes. 'Well, one of two.'

Chapter Thirty-Six

Maggie arrived home from work one Tuesday and chucked herself down on the sofa.

'Tough day at the coalface?' Jordan asked, pausing *Call of Duty*.

'Exhausting. I wonder some days how the human race has managed to breed so successfully for all these generations.'

'You wouldn't think it was rocket science.'

'Oh, rocket science is a piece of cake compared to sex, apparently. Seriously, how can combining genitals and friction be so much bloody hard work?'

'See, this is all I ever wanted in life. A beautiful woman who'd come home and talk dirty to me.'

Ibby, who'd been parking the car, came in and slumped down next to Maggie.

'Not you too?' Jordan said. 'No one who sells books and 99 Flakes for a living has any right to look that knackered.'

'The books are all right. The feature I'm writing on river dredging, not so much.' He glanced around to make sure Amelia wasn't about before adopting his grown-up vocab set. 'Christ almighty, talk about dull. I nearly nodded off into my James Pattersons.'

'So what've you done all day?' Maggie demanded of Jordan. 'Played *Call of Duty* and scratched yourself? You're wasting your life, Max.'

'Sounds like he's living the dream to me,' Ibby said.

Jordan shrugged. 'Did the hoovering.'

'Well, that's more than you did in this place when we were students, I suppose. Is that it?'

'Made dinner. Come on, what else can I do? I can't go out, can I?'

'Hmm.'

'When she says "hmm", it's usually time to worry,' Ibby told him.

'Why shouldn't he go out every once in a while?' Maggie asked Ibby. 'He can't just hide in here, never seeing the sun. He'll get rickets.'

'Because he's Jordan Nash, isn't he?'

'Exactly. And where's the last place anyone's going to expect to see the country's most famous musician while he's in hiding? Applecroft, the town that just a month ago was at the centre of a media storm around his ex. We can hide him in plain sight. Only an idiot would hide out here after what's gone on recently.'

'You know, I'm right here,' Jordan said.

They ignored him.

'What about that journalist who grilled you the night he turned up?' Ibby asked.

'She didn't seem to have any notion he was here. She just thought I might let slip where he was hiding. There's been no one since then, so even that's obviously not a popular theory.'

'Still, he's a bit bloody conspicuous,' Ibby said, scanning Jordan's tattooed arms. 'What're we going to say, that he's our friend Kevin, the country's leading Jordan Nash impersonator?'

'He doesn't have to be conspicuous.' Maggie dragged Jordan to his feet so she could examine him. 'Okay, what's with the Dark Lord of the Sith look, Max?'

He rubbed his head. 'The black hair, you mean?'

'And the brown eyes. Max Jordan had light brown hair and blue eyes. Where are they?'

'Dunno, s'pose I just got used to having the contacts in.' Jordan popped his coloured contacts out to reveal his natural pale blue irises.

'Okay, I can pick you up some dye and we'll get you back to your real hair colour. How do you feel about a beard?'

'Do I have to? It always goes a bit ginger.'

'Go on, it'll suit you.'

'Well, a bit of longish stubble then.'

'Maybe we can get you some clear-lens glasses too. You know, like those ones you wore in the first year when you went through that Jarvis Cocker phase.'

Jordan winced. 'You had to remind me.'

'I quite liked them,' Maggie said, shrugging. 'You can stop dressing in all that designer gear as well, get decked out like an ordinary Topman pleb. Ibs'll lend you some shirts.'

'Thanks very much.' Ibby nodded to Jordan's arms. 'What about the tattoos? They're the big giveaway.'

Maggie took Jordan's hands and examined them. 'The arms we can cover. These little clockwork things on the backs of the hands… hmm. Maybe we can have them lasered off.'

'Do I get a say in this?' Jordan asked. 'Hours of pain, you're looking at there.'

'You don't want to be a recluse all your life, do you?' She turned to Ibby. 'I'll talk to Nicki. She can find out about cosmetic treatments through work.'

Ibby patted Jordan's cheek. 'There you go, mate. Give it a few days and you can take us both out for a pint.'

Jordan looked thoughtful. 'Yeah. Hey, Ibs, what was that you said before?'

'I said you're buying me a pint. Don't worry, I won't forget.'

'Not that. About the country's leading Jordan Nash impersonator.'

–

Lying in the dark, Jordan held his mobile to his ear and listened to it ring.

'Jord, don't take this the wrong way but please fuck off,' Craig mumbled when he answered. 'It's two in the morning.'

'I wanted to guarantee I'd catch you alone.'

'What's so urgent? Some of us need our beauty sleep here.'

'Craig, you remember when we headlined that festival down in Dorset? There was that bloke, Ellis something. He kept hanging round outside the hotel busking our material, till you threatened him with legal action.'

'This is not a conversation for two a.m., Jordan.'

'Please, it's important. You remember?'

'Yeah, I remember. To be fair, I would've let him get away with covering the songs. It was when he started pretending to be you to cop off with girls I decided he needed shutting down.'

'He looked like me though, didn't he? I mean, he'd gone to a lot of effort, with the tats and everything.'

'The girls obviously thought so. Why?'

'I want you to hire him for me.'

Craig snorted. 'You what?'

'I want you to find him and offer him a free holiday in a private beach resort of his choosing, plus whatever financial incentive it takes to guarantee cooperation and silence.'

'In exchange for what?'

'In exchange for letting the paparazzi take as many long-lens photos of him as they feel like. I'm getting crazy cabin fever here.'

'Ah, right. Decoy,' Craig said. 'But they'll wise up quick enough when you start getting spotted in bloody Scrumpyville or whatever it's called, won't they?'

'Not necessarily, if I ditch The Look. Ninety-nine per cent of Jordan Nash is the hair, the tattoos and the clothes. Once I lose them, I can be Max again in no time.'

'Hmm. It's risky, Jord.'

'Well, what's the alternative? I can't stay indoors forever. And Maggie's right: people don't see what they're not looking for.'

Craig let out a resigned sigh. 'I'll give it a go.'

'Cheers, Craig. Oh, and thanks for doing that press conference. What took you so long though?'

Jordan could practically hear him grin. 'I was waiting for a lull in album sales. The buzz around your disappearance was doing wonders for *Sleepwalking*'s chart position.'

Jordan smiled. 'You cynical old bugger.'

'Worked though. Soon as there was a dip I announced the band were splitting and up we shot,' he said. 'So anything else you need or are we calling it a day with the body double?'

'Yeah, my guitar. Can you get it couriered to Maggie at work?'

'No problem, I'll do it tomorrow. In daylight hours. When you could've just bloody rung me. How's it going there then?'

'Good. Really good.' Jordan smiled to himself. 'Best I've felt in ages.'

'Star, I know that tone,' Craig said. 'You're holding out on me. What else?'

'I think... I'm falling for her again. Maggie.' Jordan pressed his eyes closed. 'No, I don't think anything. I know I am – I mean, I have. Or I never stopped. Something woke up inside me the day I quit coke and I think this is what it was.'

There was silence at the other end of the line.

'Craig, did you hear me?'

'I heard.'

'Well?'

'Jord, get out of that place. I'll sort you out a safehouse, somewhere you can get better without distractions.'

'I'm not leaving.'

'What happened to no dating during recovery?'

'That's advisory,' Jordan said. 'Anyway, I don't care. I'm ready.'

'I'm going to have to respectfully disagree with you there.'

'I promise you, I am. I let Maggie Nightingale out of my life once before and it was the biggest mistake I ever made. If this is my chance to fix that, I'm bloody well going for it.'

'Jordan, I don't like this. I don't like it one bit.'

'I know what I'm doing. This is right, boss, I feel it.'

Craig sighed. 'Too much feeling, not enough common sense, that's always been your problem. Anything else then?'

'There is one other thing I need,' Jordan said. 'You've got teenage nieces. What's a good present for a fourteen-year-old girl? Something special.'

'Well until a few weeks ago, tickets to see Route 69.'

'But what now?'

Craig fell silent.

'I'll have to ask one of the girls,' he said.

'I need something by the end of the month. It's Maggie's kid's birthday.'

'Leave it with me, I'll get it sorted. Look after yourself, Jord. And for God's sake, be careful.'

–

'So did you get it?' Maggie asked.

'Yep.' Nicki handed over a tube of something. 'Matched the skintone as closely as I could.'

'Good stuff, that,' Other Max said. 'It's what the hospital recommends for covering surgical scars. Should work perfectly for tattoos.'

'How's the guest then?' Nicki asked. 'What is it, three weeks you've had him there?'

'Around that,' Maggie said. 'Yeah, he's doing well. His hands have stopped shaking entirely now, and he says he hardly ever gets a craving these days.'

She had a dreamy, faraway look in her eyes, a little smile hovering on her lips. Nicki shot Other Max a significant glance.

'How about you three?' Other Max asked. 'Housesharing working okay?'

'Melie's struggled to adjust, but she's getting there. Ibby's just glad he's finally got a Player Two worthy of him. And I'm enjoying having him, obviously.'

'What's Jord's plan for afterwards?'

'Afterwards?'

'Yeah, after the heat's off,' Other Max said. 'That was the idea, wasn't it? He hides out with you guys till he's stopped being quite so newsworthy then starts building some sort of life? The press coverage does seem to be slowing down now they've milked the band split dry.'

'Well, there's no big hurry,' Maggie said. 'It's nice having him around. Plus he's paying board out of the wads of cash in his safe, and me and Ibs get our dinner on the table every night. Max is a fantastic cook.'

'Hmm.'

'What?'

'Mags, we hate to break this to you,' Nicki said, stretching an arm around her, 'but you've got all the symptoms of a woman who's falling hard.'

'Don't be daft.'

'Nic's right,' Other Max said. 'You should see your face when you talk about him. You and Jord aren't... you know, are you?'

'Oh God, not the "you knows",' Maggie said, groaning. 'We aren't what? Nipple? Orgasm? Erectile dysfunction?'

'Bonking,' Nicki said.

'We're just good friends, all right?'

'And planning to stay that way?' Other Max asked.

Maggie sighed. 'I don't know, you guys. The sensible part of me knows what a terrible idea it'd be to get involved with Max again now. He's got his problems to deal with, the nation's media are lurking behind every bush waiting to pounce on him, and on top of all that, my daughter can't stand the idea. But...'

'But?' Nicki said.

'On a more basic level, yeah, I fancy the pants off him. And it's worse than that, I really like him as well.' She watched Other Max guide Nicki onto his lap. 'And there's you two all over each other like a rash, Ibs loved up with Nat, and I seem to be the only one of us not having any sex. Which seems pretty unfair, given I'm the one who has to talk about it all day.'

'Maybe you should have sex with Jordan then,' Nicki said, snuggling back against her boyfriend. 'I mean, just sex.'

Maggie patted her knee. 'I love the way you make it sound so simple, Nic.'

'Well, couldn't you? You know, friends with benefits? Amelia wouldn't find out if you were discreet.'

'I don't think I could sleep with him on a regular basis without it ending up as more. Too much history. Too many feelings.' She paused. 'Maybe once, though.'

Other Max shook his head. 'Women. You use us as your playthings then toss us aside.'

'I know, you lucky sods.' Maggie sighed. 'No, I couldn't do it. It wouldn't be fair on Max.'

'Do you know how he feels about you?' Nicki asked.

'I have got a theory, yeah.'

'What's your theory?'

'Something I'm trying very hard not to think about.'

Chapter Thirty-Seven

'Hey, this is all right,' a newly brunette and designer-stubbled Jordan said as he watched the ink on his hands disappear under the heavy scar make-up. 'Waterproof too. Get us a vat of it, I'll go for a swim.'

'Impressive,' Ibby said. 'You can't tell the clock things were ever there.'

Maggie nodded to the door. 'Go change into the shirt Ibs lent you. Let's see the full effect.'

Jordan darted upstairs to change, returning five minutes later in one of Ibby's checked shirts.

'Well?' he said, twirling. 'How do I look?'

Ibby nodded. 'It'd make Georgia cry but it does the job. Now you just look like an ordinary handsome bloke.'

'Thanks, Ibs, you're sweet. Oh! Forgot.' Jordan reached into his pocket for the clear-lens glasses he'd bought online and put them on. 'There. Bite me, Clark Kent.'

'Bloody hell,' Maggie muttered.

'What? Do I look daft?'

'No. You look... like Max Jordan.' She shook her head. 'Wow.'

'You think I'll get away with it, now Ellis is doing time as me over in Antigua? Amelia showed me a photo of him sunbathing in his trunks in *Heat* today. I mean, of me sunbathing in my trunks.' He waved a hand mysteriously. 'Because I was never here.'

'I doubt even Sylvia would recognise you.'

'So when are you going for your first outing, Jord?' Ibby asked.

'Not till this evening. Don't want to push my luck by going out when town's busy.'

'Where will you go?'

'Somewhere I've needed to go for a long time.' He glanced at Maggie. 'Mags, are you free later?'

'Yeah, why?'

'Wondered if you could give me a lift over to Bath. Tarnmoor Crematorium.'

—

Jordan ran his fingers over the lettering on the marble tablet.

Jean Elizabeth Jordan, 1934–2003.
Much loved mother and grandmother.

Missing you.

'Not been here since the funeral,' he said quietly.

'You want me to leave you alone with her?' Maggie asked.

'No, stay, please. She always loved you.'

A woman passed close by, holding a wreath she was delivering to one of the cemetery's other residents. She nodded a friendly hello, no glimmer of recognition in her eyes.

'The new look seems to be working,' Maggie muttered when she'd gone.

'Yeah, pretty effective.'

Jordan looked at the grave in silence for a moment.

'Poxy little thing, isn't it?' he said at last. 'I should get her a new one.'

'I think "Missing You" was the best memorial you could've given her. A grave's just a place to go. A song's a living thing.'

He smiled. 'That's the sort of thing she used to say.'

'Here.' Maggie brushed a tear off his cheek.

'Thanks.'

After another moment's silence, Jordan sighed. 'Come on. Let's go home.'

'Shouldn't we have brought her some flowers?'

'Flowers are for the living, Nana always said. We'll get some for the house, where everyone can enjoy them.'

'That's a nice idea.'

'Anyway, I don't want to leave a trail,' Jordan said in a low voice. 'I'm supposed to be abroad, remember?'

'True.'

They walked back through the cemetery. The lawn was freshly mown, the scent of cut grass and wild flowers filling the air as the sun sank into the horizon. Birds sang to each other in the trees, a reminder that for the living, music – like flowers – could still be enjoyed.

Jordan breathed deeply. 'God, it's good to be outside.'

'We don't have to go straight home. How about I dump the car at the counselling centre and we walk back along the beach?'

'I'd like that,' Jordan said. 'Ages since I saw the town. Hey, is there still that eighties theme pub, Mallett's Mullet?'

'It's a cocktail bar now, Fuzzy Duck's. And the old cinema closed down. The Blue Lagoon's still there though.'

'Everything changes,' he said with a sigh.

'Everything but us,' she murmured, looking away into the distance.

When they got back to Applecroft, the day was turning to dusk. Jordan was glad. No one had given him a second glance since he'd ventured outdoors, but he still felt paranoid about being too visible.

They wandered along the seafront in thoughtful but comfortable silence, past the illuminated Victorian pier casting shimmering arrows of light into the gentle waves. After a while, Jordan took Maggie's hand.

'Why did we break up, Mags?' he asked quietly.

'Because you had to go be a star, didn't you?'

'I was an idiot.' He pressed her hand to his lips. 'I'm sorry. It's overwhelming, that kind of attention when you're nineteen. I let myself get carried away by it, forgot what was really important.'

'If Jean had been around you'd have got a proper earful.'

'Yeah,' he said, smiling. 'She'd never have let me get away with it.'

Maggie sighed. 'I was so worried about you, Max – we all were. You were grieving for your nan, up and down to London every few days, doing coke every night. No one could get through to you.'

They left the ocean to whisper alone and climbed the steps into town.

'Did I break up with you?' Jordan asked. 'I don't even remember.'

'No, I broke up with you. Well, I gave you an ultimatum: the drugs or me. When you rolled up the same night off your face again, I assumed I had my answer.'

'Did I do that?' Jordan shook his head. 'Christ, I must've needed my head examining.'

'You needed a slap. I gave you one of those too, but even that didn't break through.' She laughed; brushed away a tear. 'You broke my heart, Max.'

'And my own.' He nodded to the buttercross, silhouetted in the market square. 'Here's our old friend.'

The buttercross was a symbol of happier times, when the four of them had gathered there to drink cheap beer and share cigarettes on the long summer days after they'd first moved into Number 22.

'Shall we?' Maggie said.

'Let's.'

They sat down on the top step. Jordan turned to face her, taking her two hands in his.

'Maggie, I never wanted to hurt you,' he whispered. 'I'm sorry.'

'I wished you could've stopped hurting yourself,' she said with a sigh. 'I used to cry every night you were down in London, terrified about who you were with and what you were doing to yourself.'

He flinched. 'God, what did I do to you?'

'And when you moved out for good, all I wanted was to forget you. But I couldn't, could I?' She gave a tearful laugh. 'Because pretty soon after, every time I switched on the radio or turned on the TV, there you were. Max Jordan, the love of my bloody life.'

'Mags… really?'

'I mean, that's what it felt like at the time,' she said, dropping eye contact. 'It wasn't easy, getting over you. I think it was only having Ibs that kept me sane.'

'You probably could've done without him knocking you up while he was at it.'

'Well, it worked out for the best. Knowing I was going to have Melie forced me to hold it together.' Maggie smiled. 'You should've seen her, Max. Such a grumpy baby. So beautiful.'

'Can you forgive me?'

'I forgave you a long time ago.' She looked up at him. 'Do you forgive yourself?'

'It's a work in progress,' he admitted. 'Maggie, do you think – if I hadn't gone to London, if I'd never done a line…'

'Would we still be together?' She shrugged. 'What's the point wondering? We are where we are. What-ifs are no good to us now.'

He brought his fingertips up to stroke her cheek. 'But second chances could be.'

'It's… not the right time,' she whispered.

'I think it is. The right time to start again.'

'Max, you're still sick. You need to focus on getting better, not on me.'

'You're all the getting better I need, Lanie.'

He kissed her softly, then drew back, looking at her.

It was eerie, the transformation. With his ash-brown hair and blue eyes he really looked like Max now, her Max. Beautiful, intense, with that passionate innocence in the eyes she remembered so well.

'Max Jordan,' she whispered. 'Never thought I'd see you again.'

Her eyes fell closed as she brought her mouth back to his and let herself get lost in the kiss, in the arms that wrapped around her. An involuntary sigh escaped as he ran his lips over her neck.

'This isn't a good idea,' she whispered.

'You know, I wish you wouldn't keep saying things like that.' He combed gentle fingers through her hair. 'Can't we just enjoy the moment?'

'No, we… look, let's go home. I need to sleep on it before we take this any further.'

'I could help you sleep on it.'

'Alone,' she said, smiling. 'Melie's at home, we have to be good.'

–

When they got back, Ibby was in the hallway, putting his jacket on.

'You off on your date?' Jordan asked.

'Yep, so don't wait up, guys. I'm staying at his tonight.'

Jordan smiled. 'Hope he's stocked up on Viennetta.'

'How was the great outdoors, Jord?'

He glanced at Maggie. 'Very refreshing.'

'Where's Melie?' Maggie asked.

'Georgia's,' Ibby said. 'I took her round after dinner.'

'She's coming back though?'

'No, I said she could sleep over. Hope that's okay with you. I did ring, but your phone was off.'

'So. House to ourselves.' Jordan shot Maggie a significant glance. 'I'll get the wine open. Have fun tonight, Ibs.'

When Jordan had disappeared, Ibby started to open the front door.

'Ibs, don't go out,' Maggie said in a low voice, putting a hand on his arm.

He frowned. 'What?'

'Don't go out. Stay in with us.'

'I have to go out, Nat's got us theatre tickets.'

'Oh. Okay.'

'Why, what's up?'

'Nothing.' She managed a smile. 'I'm being daft. Go have fun.'

'You sure you're okay?'

'I'm fine. Just thought it'd be nice to hang out while Melie's not here. We could've asked Other Max and Nicki over.'

'Well, I'm sure there'll be plenty of other opportunities. She seems to spend half her life at Georgia's these days.' He scanned her face. 'You're positive you're okay?'

'I'm okay. Go on, off you go. Give my love to Nat.'

When he'd gone she went into the sitting room, where Max had poured them each a glass of wine. He was leaning against the mantelpiece, waiting.

'So,' she said brightly. '*Mario Kart* battle?'

'Lanie,' he whispered, and she knew he wasn't going to let her off that easily. Approaching, he took her cheek in his palm and kissed her.

'Max, please…'

'I know you want to.' His arms twined around her. 'I do too. So why not?'

'Because it's not that easy, is it?'

'Tonight it's that easy. Tonight's just for us. Look, the Fates have even arranged an empty house.'

'We shouldn't,' she breathed, tilting her head so he could kiss behind her ear.

'Mmm. You're really putting up a fight there.'

'Max... look, if we do this, we have to be discreet, okay?' she whispered, giving in. 'Melie can't know.'

'I'm the soul of discretion,' he murmured against her skin.

She threw her head back as he pulled her top aside to nuzzle her shoulder. 'God, do you know how long it's been since I last had sex? There've been shorter ice ages.'

'I'll be gentle with you.'

'Not too gentle.'

'You're beautiful, Lanie,' he whispered, his lips falling on the soft flesh exposed by the V of her top. 'So beautiful to me.'

She smiled. 'Bad boy Jordan Nash. I bet it'd ruin your reputation if fans found out you were this sweet behind closed doors.'

'I can be bad.' He pressed her against the wall and his hands slipped up inside her bra. Maggie moaned softly.

'So what would you tell me, if I was a client?' he whispered into the ear he was kissing.

'I'd tell you that you were doing just fine,' she breathed, helping him out of Ibby's shirt. 'Keep it up.'

'Not a problem right now.'

'So I see.'

'God, I missed you. Missed laughing with you.' His fingertips whispered over her breasts. 'Missed touching you.'

'I missed you too,' she said, loving the feel of his naked shoulders against her palms.

'Never really stopped loving you. That's why I wrote the song. I think my subconscious made me write it, to reach out to you again.'

'What?' She pushed him away. 'For God's sake, Max!'

'What? What's wrong?'

'What did you have to go and say that for? You've bloody ruined it now.'

Jordan blinked. 'Come on. You knew I felt that way.'

'You know, I was really looking forward to some nice, simple sex without having to think about anything. I can't do it now.'

'Oh, what? I was looking forward to some as well.'

300

'Yeah, well, nice job cockblocking yourself.' She grabbed her wine off the table. 'I'm going to bed.'

'Can I come?' he yelled after her.

'No! You go to your room and think about what you did. Idiot.'

—

Maggie lay in bed, glaring into the darkness.

Bloody Max. Why couldn't he just keep his big mouth shut? Her first opportunity to have sex in nearly four years and he had to complicate things by dropping the L-bomb on her.

She had to go to work tomorrow too. The first person to start whinging about their sex life was in serious danger of getting a slap. She scrunched her eyes closed, trying to banish the image of Max's bare chest.

'Oh for fuck's sake,' she muttered at last.

Maggie got out of bed, marched to Max's room and flung open the door. She stood silhouetted in his doorway, hair flowing out behind her, like the Second Coming in an M&S nightie.

'Maggie? What's up?'

'I bloody love you too, you stupid bastard. Here, shift up.'

Jordan moved over to make room for her. 'Is this a seduction? It's terrifying.'

'You just had to say it, didn't you?' she said, climbing in with him. 'Now it's not just sex. Now it's love, and that's a whole different can of worms.' She sighed. 'Sorry. You shocked me a bit, that's all.'

'Don't tell me you didn't know.'

'Maybe. I was trying not to think about it so I could have a bit of guilt-free sex with you.'

'No need to feel guilty.' His hand slid into her nightie. 'It's love, Lanie. Sex with love's the purest thing there is.'

'You're a soppy git, Max Jordan.' She ran one finger over his cheek. 'I really did miss you,' she whispered.

She surrendered to soft lips, and let herself fall.

–

'This is going to make things awkward,' she said afterwards as they lay, panting and satisfied, in a tangle of naked limbs.

'Dunno, I didn't think it was that bad.' He nibbled her ear. 'I seem to have remembered where you keep the key erogenous zones.'

'Not what I meant, as you well know,' she said, smiling.

'I did all right then?'

'Yes, you get full marks in the performance department. As if you couldn't tell.'

'Thanks. Means a lot coming from a certified professional.'

'You know what I mean though. We'll tell Ibs but Amelia can't find out. Not yet.'

'We'll be careful.' He rolled on top of her to plant a kiss on her nose. 'I love you. Okay?'

'More than okay.'

'Tired?' he whispered, sliding his hand over her hip.

'Are you kidding?' She rolled him over so she was on top. 'We've got a lot of catching up to do.'

Chapter Thirty-Eight

One Monday, Amelia got up at her extra-early summer holiday rising hour of nine a.m. Her mum started work at ten, so if she wanted a lift to the beach to hang out with her friends, she needed to be up with the world's tardiest larks. Otherwise she'd be stuck in her room all day, trying to avoid Jordan.

She went to the bathroom and picked up the toothpaste tube.

'Mum!' she yelled. 'Is this all the toothpaste?'

'Think so!' her mum called from downstairs.

'There's hardly any left!'

'We've got an extra person living here now, haven't we? Just manage as best you can and I'll pick some up later.'

Amelia scowled at herself in the mirror as she brushed her teeth with a pea-sized amount of paste.

Some of Jordan's stupid designer clothes were drying on a rack outside the bathroom and Amelia nearly tripped on it. She scowled at that too then made her way downstairs.

Jordan was making pancakes, wearing the shabby pink dressing gown of her mum's he always had on in the mornings. Her mum was stuffing ham into bread buns for Amelia's packed lunch.

'Can't you get a proper dressing gown?' Amelia asked him.

'Why, don't you think this one suits me?' he said, twirling for her.

'It's too short. I can see your pants.'

'Is it?' Jordan glanced down. 'Hmm, it is a bit.' He nudged Maggie. 'Lucky I wore pants today, eh?'

Maggie smiled vaguely, but she didn't look at him.

Amelia approved of this. She'd noticed a marked improvement in her mum and Jordan's behaviour these past few days. They'd stopped the flirty touching, and her mum no longer laughed like an idiot at every joke he made. Amelia definitely felt more comfortable leaving them on their own now.

Getting used to Jordan sharing her home was another matter. She was still finding it hard to cope with a new person, a male person, with all his habits and his stuff and his... *him* all over the place. Telly Takeaway Night, formerly her favourite night of the week, was rubbish now. She felt totally left out while Jordan reminisced about what he called 'the good old days' – the days before she was born – with her parents.

She couldn't even have her friends over any more, since Jordan's stay was so super secret. The house was basically in lockdown, with everyone they knew under strict instructions not to call round because of decorators or something. She owed Georgia about five million sleepovers and she didn't know when she'd be able to repay them.

'Pancakes before you head off, kid?' Jordan asked with a friendly smile. 'You can't sunbathe on an empty stomach.'

That was the other thing. He was always so *nice* to her. If he was horrid she could just happily resent him, but when he was all friendly he made her feel annoyed with him and guilty about it all at the same time. That was too many things to feel in one go.

'No thanks,' she muttered.

'Your mum got blueberries. And golden syrup.'

'Well... okay.' She was a sucker for pancakes with blueberries. 'But just one.'

'There, that wasn't so hard, was it?' Jordan said, sliding one onto a plate for her. 'Give it ten years and you might even smile at me.'

'You're not staying ten years, are you?' she asked, horrified.

He smiled. 'Just a figure of speech.'

'How long are you staying? Are you moving out soon?'

'Don't be rude, Melie,' her mum said, frowning.

'Was just wondering.' Amelia tucked into her pancake. 'Mum, can I sleep at Georgia's tonight?'

'No you can't. You've been staying there far too much recently.'

'Mum!'

'No, Amelia. It's not fair on Sally. You can spend time with your family for a change.'

'Fine. Whatever then.' She swallowed down the last of the pancake. 'I'm going to pack my swim stuff.'

'Just a sec,' her mum said. 'You still haven't told me what you want to do for your birthday. Fourteen's kind of a big deal, isn't it?'

'I remember fourteen,' Jordan said. 'Had my first proper snog at my fourteenth birthday party. Jojo Pippin, we went to the same dentist. Nearly got our braces stuck together.'

Maggie nudged him. 'No giving her ideas, you. So what do you think, Melie?'

She shrugged. 'Dunno. Anything.'

'We could take some of your friends out to Bristol for Laser Quest and Maccy Ds.'

Amelia curled her lip. 'No thanks. We're not nine.'

'Well, have a think, okay?'

'Oh.' Amelia produced a piece of paper from her pocket. 'Mum, can you and Dad take me to this? It can be my birthday treat if you want. It's for families but it's in a pub so I need an adult to go with me.'

Maggie took the paper from her. It was a flyer for some band, Sleek Geek, playing at The Blue Lagoon that weekend.

'It's just a band I want to see,' Amelia said. 'Some of them go to my school.'

Maggie smiled. 'Ah. Isaac Helms.'

Amelia started. 'What?'

'He's the bassist, it says here. Funny, I thought I remembered you mentioning an Isaac before.'

Amelia flushed. 'That's nothing to do with it.'

'Sorry, who's Isaac Helms?' Jordan asked.

'The older boy she likes,' Maggie told him.

'Mum!'

Maggie glanced at the date on the flyer. 'Oh, I'm sorry, sweetie, it's this Saturday. I'm away at the conference, remember?'

'Can Dad take me then?'

'He's got plans with Nat. I'm sure he'd cancel for you normally but it's kind of important, he's meeting Nat's mum and dad.'

'I could always take you,' Jordan said. 'I mean, if it's okay with your parents.'

Amelia stared at him. 'You?'

'Yeah, why not? I'd be interested to hear the band. I used to be in one myself, you know.'

Maggie frowned. 'Are you sure it's safe, Max? It'll be busy.'

'I'll be okay if I keep the glasses on. No one's even looked at me so far, I've got the ultimate in forgettable faces.'

'What do you say, Melie?' her mum said. 'Uncle Other Max and Nicki might be able to go along too. I could ask them for you.'

A short battle went on inside Amelia. Spending time with Jordan was absolutely the last thing she wanted to do, but she hadn't seen Isaac for nearly a month. Plus Jordan knew all about music stuff. Maybe he could tell her some impressive things to say to Isaac.

'Okay.' She jabbed a finger at Jordan. 'But I'm in charge, right?'

'Right,' Jordan said, smiling.

–

It wasn't much of a beach day, Amelia thought, as another fat blob of rain plopped into her ham sandwich.

It had started out nice enough. The sun had shone. Rory had turned up to challenge Amelia and Georgia to a supersoaker fight, which was a pretty fun way to cool off, although Georgia whispered her theory that it was just a ploy to get their t-shirts wet so Rory could see their bras. But Amelia was willing to overlook it, with him being a boy and everything. They couldn't help being tragic, poor things, it was in their genes.

But by lunchtime, everything had turned a bit grey. They were just tucking into their packed lunches when the first drops started to fall.

'This is rubbish,' Amelia said, shovelling the whole sandwich into her mouth before it dissolved.

'My mascara's running,' Georgia said – mainly, Amelia reckoned, because she wanted them to know she was wearing mascara. 'I'm ringing my mum.'

'Yeah, me too.' Rory's red hair was plastered to his forehead. 'Melie, you want a lift?'

Amelia thought gloomily about spending an afternoon stuck in the house with Jordan. But there was nothing else for it. She was drenched to the skin thanks to the rain and Rory's supersoakers.

'Okay,' she said, shivering.

Half an hour later, Rory's mum's car pulled into The Cedars.

'You can come hang out at mine if you want,' Rory said.

His mum nodded. 'You're always welcome, Amelia.'

'You could stay for dinner too. We've got turkey dinosaurs.'

Amelia was tempted. It'd certainly be more fun than hiding from Jordan at home. But she was wet through, and she really wanted a bath.

'Not today, thank you,' she said. 'Another time though.'

'Okay.' Rory pointed to her front door. 'Hey, who's that outside your house?'

Amelia followed his gaze. There was a woman knocking at her door. She was wrapped in a big raincoat and wearing sunglasses, but the bleach-blonde hair and fishy pout were very familiar.

Sylvia Nash.

'Dunno,' Amelia lied, impressed with her own calm.

'Could it be a journalist?' Rory's mum asked.

After the Ibbotson-Nightingale household's recent brush with fame, a protective community instinct had kicked in that Amelia found rather flattering. She'd never realised how much people liked them.

'I don't think so,' she said, hoping Rory's mum wouldn't offer to come to the door with her. 'She looks like... someone my mum knows. It's fine, I can tell her to come back later. See you, Rory. Thanks, Mrs McCallum.'

She got out of the car and headed for her house. Sylvia was hammering on the door, peering through the frosted glass.

Did she know about Jordan being there? Amelia wondered whether to phone and warn him, or ring her dad to come and make Sylvia go away.

But it was too late, Sylvia had seen her. Her too-plump lips spread into a grin.

'Is this your house, little girl?' she asked, blocking Amelia's access.

'Yes. What do you want?'

'You, actually. You're Amelia, aren't you? Your mummy's Maggie Nightingale.'

Sylvia was leaning down, adopting the patronising tone Amelia herself might use to a kid of three.

'Why do you want to know?' she demanded.

'Because I think you might be able to help me. Can I come in?'

'I'm not allowed to let strangers in.'

'I'm not a stranger, am I? I bet you've seen me loads on TV.'

'I've seen you,' Amelia said. 'You were rubbish.'

Sylvia's grin flickered.

'Now, I know you can help,' she said, screwing it back into place. 'You've heard of my son, of course, Jordan Nash. I bet you and your little friends love him, don't you?'

'No,' Amelia said, then immediately bit her tongue. That was a dead giveaway. She had to act like any normal kid who loved Route 69, like Georgia, not like someone who came face to face with the unsexy vision of Jordan in her mum's dressing gown every morning. 'I mean, yeah. Love him.'

'Then you'll know how worried I've been,' Sylvia said in a sad little infant voice, blinking back an invisible tear. 'Since he disappeared.'

'You've been in all the newspapers.'

'That's right.'

'Don't people normally go to the police when someone they love goes missing?'

Sylvia's grin was starting to look sprayed on. 'The newspapers have more reach.'

'And they pay you money, right? To give them interviews? My dad's a journalist, I know how that stuff works.'

'That's... not important.'

'Well, I haven't seen your son so I don't know why you're asking me. He was my mum's friend, not mine.'

Sylvia tinkled a laugh. 'Well no, you ridiculous child, I wouldn't expect you to have actually *seen* him. But I just bet he's contacted your mummy.'

'If he's contacted her and not you, then I guess he probably doesn't want you to know where he's gone.'

Sylvia looked triumphant. 'Then she does know where he is! And I'm sure she mentioned it to you, didn't she? You look like the sort of clever girl who always knows what's going on.'

'I didn't say she knew, I said you didn't. So that means Jordan doesn't want you to find him.' Amelia smiled sweetly. 'Otherwise he'd have told you, wouldn't he?'

Sylvia let her face settle into a scowl. 'You really are the rudest child.'

'I know all about you,' Amelia said, standing her ground. 'I know you're horrid and you left him when he was a little boy. So you can just go away and leave us alone. We don't know where he's gone anyway.'

Sylvia leaned down and stared into her face. 'I don't believe you, Amelia. I know what lying looks like, I'm a seasoned pro.'

'Well, it's true,' Amelia said, not letting her face flicker. 'It says in *Heat* he's in somewhere called Antigua. Why don't you go there?'

'I did go there,' she muttered. 'There was no sign of him.'

'Why do you want to find him so much anyways?'

'Because I'm his mother, of course,' Sylvia said, summoning a smile that didn't extend to her eyes. 'He's sick. I want to help him.'

'You just want to be famous. And you're not famous unless he's famous, and now people aren't talking about him as much so you want to find him and make him be in a band again. You don't love him like... like a proper mum, like my mum.'

'You're a child. You don't know what you're saying.'

'Yeah, fine, whatever,' Amelia said, rolling her eyes. 'But we don't know anything about where he is so you might as well go home. Bye.' She pushed past Sylvia and started unlocking the door.

'You little—' Sylvia grabbed her arm, her long nails digging hard into the flesh. 'Don't lie to me. You know exactly where he is.'

'You're hurting me,' Amelia said in a low voice, her eyes darting from side to side. If the neighbours came, there could be trouble. She had to stop anyone finding out Jordan was right there in the house.

'Where's Jordan, you little bitch?' Sylvia demanded, her face twisting. Amelia thought it looked like her true face, the one she kept hidden inside her behind the plastic surgery. It was ugly and full of hate. 'I swear, if you don't tell me what you know I'll make life miserable for the whole pack of you, you and your weird fucking parents.'

'Get *off!*' Using all her strength, Amelia wrenched her arm from Sylvia's grip and darted into the house. Sylvia tried to wedge her foot in the door and whimpered as Amelia slammed it away. Finally, Amelia got the thing shut and locked it with a trembling hand.

She ran into the kitchen, where Jordan was baking.

'Someone at the door, kid?' he asked. 'There was a lot of knocking.'

Amelia stared at him, familiar and friendly as ever. And suddenly she didn't care that Jordan was in her house, leaving his things around and flirting with her mum. All she cared about was that she was a kid and she was frightened and he was the only grown-up she trusted who was around to look after her. She burst into tears and threw herself at him for a hug.

Jordan, who'd never had to comfort a sobbing child before, patted her head in what he supposed was the proper way to go about it.

'Hey,' he said gently. 'What's up, Amelia? You're soaking wet, sweetheart.'

'Your... mum,' she gasped between sobs. 'She's... here.'

'Sylvia's here! Where, outside?'

'Yes,' Amelia whispered.

'Does she know I'm here?'

'No. She came for me. She wanted to know if Mum had told me where you were.'

'For you?'

'Yeah. But I told her I didn't know where you were and I slammed the door on her foot.' Amelia sniffed. 'Jordan, she was so mean. She swore at me and she called me names and... it was really scary.'

'She can't hurt you now. I won't let her.' Jordan looked down at her, impressed. 'You did that? That took a lot of guts.'

'Not really,' Amelia muttered, secretly pleased.

Jordan went to peep through the blinds. 'Looks like she's gone now.' He shook his head. 'She's got a bloody nerve, pardon my language. Exploiting me, that's one thing, but when she starts going after people I care about to get to me...'

'Jordan, she grabbed me. It really hurt.' Amelia rolled up her sleeve to show him the angry red welts Sylvia's nails had left in her skin. They were already starting to bruise.

'Oh my *God!*' Jordan took her arm to examine them. 'She did that to you? That—' He stopped himself. 'I'm sorry, kid.'

'It's okay.'

'It really isn't.' Jordan looked at her soaking clothes. 'You'd better get dry things on before you catch cold. I need to ring someone.'

'Who?'

'Friend of mine who's a journalist.'

'My dad, you mean?'

'That's right.' Jordan's brow knit. 'I'm going to make sure Sylvia finally gets what she deserves.'

–

'What's up? Is Melie okay?' Ibby demanded when he burst into the house ten minutes after Jordan's call.

'A bit shaken. She's just having a bath. Poor thing was shivering to the bone.'

'What happened?'

Jordan's brow lowered. 'My fucking mother.'

'Sylvia was here? How'd she find you, Jord?'

'She didn't.' Jordan scowled at the carpet. 'She came for the kid.'

'Melie? Why?'

'Sylvia's a scavenger. They always prey on the weakest. Except she underestimated her, because Amelia's a hundred times stronger than she'll ever be.'

'What happened? Tell me.'

'Sounds like Sylvia started grilling her on where I was. Melie told her to sod off.'

Ibby nodded. 'That's my girl.'

'Ibs, I'm so sorry,' Jordan said, grimacing. 'I never thought she'd drag you guys in. She hurt Melie's arm.'

'Hurt? How hurt?' Ibby said, alarmed.

'It'll bruise, but she doesn't need a trip to A&E or anything.' Jordan shook his head. 'Jesus, she's some piece of work, that woman. I feel sick every time I remember she's part of me.'

'You're you, Jord. Don't think of it that way.'

'Yeah, that's why I wanted to talk to you. I'm taking a stand, Ibby. I'm finally getting Sylvia out of my life – all our lives.'

'Okay. And where do I fit in?'

'Mate, how'd you like the exclusive on the last ever interview with Jordan Nash?'

Chapter Thirty-Nine

'What're you doing?' Amelia asked when she came downstairs the next afternoon to find Jordan sitting in her dad's armchair, tapping away at his laptop.

'Writing my memoirs.'

'Does that mean like… memories?'

'Kind of. Memoirs is what you call a book someone writes about their life.'

'Why are you writing a book?'

'I'm not, I'm writing notes on some stuff for your dad. He's doing an interview with me for one of the newspapers.'

'What'll you say in the interview?'

'Oh, I've got plenty to say,' Jordan said, looking determined. 'There's a lot about my mother the public doesn't know. The things she's done to me. And to others.'

'Are you writing it because of her coming to the house?'

'Not only that.' He looked up at her. 'How's your arm, kid?'

She rolled up her sleeve to show him the purpling nail marks. 'Kind of sore.'

'She's gone too far this time,' Jordan muttered. 'Time to give the Jordan family dirty laundry a bloody good airing.'

'Um, can I sit in here with you?' Amelia asked, scuffing the carpet with the toe of her sock. She had her own laptop under one arm. 'I'm doing homework so I'll be quiet.'

Jordan glanced up. Amelia nearly always hid in her room when she knew he was downstairs.

'Sure.'

She settled on the sofa with her laptop.

'So to what do I owe the pleasure of your company then?' Jordan asked.

'Just... you were nice to me yesterday, when your mum came. And you said she hurt people you care about, and I guess that meant me as well as Mum and Dad. And... I sort of decided I want us to be friends.'

Jordan blinked. 'Wow. There's a lot to take in there.'

'I'm sorry,' she mumbled. 'For not being nice. You were nice to me and I was mean back.'

'Well, it's not easy, sharing your home with a new person,' Jordan said, shooting her what he hoped was an understanding smile. 'I do appreciate it, you know. You asking me to stay when I wasn't doing so well.' He held up a hand so she could see how steady it was. 'See that? You helped me get better.'

'I knew it was a good thing to do. But I wasn't happy about it.' Amelia smiled. 'I am now though. You're okay.'

'High praise coming from you.' Jordan stood up and held out his hand. 'Friends then?'

'Friends,' she said, shaking it.

'So can I see what homework you're doing?'

'If you want. It's rubbish though. Can't make it work.'

Jordan sat down beside her and scanned the screen. 'Oh,' he said, blinking. 'Python. That brings back memories.'

Amelia stared at him. '*You* know Python?'

'Yeah. I was a computer science student when I met your parents, you know.'

'You?' Amelia said, in a tone of such surprise that Jordan couldn't help laughing.

'Yep, me. If the Routers ever found out there was just a big geek under the layers of rock star, I'd be finished. Lucky I already decided to quit.' He nodded to the laptop screen. 'That won't work until you put the missing equals sign in line twelve. You need two, not one.'

'Ugh.' Amelia grimaced as she fixed the code. 'I've been trying to work out what was wrong for ages. I *hate* stupid Python.'

'You say that now, but one day it'll just click and you won't be able to stop. It's like learning to read – painful as hell, but once you've mastered it you can't remember a time you couldn't do it.'

'I just can't get it. All the kids in Coding Club are ahead of me.'

'Why do you go to the club if you're not enjoying it?'

She flushed. 'Isaac. He helps out.'

'The boy you like?'

'Yeah. It's the only time I get to talk to him.' She glanced up at him. 'Jordan, do you like my mum? I think she likes you.'

'Yeah. I like her a lot, I always did. Is that okay?'

'S'pose,' she muttered.

'I didn't come to steal her off you, you know,' he said gently. 'She'll always be your mum, whatever she feels about me.'

'I know. And I like that she seems happy when you're around. But...'

'But?'

'Sometimes when you're there, it's like she's gone back to being a kid again. Like, as if I was never born.' Amelia looked down at her fingers splayed on the keys. 'I mean, as if she wishes I hadn't been.'

'Aww, Melie. Is that how you've been feeling?'

'A bit. Mum and Dad keep telling me I'm being silly, but I can't help thinking it.'

'You know it's not true though, right? Your mum genuinely thinks you're the best thing that's ever happened to her,' Jordan said. 'Last time you were out, she spent the whole night showing me baby photos. Eventually even I had to admit you were kind of impressive. To shut her up, mainly.'

Amelia's eyes went wide. 'Not where I'm in those tragic knitted cardigans my Nana Nightingale sent from Canada?'

"Fraid so.'

'Ugh! She is *so* embarrassing.'

He smiled. 'You were pretty cute though. I mean, a bit hairy.'

Amelia tapped absently at the Caps Lock key. 'It's just that when we're all together, it feels like we're not a family any more. Like you're all friends, you and Mum and Dad, and I'm the odd one out.'

'You know that's exactly how I've been feeling?'

She frowned. 'You?'

'Yeah. When I see you three all loving each other like families should, it just hammers home that I'm not part of that.'

'Does it?'

Jordan nodded. 'It reminds me I haven't got anything like that in my life. That I spent the last fourteen years – well, never mind what I was doing. But I made the wrong choices once upon a time and now… let's just say there's a lot I missed out on.' He smiled. 'But it still makes me happy to see you. Your mum and dad are good people, Amelia, they deserve good things. And you deserve a mum and dad like them.'

'You did too,' Amelia said. 'I mean, you deserved a nice mum like mine instead of a horrid one.'

'I did have one. My nana was the best mum I could've had. I guess families come in all shapes and sizes, don't they?'

Amelia nodded. Her family was a bit different to most others too.

'Do you miss your nana?' she asked.

'Every day.'

'My Grandad Ibbotson died last year. It made me feel the most sad I'd ever felt.'

'For me too.'

'I'm sorry your nana died, Jordan.'

'Thank you. I'm sorry too, about your grandad.' He nodded to her screen. 'So what do you say, kid? Will we wow gorgeous Isaac with this Magic 8 Ball program of yours?'

'You mean you'll finish the project for me?' Amelia asked hopefully.

'Nice try,' he said, smiling. 'No, I mean we'll finish it together. Trust me, by the time your mum and dad get home, you won't be able to remember a time you hated Python.'

—

'Dad,' Amelia said when Ibby got home. 'Ask my computer a question.'

'Er, okay. Who'd win in a fight between a T-Rex and the Predator, Amelia's computer?'

'Has to be yes or no, Dad,' Amelia said, rolling her eyes.

'And it's Predator,' Jordan said.

'Right,' Ibby said. 'Amelia's computer. Will meeting Nat's parents go well on Saturday?'

Amelia fed the question to her Magic 8 Ball simulator. 'All signs point to yes, it says.'

'Oh, well. Can't ask for a fairer answer than that.'

'Thanks for helping me, Jordan,' Amelia said, beaming at him.

'So how are we feeling about Python now?' Jordan asked.

'Loads better. It's fun, isn't it? I mean, when you can actually make it do stuff, like games and stuff.'

'We can work on something else tomorrow if you want. How about a simple platform game?'

'Oooh, yes please. That sounds great.'

'Isaac'll be impressed, right?'

Amelia blinked. It was funny, but she'd been so focused on getting her program to work, she'd almost forgotten Isaac. For the first time, she'd actually enjoyed coding for its own sake.

'Right. Yeah,' she said.

'By the time school starts again, you'll be way ahead.'

'I'm going to WhatsApp Rory. I bet he's never done a platform game.' She grabbed the laptop and dashed off upstairs.

'You've been helping her with her project?' Ibby asked Jordan, chucking himself down on the sofa.

'Yep. Not bad for a CompSci dropout, right?'

Ibby was silent.

'Ibs?'

'Hmm? Oh. Yeah.' He lowered his voice. 'She hasn't sussed about you and Mags, has she?'

'She's worked out there's a mutual attraction there. She doesn't know about us being together, but she's definitely coming round to the idea.'

Ibby sighed. 'We're going to have to make a plan at some point. Everything's changing.'

'But it doesn't need to change too quickly. One day at a time, eh?'

'Guess so.'

Jordan nudged him. 'How about your love life? Magic 8 Ball seemed to think things were going well.'

Ibby smiled, but he didn't answer; just picked at a thread on his jeans.

Jordan examined him. 'Ibs, are you blushing?'

'No. Get lost.'

'You are! Come on, what is it?'

'There may have been an L-word exchange at Nat's over the weekend,' Ibby confided. 'No piss-taking from you, okay?'

'Who, me?' Jordan said, grinning. 'Good news, mate. Sounds like you've got a keeper there.'

'I know. Never thought I'd find one who could cope with me.' Ibby glanced around. 'Or all of this. Course, he doesn't know I've got a megastar hiding out in the spare bedroom yet.'

There was the sound of the front door opening, and a second later Maggie joined them. Ibby shuffled up to make room for her between them.

'Evening, menfolks.' She kissed Ibby on the cheek, did a quick scan of the area, then leaned round to peck Jordan on the lips. 'No Melie?'

'She's upstairs,' Ibby said. 'Jord's been helping her with Python. Now she's carried away with her own genius and showing off to Rory over WhatsApp.'

Maggie nodded. 'Nice one, Max.'

Ibby gestured to Jordan's laptop on the coffee table. 'So what've you written for me?'

'I just slammed down everything I could think of,' Jordan said. 'Stuff I remember from when I was tiny, stuff my nana told me. When the public gets wind, it'll kill her so-called career stone dead.' He sighed. 'I'll have to pay her an allowance though. Enough to live on, at least.'

'Cut her off, Max,' Maggie said. 'She's never done a thing except cause you pain.'

'I can't just leave her to rot, can I?'

'She left you to rot.'

'Which is exactly why I can't do the same to her.' He flipped open his laptop. 'So how are we going to play this, Ibs? I'm sure any of the redtops'll snap it up.'

'You sure you want me to do this?' Ibby asked. 'I've never had anything in the nationals before.'

'Course I do, it's just how. We don't want them to work out I'm here.'

'I could pitch it under a pseudonym.'

'But then you wouldn't get your byline,' Maggie said.

Jordan shook his head. 'No, that's part of the deal. This is an Aaron Ibbotson exclusive.'

'How then?' Ibby asked.

'Supposing I got Craig to set up a photoshoot with the body double, Ellis? Lying about in a hammock sipping cocktails?'

'I see where you're going. "When I spoke with an old friend from student days, Max Jordan – better known to the public as Jordan Nash – he was sunning himself on a private beach in Antigua…"'

'"…far from drizzly Somerset, where we'd misspent our youth…"'

'Does this bloke really look enough like you to get away with it at close range though, Max?' Maggie asked.

'Not far off, with a bit of Photoshopping on the nose. I'll get Craig to set it up.' Jordan closed the laptop. 'And once it's done, I can finally get Sylvia out of my life for good.'

Chapter Forty

Amelia couldn't sleep. She'd seen something, and it was preying on her mind.

It had been late when she'd seen it, long after she should've been asleep. Her dad had gone to bed, but her mum and Jordan were up. Amelia's throat had been stinging after a day breathing the salt sea air, and she'd been gagging for a glass of something wet.

So she'd crept down the stairs, quietly so as not to wake her dad, then hovered at the door of the sitting room. Her mum and Jordan were in there, talking. Actually they were arguing, but not in an angry way. It was what adults usually called 'a discussion'.

She hadn't meant to listen. Her parents had taught her it was rude to interrupt, so she'd waited for a break in the conversation to make her presence known and ask if it was okay to come through to the kitchen for a drink.

'Max, we can't,' her mum was saying. 'There's been too much change for her lately. All that business with the press, then her dad and Nat, and you hiding out here. Plus general growing-up stuff on top. She has to be prepared, we can't just dump it on her.'

'I think she is prepared,' Jordan said. 'She practically gave us her blessing the other day.'

'Look, it's great that the two of you are getting along. But to tell her you're my boyfriend so soon...'

'I love you, Lanie, and I want everyone to know it.'

There was a pause. Amelia, too curious now to stop eaves-dropping, peeped through a crack in the door.

Oh. They were kissing. Ick. She stopped peeping.

'I want that too,' her mum said when they'd done. 'But everyone can't know, can they? Because you're... you. Jordan Nash. If you weren't, you wouldn't need to be hiding here in the first place.'

'We can tell Amelia though. She'll be pleased, I know it.'

'But her needs come first. Something like this, it makes everything different. She's got plenty to worry about already with the new term starting soon.'

'I just hate lying to her,' Jordan said. 'She's a sweet kid. Doesn't seem fair, keeping her out of the loop in her own house.'

'Look, give it a month, let her settle into the new routine at school. When we've got a plan for what happens next, then we'll talk to her. Okay?'

'If that's what you think is best.'

'Thanks, Max. I love you.'

'Love you too, darling.'

They fell silent, which Amelia guessed meant they were kissing again.

She crept back upstairs. She filled the toothbrush glass at the bathroom tap and swallowed some minty water to ease her throat, then went back to bed.

It was funny, she reflected, as she lay thinking. She didn't feel how she'd expected she would.

Everything was changing, and yeah, that was scary. But the changes at home didn't seem nearly as terrifying as the other big changes she was about to face. Turning fourteen. Year Ten. GCSEs...

That was the thing. When you were growing up, every day meant change.

She did like Jordan, now she'd got used to him being around. She liked how her mum smiled and laughed all the time, and let her get away with stuff she couldn't before, because Jordan was making her happy. She liked how he was friends with her dad, so she knew he'd never try to take his place the way Dan had.

Another boyfriend might do though. No, if her mum had to have a boyfriend, it was probably best if it was Jordan. He understood how their family worked.

Pretty soon, she heard her mum brushing her teeth and going into her bedroom. Amelia waited until she heard Jordan go to his room, then sneaked out and knocked on her mum's door.

'Another late-night visit,' Maggie said when she opened it. 'What is it this time, Melie?'

Amelia plonked herself on the edge of the bed. Her mum sat down next to her.

'Mum, I wanted you to know... something.'

'At this time of night?'

'Yeah. It's been keeping me awake.'

'What's wrong, my love?' Maggie said, looking concerned.

'I just wanted to say... I like it when you laugh a lot and you're happy.'

'Aww. Sweetness.' Maggie ruffled her hair. 'Did you come in just to tell me that?'

'No. I wanted to say as well that I don't want to do Telly Takeaway Night tomorrow.'

'I thought you loved Telly Takeaway Night.'

'Yeah, but I think it's weird for Jordan. He feels left out.'

'I'm sure that's not true.'

'He does, I know it. I thought we could play *Trivial Pursuit* or *Mario Kart* or something instead, so we can all join in.'

'Melie, are you saying you want him to feel like he's part of the family?'

'I guess. I mean, he's staying here, so he sort of is. And he's your friend so... I want to be nice to him. Not ruin you being happy.'

Maggie pulled her into a hug. 'Amelia, you're amazing. You know that?'

'I'm just me,' Amelia mumbled.

'Exactly. You're just wonderful little you. Now go to bed, it's late.'

–

'...and don't eat nothing but rubbish while I'm away,' Maggie told Amelia as she prepared to leave for her conference the following Saturday. 'I've told Max to keep an eye on what you put in your packed lunches. Don't walk to the beach on your own, don't stay up too late – oh, and if anyone knocks at the door when there's no adults around—'

'—don't answer it, I know,' Amelia said, rolling her eyes. 'You're only going for two days, Mum.'

'If you need anything and you can't get hold of Dad then ask Max, or give Nana or Aunty Beth a ring. I'll call you after the gig to check you got home okay.'

'Mum, just go already. I'll be fine.'

'Okay.' Maggie still looked hesitant. 'You're sure though?'

'I completely promise I won't have a wild party or burn the house down or anything.'

Maggie gave her a goodbye hug. 'Are you going to the beach today?'

'Yeah, Rory's mum's going to drive us.'

'Well, let Max know and he can pick you up from there. Uncle Other Max and Nicki are meeting you at the pub. And remember, don't call Max his proper name when people are listening. Call him... John.'

'John. Right.'

'Have fun, my love.' Maggie gave her daughter a kiss and headed down the drive to the car.

'You too!' Amelia called after her, although a counselling and psychotherapy conference sounded like the ultimate in boring to her.

Whereas she was going out tonight to have some real fun. This evening, she'd finally get to see Isaac again. Playing his guitar too – how sexy would that be? The worst thing was going to be counting the minutes until it was time.

–

Amelia was hanging out with Georgia near her dad's ice cream van when she spotted Jordan, dressed in one of her dad's shirts and a pair of sunglasses. She waved to him.

'Is that your mum's new boyfriend then?' Georgia asked.

'Yeah.'

Georgia shot him an uninterested glance then resumed scrolling her Instagram feed.

'What do you think, Georgie?' Amelia couldn't help herself. 'Good-looking?'

'God, no! I mean, maybe to your mum, but he's like a hundred. What's he called?'

'Jo – er, John.'

'You like him?'

Amelia shrugged. 'He's okay when you get used to him.'

'I can't believe your mum dumped Jordan Nash just to end up with someone ordinary like that.'

'Maybe Jordan Nash is ordinary. Maybe all famous people are.'

'Jordan could never be ordinary,' Georgia said fervently. 'You know, him and your mum could've been married by now. How fierce would that be? You'd be epicly rich.'

'Yeah, except I'd never have been born, would I?' Amelia grabbed her beach bag. 'Right, I have to get ready.'

She fumbled for some pink lip gloss, slicked a bit on and checked her reflection in her compact mirror.

She'd been hoping a day by the sea would have resulted in the coveted beach waves that were the in thing this summer, but she wasn't sure she'd quite pulled it off. Her hair mainly just looked fluffy. She did have a nice, deep tan though, plus a gorgeous new midi sundress her mum had bought her to wear over her bikini. If Isaac did spot her in the crowd, she wanted him to think she looked pretty but beach-casual – like the sort of girl who could pull off any old look without even trying. Boys never seemed to realise how much hard work it took to look effortlessly pretty.

'What do you think?' she asked Georgia when she's pulled on her new dress, giving her a twirl.

Georgia eyed her critically.

'Not bad,' she said at last. 'You look older with your hair like that.'

Amelia beamed.

'WhatsApp me later, tell me all about the gig,' Georgia said. 'Wish I was coming.' Georgia's mum was rather less liberal than Amelia's parents when it came to the idea of her fourteen-year-old daughter spending the night in the pub.

'Okay.' Amelia grabbed her bag. 'See you tomoz.'

She headed to the Chilled Reads van. Jordan was leaning against the counter, chatting to her dad.

'So. First gig. You excited, Melie?' her dad asked when she joined them.

Amelia shrugged.

'That means yes,' Ibby told Jordan. 'Thanks for taking her, mate. Sorry I can't come. Big night for me and Nat.'

'Do you think his mum and dad'll like you?' Amelia asked.

'What's not to like, right?'

'Good luck, Ibs,' Jordan said, slapping his arm. 'Come on then, kid. Let's go see if Isaac's good enough to make me cry into my guitar.'

They set off for The Blue Lagoon. Amelia was silent. Something Georgia had said before had got her thinking.

'What's up, Melie?' Jordan asked. 'Not missing your mum already?'

'No.' Amelia stared at the pub as it loomed into view. 'Hey. Could you buy that pub?'

Jordan blinked. 'Er, I guess so, yeah.'

'Could you buy… a horse?'

'I don't want a horse.'

'Yeah, but could you?'

'Why not? I could keep it in my new pub and make insulting comments about the length of its face. What's the sudden interest in me buying things?'

'Just wondered how rich you were,' she said, shrugging.

He laughed. 'Why, are you after a loan?'

'I was thinking about you and my mum. Because if you got married then she'd be rich too, wouldn't she? And we'd never have to worry about being poor again like when I was little.'

'Are we getting married now? Nice to know you've planned it all out.'

She looked up at him. 'I know, you know.'

'What do you know?'

'About you and Mum.'

Jordan looked taken aback for a second. Then he smiled.

'So are you mad at us for keeping it secret?'

Amelia shrugged. 'A bit. But I don't mind if she's happy.'

He gave her shoulders a squeeze. 'Thanks, kid. That'll please your mum, she's been worrying herself daft about how to tell you.'

Inside the pub, Jordan nodded hello to Other Max and Nicki, who'd claimed a table for them in a sheltered corner, and headed to the bar.

'Pint of Best please, and a Diet Pepsi for this one,' he said to the barmaid. Amelia noticed he changed his voice slightly, giving it a faint Scottish lilt.

The barmaid blushed a little as she started pouring their drinks. Amelia rolled her eyes. She knew what that meant. Well, the woman could keep her hands off. Jordan was her mum's boyfriend, he wasn't on the market.

'I suppose you get this all the time, but from a certain angle you really remind me of someone,' the woman said.

'Yeah, I've been told that before.'

Amelia tensed. Could the woman have recognised him, even with the glasses?

'Jamie Fraser,' the barmaid said. 'You know, from *Outlander*? If your hair was a shade redder you'd be the spit of him.' Amelia let herself breathe again.

Jordan blinked. 'Oh. Right.'

'So is this your daughter?' the barmaid asked, sliding over their drinks.

'No, I'm a family friend.' Jordan smiled his most charming smile as he handed her a tenner.

'Actually he's my mum's boyfriend,' Amelia said, crossing her arms.

'I see,' the barmaid said, sounding disappointed.

'We're here for the band,' Jordan said. 'What time are they on?'

'Not long now. They're just warming up in the function room. Trembling like whippets with stagefright, poor boys.'

'Mmm, I bet they are.' Jordan winked as he took the drinks. 'Cheers, sweetheart.'

'I saw that,' Amelia said as they made their way to the table.

'Saw what?'

'You. Flirting. Don't think I won't tell Mum.'

'I was flirting my way out of trouble,' he whispered. 'She was five seconds from working out who I really reminded her of.'

'Hmm. How come you went Scottish?'

'I am Scottish. A bit. My nana was Scottish.'

'You're not normally Scottish.'

'Well, maybe I'm only Scottish when I'm Jamie Fraser.'

When they reached the others, Jordan leaned over the table to shake Other Max's hand. He and Nicki had been round a few times since the fateful night Ibby had discovered Jordan drunk in the porch, but it had been a couple of weeks since they'd all seen each other.

'You're looking well, Jord,' Other Max said.

'You have to call him John,' Amelia told him in a whisper.

'Sorry, Melie,' Other Max said, smiling. 'Er, John, mate. You're looking well there.'

'Thanks.' Jordan sat down with his beer. 'I'm a new man these days. Even quit smoking, I'm sure you medical types'll approve.'

Nicki shook her head. 'I still can't get over how different you look.'

'Yeah, I'm channelling Jamie Fraser apparently.'

'Oh, I like him,' Nicki said, a dreamy look in her eyes.

Other Max nudged her. 'Oi. You've got your quota of ginger blokes.'

'So what's this band then, Amelia?' Nicki asked. 'They'd better be good. I painted my nails for this.'

'They will be,' Amelia said.

Jordan glanced towards the group of boys setting up their equipment. 'Which one's your one, Melie?'

'It's the bassist,' Other Max said.

'The one with the glasses?' Nicki squinted at the skinny, nervous-looking teenager in the oversized glasses. 'He's a bit old for you, honey.'

Amelia groaned. 'Did my mum tell everyone about it?'

'Actually your dad told us,' Other Max said.

Jordan shook his head. 'Worst parents ever.'

'So you're in loco parentis tonight then, Johnny,' Other Max said. 'You going to grill this Isaac on his intentions?'

'No, but I might have to find out who his favourite Harrison Ford character is,' Jordan said, shooting Amelia a grin.

But she wasn't paying attention to their teasing now Isaac was in her sights.

He was even more beautiful than she remembered. His hair had grown a bit and he was forever pushing it out of his eyes in that way that just made her melt. He was super tanned after the hot summer they'd enjoyed too, his green eyes sparkling as they peeped from nut-brown skin.

He smiled and waved when he spotted her staring. Flushing, Amelia waved back.

'You've gone a very funny colour, you know,' Jordan said.

'Shut up. Haven't.'

'What happens if his band's rubbish? Will you go off him?'

'No,' she said, rolling her eyes. 'I can't just *go off him*. It's deeper than that.'

'Okay,' Jordan said penitently. 'Sorry, I didn't realise it was as deep as all that.' He groaned as the band started their first song. 'Oh God. No one told me they did covers.'

'You know, I think I actually prefer this version,' Nicki said to Other Max.

He nodded soberly. 'It's pretty much definitive.'

Jordan tried not to grimace as the band gave his first hit, 'Missing You', a thorough going-over.

It was always weird, hearing someone else singing lyrics that had a particular meaning for the writer. Sleek Geek weren't exactly bad, but... well, they sounded like what they were: a schoolboy band. In a pub. Singing about his nana.

'Is it weird?' Amelia asked, as if reading his thoughts.

'A bit.' Jordan lowered his voice. 'They won't know this, but I wrote that song for my nana after she died.'

'Why write her a song after she'd died? Then she wouldn't hear it.'

'But I would. I like to write songs for people I love.'

'Like you did for my mum?'

'Yeah,' he said quietly.

'Do you love her a lot?'

'You want the truth, Melie?'

She shrugged, which Jordan had worked out by now was Teenager for yes.

'I do love her a lot,' he said. 'More than I've ever loved anyone, in fact.'

'Will you get married?' Amelia asked, wide-eyed.

Jordan hesitated a moment. 'I hope so, yes. If we did, how would you feel about it?'

'I don't know. I'd have to think about it.'

'Okay. You let me know, all right?'

Other Max raised an eyebrow at Nicki.

There were a couple more covers and then the band launched into something of their own, with Isaac taking lead vocals. Amelia listened hard to the lyrics, wondering if he'd written them.

'So is he good?' she demanded of Jordan when they'd finished. 'He's very shouty. That means he's passionate, right?'

Jordan smiled. 'Sorry. Not if he's not making me believe it.'

Amelia's face fell. 'So he's not good?'

'His performance is okay. He just needs to find something he genuinely believes in rather than faking it. At the moment all he's got are Route 69 covers and copycat songs. That's Jordan Nash's rage, not his.'

'What used to make you angry?' Amelia asked. 'Mum said you used to write angry songs all the time.'

'Oh, injustice. Inequality. The underdog, you know?'

'Like, when things aren't fair?'

'Yeah. I hated to see anyone beaten down. Thought I could change the world with my songs.'

'Why don't you sing those songs now?'

'I grew up,' he said quietly. 'I still cared, but… you get jaded, after a while. You shout and you shout, and things stay the same.' He glanced at her. 'How about you, kid? What pisses you off?'

She pondered a moment.

'People being mean to my dad. Because he's gay, I mean.' She frowned. 'And things do change a bit, don't they? Because before the sixties you couldn't even be gay without going to prison. Like that was the *actual* law. And now you can, right? And you can get married and everything. Even if some people are still mean, the law's been made more fair.'

'Yeah. I suppose it has.'

'And like, women. Once women couldn't vote or do anything. And now they can, because some people called the suffragettes stopped eating and jumped in front of horses and stuff until people had to listen. So one person can change things. Even if it doesn't seem like it at the time.'

Jordan smiled. 'You know, Melie, you're pretty smart for someone so short.'

'I know,' she said, flicking her hair.

Other Max stood up. 'Time for a drinks run while they're between songs. Give me a hand, John Boy?'

'No flirting with ladies!' Amelia called after Jordan as he headed to the bar.

Jordan nudged Other Max. 'Looks like I'll just have to flirt with you then.'

'That kid'll be your stepdaughter soon if you keep on like this,' he said in a low voice.

'I hope you're right.'

'Here, come outside. I want a word.'

Jordan followed Other Max to the empty beer garden.

'What's up, mate?'

'Look, Jord, are you sure about all this?' Other Max demanded, exercising an old friend's right to speak bluntly. 'You waltz back into Maggie's life after nearly fifteen years, and within months you're talking love and marriage? It's a bit scary.'

'I've wasted enough time,' Jordan said, shrugging. 'You know how many of the last fifteen years I can actually remember? While you lot were here building lives, I was passed out in some stranger's bed or sobbing in a hotel room. Now I'm finally happy, and I'm not letting a single minute get away from me.'

'What about Mags?'

'I'm hoping she feels the same.'

'I mean, you don't just get to pick your old life up again,' Other Max said, resting his hands on Jordan's shoulders. 'Don't get me wrong, Jord, everyone's glad you're back. But we've done a lot of living in the last fifteen years, you can't just pretend that didn't happen.'

'I'm not trying to, am I?'

'Aren't you? Moving back into The Cedars, playing happy families with the kid? I can't help worrying.'

'You worry too much.'

'I'm serious, Jordan. You know, Mags was a state when you guys broke up. And then a baby came along. She was twenty, broke, her parents had just emigrated to Canada. If it hadn't been for Ibs, God knows where she'd be now.'

'I know. And I want to make up for it. I won't hurt her again, I promise.'

'Hm.'

'I'll look after her this time. Amelia too. The one good thing to come out of the last fifteen years is that I can afford to give them a decent life.'

'And what about Ibby? They're his family.'

'There's room for us both, isn't there?'

Other Max looked at him for a moment. 'Did Mags tell you about Dan?'

'The ex who didn't get on with Ibs. What about him?'

'It was a bit more than not getting on. He tried to push Ibs out entirely, until Maggie gave him his marching orders. Thought he could take the father's place in the family.'

'She knows I'd never do that.'

'Yeah, but does Ibby know?'

'We're mates, aren't we? Ibs knows we're on the same side.'

'Hmm. He's a laid-back guy, but I'm not sure I'd be a hundred per cent happy if I was suddenly sharing Daddy duties with another bloke under my own roof. Just take a bit of friendly advice and keep an eye on it.'

Chapter Forty-One

Shortly after he'd gone to stay at Number 22, Jordan had set up a subscription to all the major tabloids so he could keep an eye on the latest news about himself. They landed on the hall carpet every morning with a series of dull thuds.

That was how Jordan knew he'd moved from Antigua to Brazil – Ellis had fancied a change of scene, presumably – that Jake would be releasing his first solo single in the autumn, that Riley had been in court for drunk-driving, and that thanks to Craig's machinations, *Sleepwalking* was still top of the album charts.

Now that Jordan Nash's location had been accounted for and he didn't appear to be doing anything more interesting than getting a tan, the press had started to lose interest. The pap photos were fewer, the column inches negligible. Fame was always fickle and Jordan was hopeful that in another six months, the world would have moved on from Jordan Nash. The only downside to the interview he'd given to Ibby was that there was likely to be a fleeting renewal of interest in him.

He did have a plan, kind of. He knew he couldn't stay in Maggie and Ibby's spare bedroom forever. He'd asked Craig to put the big house in Devon on the market and he was keeping an eye out for properties in Applecroft. When the heat was off he'd get his own place, close to Maggie, and they'd take it from there.

After his conversation with Amelia in the pub, he'd started looking at engagement rings too. He knew it was early days but he couldn't help it. Jordan had never felt so sure about anything as he did about the fact that Maggie Nightingale was the only woman for him – she always had been. He'd lost her once, when he'd been too young and stupid to realise her full worth. He sure as hell wasn't going to do it again.

It was an unremarkable Thursday when the story broke. Ibby had got an exclusive in the *Daily Recorder*, one of the most widely read of the redtops.

Shameful past of Jordan Mum! the headline screamed. *Star tells all in sensational final interview.*

It was accompanied by a photo of him – well, of Ellis being him – and another of a drunk-looking Sylvia at some party.

Jordan grimaced. He knew Sylvia needed to be outed as the terrible mother she was, but it didn't give him any pleasure. Until now, the story of his early life was something he'd taken pains to keep private.

He flicked to the inside spread. Yep, it was all there. How Sylvia had met his dad in a squat they were sharing with a bunch of other addicts. How she'd abandoned Jordan to be raised by his grandmother in Bath. How she'd encouraged his dad to greater and greater excesses until he'd died of an overdose. How she'd reappeared in Jordan's life only after he'd become a star, and used him to fund her lifestyle ever since. And plenty more besides. He'd kept some stuff back – he didn't want to humiliate her for the sake of it – but there was more than enough to ensure she'd never be able to trade off the Jordan Nash name again.

He rang Craig.

'So has she been in touch?' he asked.

'What do you think?' Craig said. 'My PA's phone's been ringing off the hook.'

'What did you tell her?'

'Haven't got back to her yet. What do you want me to tell her?'

'That I'm done with her,' Jordan said. 'I'll support her financially but that's it. Two grand a month paid straight into her bank account on the condition she never contacts me again, or the press. One strike and she's out, Craig, make that absolutely clear. I'll cut her off with nothing if she comes near anyone I care about again.' He paused. 'And tell her... tell her I'm sorry. But she really should've left the kid out of it.'

'You don't have to pay her hush money any more, Jord.'

'It's not hush money. It's... I just want to make sure she doesn't struggle.'

'Well, you're a better man than I am, star,' Craig said gently. 'Okay. I'll pass all that on.'

'How's Ellis? Still enjoying being me?'

'Yeah, living it up on a private beach in Rio at the minute. The press'll get wise eventually though.'

'I'm hoping they'll lose interest before they suss it out,' Jordan said. 'Oh, cheers for getting Amelia's birthday present sorted. And the guitar.'

'Have you written anything yet?'

'Not yet. Waiting for inspiration to strike.'

'Anything else you need?'

'Not at the moment.' He paused. 'Craig, have you got a suit?'

'Eh?'

'A suit. Something smart.'

'Course. Why?'

'I'm going to ask Maggie to marry me.'

'Bloody hell!'

Jordan smiled. 'Yeah, I know. See you, boss.'

When Craig had hung up, Jordan glanced at the newspaper again. It didn't make him happy, but there was a closure to it. Sylvia was gone. The last thing that had tied him to Jordan Nash had been obliterated.

He was free...

Jordan folded the newspaper carefully, carried it upstairs and locked it in his safe. Then he picked up his guitar.

He wasn't Jordan Nash any more. He was Max Jordan. What did Max Jordan write songs about?

He remembered Amelia – her firm belief one person could change the world. He'd been idealistic like that once.

That was it; he'd write a song for the kid. A protest song, something to right wrongs. Grabbing a notepad, he scribbled down a title and started to write.

–

When Ibby got home from work, he found Jordan and Amelia sitting on the sofa. Amelia had Jordan's guitar in her lap and Jordan was writing in a notebook.

'What're you two up to?'

'Jamming,' Jordan said.

Amelia beamed at him. 'Dad, it's *so* cool. Jordan's written a song for us. And I helped.'

Ibby blinked. 'Us?'

'Yeah, it's called "Standing Up". It's about not giving in to bullies and stuff.'

'You want a performance, Ibs?' Jordan asked. 'Melie and me have formed a supergroup. She's learnt three chords today.'

'Excellent, she can join Status Quo.'

'She's a natural actually. Picked it up in no time.' Jordan nudged her. 'Come on, kid. I'll sing, you play.'

They started the song, Amelia hesitantly navigating her way through her three chords while Jordan sang.

When they were done, Ibby nodded. 'Nice lyrics, Jord. You're back in Pheasant Pluckers territory there.'

'That was the idea.'

'Hey, Dad, we should play it for Nat,' Amelia said. 'He could use it for his campaign song.'

Ibby laughed. 'Right. "How do you like this song? Oh and by the way, this is Jordan Nash, he's hiding in my house. Keep it under your hat, eh?"'

'Has Nat got a campaign?' Jordan asked.

'Yeah, Over It. They're leading the battle against homophobic discrimination in Applecroft and the surrounding area, up to and including Hesham but stopping just short of Portishead.'

'Are you part of it?'

'Not my thing really. I can't do what Nat does, the public speaking and everything, I haven't got the nerve.'

'Jordan, you should join,' Amelia said, her eyes sparkling. 'You could write songs for them.'

He smiled. 'I'm in hiding, Melie. Or have you forgotten?'

'Yeah, okay, but when you're not though.'

'Maybe I will.'

'So are we going to the caff then, Melie?' Ibby asked. 'Thursday means hot chocolate day.'

'Do we have to?'

Ibby frowned. 'Well no, we don't have to. Why, are you too big to hang out with your dad now?'

'No, I just want to practise the song a bit more. I can do nearly all the chords perfect now.'

'Oh. Okay.'

Amelia looked up at him. 'We can go to the caff any time, Dad. We'll go at the weekend.'

'All right. How about I make dinner while you practise then?'

'All sorted, mate,' Jordan said. 'Bangers and mash ready to go. Your favourite, right?'

'Yeah. Thanks.'

Amelia was already strumming at the guitar again, trying to remember where her fingers needed to go.

'I'll be upstairs then,' Ibby muttered, although it seemed like no one was really listening. 'Have fun, guys.'

Jordan had left his slippers at the top of the stairs. Ibby kicked them out of his way.

—

'You're very quiet tonight,' Nat said to Ibby as they lay in bed that evening. 'Something up?'

'Oh, nothing. Nothing important.'

'Come on, Ibs.'

'Maggie's got a new boyfriend,' he said glumly.

'That's good, isn't it? Now you've got one each.' Nat trailed his fingers over Ibby's bare chest. 'Or do you not get on with the guy?'

'No, I do. He's a mate actually. It's just… dunno. Mags is all loved up, this bloke's practically living at ours, and now he's started bonding with Amelia…'

'You're not jealous?'

'I'm feeling a bit surplus to requirements in the old lord and master department, that's all.'

Nat rolled over him and nuzzled into his shoulder. 'They're your family. They're not going to trade you in for a newer model, are they?'

'I know. Just being silly.' He smiled as Nat started kissing his ear. 'You know, it's a terrible faux pas to seduce someone while they're unburdening.'

'I had no idea. Better stop then, eh?'

'Don't you dare.'

'Try not to worry about it, Ibs. I know it's scary, things changing, but it's all good change. Maggie's happy, Amelia's happy, you're happy. That's what matters.' Nat glanced up. 'You are, aren't you? Happy?'

Ibby smiled. 'Yeah.' He ran soft fingers over Nat's cheek. 'Yeah,' he whispered again, claiming his lips for a kiss.

Chapter Forty-Two

'So, how does it feel?' Maggie asked when Amelia stumbled yawning into the kitchen the next day.

'How does what feel?'

'Well, fourteen.' She gave her daughter a hug. 'Happy birthday, sweetheart. And if you could stop growing up now, me and your dad would both appreciate it.'

'Can we do presents, Mum?'

'I thought we could wait until the barbecue.'

'Oh, what? That's ages!'

'You want Uncle Other Max and Nicki there, don't you? Come on, everyone's taken the day off work specially.'

'Okay,' Amelia muttered.

'Thanks for suggesting this, Melie. I know you'd probably rather celebrate with your friends than be stuck with the old folk.'

—

Amelia's birthday barbecue was a small affair, just her parents, Jordan, Other Max and Nicki – basically the only people who knew Jordan was hiding out at Number 22. It was a shame she couldn't ask her friends, or Nat or Nana or Aunty Beth, but that was the price she'd offered to pay in exchange for having Jordan there.

At least it was a glorious day for it. The garden smelled of charred meat, beer and mayonnaise, smells of the dying summer, and after an hour of being spoilt and petted, Amelia had to admit she was quite enjoying herself. She and Jordan played the song they'd written, which drew appreciative applause from the other adults. She beat Nicki at lawn skittles, and her mum let her have a glass of prosecco to toast her new grown-up status.

Her dad seemed a bit down though. Amelia wondered if he was upset because Nat couldn't come. Or maybe he was sad about her growing up, she knew adults could be weird about that. She'd caught her mum having a little cry in the utility room earlier.

'Okay, Melie. Time for presents, you'll be pleased to hear,' her mum said when they'd finished eating. 'Come on, sit in the middle and we can watch.'

'Do I have to?'

'Yes you do. We've spent good money and we want to see the look of childlike joy on your little face when you unwrap them.'

Amelia humphed a bit before doing what she was told.

'This is from me,' Jordan said, handing her a parcel.

Amelia ripped off the paper. Inside was a book called *Fun Python Projects for Kids*.

'Oh, cool!' she said. 'Thanks, Jordan. Will you help me with them?'

'That's the plan.'

Next she opened Other Max and Nicki's present, a bottle of her favourite Midnight Fantasy perfume.

Maggie smiled at Nicki. 'Your choice, right?'

'How did you guess?'

'Heh. Last year Other Max got her a pair of sheepskin slippers.'

'They were very nice slippers,' Amelia said loyally. 'Really, er, warm.'

Other Max laughed. 'Thanks, Melie. Still, I think I'll let Nic be on present-choosing duty from now on.'

Amelia looked expectantly at her parents.

'Did you get it?' Maggie asked Ibby.

'Me? I thought you were getting it!'

Maggie grinned at the look of dismay on her daughter's face. 'We're just teasing, sweetie. Course we got it.'

She handed over a parcel.

'Arghhh!' Amelia squeaked when she opened it to find the long-desired iPhone. 'You guys *rock!* Thank you thank you thank you!'

She gave them both a hug. Her dad, she noticed, gave her an extra tight squeeze.

'And this is from Nat,' Ibby said, giving her another package. 'He wanted to get you a case for it so I helped him pick out something suitably sparkly.'

'That was nice of him. Tell him I said thank you.'

'You can tell him yourself. He's invited me, you and Mum to his house next week for a film night on his legendary telly.'

'Well, I think we're finished,' Maggie said when Amelia was done opening things. 'Ibs, can you fetch everyone more drinks?'

'Just a sec,' Jordan said. 'I've got another present. I wanted to get a "thanks for having me" gift on top of the birthday one.'

He handed Amelia an envelope. Inside was a card bearing a picture of a monkey with big googly eyes. She opened it, and her own eyes quickly went googly too.

'Oh my God,' she whispered. 'For me, really?'

'Really. Three front-row tickets for you, a friend and whichever parent draws the short straw.'

'Oh my God!' she said again. 'Jordan, you're the best! Thank you *so much.*' She threw herself at him for a hug and he laughed as he patted her back.

'What did you get her?' Maggie asked him.

'Little Mix tickets. My source told me they were pretty high on most fourteen-year-olds' wish lists.'

Ibby shook his head. 'You shouldn't spend so much, Jord.'

He shrugged. 'Nice to see my ill-gotten gains making someone happy.'

Amelia was so happy she was almost in orbit, in fact. An iPhone and front-row tickets to her favourite band! Fourteen was looking pretty good so far.

'Mum, can I go set my new phone up and tell Georgia about Little Mix?' she gabbled in one breath.

'Go on then.'

When she'd disappeared, Ibby stood up.

'I'll get everyone another drink.'

In the utility room, he rested his head against the beer fridge. His throat felt tight, and he could feel a sob fighting to get out. God, he wasn't going to cry, was he? Not now...

A hand materialised on his shoulder.

'What's up, Ibs?' Jordan asked.

'Nothing.' Ibby summoned a smile. 'Just an emotional day. Go back to the garden, I can manage these.'

'You sure it's nothing? You haven't seemed your usual merry self all afternoon.'

Ibby sighed. 'Did you have to get her those tickets, Jord?'

'I wanted to get her something good, to say thanks for asking me to stay,' Jordan said, sounding surprised. 'That's okay, isn't it?'

'You should've checked with me and Mags first.'

'Sorry, mate, I didn't think.'

'The thing is, Jordan, those tickets are the kind of thing the two of us would have to save for ages to be able to buy her. The iPhone was a huge deal because we just can't afford to get her big presents very often. Then you waltz in flashing the cash, spoiling her in a way we never could. You see where I'm coming from?'

'Honestly, Ibs, I wasn't trying to flash anything. I just wanted to get her something that'd make her happy. She's a good kid.'

But Ibby wasn't listening. The floodgates had been opened, and he couldn't stop until all his frustrations had spilled out.

'Do you think you can buy your way into our lives, Jordan, is that it?' he demanded. 'When are you moving out anyway? You've been here nearly six weeks.'

'I didn't—'

'Because you know, lately it seems there's been a lot of what can only be described as Max Jordan getting his feet under the table. And that's my fucking table, all right? My house, my daughter, my... Maggie.'

'Come on, Ibs, this is daft. We're not falling out over Little Mix, are we?'

'No, we're falling out over you.' Ibby shoved him aside. 'Tell you what, bugger this. I'm going for a walk. Try not to claim whatever's left of my life while I'm out, eh?'

He stomped out, Jordan staring after him.

'And by the way, you peaked in the mid-noughties!' Ibby called back as he slammed the door.

He marched straight over to Nat's and hammered on the front door.

'Nat, I've had an epiphany,' he said when his boyfriend answered.

'Right. Have you got cream for it?'

'I want to join Over It. I want to strip to the waist, paint my face with the rainbow flag and run screaming into battle like William Wallace.'

'Now there's a sexy image. Here, come in.'

Ibby followed him inside and chucked himself down on the sofa.

'Okay, what's brought this on?' Nat asked, sitting down next to him. 'I thought you didn't do public campaigning.'

'Yeah, well, that was before,' Ibby said. 'I mean, you always think someone else'll fix it, don't you? Some mentor, some Yoda or Dumbledore with all the answers. We make a god of the wise father-figure but truth is, there is no one with a master plan. There's just people; flawed, fucked-up human beings trying to make the best of what life chucks at them. Gandhi was a screw-up in his personal life, wasn't he? Hell, even Nelson Mandela was into the Spice Girls. I bet they were making it up as they went along just like every other hero. And if I have to be a hero to make my kid's life a bit less shit and my own a bit more memorable, then bloody well bring it on. I'm Che Guevara, face of the revolution. So… there.'

Nat raised an eyebrow. 'You quite done, Che?'

'Probably.'

'Then how about you tell me what this is really about?'

Ibby dropped his head to Nat's shoulder. 'Had a bust-up with Mags's new bloke.'

'And that's made you go all crusadey, has it?'

'It's just the way Melie looks at the guy, like he's the sodding messiah or something, because he's got the guts to speak up about stuff. I want her to look at me like that.'

Nat stroked his hair. 'Come on, tell me what happened. What did Maggie's boyfriend do?'

'He wrote a song about standing up to bullies. Him and Melie wrote it together.'

'Is that something to get jealous about?'

'He bought her Little Mix tickets for her birthday too. Never seen her so happy.'

'Then maybe you should be happy for her,' Nat said gently. 'I'm on your side, lover, you know I am. But it sounds like this is about Amelia, not you.'

'I know.' Ibby choked on a sob. 'Oh God, I'm pathetic. Wanting to keep the two of them all to myself.'

'It's a natural instinct. But I'm sure there's room in Amelia's life for this guy, just like I hope there'll be room for me. Did you talk to Maggie?'

'No. I've been bottling it up.'

Nat nodded. 'That's always healthy.'

He sighed. 'I've made a right mess, Nat. Shoved him and everything. What'll I do?'

'Well, you might start by apologising.' Nat leaned round to give him a kiss. 'Go home now and make it up with him. I'll ring you later.'

When Ibby turned the corner into the market square, he spotted a familiar figure sitting on the steps of the buttercross.

He approached and sat down too. Wordlessly Jordan held out a fist, and Ibby bumped it in greeting.

'Ibs, I'm so sorry,' he said.

'What, you're apologising to me?'

'Yeah.'

'You don't need to do that, Jord. I was on my way home to apologise to you. I'm the one who Hulked.'

'No, it was my fault. You and Mags have done a lot for me, helping me get my life back on track. I never meant to pay you back by making you feel I was trying to take your place. Other Max tried to warn me, but...' Jordan's eyes dropped. 'It was nice, that's all, playing families. Melie's a great kid.'

Ibby smiled. 'She is, isn't she?'

'You guys have done a fantastic job with her. And I want you to know I get that you're her dad, and whatever happens with me and Mags, I won't ever forget that.'

'Thanks, mate.' Ibby sighed. 'And I'm sorry I shoved you – that was pathetic. A grown man getting jealous because he doesn't like sharing his toys.'

'Friends again?'

'Friends again.' They shook hands.

'Ibs? Can I ask you something?'

'Course.'

'You and Maggie, when you... you know. What was it like?'

Ibby frowned. 'Why is everyone so interested in that? Don't you people have sex lives of your own?'

'It's just so weird to think about. You two are like brother and sister.'

'Well, we all do daft things when we're young and hammered. You know that.'

Jordan was staring at him. Ibby ran a finger under his collar, suddenly uncomfortable. He could feel his cheeks getting hot.

'Hey, you fancy a game of pool at the Lagoon before we head home?' he asked. 'Melie won't miss us for an hour now she's on Planet iPhone.'

Jordan stared a while longer before he spoke again.

'Okay. I'm going to say something. An idea that's been building since you stomped out.'

'Seriously, I could murder a pint. Let's go, eh? I'll text Maggie and let her know where we are.'

'Maggie.' Jordan blinked a few times. 'You never did sleep with Maggie. Did you?'

'What?'

'You can't have. You can't have had sex with Maggie.' He was staring straight ahead, almost talking to himself as he followed the rabbit hole of his thoughts deeper. 'It's just not possible.'

Ibby laughed. 'I'm pretty sure it is.'

Jordan shook his head. 'God, I've been blind. You don't sleep with girls. Like you'd ever sleep with Maggie. Like she'd sleep with you!'

'Jord, what are you wombling on about? Come on, I'll let you buy me a beer.'

But Jordan had finally reached the bottom of the hole.

'Jesus, then the kid, she can't be – I mean, August. Mags said she was two months premature but it's bollocks, Ibs, isn't it? Because I left in February and if you two didn't – it means she has to be—'

'Don't say it.' Ibby made eye contact now, pleading. 'Please, Jordan. You don't have to say it.'

'You know I do.' Jordan shook his head again, as if there was something in his ears he needed to shake free. 'Amelia. She's… mine.'

Chapter Forty-Three

Jordan flung open the front door and marched into the house.

'Maggie! I need to talk to you!'

'Jord, please don't blame her,' Ibby panted, hot on his heels.

Jordan stomped into the kitchen, then checked the utility room. There was a note on the beer fridge.

Driving Nicki and Other Max home, back soon. Hope you're friends again. Mags x

'Jordan!' Ibby said, catching up with him. 'Look, let's talk about this.'

'You took my life, Ibby. My girlfriend, my kid, my fucking life!'

'The one you didn't want, you mean?'

'When did I ever say that?'

'You threw it away, didn't you? Shut us all out? You wanted to be Jordan Nash more than you wanted anything else.'

'Bullshit I did. You took my life and you lived it for me without ever telling me it was mine by rights. Christ, you even took my bloody room! It was my road to travel and you... you stole it.'

'Yeah, well it's not about you, is it? Not everything is, you'll be amazed to learn.' Ibby stared him down. 'Where were you on the thirty-first of August 2004, Jordan?'

'What?'

'Just tell me.'

'Well, I was... on the road. The album tour for *Mix Tape*.'

349

'Shitfaced on coke, right?'

Jordan flushed. 'Yeah. Not that I remember much.'

'I do. I can replay that night in perfect detail. I remember because it was the night my daughter was born.' He held up a hand to stop Jordan interrupting. 'That's right, my daughter. It's the night I held Maggie's hand and we promised each other we'd make sure her baby always had a happy, loving home and family. A nice, normal, healthy one so she could grow up a nice, normal, healthy kid. You of all people have to appreciate that.'

'It wasn't your decision to make.'

'No, it was Maggie's. I offered to parent with her if she wanted to keep the baby and she chose between that and terminating the pregnancy.'

'Why would you do that?'

Ibby shrugged as if the answer was self-evident. 'Maggie.'

'I had a right to know, Ibby.'

'And what would you have done?' he demanded. 'At fucking nineteen? Would you have chosen Maggie and the baby, then spent your life resenting them for robbing you of your big break? Or would you have chosen Jordan Nash, and dragged the two of them into that screwed-up world with you?'

'Don't make out you were doing me any favours.'

'I'm not. I'm saying, these are the questions Mags had to ask herself back then. Pretty weighty ones for a girl that age, but she was always strong. I think she did herself proud.'

Jordan sank into a garden chair and buried his face in his hands. His anger dissipated as quickly as it had appeared, but the empty pain in his chest remained.

'Where do we go from here, Ibs?' he whispered.

Ibby rested a hand on Jordan's shoulder. 'We could have a drink together,' he said quietly.

'I could use a drink.'

'Me too.' He grabbed a couple of cans from the fridge and handed one to Jordan.

Jordan looked up, his eyes soaked. 'I missed everything. Maybe I was too much of a fuck-up to be a dad, but she was mine and I... missed it.'

Ibby sighed as he took a seat opposite. 'You know, I've been lying about it so long, I think I'd actually started to believe I did sleep with Maggie. My subconscious's way of silencing a guilty conscience.'

'Did you feel guilty?'

'Course I did. We did what we thought was best for Amelia, but she was your baby.'

'But she's your daughter.'

'What will we tell her, Jord?'

'Do we have to tell her anything? Obviously I want a relationship with her, but maybe I could just... you know, be Uncle Jordan or whatever.'

'Too late,' a tearful voice said from behind the door.

The two men looked at each other.

'Oh God,' Ibby whispered. 'Melie...'

—

'Hello?' Maggie called when she got home. 'Did you two boys make up?'

'Up here,' came a quiet voice.

She headed upstairs. Ibby was sitting on the carpet outside Amelia's room, his face bone-white.

'Oh my God!' she said. 'What happened? Did Melie shut herself in?'

'She knows, Mags.'

'She...' Maggie's face drained of blood. 'No. No! How can she?'

Ibby knocked on Amelia's door. 'Sweetie, won't you please open up? Mum's here too.'

'Go away,' came a choked voice. 'I don't want to talk to liars.'

'Melie—'

'Leave me *alone!*'

351

'Ibs, how did she find out?' Maggie whispered.

'Jord worked it out. He's down in the utility room waiting for you.'

'And Melie...'

'Overheard us talking.' He swallowed a sob. 'Oh God, Maggie, what happens now?'

Maggie slumped to the floor. Instinctively they reached for each other, and Ibby rested damp eyes against her neck.

'I hoped we'd never have to do this,' she whispered.

'But we always knew we might.'

'Yes, but... it's her birthday.' Maggie gasped out a sob of her own. 'Ibs, it's her birthday.'

'I'm sorry. Let you down, didn't I?'

'No. No, you could never do that.' She wiped her eyes and got to her feet, professional-counsellor Maggie shoving panicked-mum Maggie to one side. 'Right. Up you get. Our daughter needs us.'

Ibby stood too and Maggie rapped on the door to Amelia's room. 'Melie, it's your mum. Can we come in and talk?'

'No. Go away.'

Maggie hesitated. They'd always told Amelia that her bedroom was her own space, never to be invaded without her express permission. They knew how valuable privacy was to kids her age, and they'd wanted her to understand that respect for personal space was important.

But this was a special case. Gently, Maggie pushed open the door.

Amelia was lying on the bed. She wasn't crying any more, but her face was white. She kept her eyes fixed on the ceiling as her parents sat down either side of her.

'Is it true then?' she demanded.

Maggie glanced at Ibby, who gave a slight nod.

'Yes,' she said in a whisper. 'It's true. I'm sorry, my love.'

'But it doesn't change anything,' Ibby said.

'You're not my dad,' Amelia whispered. 'How can that not change anything?'

Ibby winced. 'Sweetie, please. Please don't say that.'

Amelia gave a tight little laugh. 'Yeah, listen to me, just saying the truth. I guess that's hard for you and Mum to understand, right? Because you love telling lies so much?'

'Amelia, we need to talk about this properly,' Maggie said, struggling to keep desperation out of her voice. 'Won't you let us explain?'

'Will Jordan come to live with us for good now? Instead of Dad?'

'Melie, there's no instead. Your dad's still your dad, same as before.'

'Except it isn't the same, is it?'

'Look, you need to understand. Back when I found out I was having you, things were—'

'Liars!' Amelia burst out, gripping her head in her palms. 'Liars, liars, liars, *liars!* All my life you've been telling me stupid lies and you... you didn't even care, like it didn't even matter it wasn't real. Like it didn't matter if I knew what was real or not.'

'Of course we cared. We were trying to keep you safe,' Ibby said, casting a frightened look at Maggie. 'Please, sweetheart, calm down a little.'

'So, what, you tried to keep me safe by never telling me anything that was true? That's not safe, it's... pretend. You made me live a make-believe life, you made me a game or... like a doll instead of a person.'

'Sweetie, that isn't true,' Maggie said. 'If you knew how things were when I first learned I was pregnant, the choices I was faced with...'

Amelia turned wet eyes to her mother. Maggie flinched at the betrayal shining from them.

'You mean choices like making me go away, right? Like an abortion?'

'I never wanted that,' Maggie said quietly.

'So you didn't think about having one?'

'I thought about it. I was young, afraid. But I didn't want it, I wanted my baby.' She stretched out a hand to Ibby, who gave it a squeeze. 'We both did.'

'How do I know you're not lying now?'

'We'd never lie about that.' Ibby reached out to hug her, but she pushed him away.

'How can I believe anything? I can't ever believe you again.' Amelia burst into tears. 'Get out of my room,' she whispered.

'Sweetheart, please—'

'I said, get out! It's my room, isn't it? It's still my room, right?'

'Of course it's your room,' Maggie said. 'Always.'

'Okay, if it's my room then I don't want you and Dad in it. I want everyone to leave me alone. And I want Jordan to go away and never come back.'

'Melie—' Ibby said, but Maggie raised a hand to silence him.

'Okay,' she said gently to Amelia, who was face-down on her pillow, lost in a fit of gasping tears. 'If space is what you need, we'll leave you to have a cry and calm down. But we promise you, everything's going to be all right. Just remember that we love you.'

Ibby ran a soft hand over her hair.

'When you're ready to talk, we'll be right here,' he said gently. 'You'll always be my little girl, Amelia. Nothing can change that.'

Maggie led Ibby to his own bedroom and closed the door. As soon as they were alone, he burst into tears and she wrapped him up in a hug.

'We can fix this,' she whispered.

'How? She hates me. Did you hear her say I wasn't her dad?'

'She hates us both right now. It's a shock, that's all. Give her half an hour, then she'll have cried it all out and we can talk properly.'

'But how do we fix it? I can't lose her, Maggie.'

'She's afraid. Scared everything's going to change. We need to show her we're all on the same side.'

'"We" as in—'

'The three of us. It has to be the three of us from here on in.' She drew a deep breath. 'I need to have a talk with Max.'

'He's hurting too, Mags. Hell of a lot.'

'I know. Everything's a mess.' She brushed a tear off his cheek. 'Ibby. Love you, okay? We'll fix this, I promise.'

Ibby flashed her a watery smile. 'Yeah. Love you too.'

Chapter Forty-Four

Maggie headed downstairs, dreading the conversation she was about to have – a conversation she'd hoped would never happen.

She'd known there was a possibility, when they opened their lives to Max again, that the secret might come out. But it had seemed a remote one. Other than her or Ibby letting something slip, which she was certain they never would, there was no reason he should suspect anything: no family resemblance, no one else who could tell.

In stories, secrets always hung heavy on the keepers, preying on their minds until the weight of guilt became too much to bear. But if Maggie had felt any guilt about lying to Max and Amelia, it had been choked out by the absolute certainty she and Ibs had acted in their daughter's best interests. And The Lie had become so much a part of their lives, it almost seemed more true than the truth.

Until now.

In the utility room, Max was standing with his hands in his pockets, facing away from her.

'Hello, Magdalena.'

'How did you know?' she whispered.

'Ibby. He's not such a cool liar as you. No one gets that upset just over Little Mix.'

'Max, I'm so sorry.'

'You and me both. How's Amelia?'

'Hurt. Angry.'

'I can relate. Poor kid.'

'Max…'

He turned to face her, his cheeks wet with tears. 'It's okay,' he said quietly. 'I'm not angry. Not any more.'

Maggie came forward to embrace him, but he waved her back. 'No, I don't think I want to be held right now,' he said in the same quiet voice. 'I think I deserve some answers, don't you?'

'It was never about you, you know. It was always about Amelia. I'm her mum; it's my job to put her first.'

'Why didn't you tell me?'

Maggie sighed. 'That's the thing, Max, I did tell you. I told you the week before you moved to London.'

'What? No you didn't.'

'Yes I did. I told you I'd missed a period and you could choose to quit coke and be a part of our baby's life, or you could choose the drugs.' She laughed. 'You were so off your face you could barely take it in. Then you followed it up with a bender of such epic proportions, you clean forgot the whole conversation. That told me everything.'

He dropped his gaze. 'Did I do that?'

'You did.'

'Tell me what happened next.'

'You went away. I spent weeks wrestling with the idea of an abortion. I wanted the baby, but I was young, I had nothing. My family were far away in another country. God, I was so afraid.' Her mouth flickered. 'And Ibs stepped up. My rock.'

Jordan pushed his fingers into his hair. 'But fifteen years – fifteen fucking years! How am I even supposed to get my head round that? You had my kid, and you lied to me, and you kept on lying to me, even after we—' He shook his head. 'Do you know I was about to ask you to marry me?'

'What?'

'I've never been so happy as I have this summer, Maggie. All I wanted was to keep you in my life, all three of you. For us to be a family.' He snorted. 'I had no idea we already were one.'

'I did lie to you,' Maggie said in a low voice. 'And you know what, Max? I love you, I really do. I've never loved anyone else. But I was going to keep right on lying to you.'

'Why? I'm clean now. I could be a dad, I could… do it right this time.'

'But Amelia's got a dad, hasn't she? I swore to Ibs when he offered to parent with me that he'd be the baby's dad, legally and in every other sense. We promised we'd never breathe a word, ever, to anyone. I owed him that much.' She looked away. 'I owe him everything.'

'So no one knows except you two?'

'Ibby's family know. I mean, they know he's not Melie's biological father, they don't know it's you. Other Max suspected, I think, but he never said anything.'

Jordan slumped into a chair. 'I don't know how to deal with this. Who I can trust.'

'You can trust us,' she said gently. 'We took you in. We care about you.'

'That doesn't make it all right, Mags.'

She reached out to rest a hand on his shoulder, but he shrugged it away.

Maggie blinked back a tear. He looked so broken; she just wanted to make it better. That was her job, making things better. And yet… she couldn't, could she? Because she was responsible.

She still felt she'd done the right thing, but Jesus, what a mess it all was. Amelia crying in her room, swearing she'd never forgive them. Max crying here in front of her, unable to cope with this new reality. Ibs terrified of losing his daughter for good. What should she do? She had no idea how to fix it, how to bring them all together.

She sank onto the upturned laundry basket and rested her head on her palms, wondering how the hell she'd ever managed to get herself into this mess.

Maggie glanced at her watch. Half an hour late. They were about to have the most important conversation of their lives and he was half an hour late.

'Jesus,' she muttered when Jordan finally stumbled into The Blue Lagoon and took a seat opposite her. 'Max, look at you.'

'Hiya beautiful,' he said, beaming. 'Happy eight-month anniversary.'

Unsteadily he leaned across the table to kiss her, but she held him back.

'Take those sunglasses off,' she said.

'What?'

'Take those bloody sunglasses off and let me see your eyes.'

Jordan hesitated before removing his dark glasses and putting them in his pocket.

'There. Happy now?'

Maggie laughed and buried her face in her hands. 'You're wasted. You're fucking wasted again. Christ, Max!'

'Awww, come on, Lanie. So I had a few drinks, what's wrong with that?'

She examined him, taking in the engorged pupils and powder traces around his nostrils. 'Yeah, and what else did you have?'

'Baby, don't lecture, please. Let's have a nice romantic night, eh?'

Maggie pushed her orange juice away. 'Right. You stagger in forty-five minutes late, off your face on God knows what combination of substances, and I'm the one being unreasonable.'

He blinked. 'Am I late?'

'Yes. Didn't you get my text?'

He stared at her, struggling to focus. 'Mm. Something you need to tell me. Wassup?'

'It's... right. Okay.' She lowered her voice. 'I'm late.'

He snorted. 'No you aren't, you've been here forty-five minutes.'

'Not late like you're late, late like... I'm nearly three weeks overdue, Max.'

He stared at her.

'Are you hearing me? This is serious.' She reached out to take his hands. 'I need you with me for this. I can't deal with it on my own.'

'I… what? But… I'm moving to London next week.'

'I know. That's why we need to talk. Work out what we're going to do if it's really… you know.'

He'd started swaying slightly. Maggie frowned.

'Just how many drinks did you have?' she demanded.

'Dunno. Maybe… maybe more than a couple.' He slumped forward onto his arms.

'Max, if this is what I think it is, if I do a test and it's positive – even if it's not, I can't…' She blinked back a tear. 'I love you, I do, but I can't live like this.'

'You said… wouldn't make me choose…' Jordan mumbled.

'I said I wouldn't ask you to abandon your dreams. What I am asking is for you to make a choice: the drugs or me. Me and your baby, possibly. Which is it going to be?'

There was no answer.

'Max?'

'This is… it's too much, Lanie. I can't deal with this now.'

'Fine.' She stood up. 'I'll be at home when you're ready to talk. But if this happens again, one more binge…' She swallowed a sob. 'I think you know what that'll mean.'

When she got back to The Cedars, Ibby was waiting for her.

'Well?' he asked. 'What did he say?'

'He was off his face again, Ibs. I'm not even sure he properly took it in.' She blinked back a tear. 'I think… if he can't clean himself up, it has to be the end, doesn't it? And there might be a baby coming and Mum and Dad are gone and… shit, Ibby, I'm nineteen years old and I'm scared to fucking death. I can't bring up a kid on my own. If Max isn't going to step up, I'll have to terminate.'

'Hey.' He wrapped her in a hug. 'Don't worry, Mags. We'll fix this together, okay? You've still got me.'

With trembling fingers, Amelia tapped the number she'd found online into her new iPhone.

Jordan wasn't her dad. Okay, maybe he was the one who'd made her, but she already had a dad. Aaron Ibbotson was her dad.

But… he'd lied to her. Both her parents had lied to her, literally her whole, entire life – her made-up, accidental life that no one had really meant for her to have in the first place. She'd never felt this confused and betrayed, the impotent anger so strong it made her chest ache.

And Jordan – if he was her biological dad, did that mean legally he could take her off her real dad, stop her seeing him? She'd heard them arguing, before. If they weren't friends any more, maybe Jordan would try to take Amelia and her mum away with him. Just the thought of it made her feel physically sick.

She wasn't thinking clearly. All she was thinking about was rage – and revenge.

'*Daily Recorder*?' the female voice at the other end of the phone said.

'Um, hi, is that the newspaper?'

'That's right. Can I help?'

'I wondered if you wanted a story. An exclusive.' Amelia knew from her dad that 'exclusive' was a good word to use. 'It's about Jordan Nash.'

'Jordan Nash?'

'Yeah. Because… I know where he is. He's not really in Brazil, that's just someone who looks like him.'

'Seriously?' The woman sounded excited now. 'Hang on, let me get my boss.'

A second later a man's voice, less friendly than the woman's, spoke.

'What's all this about Jordan Nash then?'

'I know where he is,' Amelia repeated. 'And I think you should come and make him go away. I want him to go away.'

'Where is he?'

'He's at my house. 22 The Cedars, Applecroft. That's in Somerset.'

The man laughed. 'Okay.'

'Really he is. My mum's Magdalena from that song. He's been hiding here ages.'

There was a long pause.

'This better not be a hoax, kid,' the man said at last.

'It's not.'

'And your name is…?'

'Amelia Ibbotson-Nightingale.' She took a deep breath. 'I'm Jordan Nash's secret daughter.'

Chapter Forty-Five

Ibby was lying on his bed. Maggie lay on her back next to him, and Jordan on his other side.

'We can do this, people,' he said for about the third time.

'How?' Jordan asked. 'I mean, you keep saying that, but seriously, Ibs, how?'

'We have to do it for Amelia.' Ibby reached for Jordan's hand and took Maggie's on the other side. 'If she's got two dads now, we'll... work round it, that's all.'

'Work round it. Okay.'

'Yeah. Like they did in *Three Men and a Baby* and its underrated sequel.'

'Harrison Ford wasn't in that, was he?'

'I had a youthful dalliance with Tom Selleck. He meant nothing to me.'

'Not the time for jokes, you guys,' Maggie said sternly.

Ibby sighed. 'Sorry. Gallows humour. Think she'll ever forgive us, Mags?'

'Eventually. We just need to show her the three of us can work together.'

'Jord, you in?' Ibby asked.

Jordan, who still had a serious case of bombshell-shock, managed to nod his spinning head. 'I'm in.'

'Come on,' Maggie said. 'Let's go see if she's stopped crying. Poor baby, she's not having much of a birthday.'

They headed to Amelia's room and Maggie knocked gently.

'Sweetie? You ready to talk yet? We're all here, Max too.'

'No,' Amelia sobbed from behind the door.

'We won't come in if you don't want us to. But I promise you, everything's going to be okay.'

'Why should I believe what big fat liars say?'

'They lied to me too, you know,' Jordan said. 'But I'm not angry, Melie. I know why they did it.'

'Why?'

'Because of me. I wouldn't have been a good dad to you, not then. I was taking a lot of drugs and… doing other bad stuff. I was an idiot.'

'You're not my dad anyway. Not properly.'

'No, your dad's your dad. But I'd like to be something too, if you can find room for me.'

She snorted. 'So I'd have two dads? That's just weird.'

'They did it in *Three Men and a Baby*,' Ibby said.

Jordan nodded. 'And its underrated sequel.'

There was silence for a moment.

'I'm not going to replace your dad,' Jordan said, sensing the silence might be a good sign. 'But I'd still like to be a part of your life, Melie.'

'You know we all love you,' Maggie said. 'So much, my love. We told a lie because we'd promised to keep you safe and happy, that's all.'

'Dad, why did you want to be my dad?' Amelia asked quietly.

'Because of your mum,' Ibby said, smiling at Maggie. 'She was in trouble, frightened. I loved her a lot and I wanted to help. And… for you.' His voice cracked. 'Melie sweetheart, I might not have given you any genes, but you're still the most amazing thing I've ever done. I didn't make you, but I chose you, and I love you so much. Don't shut me out.'

There was silence. Then the door opened a sliver and a tearful face peeped out at him.

'Dad,' Amelia whispered. 'I think I've done something really stupid.'

Maggie put a protective arm around Amelia as they hid in her bedroom with the blinds down. There was a lot of noise outside, flashing cameras, loud voices, and a constant hammering at both front and back doors. She could just make out the voice of Mrs Pinkerton next door, pleading with the pack of journalists and paparazzi who'd once again descended on the neighbourhood to sod off back where they'd come from.

'Mum, I'm so sorry,' Amelia whispered.

'It's okay, sweetheart. Don't you worry about it.'

'How many now, Ibs?' Jordan asked.

Ibby peeped through the blinds. 'Jesus, loads. And... Jord, there's a helicopter.'

'Shit, really?'

'What did you tell them, Melie?' Ibby asked, keeping his voice gentle.

Amelia swallowed a sob. 'Everything. Dad, I told them everything. About Jordan being here and Ellis not really being him and...' She avoided making eye contact with Jordan. '...and about him being my biological dad.'

'Which newspapers?'

'All of them. I rang all the big ones. And I said it was an exclusive so they'd come.'

'No wonder they sent the helicopter,' Jordan muttered. 'That's some story you've given them, kid.'

'Are you mad with me?'

Jordan forced a smile. 'No. No, I'm not mad.'

'What do we do?' Ibby asked. 'They won't give up till one of us goes out there.'

'I'll go. It's me they want.'

'Oh no you don't.' Maggie pushed him onto the bed. 'You stay right there, Max, you're grounded.' She squared her shoulders. 'I'm going out.'

'Mum, don't!' Amelia whispered.

'It's okay, sweetie.' Maggie managed a smile. 'I've got mum rage, that'll scare them off. No one sieges my home and gets away with it.'

'But what'll you say?' Jordan asked.

'I've been lying to my nearest and dearest for fifteen years, I'm sure I can manage a few journalists. Just a sec.'

She left the room, returning a minute later in her dinosaur onesie.

'All right, boys, stay up here with Melie. I'm about to give the performance of a lifetime.'

She headed downstairs and flung open the front door. Immediately loud voices assailed her.

'Miss Nightingale, where is Jordan Nash?'

'Is it true you had his lovechild?'

'Is he here now?'

Maggie blinked, doing her best to look as if she'd just woken up. 'What? What is all this?'

'Where's Jordan, Maggie?' a journalist near the front called out.

'How the hell should I know? Brazil, last I heard.'

'We had a tip-off he's here in Applecroft.' The man's eyes narrowed. 'Right here under your roof, in fact.'

'I can promise you, under my roof is the last place Jordan Nash would ever be welcome.'

'Your daughter says otherwise,' came a voice she recognised. It was Julia, the girl who'd pumped her for information the night Max had shown up. 'She gave my editor quite a story.'

'Amelia?' Maggie groaned. 'Oh God, she didn't.'

'Well?'

'Sorry, Julia, but I'd say you've been the victim of a prank call. It's all the rage with my daughter's friends this summer, she's been grounded three times for it.'

'She said her father was Jordan Nash.'

'You what?' Maggie laughed. 'Wish he bloody was, I could get a pool put in with the back child support.'

Julia looked uncertain, but the man who'd spoken before flashed Maggie a cynical smile.

'Oscar-worthy, but no cigar, I'm afraid. I've interviewed everyone from dope-cheat sports stars to MPs on the fiddle. Buggered if I'll have the wool pulled over my eyes by some suburban housewife dressed as fucking Godzilla.'

'Er, one, I'm a relationship counsellor, and two, it's a stegosaurus,' Maggie said. 'Look, why would I lie? If I had a claim on the Nash fortune, don't you think I'd be straight in there?'

She was hoping that might appeal to their mercenary little gutter-press hearts, but the man was tenacious.

'Where is Jordan Nash, Maggie? I know you've got him hidden here somewhere.'

Behind her, the front door clicked open.

'You're wrong about that,' a deep voice said. 'Jordan Nash isn't here. But Max Jordan is.'

Jordan came to stand beside Maggie. Ibby took his place at Jordan's other side, Amelia gripping her dad's hand.

'Max, what do you think you're doing?' Maggie hissed.

'It's time, Lanie. I've been hiding long enough. The three of us talked and we decided we should face them together.'

'Max—'

'Look, I know we've got major stuff to deal with, and that won't be easy. But right now, what we need to be' – he held out a hand to her – 'is a family.'

Maggie hesitated. Then she nodded.

She took the hand he'd offered and Jordan held out another to Ibby. The four of them faced the pack defiantly, hand in hand.

'Just what are you hiding from, Mr Nash?' one hack demanded.

'Are you living in a ménage à trois?'

'Is this your daughter?'

Flashes popped all over the place, making Amelia shield her eyes. But she didn't wince. She just kept a tight hold of her dad's hand, knowing this was what they needed to do. It was the four of them against the world. She got that now.

'No, she's this guy's daughter,' Jordan said, nodding to Ibby. 'Although genetically speaking, yes, I'm her father.'

There was a clamour of voices, all yelling different questions. The mob surged closer, but Jordan didn't move.

'Do you lot want this statement or what?' he yelled over the noise.

There was a lull as the pack waited for him to speak.

'Right. That's better,' he said. 'So, here's your story, and when you've got it I hope you'll kindly leave us to ourselves. It's the kid's birthday today and she'd like to enjoy her cake in peace.'

There were mutterings as the pack scribbled frantically into notepads.

'See, we could hide in the house from you, but I've been doing that for ages and I'm a bit bored,' Jordan said. 'And me and Amelia here wrote a song yesterday called "Standing Up", about not giving in no matter how scared you are. So I'm going to give you your story, then I'm going to get on with the rest of my life. Meet the family.' He drew Maggie forward. 'This is Maggie. You know who she is because like an insensitive twat I went and wrote a song about her. Anyway, that worked out pretty well, since it turns out she's my soulmate. And she's going to marry me.' He glanced at Maggie. 'You are, aren't you?'

She shrugged. 'If you want.'

'Right, great.' He nodded to Ibby. 'This is our best friend Ibby. His favourite things are Indiana Jones and Wall's Viennetta, and he's been the best dad to Amelia anyone could be – better by far than I would've been. But you know my story.' He reached round Ibby to squeeze Amelia's shoulder. 'And this is Amelia. If any of you so much as come near her, you'll have the full weight of the law thrown at you. Don't ever forget that.' He glared at them for a moment, then grinned. 'Sorry, but I'm entitled to be a bit protective, right?'

There were excited murmurs as more cameras flashed.

'These three took me in when I was a mess and gave me my life back,' Jordan said. 'They saved me, and I don't ever intend to let them go again. That's all I have to say.'

'So is this it then, Mr Nash?' one of the journalists asked. 'Are you really giving it all up – fame, wealth, everything?'

'I really am. And the name's Max Jordan.'

Epilogue

One year and two months later...

'So, guys, what do you reckon?' Ibby asked, kneeling next to the paint swatches he'd sloshed on the wall of the new nursery. 'We've got pastel yellow or pale green, lovely and gender-neutral. Nat and Beth voted yellow, Nic and Other Max favour the green, so it's even-stevens at the moment.'

'Hmm,' Maggie said, one hand on her baby bump and Jordan's arm around her shoulders. 'What does Melie think?'

'She hasn't seen them yet.'

'I don't see why we couldn't have blue,' Jordan said.

'What if we have a girl though?' Ibby asked.

'Girls like blue, don't they? It's Melie's favourite colour.'

'This week,' Maggie said, rolling her eyes. 'Okay, I'm voting yellow. Reminds me of ducklings.'

There was a knock at the front door of Number 22 next door. When there was no answer, the knock moved along one to Number 24.

'Melie! Georgia's here for you!' Jordan yelled.

Life had changed a bit for the little family at The Cedars, but they hadn't lost any of the sweet things. When Mrs Pinkerton had called round eight months ago to tell them she was planning to put her house on the market and join her daughter in Brighton, the old lady had found herself walking away with a rather dazed look on her face and a cheque signed by Jordan for the house's full value – and then some – in her pocket.

It was all just perfect for the now fifteen-year-old Amelia. With her mum and Jordan at Number 24 and her dad and Nat in the old place at Number 22, she was loving having two bedrooms with enough walls to accommodate her current obsession with mood boards.

'Come say bye before you shoot off,' her mum called.

Amelia came dashing into the nursery, a slice of toast poking from her mouth as she struggled to fasten her school tie.

Jordan shook his head. 'Come here, kid. You're ballsing that right up, aren't you?' He undid the messy tie and fastened it neatly for her.

'Thanks, Jordan,' she said through a mouthful of toast. 'Hey, is it okay with you guys if I go to the cinema with Rory tonight?'

Jordan quirked an eyebrow. 'Rory now? What about Isaac and his perfect hair?'

'You're way behind, Jord,' Ibby said. 'There was Ashley and his cheekbones to die for after Isaac. Then came Luke and his totally adorbs glasses.'

'So what happened to him, Melie?' Jordan asked.

She shrugged. 'He got contacts.'

'Oh, how fickle is youth,' Maggie muttered.

'So can I, Mum? Pleeeeease?'

'Ask your fathers.'

'Why does she have to ask us?' Ibby demanded.

'I think Mags just likes saying that,' Jordan said. 'I don't see why not. What do you say, Ibs?'

'As long as she's home by eleven. You're at ours tonight, Melie, don't forget. You can ring if you need a lift.'

'Thanks, Dad.'

Ibby nodded to the paint swatches. 'What do you reckon then?'

'Green,' she said firmly. 'The yellow looks like scrambled-egg sick.'

'Your mum thought ducklings.'

'Yeah, if someone had sicked up scrambled egg on them. Right, bye, everyone.' Amelia leant down to kiss her mum's bump. 'Bye, baby sis. Be good.'

'You know, it could be a boy,' Maggie said.

'No way. Then we'd have four boys and two girls.'

'Good point.' She tapped her belly. 'Hear that, baby? Better work on growing some girl bits in there.'

'Pay no attention,' Jordan whispered to the bump.

He followed Amelia downstairs to wave her and Georgia off. A Yodel driver passed the girls as they walked down the driveway to Georgia's mum's car.

'Parcel for a Mr Jordan,' he said.

'That's me.'

The man stared. 'Hey. Aren't you... you're never Jordan Nash?'

'Used to be, yeah.'

Jordan found he got recognised more since he'd ditched the fake glasses and stopped covering his tattoos, but he wasn't famous enough now to be mobbed. People often wanted photos or autographs, but he could cope with that since the press had lost interest in him. That had happened quickly enough when they'd realised his quiet new life in the suburbs was about as far from rock and roll as you could get.

'What happened to you, man?' Yodel guy asked. 'You had the lot, didn't you? Then overnight you just disappeared.'

Jordan smiled as he signed for the parcel, containing a set of baby grows for their new addition. 'I realised there was something I wanted more.'

'So you don't regret giving it all up?'

'Not an ounce.'

'Shame for your fans though, eh? My missus went to all your gigs. She cried her lungs out the day the band split.'

'Well, she can still hear me. Second Friday of the month I do acoustic sets at The Blue Lagoon in town.'

The man blinked. 'You're playing pub gigs? You guys used to fill arenas.'

'I like to keep things low-key these days,' Jordan said. 'I set up an indie label under my own name. The new material's a bit different from my Route 69 stuff but I'm proud of it. Tell your missus I'll be performing as Max Jordan if she wants to look me up.'

'Cheers, I will. Hey, can I get a photo of us? It'll make my Shelly's day.'

'Sure.'

After posing for the selfie, Jordan closed the door and went back upstairs.

'We're going with the yellow,' Maggie told him. 'Melie's talking out of her backside; it looks much more like ducklings than sick. Plus, my vote counts double because hours of painful labour.'

'I also favour the yellow,' Ibby said. 'Smells like cheesecake.'

Maggie shook her head. 'It does not smell like cheesecake, Ibs, it smells like Dulux.'

'Seriously. When I look at it, I smell lemon cheesecake. I think I might have that colour sensory thingy where it triggers your nasal receptors.'

'You are making that up.'

'Honestly, it's a real thing. Google it.'

'I could live with the yellow.' Jordan pulled Maggie to him and planted a soft kiss on her lips. 'You know how much I love you?'

'Ahem,' Ibby said.

'Yeah, mate, love you too.'

'I actually meant you might like to get a room. But thanks.'

'What was that in aid of?' Maggie said, smiling.

'You. Us. Everything. You saved me, Lanie.' Jordan glanced at Ibby. 'Both of you. Melie too.'

Maggie stroked his cheek. 'Couldn't just give up on you, could we?'

'Anyone else would have.'

'Not us.' She returned the kiss he'd given her. 'So you're happy?'

'Happiest I've ever been.'

'We're a funny sort of family, aren't we?' Ibby said, smiling.

'Yeah.' Jordan rested a hand on his shoulder. 'Wouldn't have it any other way.'

A Letter From Lisa

Hi, it's Lisa here. I just wanted to say a massive thank you for choosing to read *When You Were Mine*. I really hope you enjoyed spending time with the characters as much as I did while telling their stories. All of them felt so real as I was writing, with voices all of their own, and I hated to say goodbye when I finally wrote The End for Maggie, Ibby, Amelia and Jordan.

If you enjoyed this book, I'd absolutely love to hear your thoughts in a review. These are invaluable not only for letting authors know how you felt about the story, but also for helping other readers to choose their next read and discover new writers.

I suppose the theme of this book is family and what makes it, something that is close to my heart. On their journeys, the four main characters come to learn that when love is present, a family can be whatever you make it. While weighty issues such as grief, addiction and homophobia are dealt with, I wanted the central characters' strong principles, their love for one another and their sense of humour always to shine through.

If you would like to find out more about me and my books, or contact me directly, you can do so via my website or social media pages:

Facebook: /LisaSwiftWrites

Twitter: @LisaSwiftAuthor

Web: www.lisaswiftauthor.co.uk

Thank you again for choosing me and my book. I hope to see you again for the release of book two next year!

Best wishes,

Lisa

Acknowledgments

The biggest thank yous have to go to my hard-working agent, Laura Longrigg at MBA Literary Agents, without whom this book (along with many others) would never have come to be and to whom it is dedicated, and to the utterly amazing Keshini Naidoo, my editor at Hera, whose editorial input has made the story at least 110% better.

I'd also like to thank the following talented author pals, who've all helped enormously in shaping the story: Mandy Baggot for her suggestion of Brendan Urie of Panic! at the Disco as a contemporary of Jordan Nash; Terri Nixon for pointing me in the direction of the Moody Blues song 'Your Wildest Dreams', which provided the lyric that inspired the title of this book; and my fabulous music-loving beta reader Katey Lovell for once again providing sterling input in making this book the best that it could be.

Shout-outs to all my supportive writer friends, especially my fellow Yorkshire romance scribblers, Rachel Burton, Victoria Cooke, Rachel Dove, Katey Lovell and Rachael Stewart; the Authors on the Edge, Sophie Claire, Jacqui Cooper, Helena Fairfax, Kate Field, Melinda Hammond, Marie Laval, Helen Pollard and Angela Wren; the Airedale Writers' Circle, and the ever-helpful members of The Savvy Authors' Snug on Facebook.

And of course, long-suffering friends and family – my live-in beta reader and squeeze of thirteen years and counting, Mark Anslow; friends Robert Fletcher, Amy Smith and Nigel and Lynette Emsley; and the sprawling masses of the Firth, Braham and Anslow clans around the world. Not to mention all my colleagues at Dalesman Publishing, always unwavering in their support for me and my books.

I have to mention too the Romantic Novelists' Association. I'm proud to have been a member of this organisation for several years now, and would like to thank them for the invaluable support and resources they provide to both aspiring and established authors. A special shout-out as well to my fellow members of the RNA's Rainbow chapter, which provides support for RNA members who identify as LGBTQIA+ and/or write novels featuring LGBTQIA+ characters.

And finally, the amazing team at Hera, who gave this book its perfect home and brought it out into the world – thank you so much to Keshini, Lindsey and the gang! It's been a pleasure to work with you all.